David Stanlake was born and brought up in the north of England and has been fortunate to live in Scotland for the past forty years. He has lectured in social studies and has previously written about social care issues in the early medieval period. As an antidote to this, he has turned in retirement to writing fiction with a particular interest in the espionage genre. *A Cause to Die For* is his first published novel.

Nam amores vitae meae prima et ultima.

David Stanlake

A Cause to Die For

AUSTIN MACAULEY PUBLISHERS™

LONDON • CAMBRIDGE • NEW YORK • SHARJAH

A CIP catalogue record for this title is available from the British Library.

ISBN 9781528920315 (Paperback)
ISBN 9781528920339 (ePub e-book)

www.austinmacauley.com

First Published (2020)
Austin Macauley Publishers Ltd
25 Canada Square
Canary Wharf
London
E14 5LQ

I am grateful for the help of many friends who have encouraged me and offered all kinds of support throughout the writing of this book. Without their wise advice and expertise, I would all too often have lost my way. I also pay tribute to the thousands of refugees who struggle against daunting odds to make a life for themselves and their loved ones. Their story is the basic fabric of this tale. Finally, I marvel at the professionalism and bravery of my publishers! Any errors in the book are entirely down to me.

Chapter One

Sicily
1 April 2015

The watcher on the cliffs had been staring out to sea for several hours. A grey dawn had given way to a grey April morning. Scanning the horizon in an arc from east to west, he was growing impatient. A cool offshore breeze blowing down from the mountains was beginning to catch at his clothes and make him shiver. As far as he knew, the boat had left Zuwara on the Libyan coast last night as scheduled. With any luck, it would have a trouble-free passage. It would be overloaded, well in excess of its capacity, in the nature of the trade that was to be expected. But this time, the traffickers were taking a calculated risk. The watcher knew that if it failed to pay off and the boat foundered, their backers were likely to take a swift and savage revenge. This was no mere rubber dingy like so many that were put to sea but a seaworthy fishing vessel— its hold filled with a human cargo and a monetary value many thousand times in excess of its usual haul. But with the weather likely to hold fair and reasonable cloud cover, there was every chance of making it across without the need to call for help. Recent history showed that most of those who failed to make the crossing became the victims of sudden storms and overloaded craft. That could happen at any time. Thousands had perished in the attempt and still they came, undeterred. A passage paid for—but without guarantees—a passage driven by desperation. The watcher knew all about that. Desperation drove him too. Pray God, this time there would be no mishap. Among the flotsam and jetsam of the cargo there were some very special items.

He shivered, pulling his trench coat closer to him and reaching for his lighter lit up again. On the cliff road behind him, a military transport vehicle was parked waiting. Looking back towards it, he glimpsed the glow of a cigarette behind the windscreen. Karim had wisely opted to stay in the shelter of the cab. A silent man, preferring the company of his own kind. The watcher had no idea where he came from, somewhere deep in the North African deserts; one of the lucky ones, he'd made it over in a rubber dingy. Now he'd become part of the operation. Karim was the Caliphate's man—but then, wasn't he as well? He turned back to searching the horizon.

When the vessel arrived, the work would begin. This was his part of the deal, struck months ago in the back room of a seedy Maltese lodging house. *You will pick up a group of twenty jihadis. They must be taken off first, before the rest of the passengers are disembarked. That is vital. Take them up the cliff path from the beach to the truck waiting at the top, then move them to the safe house.* Safe, more or less, because the farmhouse deep in the central highlands of the island belonged to him, had been in his family for generations, long since abandoned, and now part of the deal. Then the call from a public pay phone. *This is to let you know the population of the Republic of Italy has just increased by a further six hundred destitute human beings. No, you don't need to know my name. You will find them...* And that was only today's delivery and at this landing point; one of many around the littorals of the world's largest graveyard! He'd questioned this; surely the authorities would find out soon enough. Why stir things up? The Arab told him that questioning their decisions wasn't part of his job. *Be glad we're giving you a smokescreen. When the authorities turn up, it'll be all hell down on the beach and no one will give a shit what you're up to.* So, to all intents and purposes, his problems would come to an end. He'd be paid, well paid. The Arab was cutting, *don't worry, we'll make sure you earn it.* A cog in a complex machine. All he had to do was get the plan right. He knew it wasn't destined to be that simple.

To begin with, the price of failure didn't need to be spelt out. In the smoke-filled room, the eyes of the Arab had bored into him. Two others sat in the shadows, watching, saying nothing. He could feel the intensity of their presence. The message was clear enough. The Caliphate had a well-publicised method of dealing with those who failed. Images of black-clad soldiers, their victims kneeling before them, were becoming all too familiar. *Had he any questions before the deal was finalised?* He had but preferred to keep them to himself. For a start, the use of a redundant property on his estate was not without complications. Sicilian society may have had a long history of *omertà* but at the beginning of the twenty-first century, it couldn't be guaranteed. Old allegiances, if not quite dead, failed to command the same respect as previously. It was to the state that people looked for protection these days rather than the local landowner. He hoped to God that tenants on his land would know when to hold their tongues.

In the course of the meeting, he'd tried to explain that vigilance had been stepped up, the state was struggling, trying to accommodate the tidal wave of immigrants. Transit camps were overstocked and it was impossible to keep track of every individual. Some would disappear the moment they reached dry land to try to make it on their own. And they hadn't yet reached the mainland of Europe! Swarming all over the country. Likely to turn up anywhere. Long accustomed to invaders, it might be something of a novelty in the islanders' experience that this latest batch sought sanctuary rather than conquest, but even charity had its limits. What if the presence of foreign terrorists was even suspected? Certain elements on the island might have something to say about that. Cosa Nostra! We have our causes too. They didn't want to listen. As far as they were concerned, it was his problem now. The Arab, known as Al-Azhar, was scathing. *That's what we're paying you for, isn't it? We said you'd earn it! Now shake on it, a solemn and binding pledge. Once given, not to be retracted.* So, the pledge was confirmed and twenty trained jihadis, waiting to leave the shores of Libya, were to be spirited away. The Caliphate's crusade against the 'Christian' West galvanised with a new energy for *jihad*. A crusade that had, moreover, taken advantage of the mayhem that Western powers proclaimed as an opportunity for hope, optimistically described as the Arab Spring. The irony was obvious. Spring came in different ways in different places.

Since the fall of the despotic and eccentric Muammar Gaddafi and the end of his 42-year rule, the oil-rich desert state of Libya had descended into political chaos. If despotism had proved anything, it was evident that it had at least stood for a type of stability. Forty-two years were forty-two years. In the new Libya, stability was to prove elusive. Within the space of two years, Libyans found themselves with two rival governments as Islamist and secular militias struggled for power and central authority collapsed. It was proof, if proof was needed, that the transition from despotism to democracy, as European history knew only too well, is not achieved without serious bloodletting.

He stamped his feet and paced up and down trying to encourage some warmth into his limbs. Then the corner of his eye caught a speck on the horizon. As he watched, it grew bigger and gradually assumed the shape of a vessel moving sluggishly, well down in the water, rocking noticeably from side to side as though its cargo was shifting about causing a lack of stability. He signalled to Karim. The Arab climbed out of the cab and sauntered over.

"It's here, thank God."

The Arab spat. The Sicilian thought he heard him mutter "*Inshallah*" under his breath.

"You know what to do," he told him. "Get them into the truck as quickly as possible. Before the passengers are let out."

"You think they don't know?"

"What?"

"The passengers. You think they don't know who's on board?"

"It doesn't matter. That's not the point."

"They know. They don't care."

"We need to keep them apart."

"They don't care as long as they get here."

"It's to protect identities."

Karim shrugged, as if that mattered. "Whatever you say."

"It's what was agreed."

"Whatever."

"Let's get on with it." *And get the hell out of here.*

He scrambled down the rocky path to the beach where an ancient wooden jetty ran a few yards out into the bay. After what seemed like an age, the boat eventually came alongside and a couple of seamen leapt ashore, throwing ropes around bollards and the engine was cut. On the upper deck, a group of men lining the rails began to climb over and jump down onto the jetty. Karim greeted them, brother to brother, "*As-salamu alaykum*," receiving the traditional response as the men began to gather around and embrace him.

11

Suddenly, there was a furious hammering from one of the hatches and before he could be stopped, a seaman on board rushed over, pulled the canvas covers off and released the bolts. The Sicilian shouted out but it was too late and no one heard him. As the hatches burst open, the little vessel began to disgorge its contents. The sounds and smells that emanated from the ship's hold impinged on the morning air. The Sicilian hadn't experienced anything like it before—this legacy of desperate clamour mingled with the stench of human bodies and worse. At heart a refined man, he fought off the urge to throw up and shame himself. Suddenly, the beach was full of men, women and children huddling together in fear and uncertainty. A black African in a rolled neck sweater and a peaked cap approached him.

"Signor Galiano?"

"*Si.*"

"Well, here's your cargo, not quite complete. Two died on the voyage. A pregnant woman whose birth pangs came too soon and an old man who would never have travelled in the first place. They were 'buried' at sea! Another couple of dozen were, let us say, transferred to alternative arrangements."

He glanced at the group of men who were now beginning to form up close to Galiano. "They were encouraged to embark on a dingy and make their own way. With an outboard motor," he added, but thinking, *without enough fuel.* "Soon after we left them, there was an explosion." *So the lack of fuel wouldn't be a problem.* The captain shrugged. *Waste of a good dingy and for what?* Galiano couldn't think of what to say; what was the point of it all? To settle a score, right an ancient wrong, or simply an atavistic response from deep in the folk memory of Islam. The Great Sea alone knew that nothing of significance had taken place in the middle of that night. She had merely opened her arms to receive her reluctant lovers in a cold embrace. Some of the men around Galiano edged closer to the captain. One of them spoke up, a bearded, broadly built man, thirties-something, with the look and tongue of a Libyan, fresh from a desert training camp and eager to show it.

"Christians!" he spat the word out. "Ethiopians! Crusaders! Enemies of the Prophet. They could have converted or paid for protection. They made their choice. It was the will of Allah."

"*Inshallah*," came murmurs of agreement from those around him and the captain fell silent.

Suddenly from close by, there was a penetrating scream. A woman clutching to her side a young boy of maybe nine or ten broke away from the small group she was with and ran towards the speaker. "Murderers! Murderers!" The man who had spoken stepped forward, his t-shirt tight across his chest, his jacket blowing open in the rising breeze. For a moment, he looked at the woman as if he couldn't believe that she had dared to raise her voice, then reached out and caught her a blow on the side of the head. She fell at his feet and lay in the sand sobbing. The child stood frozen to the spot. Galiano noticed a dark patch had formed at the front of his shorts and wetness was running down his leg.

"Her husband was in the dingy," said the captain.

"So, bitch, join him in hell!" He took out a gun from inside his jacket, cocked it, pressed it to the back of the woman's head and fired. As the sound ricocheted around the cliffs, a pall of silence fell on six hundred people. Then he turned to the child.

* * *

Venice
1 April 2015

Several hundred miles to the north, the weather that April morning was altogether more benign. Spring sunshine blessed the city of Venice nestling at the heart of its peaceful lagoon. Already a floodtide of visitors had begun to swarm about the calles and piazzas. To the despair of more elderly residents but, no doubt, to the hopeful anticipation of those whose livelihoods depended on the passing trade. It was a tension to which the city had long become accustomed. The ability to endure with a certain kind of indifference what in the short term meant survival but, in the end, might bring the city to its knees. That's if the floods didn't get there first. But with money in the pocket, there was always the hope of escape to *terra firma* or perhaps a final feast as the waters closed overhead. Given a choice, most born and bred Venetians would opt for the feast.

Lavinia Dyer settled herself at a table for two in the morning sun, ordered her coffee, took off her sunglasses and surveyed her fellow customers. Outside on the pavement, it was all tourists, drawn not from the thousands of day trippers who packed into the city and mostly made for the cafes and ice-cream bars close to Rialto, but those who had discovered or been told that Da Gino's was one of the places where proper Venetians took their coffee. A group of four arrived and settled at the table next to her. There was a 'knowing' air about them. *We'll show you the place to go.* Indoors, a different atmosphere— the conversation around the counter was *Veneziano*, loud and excited. Last night, the national football team had narrowly lost and local views as to the reasons why were many and hotly disputed. Lavinia Dyer smiled—Italian enthusiasm for football as ever undimmed. A journalist of thirty years standing and with a professional reputation second to none, she was in pursuit of a different kind of story. An irritation, as she was meant to be on holiday.

"I hear you're planning to go to Venice next week. Art or romance?" Her chief had hovered somewhat diffidently in the doorway of his office.

"Come on, Ferdy, whatever; do you really suppose I would admit to anything in this place? I sometimes think gossip was invented here. Just interested in my welfare or is your question loaded for some other reason?"

"Sorry, Lavinia, I wasn't prying..." Ferdy Keymer laughed nervously, "...as you've guessed, there's a motive behind my question."

Dyer sighed, *and your motives are never disinterested.* Keymer came into the room, pulled forward a small armchair and sat down. "Church politics."

13

Dyer looked at him enquiringly. "There's a topic for a Friday afternoon! You'll have heard of Father Antonio Marcetti?" he continued. "Who hasn't these days? Embraced by Pope Francis and distrusted by the Curia."

"Well, that's quite a recommendation to begin with," observed Dyer dryly.

"Popular opinion agrees with you. One of our competitors calls him 'the people's favourite friar', no prizes for guessing who!"

"So what's our interest?"

"Two things. His views on the migration crisis in Europe are not being well received in some quarters. No surprises there. The politicians are jumping up and down, not just the Right Wing and not just in Italy. Behind the scenes, there's been pressure on the Vatican to rein him in. I'd like us to be more involved in the issue. It's a global problem, one we've got on our own doorstep. I see a crisis looming here. Another administration might have different views about dealing with it. You've had some experience. It came up in your Mexico interview, yes? With El Presidente."

"We touched on it, that's all."

"Nevertheless, Lavinia, you probably know more about it than anyone else on the paper."

"I don't know anything about Marcetti, bar a lot of media speculation."

"He's been a firebrand in the Catholic Church for years. Migration is only his latest passion. He's carried a torch for reform of church practice since he entered Holy Orders. There was a headline in *Corriere della Sera* last week, '*Dominican seeks Social Justice*'. And that was about abortion!"

"Reminds me of that Italian monk in the Renaissance...I can't think of his name...you know who I mean...made so much trouble," said Dyer. "The one they put to death!"

"Savonarola. Good comparison. He has the same passion and the same intellectual power. And knows how to use them. I imagine the Curia feels similarly inclined!" Keymer gazed out of the window behind Dyer at the Manhattan skyline hazy in the late afternoon sun. "Like Savonarola, Marcetti's also a Dominican. To complicate matters even further, he's being strongly tipped to be the next Master General of the Order. When the present incumbent steps aside, it's said His Holiness would entirely approve of Marcetti's election by the General Chapter. Not that Francis would want to be seen interfering. Not his way. But it would place Marcetti in a very powerful position. The Master of the Order of Preachers commands tremendous respect and with Papal backing, he would be virtually unassailable."

"High politics in the church are all very well, Ferdy, especially on a Friday afternoon. What exactly has my visit to Venice got to do with it?"

"That's the other thing I was going to mention. The week after Easter, Marcetti is preaching in St Mark's Basilica at the Installation of the new Patriarch. Old friends from seminary days. Thought you might try for an interview. Your being on the spot seems too good an opportunity to miss."

"The world's press and its wife will be there. I'll need more than even this paper's good name to get anywhere near. Who do we know in the Patriarchal office?"

"Well," Keymer hesitated, "I thought you might be seeing Casamassa."

"You're a cunning bastard, Ferdy, and no, I have no plans to meet up with Matteo, next week or any other time."

"Take it easy, Lavinia, it was just a thought." Keymer got up, headed for the door. "By the way," he added over his shoulder, "I've got you a ticket to the Installation; the rest will be up to you," and beat a hasty retreat.

While the novelty of a new assignment no longer seemed to excite her interest, there was something about Antonio Marcetti that Dyer found intriguing and slightly disturbing. She thought it over. A man who so sharply divided opinion was worth probing. But what dangers lurked beneath the surface of such a complex and volatile personality? The possibility of a meeting and an interview carried a certain allure. She picked up her iPhone and sent a text to the *Reuters* man in Venice.

As the visitors streamed past her along the Calle Nuova, Lavinia Dyer contemplated the week ahead with mixed feelings. Over the last few months, her job had started to lack its old sense of fulfilment. The adrenaline she counted on as necessary for a top-ranking investigative journalist seemed to be ebbing away. Virtually every major prize that the profession handed down, including last year's Pulitzer, had fallen into her lap and she knew the paper regarded her as its most distinguished asset. On the wrong side of fifty and a single woman, Dyer accepted that she had traded the normal expectations of a settled home life for one that was nomadic but often exciting and full of surprise, which was, she supposed, the compensation. She'd come a long way since student days at Princeton. They'd pressed her to stay on, but she'd secured a place at the Harvard Business School and then entered journalism still in her early twenties. Before she reached thirty, the *New York Times* had head-hunted her. From then on, there was no looking back. Assignments took her back and forth across every continent, into every war zone on the planet. There was scarcely an international leader she had not interviewed and certainly more than one who, in good newspaper speak, had been drawn into 'a frank exchange' by a combination of good looks and a very sharp intellect. Of course, there had been relationships, usually without much emotional involvement on her side and always transitory. Now middle age was upon her; she felt its onset even if the outward manifestations were for the moment held at bay. Lavinia Dyer was still a remarkably good-looking woman, easily mistaken for ten years younger. She had come to Venice because she loved the city, knew it intimately, felt more at home than in New York. At one time, she had even contemplated buying an apartment there. Until Matteo, that is.

Matteo Casamassa, director of one of the most prestigious art collections in Venice, a man with connections and hence a coveted contact for any journalist worth the salt. He and Dyer had met at the opening of a major exhibition two years ago. '*Venetian Art of the High Renaissance*' was heralded a triumph and

Casamassa's reputation, which scarcely needed enhancing, soared to Olympian heights. An impromptu interview with Lavinia Dyer appeared in the *New York Times*. The international art scene hailed him as one of its golden boys. Thus, began an affair intended by the participants to be conducted in clandestine conditions; Casamassa had a wife and three children. Fortuitously, as matters turned out, it entirely escaped public notice—no minor achievement in a city as small and gossipy as La Serenissima. It did not, however, escape the notice of Signora Casamassa. After a month, Dyer retreated hastily to New York and Casamassa followed. Not, she was later to discover, out of love but to inspect the legacy of a wealthy collector from which his gallery was to benefit. And there it ended as suddenly as it had begun, one evening over dinner. His wife had delivered an ultimatum: Stop it now or public exposure. No recriminations, *cara*, a wonderful time while it lasted. But Dyer had invested far more in the relationship than even she'd realised. If she'd been capable of rational thought at that moment, she would have suspected the bluff. Giuliana Casamassa was not the kind of woman who'd do anything to place her own position in society in jeopardy, even to the extent of tolerating the latest in her husband's long line of affairs, especially as they were not characterised by longevity. Despite everything, Dyer threw herself into her work and an assignment cropped up that took her to Mexico City, culminating in a high-profile interview with the President of the Republic. That saved her sanity and her self-respect. And it didn't do her reputation any harm.

Now she was back in her former lover's home city and knowing it was too much to expect, in search of a favour. Matteo regularly attended mass in the Basilica and was well acquainted with members of its clergy; he would be the obvious route to a contact in the Patriarchal palace. It might work if she could contrive an accidental meeting before the Installation; a dangerous proposition for a middle-aged ex-lover whose feelings were still bruised from the last encounter. She was counting on her *Reuters* colleague to help pave the way. Dyer sighed, signalled the waiter and ordered another *macchiato*.

* * *

London, the Foreign Office
2 April 2015

A discreet knock on the panelled door and the male secretary entered the room without waiting for a response.

"Sir Peter Glendower, minister." He stood aside to admit a tall grey-haired man with a walking stick.

"Sir Peter, come in. Please have a seat," indicating the buttoned leather armchair in front of the enormous desk. "Good of you to come at such short notice."

"Your secretary sounded urgent."

The Minister of State for Foreign Affairs, a small overweight man in his forties with a red face, a shock of red hair and an anxious expression, rose from his chair with difficulty and leaned across to shake his hand. It was, Glendower noted, distinctly clammy. But then the minister had only been in post a few weeks and was probably struggling to come to terms with his new job. In his long Civil Service career, he'd seen political appointments come and go; most needed their hands held at the beginning and many for the duration of their office. This one was still an unknown quantity with no previous experience in the thorny field of British foreign affairs. Still less of the security services. Not that that was necessarily a disadvantage. The less they knew, the more they might listen to advice. *Some hope of that!*

"Urgent, yes, I suppose so. I'm learning that in this job, everything's urgent today; whether it remains urgent tomorrow is not so certain. However, the Foreign Secretary assures me that the matter we have to discuss today is both urgent *and* top priority," he frowned and shuffled the papers in front of him. "You'll be aware that next week, he's attending the EU foreign ministers' conference in Brussels on the migration problem. He'd like to reassure his colleagues that the British Government is ahead of the game."

"Understandable. I take it government policy isn't about to change."

"Well, there's a need for reappraisal. A sharpening up of our focus, a different approach. Immigration statistics bring small comfort. But, that apart, what's bugging everyone at the moment are the press reports of this Italian monk. The allegations he's been making."

"The Dominican, Marcetti. He's been on our radar for some time."

"He has?"

"Yes."

"How did that happen?"

"In the time-honoured way. An overheard conversation. We have someone in the household of the Nuncio, the Vatican's diplomatic representative."

"And?"

"Senior members of visiting religious Orders usually drop in as a matter of courtesy."

"Lucky for us, they do."

"Indeed, minister."

"May one enquire what you've been doing about it?"

Glendower could tell the minister was eager for details. He was having none of it.

"Kept him under surveillance when he's been in the UK."

"That's it?"

"There's little else we can do."

"Well, the guy needs to put up and name names, or shut up."

"I doubt he'll do either. He's been a thorn in the Vatican's side for a long time. The Curia doesn't like the *status quo* being upset. But it hasn't been able to silence him."

"Why doesn't his Order shut him up? I thought monks were meant to be under some sort of obedience."

"It's said he has the Pope's backing. A formidable ally."

"A bloody pain in the backside."

Glendower resisted the temptation to ask to whom he was referring. The minister was noted for plain speaking and anything was possible. He was beginning to warm to his subject.

"Even His Holiness must see the potential for damage to the church's reputation. This allegation—that some members of the EU are funding the people traffickers. For God's sake, what the hell does that mean? Some new kind of overseas aid? Who's he got it in for; has he got a grudge or something?"

"He enjoys causing shock waves," observed Glendower mildly.

"What about this claim of a secret campaign to provoke a backlash about the numbers of migrants coming into the EU?"

"It's feasible. The signs are there. Some of the media know how to fire up public opinion. Even over here. The right-wing press in Germany has already been demanding the forced repatriation of migrants with military backing."

"Umm, I've seen it. Send them back to where they came from, regardless of the reasons they came in the first place. Starvation and persecution no bar, to hell with the consequences. Sounds familiar coming from that lot."

"There's a plausible theory behind it. Pay the smugglers to pile them in, sit back and wait for the reaction and then have a neat political solution ready to hand. Up to a point, we've been there before."

"Rather savvy for a monastic, wouldn't you say?"

"He's had a lot of practice. Been at the forefront of this issue for a long time." *A lot longer than you, my friend.*

"Sooner or later, there're going to be some nasty reactions."

"Already are, Minister. Hungary's closed its borders, the southern Balkans are talking about doing the same. Here, it's becoming an issue. Demands are growing for a referendum on Europe. Immigration's bound to loom large if that were to happen."

"Yes, well, there are things we will need to consider in any case."

"Part of a reappraisal?"

The minister coughed and looked embarrassed. "Perhaps we should skip that. Still under discussion in the cabinet."

"Naturally. There are dissenting voices, of course."

"Huh! A few Church of England bishops? I've read it. Typically, naïve. But then, *realpolitik* was never their forte. Getting back to Marcetti, he must believe he's got evidence."

"Presumably. Doesn't strike one as a fantasist. Insider information?"

"That's where your department comes in. We've no idea if he's about to make public who's involved. Top priority is to trace his source. Find that and we may be able to find who's supposed to be bankrolling the smugglers. As for the claim that the British government's behind the whole enterprise, the Prime Minister isn't exactly taking that on the chin."

"No, I imagine not. We could be getting into very dangerous territory here. If there's any truth in it, we're looking at someone who believes they're representing the unofficial views of the most senior levels of government."

"Umm," the minister looked thoughtful. "So, someone with influence. A power behind the throne. I can think of one or two."

"And access to very large sums of money; private funds, I assume."

"God forbid taxpayers' money being diverted onto human trafficking. That would play well with the public, wouldn't it?"

Whatever was going on, Glendower thought, *there's no question which way the wind is blowing. The newly elected government with its slender majority thinks its very survival under threat. And so it may be.*

"Minister, don't forget; we're not standing alone on this. Some of our European colleagues are being targeted by the same accusations. We need to talk to them. They may have information that would be valuable."

"I want you to handle this. The PM has already made it clear that nothing official is to be countenanced. This is a job for the Intelligence Services. We don't want to stir up a worse hornet's nest than we have already."

"Informal approaches to our fellow services on the Continent would be more prudent in the circumstances. Some of our EU partners can be extremely sensitive. The UK is not universally trusted. I take it the Foreign Secretary believes there's no doubt we're on Marcetti's hit list. Why is that, I wonder? Who else does he suspect is likely to be named?"

The minister declined to answer. Either he didn't know the answer or had been told to keep his mouth closed—most likely the latter. *Typical of a new administration*, thought Glendower. Tie the hands of the security services in the interests of so-called open government (a manifesto pledge!) and then expect miracles to be performed. If there was a favourable result, *aren't we the clever ones*; failure, and *we knew nothing about it, but please accept that heads will roll, beginning, my dear Sir Peter, with yours.* And if the failure was really bad, think purge! When a government was on the run, any kind of treachery was par for the course.

Glendower took a roundabout route back to his office, heading for St James's Park needing time and fresh air to take stock of his meeting. The minister was running scared and not simply through inexperience. Clearly, he was being leant on from above and Glendower wanted to know why; did the Foreign Secretary know more than he was admitting to or did he at least suspect how the Dominican might be obtaining his information? Beyond that, the guesswork was too horrifying to put into words. How far was the new administration prepared to go? What was it the minister had said, *Government policy on immigration needed reappraising? A sharpened focus? A different approach?* Glendower sensed that behind the deceptively bland phrases lay a covert and well-conceived strategy. One that might carry frightening consequences.

The park was quiet for the time of year; the thin April sunshine lacking in enough warmth to tempt out the normal crop of lunchtime picnickers. Office workers and a few tourists, young couples strolling but virtually nobody lounging around on the grass under the trees; summer habits still far off. Along the path by the lake, a group of young schoolboys in their red blazers and caps chirping like birds were hurried along by a harassed-looking young female teacher. "Come on, don't dawdle; we'll be late for the show." One child smiled up at the grey-haired man with a walking stick as they passed by. Glendower returned the smile but felt a chill on his heart. A spare man in figure, his face pallid, cheekbones prominent, his well-cut suit was beginning to hang loosely round the shoulders indicating that this was a man marked down by illness. What kind of society, he wondered, were these children going to inherit? One where political leaders were willing to deal in death and where ethnic cleansing was public policy, secret doctrines that were about to receive worldwide currency, the twentieth century resonating with a terrifying familiarity, a corpse refusing to allow itself to be buried. Emerging onto Birdcage Walk, he consulted his watch and hailed a taxi.

Back in his office, he asked his efficient young secretary to contact Milo Standish. Less than ten minutes later, Standish entered the room and was waved to an armchair by the window where Glendower joined him.

"Milo, I need you to find someone, maybe more than one. Hidden, in all probability, in plain sight. Not many leads at the moment but that may be about to change." So ensued a summary of his meeting and the bare facts as known— no commentary, no personal opinion. When he had finished, he relaxed, leant back in his chair, formed a pyramid with his hands, rested his chin upon them and waited. Standish remained silent, seemingly lost in thought, gazing out of the window at the plane trees along the river already bursting into leaf. The only sound in the room was the ticking of the Boule clock on the desk, the Chief's pride and joy. In his early forties, with dark hair greying at the temples, pronounced crow's feet at the corners of his pale blue eyes, there was a latent alertness about him, a pent-up energy waiting to be released. It was well-known in the intelligence community that Milo Standish's particular expertise lay in the field of information analysis. Therefore, a careful, well-considered man. Eventually, he spoke up quietly, weighing his words.

"How long have you and I worked together, Chief? It must be getting on for twenty years. How many times have you presented me with a situation that required all our ingenuity, yes and cunning too, to deal with a threat to our national security? Sometimes, I tremble to think of the risks we took, usually calculated, but not always. Most of the time, we were lucky. Usually, we thought we'd made a difference for the better. I've often had doubts about that but holding onto it has kept me going. We've had our share of rotten apples too. We both know we have to pick through the barrel from time to time. This time, which barrel do we look in?"

"All of them, I guess."

"Reaching the ones at the top isn't going to be easy."

"None of them are sacrosanct, Milo. Whatever access you'll need, you have in my name."

"And the consequences?"

"I'm head of the service. They fall on me." He looked thoughtfully out of the window, watching a river bus making its way down from Putney to Canary Wharf. "I somehow imagined that in forty years, I'd seen most things. But…this abuse of humanity. Exploiting the lives of innocent refugees, all the makings of a modern holocaust. It takes depravity to a whole new level." He eased himself out of his chair with difficulty and walked over to a side table. "Glass of sherry?"

"Thanks."

"So, where do we go from here?"

"From what the minister has told you, we have to assume that the UK's about to be branded an international criminal. If that's not putting it too strongly. He may have overstated the situation. Let's face it; ministers are inclined to do that. Truth is, we don't know. From the little we do know about Marcetti, he has a tendency to indulge in the histrionic. But perhaps only if he thinks there'll be a payoff. I don't know what he hopes that might be in this case."

"Simply to be proved right. Job satisfaction." Glendower gave a dry laugh.

"My instinct is that it would matter little either way. After all, it's the internet age. No escaping that. Accusations of this kind, true or not, will come out and we have to live with them. That's got to be our starting point. If other governments are involved, it's not independently. That would be a coincidence too far. To be blunt, I see all the hallmarks of a conspiracy."

"Hm. I've been thinking along the same lines. We've had Marcetti under surveillance for a while. Anything come of it?"

"Not enough to justify it, really."

"How many have you got on it?"

"Only one. Young part-time recruit. Trying him out. He's good."

"How long's it been?"

"Six months."

"Are you going to close it down?"

"Not now, I'm not. I've something a bit more ambitious in mind."

Glendower smiled and got up to refill their glasses. "Why do I feel you're about to let me in on something?"

"Let's just say, Chief, with your permission, I'd like to take a post-Easter break."

"Great idea, Milo. Venice is very nice at this time of year. Hope you don't mind the suggestion."

Standish laughed, "Grateful for it. Hear there's likely to be some good preaching in Saint Mark's next week!"

"May it be good for the health of your soul! Now tell what you've got in mind."

When Standish had finished, Glendower stood up, stretched his aching limbs and finished off his glass of sherry. "I could do with a breath of air. Care for a stroll?"

Leaving the building by a side entrance, the two intelligence officers walked across the forecourt down towards the river. Boats plied to and fro under Vauxhall Bridge; traffic on the bridge itself had come to a temporary halt. A cool breeze blew off the river and Glendower momentarily shivered and pulled his coat closer.

"You all right, Chief?"

"Feel the cold more these days." He'd listened intently up in his office while Standish outlined his plan. "A number of risks, Milo, right?"

"Right."

"Worth it, if it works."

"Might make him stop and think."

"The Marcettis of this world rarely stop and think. Don't want to see the bigger picture in case it spoils their fun. Your instincts are right, though. Marcetti has to be the priority."

"We need to know what he knows, or claims he knows. And how he came by it."

"So, a meeting? That might take a stroke of luck. The Press will be hanging on his every word."

"I'm hoping the new Patriarch of Venice will play ball. He owes me a favour!"

"Leaving Marcetti aside for the moment, we've got a homegrown conspiracy on our hands. I'd like to come at it from both ends at once and use the time you're away to put a few options together. Might be of help when you get back."

Standish leaned against the balustrade, looking up at the fortress-like building.

"Behind any conspiracy, there's an alliance of interests. And behind that, there'll be big money. It's often said, 'follow the money'. The question is, why? Why invest enormous sums in a dangerously high-risk venture?"

"It's happened before. As long as the right conditions are there, it's not as difficult as one might imagine. Social change is the catalyst to political change. The lesson of twentieth-century history. Potentially, the migrant problem is the greatest social problem Europe's seen since 1945. It's this century's first lesson in geo-politics. Have you seen the latest estimates?"

Standish shook his head.

"Five hundred thousand waiting to cross the Med from North Africa alone. Then there are those trying to get into Europe from Syria and elsewhere. Work out the figures. A thousand quid a head for the smugglers, minimum. Perhaps double it. Plus, the commission from their backers. One way or another, that's an awful lot of cash swilling about."

"Whoever's doing the bankrolling must be expecting a bloody big pay-off."

"Naturally. The risk has to be worth it."

"Political power?"

"It's a fair bet. We shouldn't underestimate the resurgence of the Far Right. Even on the other side of the pond. My guess is that our conspirators are positioning themselves to take advantage of how the wind is blowing. Stage one is destabilisation, which is happening as we speak."

"Stage two…?"

"Think the unthinkable. Milo, I'm aware of the fact I'm asking you to take on a job where the parameters aren't easy to define. That's not the way we normally work. You realise, of course, I might not be around to hold the torch. All the indications are that my time is limited. God willing, I'll stay until the last possible moment."

Visibly moved, Standish ventured the question, "Are you sure you want to do that?"

"I've no reason not to. I'm not a family man. No ties, except the Service," he smiled. "So, my friend, good luck. Send me a postcard!"

"I certainly will," said Standish.

* * *

The City of Enna, Sicily
Good Friday, 3 April 2015

A solemn procession of white-hooded figures wound its way through the silent crowd-lined streets of the city of Enna. Beneath the hoods, each figure wore the distinctive habit of the Confraternity of the Holy Shroud, emblazoned with a scarlet cross, denoting its ancient connection to the Knights Templar. The Good Friday procession was nearing its climax as it drew closer to the Duomo. It had left the baroque church of St Joseph of Aramathea two hours previously, bearers carrying on their shoulders an ornately carved and gilded frame within which hung a replica of the Shroud of Christ. As the procession approached the cathedral, all the other confraternities stood waiting silently, together with an enormous black-veiled statue of the grief-stricken Madonna. Then the bright red capes of the Confraternity of the Passion moved forward in unison, carrying on scarlet cushions the symbols of Christ's suffering—the whip, the nails, the soldiers' dice, the crown of thorns and a live heavily sedated cockerel representing St Peter's betrayal.

As the Holy Shroud Confraternity made its slow progress, one pair of eyes at the head of the column, peering through the twin slits in its white hood, scanned the lines of onlookers. Luca Galiano had been a member since boyhood and still maintained his family's long tradition of leading the cortège into the splendid baroque basilica for the commencement of the Good Friday mass. The annual ritual had become second nature to him. His mind strayed to the twenty jihadi fighters penned up thirty kilometres away in a series of remote farm buildings at Altrabia. The journey, a week ago, from the landing place in an ex-army truck had passed without further incident. What occurred on the beach was unfortunate and unforeseen. Two bodies to be disposed of and six hundred frightened and volatile refugees cowed into temporary submission. But who knew for how long. Sooner or later, someone would be emboldened to talk, and talk eventually would reach the ears of the leaders of the Soldiers of the Caliphate. The possible consequences were too hideous to contemplate. Galiano shuddered; matters were running out of control. Al-Azhar had impressed upon him, in no uncertain terms and with scarcely veiled threats, the absolute imperative of secrecy for that part of the operation. But already the Catania police had discovered the shallow graves. He knew that no blame could be attached to him for the murders of the woman and child. He also knew that that would count for nothing where Al-Azhar was concerned. The fighters should have been removed from the beach before the rest of the migrants disembarked. Damn that captain; too eager by half to distance himself from the plight of the Ethiopian Christians. Well! No doubt he too would become a casualty of the terror war! The Caliphate would see to that.

Darkness fell quickly on the city. Galiano led his procession up the long flight of steps to the great entrance doors. Here, the crowds had been kept well back to allow the confraternities room to assemble and form up with their sacred objects before entering the cathedral. A movement among the onlookers caught his attention. A white-shirted man was trying to push forward as if to gain a better vantage point, followed by two others; a couple with a young child obligingly shifted to one side to let the strangers through. But a police officer stepped forward, stretching out his arms to forestall the manoeuvre. They hesitated, drew back slightly and waited. Galiano passed out of their sight into the Duomo, his confraternity behind him. He murmured a silent prayer of thanks for the protection of his hood; it was inconceivable that he'd been recognised. The man in the crowd was Al-Azhar. One of the others was the armed terrorist on the beach, called Mahsoud. Galiano's anonymity was destined to be short-lived. As they moved down the nave towards the high altar, the white hoods were removed prior to the adoration of the holy images. Behind them, the cathedral was filling up—first the other confraternities laying their images to either side of the glass coffin, borne by the Confraternity of Sanctissimo Salvatore, then last of all, members of the public crowded in behind to take whatever vacant space was left. Galiano, in a sudden spasm of panic, turned to his companion in the procession, keeping his voice low, "Take over, I have to leave, say nothing."

"Luca, you're ill?"

"Say nothing! You know what to do." Slipping in front of the other robed figures at the altar steps, he moved quickly towards a side door that led to the cathedral sacristy. A party of acolytes emerged with smoking censers at that moment. He nearly collided with the leaders. One of them, an older man, looked alarmed and started to say something but Galiano pushed past him and made for the passage that led to the outside door, pulling off his robes as he went. He paused to bundle up the garments and stuffed them in the bottom of one of the great *armadios* that lined the walls of the room. The street was mercifully dark, illuminated only from one end by the lights from the piazza. He turned to his left and the shadows enveloped him.

Outside the cathedral, a group of three men stood in the entrance porch to the right of the main doors, their voices muffled by the chanting of the congregation inside. On the curving steps below them, a crowd of onlookers, mostly tourists, craned for a view of the rituals taking place. The cathedral was tightly packed—worshippers spilling out through the great doors mingling with those who had been unable to gain access.

"He was there?" inquired the beach fighter, Mahsoud. "You can be certain?"

"He was there," came the answer, "he's always there, at the head of his confraternity."

"So now we wait for him to leave, without his mask, if Allah wills it."

"By all that's holy, are you crazy?" interjected his companion. "With these crowds of infidels, you'd never get near enough to strike with a knife."

"Watch your tongues," said Al-Azhar.

"So what do you intend?"

"Nothing. We do nothing now."

"Nothing?"

"Nothing, I tell you. Hear me well. He knows we are here. We could not see him but he saw us. A warning has been given. That was the point of all this. It will suffice this time. We have no proof it was Galiano who reported the deaths on the beach. He is still of use to us. He will be watched at all times. With your companions holed up on his property waiting for transfer, more bloodshed would accomplish nothing. It has already compromised us unnecessarily," he added with a meaningful look at Mahsoud. "Come! We return to the farm. There is much to do before this night ends."

The house of Luca Galiano was close to the city centre. An old villa built in the seventeenth century of unpretentious appearance with peeling grey stucco, it overlooked the vast plain that stretched into the distance. The province of Enna lay at the centre of the island of Sicily and its eponymous capital city had been built on the summit of a gigantic hill. Surrounded on all sides by precipitous cliffs rendering it almost wholly inaccessible, it was one of the most remarkable natural fortresses in the world. An enterprising Barone of Galiano had chosen the site of his family's town house well—at the end of a narrow street and easy to spot the approach of strangers, but not the best escape route if one was required. Tonight, the house was deserted apart from the presence of one ancient retainer who acted as guardian and gatekeeper; the remaining staff of three women was busily occupied in the cathedral with their Good Friday devotions, a ritual unthinkable to miss. Galiano's sudden arrival caught the old fellow unawares and confused; surely the ceremonies would have barely begun?

"Barone! Why are you home? Has something happened?"

"It's all right, Seppi. Don't be alarmed. I have to go away unexpectedly. I must pack a few things and then leave. Please fetch the car and have it ready for me. When the others return, you will explain my change of plan."

Galiano's household was well accustomed to the flexibility of their employer's arrangements. Despite the usual grumbles normal between domestic staff, the resulting inconveniences were accepted with resignation. It had not been so, of course, in the old days of his much-revered parents. The daily rituals of life followed a predetermined pattern, unvaried throughout the year and surprises were few. But times had moved on; after the premature death of Galiano's wife, the two children, now grown up, had left home—the daughter to Palermo to marry and then move to the USA, and the son to work in Milan. Life for him had begun to change as well. A chance meeting with an Arab businessman in Malta where the family had property interests produced quite unforeseen results. No doubt at all the man was suave but seemed cultured and intelligent. He had spoken knowledgably about financial affairs and clearly had experience in managing a considerable property portfolio with investments in half a dozen countries around the Mediterranean. He could perhaps be of some assistance to the Barone and at the end of an alcohol-fuelled evening, Galiano was encouraged to admit that his own business affairs were somewhat in the doldrums. He was open, therefore, to suggestions. Any interesting enterprise would be worth consideration. Enough for tonight, the Arab had concluded, good business required cool heads. So, no further discussion until tomorrow; with a new dawn would come a new clarity! They would meet over lunch; that would suit the Barone? A courteous offer to drive Galiano back to his hotel was accepted with grateful thanks and the chauffeur, a model of impeccable manners, even escorted the Sicilian to the door of his suite. Crossing to the bedroom his clothes came off as he staggered drunkenly to the generous-sized bed, sinking down with relief. The appearance from nowhere of a naked boy in his early teens who promptly climbed onto his lap occasioned only the slightest surprise. *What on earth*, he thought hazily, *did his young son think he was doing here?* Suddenly, the bright flash from a camera startled him. Then he passed out.

The shortest route to the coast and on to the ferry terminal at Messina would have taken Galiano within two kilometres of Altrabia, too close for comfort, a risk of being spotted on the road by the trio from Enna. He decided on the longer journey via Catania. With luck and no delays in crossing to the mainland, he would be at the remote Calabrian estate in the early hours of the morning. San Vibio belonged to a distant relation, a childless widower in his late eighties now being cared for in a residential home in Cosenza, of whom Galiano was the sole heir. The old man had handed the hunting lodge over years ago, pleased to be free of the responsibility for its upkeep. A safe retreat, not even known to his staff in Sicily, he used the place from time to time during the course of his marriage as an escape from the trials of family life and a convenient venue for entertaining the occasional girlfriend. Maria, the elderly housekeeper, and her husband Gino who acted as guardian, the sole members of staff on the premises, were unfazed by his sudden appearances and tolerant of his house guests. Traffic was light at this early hour and the journey from the ferry port of San Giovanni north was uneventful. Galiano left the main coastal highway and turned onto a minor road that led deep into the Calabrian hills.

* * *

Altrabia
3 April 2015

At the remote farmstead, Raschid Al-Azhar was addressing his contingent of the Soldiers of the Caliphate. They were about to embark on the next stage of their mission, he told them. Infiltration was a delicate exercise. The strategy would be to release them in pairs over the next week or two to avoid attracting attention. They would be conveyed to various port cities around the Sicilian coastline, from where they would embark on a variety of ferry routes to destinations on the Italian mainland. After that, infiltration into the capital cities and some of the main tourist locations throughout the European Union was a matter of time and planning. Use of existing networks with resources would be made through contact with local imams with known sympathies for the Caliphate's cause. But that was several stages ahead; his immediate concerns were twofold. First, they must ensure that their presence on Sicilian soil remained secret. So no wandering from the farm into the surrounding countryside. And secondly, they needed to keep themselves occupied. They were fresh from a training camp in the harsh conditions of the Libyan Desert. They'd achieved a level of physical fitness that must be maintained. He understood how eager they were to begin their glorious work. They must do nothing to put that at risk. He then drew Karim to one side for a private talk. Hotheads like Mahsoud, he said, posed a particular problem. Not averse to stirring up others, his continued presence at the farm could only spell trouble, which might have catastrophic results. He must be moved on as soon as possible.

Easter weekend saw the first real surge in tourism as the forthcoming season got underway and traffic across the Messina Straits was heavy in both directions. Among the usual mass of cars and caravans, a final smattering of commercial vehicles hastened to get home. Tour coaches from across the continent crowded the waiting areas on both sides of the channel. One coach belonging to a tour company in Catania was filled with some of the migrants who a few days before had landed on the southern Sicilian beach. After initial processing, they were now destined for one of the over-crowded detention camps on the mainland in an attempt to relieve the pressure on the island's three centres. Mahsoud and his travelling companion, carrying only light hand luggage, strode past heading for the *imbarcadero* for foot passengers. Deep in conversation, they were unaware of being recognised or that their progress was being watched from the coach by one passenger in particular. A man who, like the others travelling with him, had landed from a Libyan fishing vessel and had witnessed the cold-blooded murder of a woman and child. A man who, despite being a refugee in search of a better life, was not afraid to speak out. The woman volunteer in the holding centre had listened to him with sympathy. Her eyes had filled with tears but behind the tears was a grim determination and she had called the police and sat with him while he told his story.

* * *

Rome-Venice Express
6 April 2015

A black-suited figure joined the queue of those waiting to board the mid-morning express from Rome to Venice. Carrying only a briefcase and a small valise, his first-class seat had been booked in advance—a concession by his superiors, not normally granted, for a member of the Dominican Order whose photograph regularly featured in the press and had even appeared on the front cover of *Time*. It helped to insure a degree of privacy and hopefully avoided the necessity of unsolicited conversation. His civilian dress, by its anonymity, also afforded some protection from the more importunate members of the public. Traditionally, members of the Order wore a white habit with black cloak and were instantly recognisable, as an ancient wit had once remarked, as the Domini Canes—the Hounds of the Lord. There was still at least one member of the Order on the staff of the Congregation for the Doctrine of the Faith, the modern successor to the Inquisition. These days, members of the Order fulfilled a rather different function than hunting down and burning heretics. There were some in the Vatican who were wondering why they hadn't bothered to tell Marcetti. His evangelising zeal coupled with a formidable intellect had been spotted early on by his superiors and got qualified approval. But when his name began to appear in the headlines, a warning bell began to toll. Trying to curb in the young friar a tendency to find himself in the spotlight proved challenging. Centre stage was exactly where Marcetti was most comfortable and from where he was most reluctant to be dislodged.

"Your gifts are already acknowledged, my son," remarked his spiritual director. "You must beware of self-advertisement. The Order does not wish to stifle enthusiasm or restrict your development as an effective preacher of the Gospel but your voice is merely a vehicle through which God speaks. It is His message the faithful need to hear. We're only servants, day-labourers in the vineyard. You hold strong, dare I say, radical views on a number of subjects. Can you be certain you represent the mind of the church, let alone the mind of your Order? Some members of the Chapter have expressed reservations. It is a fine line you tread, remember that."

Undeterred by his confessor's admonition, Marcetti had driven himself even harder, espousing a variety of causes unpopular with conservative tendencies in the mainstream church but—as might be expected—widely applauded in the left-wing secular press. The status of women in the Catholic Church and in other cultures; the problems posed by alternative lifestyles;

abortion and contraception; in all these, his voice challenged traditional wisdom and incurred the censure of his superiors. 'A prophet is not without honour except in his own country and amongst his own people,' a well-known journalist had quipped. It seemed to Marcetti a fair summary of official reaction, but the zealot in his character overrode opposition. Eventually, his intellectual rigour and persuasive oratory won him grudging respect. His younger co-religionists in the Order gave him their tacit support. Here was a priest with fire in his belly and evangelistic fervour in his heart, something of a rarity these days. Like the dragon of the Apocalypse, he would breathe that fire on the ungodly, however exalted their status. Those who stood in its path would be consumed. What was less clear to his critics was the question of who divided the sheep from the goats, the ungodly from the godly. Many suspected that it was Marcetti himself who determined where the blade should fall.

"He claims to be a spokesman for the righteous anger of God," complained a senior member of the Order.

"That's some claim," voiced another. "Can we be certain that he is truly a prophetic voice for the age in which we live?"

"There's an arrogance in his manner," said the friar sitting beside him in Chapter. "This is a pluralistic society. There are many shades of opinion. Our duty is to listen to voices that often conflict with our own."

"God's anger at the excesses of human folly has always been a crucial part of our preaching," countered another. "It was the reason our Order was founded."

"But it should always be tempered by love," observed the Master mildly. "It is that that disturbs me. I feel the anger but see less of the love."

Settled in his seat in an otherwise empty carriage, Marcetti took his copy of *Corriere della Sera* from his briefcase and began reading. As the express slipped almost noiselessly northwards to Florence and Bologna, he soon found himself nodding off to sleep lulled by the gentle motion. Exactly what roused him some time later he was never sure—perhaps the gradual slowing down as the train approached the outskirts of Bologna. He opened his eyes to see a figure standing in the aisle in front of him. The youth who looked scarcely out of his teens was smartly dressed in a dark blue two-piece suit and a white shirt, tieless but buttoned at the neck and with short neatly cut hair. *He had the appearance*, Marcetti thought, *of a student waiting to be interviewed for an internship*. Hesitant almost bashful in manner, he seemed about to apologise for disturbing the older man's sleep.

"Monsignor Marcetti?"

"Just 'Father', my son."

"But you are the Dominican priest we hear so much about."

Marcetti smiled and shrugged. "How may I assist you, young man?"

An almost imperceptible change in manner, a tightening of the facial muscles, a slight squaring of the shoulders, a few beads of perspiration forming on the dark-skinned brow. Not the bashful youth anymore. Marcetti, experienced in the way students presented themselves in challenging

29

situations—the subtle accommodations they made with their body language saying, I'm equal to this moment—detected a change of mood and waited patiently for the youth to continue.

"You are a crusader, an enemy of the Prophet, you have crushed my people for too long. Now is the hour of your martyrdom." Words carefully rehearsed, learned by rote, almost a mantra, prelude to an act that was to follow. Slowly, he took from his pocket a short-bladed knife and advanced a step towards Marcetti. At that precise moment, the door at the end of the carriage opened and the conductor appeared followed by another man in railway uniform. For a split second, the youth hesitated, then turned on his heel and raced down the carriage in the opposite direction.

"Signor!" the conductor cried out and hurried to his passenger's side. "Was that a knife? Were you threatened? Are you harmed?"

"Threatened, yes. Harmed, no, my friend."

"The Mother of God be praised. Signor, excuse us, we must find him. The other passengers! Aldo," to his companion, "call the *carabinieri*! We're coming into Bologna."

When the Rome express pulled into Santa Lucia Ferrovia in Venice at the end of its journey, it had succeeded in making up most of the delay caused by the search for Marcetti's would-be attacker. Of course, no one had been apprehended in Bologna, the timing of the confrontation nearly perfect. Arrival at a busy station, platform crowded with passengers waiting to board for the final leg of the journey. Easy enough to slip through and leave the concourse before the victim had been discovered and disappear into the crowds of the city, one face among hundreds. A senior officer of the *carabinieri* had travelled with Marcetti for the remainder of the journey taking a statement, a description of the youth and discussing the security implications of his visit to Venice.

"How long are you planning on staying in the city, Father? We can offer you some protection but you will appreciate it will be all but impossible to guard against an attack on the street. This is one of the busiest tourist venues in Europe and you are staying in the residence of the Patriarch at the very heart of the world's most famous piazza. If I may respectfully offer a word of advice, remain indoors. In the Basilica we can protect you; there'll be a heavy police presence at the Installation with so many distinguished guests attending."

Consigned to the care of two armed officers of the local force, Marcetti was escorted to a waiting launch moored at the foot of the steps in front of the station on the Grand Canal. On the opposite side, a large party of Japanese tourists were clustered around a guide in front of the church of St Simeon Piccolo, drinking in every word and cameras at the ready. His eyes were drawn to a group of students. Two boys among them were sitting on the edge of the quay, poring over a map and laughing together; his mind travelled back to his first visit to the city forty years ago with his friend, Salim. In the city, it had been hot and humid with not even a breath of wind to stir the air. So the Syrian boy had suggested a trip on the *vaporetto* out to the island of Torcello. Out on the lagoon, he'd said, there's always a refreshing breeze, the place to escape to when the city got too much to bear.

"And Torcello you have to see; it's special."

"What's special about it?"

"Wait until we get there; it'll blow your mind."

He'd laughed, "You've been listening to too much Dylan."

"Who doesn't? Seriously though, it's amazing. My mother took me there on my first visit to Venice when I was fourteen. You'll see what I mean."

And Salim, the friend of his youth, the Syrian boy with a Catholic mother and a Muslim father, had shown him the wonders of the cathedral of Santa Maria Assunta with its dazzling mosaic of the Blessed Virgin.

"It's called the hodegetria. I'm not sure what that means. Your Greek's better than mine, Antonio."

So Marcetti had told him. "It means 'showing the way'."

"Well, she does show the way. Her image stays in the mind long after you have left it behind. Maybe that's it. You come back to it years later to find it still beckons. She seems to be leading you somewhere you weren't expecting. Weird in a way."

The following semester, after he'd returned from seeing his family in Calabria and Salim got back from a visit to his father in Damascus, a tension had unaccountably sprung up between them. Nothing either of them explained or discussed, but they saw less of each other and somehow went out of their way to avoid each other's company. Then one day—halfway through the semester—Salim disappeared from the university and was never seen again. Father Pascal, the boys' tutor, told him that Salim had returned to his family in Damascus.

As the launch sped under the Ponte Scalzi and headed along the Canal towards Rialto, Marcetti shivered, thinking of the hatred in the youth's eyes as he had confronted him on the train. Up to now, he knew he'd been protected. He owed that to the Order. It had allowed him the freedom to pursue his campaigns for social justice, conducted largely through the media. Not all his brothers had supported him. Some shrank from the exposure he'd brought upon the Dominican life. Bad publicity, one had accused him, like relighting the fires of the stakes. Now those same fires were creeping close to his own feet.

31

Chapter Two

The Grand Canal, Venice
6 April 2015

Lunch on the canal-side terrace of the Hotel Regale, a short step from the Piazzetta, was always an interesting experience when one's companion was the resident *Reuters* bureau chief, Efrem Seiler. There was no sign of him when Lavinia Dyer had arrived, so she was ushered to a reserved table for two set against the front façade of the hotel. It gave a commanding view of the other diners to her left and right. Seiler was a consummate professional who left nothing to chance and never let an opportunity to see and be seen pass him by. Dyer was in no doubt that he had specifically requested the seating arrangements. A glass of *prosecco* appeared as if by magic and she settled down to observe her fellow guests—the habit of a lifetime in journalism—a mixture of quietly well-healed regulars, a large group of adventuresome tourists mostly from the Far East and a smattering of trans-Atlantic money. Her attention turned briefly to a table of four in the far right-hand corner of the terrace. There was a familiarity about the man sitting with his back to her and as he half-turned to address the attractive blonde seated to his right, she realised with a jolt that it was none other than Casamassa. Her instinct was to get up and leave but curiosity held her back and a moment later, Seiler was at her side, all smiles and customary charm, solicitous as always for her well-being and chattering like an excited child.

"Lavinia! A thousand pardons. To keep you waiting so! A mad morning, my masters! As ever, your usual ravishing self. I trust the view from here has been worth the wait."

"The view from here, Efrem, has always been perfect, if a little tarnished today," observed Dyer dryly, nodding towards the company at the corner of the terrace. "I take it that, unlike the table booking, you didn't set that up as well. I know you're more than capable of orchestrating a little lunchtime drama!"

Seiler glanced quickly over and gave a brief laugh. "My dear, I'm wounded you would think that of me, but you know my hack's creed. Never miss an opportunity." He lowered his voice, "Even ex-lovers might have their uses."

"You're outrageous, Efrem, as usual. Seriously, I do need a favour and our distinguished director might be the one to grant it. I just can't for the life of me imagine why he would. Let's order first, I'm famished, and then I'll tell you all about it. Well, you know me…perhaps, not *quite* all!"

"And you know me. What I'm not told I can usually guess…or make up! So lunch, and business can wait!"

Pleasantries saw them through their meal and before coffee was brought, Dyer excused herself and headed indoors to the ladies' room. On her return, she noticed that the Casamassa party had already left.

"So," she quipped, "the exigencies of nature lead to another lost chance! Every journalist's nightmare. Did he speak?"

"Briefly. To introduce his guests. Compatriots of yours. They've come to view their late relation's bequest to the gallery. He was all over them like a rash! And he knows you're in Venice. He enquired after you. Now Lavinia, what's going on? I don't imagine you are here for the sights. Venice is almost a second home."

"Even the American press can make some mileage out of the Installation of a new Patriarch. Especially when the guest preacher is none other than our twenty-first century revolutionary monk. Fireworks from the pulpit of S. Mark's Basilica! That's surely a show not to be missed."

"I might have guessed as much. Well, if it's fireworks you're hoping for, don't be too disappointed. I'm told our distinguished visitor is for once a bit subdued. Hard to imagine, isn't it! There was an ugly little incident on the train from Rome. It hasn't been on the wires. An Asian youth accosted him and threatened to slash his throat. Or so they say. Only the conductor's intervention prevented it. Not the first threat he's received, I imagine, but when you're as outspoken as Marcetti, you're a sure-fire target. Extremists of every hue must be queuing up. I'm told it's shaken him. A face-to-face confrontation, not simply a poisonous letter or a cranky phone call, which we've all had. Guaranteed to unbalance, that's part of the calculation. The only surprise to me is that it hasn't happened sooner!"

"I wonder, though, where the threat actually came from."

"What are you getting at, Lavinia?"

"He's certainly stirring the political pot this time. Not too difficult to dress it up as something else. The French and Germans are smarting but publicly keeping their heads, whereas the British press has openly excoriated him. Think about it. Any one of them could have set it up."

"To scare the hell out of him? If that's the case, on balance, my vote would go to the Brits."

"Surprise, surprise! But I think you're right. There can be a very nasty streak in them sometimes."

"I don't often hear you badmouth your Anglo-Saxon colleagues. I suppose they're frightened he's going to name and shame them. Expose yet another instance of British hypocrisy. In any case," he added with a vicious smile, "they're notoriously anti-Catholic." Seiler's views on the British establishment were at one time no secret among the journalistic community. During his *Reuters'* stretch in London, his outspoken comments had offended Fleet Street and he had been young and naïve enough not to know when to hold his tongue. It affected his career when charges of a lack of objectivity were levelled against the news agency. He'd learnt the hard way that memories were long in his profession.

He shrugged now and changed tack. "You'll have heard what happened in Sicily. The bodies of a young woman and child have been found in shallow graves on a beach somewhere near Catania. Shot through the head. The word is that a boatload of migrants had recently landed there from Libya. Why would they murder two of their own? Or if not, who did? A woman and child!"

"It hadn't made our press before I left the States, but I've caught up since. Efrem, what are your contacts like with the Patriarchal Palace?" asked Dyer, her mind for the moment on other matters.

"Strictly professional and right now, distant. They're keeping the media at arm's length this week. Casamassa's your best bet. The new Patriarch's giving a reception tonight. He's bound to have been invited. I tell you what. Let's go and look at his new acquisitions together. I ought to anyway and I can hold your hand."

"I'm not sure I can face the embarrassment of a meeting. Believe it or not, Efrem, these days I'm not as courageous as I used to be."

"Come on, Lavinia. The place will be crowded and we have the perfect excuse. It's our job, after all! The problem will be getting a private word with him. Don't worry about Giuliana; she never goes near the place except for Private Views. The good wife likes to be seen playing her role but only when the media are there to comment favourably. She's paid court to them to very good effect. To be frank, he doesn't know how fortunate he is. Most women would have dumped him long ago, but social cachet is a principle of life for our Giuliana and the director's wife enjoys plenty of that."

"Most women would rarely get the opportunity to dump Matteo. He's the first to exit stage left or hadn't you noticed!" observed Dyer dryly.

Casamassa's gallery occupied the *piano nobile* and principal floors of a renaissance palazzo overlooking the Grand Canal. The vaporetto journey, packed with tourists, was mercifully short—only three stops—so Dyer and Seiler remained on deck jostled uncomfortably by student rucksacks and tourists eager to take selfies, apparently more interested in seeing themselves than the city they had come to visit. Local residents mostly seated inside were easy to spot from the somewhat resigned expressions on their faces.

"Hell's teeth!" growled Seiler as they fought their way onto the landing stage. "This benighted place is becoming all but impossible. They'll soon have to be issuing day tickets just to come into the city. In fact, the sooner the better! Show your press-pass at the door and we can go straight through."

As Seiler had predicted, the gallery was packed with visitors. So much so that the staff on duty in the ticket booth were letting in only a limited number at a time as others left. Press, however, was recognised and courteously waved in with an apology for the crush. "Dottore, Dottoressa, how good to see you again, please come straight through. I'll let Professore Casamassa know you are here. He'll wish to greet such distinguished members of the press," and with a polite bow and a somewhat theatrical flourish of his hands, the attendant was gone. Dyer raised her eyebrows at Seiler as they made their way to the *piano nobile* overlooking the Canal. The newly acquired canvasses were displayed on four large easels in the sixteenth-century salon. A roped-off walkway shepherded members of the public past the canvases, which were lit from above. Huge windows overlooking the Grand Canal had been shuttered for protection from daylight.

"It hasn't been finally decided where they will hang. Maybe not in here but in a smaller room of their own," a suave professional voice sounded behind them. Dyer turned to see a smiling Casamassa, for once looking almost diffident but clearly unsurprised to see his two visitors. "Lavinia, Efrem, welcome. Lavinia, I am so sorry to have missed you at the restaurant. I heard you were gracing us with your presence. You're here perhaps for a few days? Not just work, I trust."

From the coolness of her manner, it would have been difficult to read Dyer's inner feelings, nor was she very sure herself of what they were. She smiled with a formal politeness. "Some relaxation, I hope Professore, but work is never far away as I'm sure you know. I'm covering tomorrow's Installation for the paper but if the opportunity presents itself, I'm hoping to get a few minutes conversation with our distinguished preacher."

"I understand he is restricting his time in the city and leaving the morning after. However, the Patriarch's reception tonight would be the best opportunity."

"That's not something I have an entrée to. My official presence is limited to the service in the Basilica."

"Lavinia, I would be delighted if you would come as my guest."

"Too kind, Matteo. But too much of an imposition."

"My dear Lavinia, there's absolutely no problem. I have two spare invitations. My wife has taken the children to visit their grandparents in Merano. So Efrem, unless you have an invitation already, can you be persuaded to accompany us? I'm sure Lavinia would be glad of your company. I'm likely to be monopolised by half the room wanting to talk about these new acquisitions."

Seiler positively glowed. "I would be honoured, though I think our press credentials had better be kept on a back burner. I believe the Patriarchal office is rather sensitive just now, at least as long as its Dominican guest is in residence."

"That's settled then. The reception begins at six. Why don't we meet at Florian's at five-thirty? And now, if you'd excuse me, I must return to my guests. So, until later," and with a deprecating smile and handshakes all around, he departed.

* * *

To the north of the Basilica of St Mark's and largely unnoticed by tourists lay the small Piazzetta dei Leoncini dominated by a monochrome white neo-classical building that, since its completion in 1850, had been the residence of the Venetian Patriarchate. Up to 1807, the cathedral of the city of Venice had been the basilica of St Peter in Castello and St Mark's had been merely the private chapel of the Doges until the Republic fell to Napoleon in 1797. It had always been a fascination of Dyer's that possibly the second-most famous church in Christendom after St Peter's, Rome had only embraced cathedral status so late in its history. Crossing the piazza still alive with tourists, though the day-trippers had already left and a light misty rain was blowing in from the lagoon, she made this observation to Casamassa and Seiler.

Casamassa laughed lightly. "I suppose that's something we have to be grateful to Napoleon for; otherwise, right now we'd all be trekking out to Castello to the old patriarchal palace! Have you ever been out there? I imagine the Doges and the Great Council were determined to keep the influence of the church as far away as possible and the island off Castello seemed about right. It's always seemed remote from the life of the city. Perhaps Father Marcetti would have attracted far less attention there and been easier to keep an eye on."

"That would scarcely have pleased him. I've never known a churchman who thirsted more for the oxygen of publicity," remarked Seiler waspishly.

"'Drunk with the rhetoric of his own imagination'. Who was that said about?" mused Casamassa.

"Most politicians I've ever come across, and clergy too," added Seiler.

"Actually, I think it might have been about Napoleon. I can't for the life of me think who said it. Come, my friends," said Casamassa, taking Dyer's arm and guiding her up the main entrance steps of the palace. "Here we are. The reception is being held in the Tintoretto Hall; that in itself is worth a visit."

The Tintoretto Hall had been so named after an earlier patriarch had had the foresight to acquire custody of a cycle of eight oils by the artist illustrating the life and martyrdom of St Catherine of Alexandria. Already, the hall had begun to fill with guests. White-jacketed attendants glided among them bearing trays of the best *prosecco* and *canapés* provided by one of the finest restaurants in the city. At the door, the new Patriarch in his scarlet soutane and members of the Basilica clergy lined up to greet their distinguished guests on arrival. Of Marcetti, however, there was as yet no sign. Casamassa drifted off to pay court to some of his fellow citizens. On occasions such as this, Dyer reflected, Matteo Casamassa shined, clearly enjoying the attention being lavished on one of Venice's most eminent and much lauded gallery directors. One might almost think, she discreetly whispered to Seiler, that the reception had been staged for his personal benefit.

"Oh!" said Seiler, "hasn't it been? The great and the good of La Serenissima seem to think so!"

"Efrem Seiler, unless I am much mistaken," a rich deep English voice sounded behind them and they both turned to a tall good-looking man holding a full glass of *prosecco* who had apparently just arrived.

"My God, you gave me a fright. Milo Standish. How long has it been? Five years?"

"Nearer ten, I suspect."

36

"Ten years—can it be possible? On one of my flying visits to London. Time has clearly been kinder to you than to me. But, please, allow me to introduce my colleague, Lavinia Dyer of the *New York Times*."

"Miss Dyer, I'm honoured. Your distinguished work is, of course, well-known."

"How do you do?" Dyer smiled and held out her hand.

"I take it you are both here in an official capacity?"

"Not at all. We've been fortunate to come as guests of Professor Casamassa, the Director of Venice's Gallery of Renaissance Art."

"Ah yes. I hope to view his new acquisitions while I'm here. Have you seen the paintings, Miss Dyer?"

"Yes, I have, this afternoon. They are a great feather in the cap for Venice and for the Director."

"A generous gesture. We are all the beneficiaries. Will you be reporting for your paper on how they've been received?"

"The legacy came from a fellow countryman of mine, a New Yorker in fact. The paper's going to run a feature by prior agreement with the Gallery's trustees. Our Arts critic will be coming over."

"It's good to know there'll be international coverage."

"But Standish," said Seiler, "what brings you to Venice? Hardly work, I imagine."

"On the contrary," Standish replied swiftly, "I'm representing the British Embassy at tomorrow's Installation. My government likes to be seen supporting the leadership of the Church on these occasions. There are a good many of our fellow countrymen and women in the expatriate community here."

"Since when has the British Government been so solicitous of the Catholic Church? Is His Holiness breathing a fresh wind of peace and harmony even over your damp islands?" Seiler gave a sly smile.

"Much has changed since the days of your London posting, my friend. Though I doubt whether even Papal peace and harmony can change our climate!"

"Time, Efrem, to forgive and forget," interjected Dyer, "that's if you want to be 'on message' these days! Don't you agree, Mr Standish?"

"And do you suppose that Father Marcetti is 'on message'? From what I hear, the British Government is less than enthusiastic about our famous Dominican friar. Peace and harmony might well prove to be in short supply." Seiler was warming to his subject.

"Have you met tomorrow's preacher, Miss Dyer?" Standish adroitly avoided commenting.

"Unfortunately, not. But I'm hoping for an introduction this evening and if circumstances permit, a private word or two."

"You may find Father Marcetti's become rather more reticent of late. His stay here is to be brief. I'm told he's leaving the day after tomorrow. Well, excuse me, business calls! Courtesy demands that I convey my country's formal greetings to the Patriarch and his retinue, but I don't believe the Friar has appeared as yet."

"I think," said Seiler, "that's about to change."

There was a sudden movement around the entrance doors as the new Patriarch left his place and swept down the hall, his chaplain and another cleric at his side, and crossed to a doorway at the far end from where a figure had just emerged. Dyer glimpsed a lean man of average height, short, cropped grey hair and in his sixties, not in typical Dominican habit but in the more normal clerical dress of plain black suit. The Patriarch stretched out his arms in a brotherly embrace, took his friend by the arm and led him on a circuit around the reception hall.

"It's now or never," murmured Seiler in Dyer's ear and turned to Standish who had, however, drifted away to speak to a fellow guest. It was some time before the clerical party approached the journalists and Casamassa had by this time joined the group, in conversation with a white-haired elderly cleric with whom he appeared to be on familiar and excellent terms. "The Canon Chancellor, I believe," whispered Seiler. As they drew near, Standish reappeared at their side.

"Ah! Mr Standish," the Patriarch gave a warm smile and extended his hand. "A pleasure to see you again. Welcome to the representative of Her Majesty's Government! Mr Standish and I have met before. At an embassy reception in Rome a few months ago," this to the members of his party, and then to Standish, "May I present my good friend, Father Antonio Marcetti of the Order of Preachers."

Marcetti stepped forward, hand outstretched, "I am delighted the British Government should see fit to mark His Grace's translation. Venice's Patriarchate is one of the most important Sees in Italy. My Order is also honoured by your presence, Mr Standish. This is a deeply troubling time for the whole continent of Europe. We attach great value to all opportunities for expressions of goodwill between our countries and our churches."

"And I am privileged to meet you, Father, and most happy to convey your sentiments to my Ambassador."

"Antonio, you and Mr Standish will have an opportunity later to get better acquainted. He's joining us for dinner," said the Patriarch.

"Your Grace," interjected Standish, "may I present two distinguished members of the international press corps. Miss Lavinia Dyer of the *New York Times* and Mr Efrem Seiler of *Reuters*, both here this evening in an entirely private capacity."

The Patriarch raised his eyebrows. "As *private* individuals," the emphasis was too marked to miss, "their presence is of course welcomed."

As he took her hand, Marcetti gave Lavinia Dyer a level stare. His large pale blue eyes were widely set and searching, conveying the impression of a man who knew what he wanted and exactly how to get it. A man with a mission, perhaps, not one to be easily diverted. Behind him, her eyes encountered Casamassa's and a look she couldn't quite work out, almost verging on envy.

"Miss Dyer," Marcetti was saying to the Patriarch, "is preceded by a quite formidable reputation as an interviewer. To be on the receiving end is so far a pleasure denied to me...but who knows?"

"I am not here tonight as a journalist, Father, and would not dream of trespassing on His Grace's hospitality."

"Nevertheless, Miss Dyer, your probity and, if I might say so, the quality of your work, which I'm well acquainted with, encourages me to feel that there might be a way in which we could be of service to one another. Those of us who find ourselves in the public eye these days always need an honest interpreter. A rare commodity in a media-hungry world. My time in this beautiful city...what has it been called, Giancarlo?" he smiled at the Patriarch, "the 'Queen of the Adriatic', much more even than that I think, my time here is sadly limited. However, I would be glad of a few minutes of your time, Miss Dyer, if you are willing."

The Patriarch intervened, "If Miss Dyer is able to present herself here after the Installation Mass?" As the Patriarch's party passed on, Casamassa smiled and nodded to the journalists.

"The success of your evening," Seiler observed acidly, "he lays entirely at his own door. Be careful, my dear, our distinguished director has a distinctly predatory look about him. Did you notice the expression on his face when Marcetti was speaking to you? Come on, I've had enough of our Holy Mother Church for one evening; let's see if Harry's Bar can find us a dinner table!"

* * *

In a small private dining salon at the rear of the Patriarchal palace, four men sat at a table. Two windows looked out on the Rio Canonica canal and the remaining walls were hung with the portraits of previous incumbents, serene or severe as the painter of the time saw them. The atmosphere was informal but not exactly convivial, restrained by the presence of two habited nuns who silently plied back and forth serving the simple dishes but leaving the diners to pour their own wine. Conversation was restricted to general observations about the evening reception that had just taken place.

The Patriarch seemed satisfied. "All aspects of the Archdiocese's life seem to have been represented tonight," he observed. "Probably one of the few opportunities they have to meet one another in a setting such as this. There is much value in that and I trust we shall encourage further gatherings." He turned to his chaplain, "Perhaps, Ennio, you would give some thought to this and draw up a list of possible occasions when we might repeat the exercise. I want to open up the use of the palace much more for ordinary people. They should be made to feel at home here. Of course, not all events need to be quite as lavish as this one has been!"

The chaplain coughed discreetly, "Your Grace will no doubt soon discover that the Archdiocese's financial affairs..." he hesitated in mid-sentence, "require careful handling."

The Patriarch laughed. "And no doubt," he said to his two guests, "Ennio will be telling me in no uncertain terms that we have little scope for fun! Good stewardship is important but so is our outreach to others. I don't want to lose this initiative. Now Ennio, there are one or two matters I need to go over with you before tomorrow. Antonio, Milo, please excuse us. We shall leave you to your conversation but feel free to join us for coffee in my study when you are ready."

When they had left the room, Marcetti smiled at the diplomat and refilled their glasses.

"A good vintage from the Veneto." He settled back in his chair and continued, "Giancarlo is the master of tactfulness. Back in our days as seminarians—you know he is also a Dominican—he developed a reputation for being able to discern the dynamics of a group before its individuals were even aware that they were a group! But as to our own dynamics, your official role in tomorrow's proceedings I understand but your private agenda is more of a puzzle."

"Yet you believe I have a private agenda and you would like me to declare it."

"This is not a confessional, Mr Standish. But I hazard a guess that our meeting this evening hasn't occurred by mere chance. I take it you requested it."

"His Grace was kind enough to accommodate me. It was his thanks for a small service I had been able to render earlier this year."

"And I'm happy to abide by his judgment. So how may I be of assistance? Let us not waste time by, how do you call it, beating around the bush!"

"Indeed Father," Standish paused and took a sip of his wine. "I don't have to tell you that my government feels poised on the brink of a precipice; an international scandal would not be expressing it too strongly. You are aware of the rumours that are flying around and that you yourself are being identified as, what these days, is called the 'whistle-blower'. It's being claimed that you are intending to release a statement about the nature of British involvement in the illegal movement of refugees."

Marcetti frowned. "No one can say where such rumours originate. It may not be profitable to pursue enquiries in that direction. As to the 'why' they do, that confronts us with an altogether more interesting question, albeit a complex one. I want to suggest to you that Britain is not alone in being the subject of these matters; at least two others of her European partners stand in what you would call 'the firing line'."

"We're aware of that. We wouldn't wish to imply that you are singling out the United Kingdom. However, we would clearly like to know the source of your information. Whether we would be prepared to share that with our partners, I can't tell you. That decision lies outside my remit."

"And what is the precise nature of this remit?" There was an edge to Marcetti's question that Standish didn't fail to register.

"At this stage, purely exploratory. However, there's a belief in Britain that the migration crisis is being used to further the interests and political aims of certain groups across the European Union. Some of these groups are well-known to us, others less so. They hide in the shadows only to emerge by innuendo and threat. I have been asked to define the nature of that threat."

"And to do so, you require information you believe I may possess?"

"Anything you are able to share with me would be of value, Father. My government needs to assess the extent of any danger we might face and, if possible, identify the factors—external and internal—that contribute to it. The security of our people is our chief concern."

Marcetti leaned back in his chair, toyed with the stem of his wineglass and pursed his lips but he remained silent as Standish continued, "Are you able to confirm the reports in the press that intelligence has reached you suggesting, perhaps no more than that, that sources in the UK and—we're led to believe—at least two other member states of the EU are directly involved in making substantial funds available to certain individuals for the transportation of refugees across the Mediterranean to the mainland of Europe? 'Individuals' operating illegally out of North Africa."

There was a long silence as Marcetti stared down at the table. Eventually, he sighed, raised his head and looked directly at his fellow guest.

"My intelligence indicates that."

"Do you place reliability on it?"

"Without hesitation."

"How much further are you prepared to go in identifying this source?"

Again silence, then, "Mr Standish, Milo, if I may and, please, I am Antonio. Let us try to communicate with one another as friends and allies in a common cause." Standish raised his hand in agreement.

"This intelligence, if we can rightly call it that, came to me a little over a year ago. As the result of a visit to my Order's principal house in Rome of a penitent wishing to unburden their conscience. Knowing my very public involvement in the migration debate, this person had specifically requested an interview with me. The Master General reluctantly agreed. He would not normally have countenanced my participation. The Order does its best to shield its members from unnecessary exposure. It was made clear that it was to be an initial interview only. At that point, the Sacrament of Penance—confession, that is—was not discussed; indeed, it was not known if it would be appropriate. Even so, our discussion was to be conducted under conditions of confidentiality. I'm sorry, Milo, if I labour the distinction. Not easy for a layman perhaps to appreciate."

"An interview, I suppose, would leave open the possibility that its content could be shared with a third party. In certain circumstances," said Standish.

"That might be the case. In certain circumstances. The secrets of the confessional couldn't be. They are absolute."

"I take it your client was willing to go ahead on that basis."

"Yes. And that interview has so far remained a close secret."

"And now?"

"Now there are issues arising that cast a different light on things."

"What kind of issues?"

"Sensitive ones that go beyond the individual."

"Are we talking politics?"

"Politics come into it. But before I say any more, I need something from you."

"Go ahead."

"I want a promise that nothing I tell you tonight will be used to endanger the client's safety."

A pause while Standish considered. "That's an enormous undertaking to give. I've no idea what the implications would be if, for example, the safety of others became an issue. I won't give false assurances. Matters may not remain in my hands. I'd do everything in my power. I can't say more than that."

"As long as we understand each other. This is one very vulnerable individual. The client's a devout Catholic, married to an international businessman. An Englishwoman."

"Do you have a name?"

"Sorry. A step too far. No names or details that might identify her. I can tell you that she lives in London and has grown-up children."

Standish smiled, "That much to go on!"

"The British Intelligence Services have ways and means."

"I can't answer for that."

"Naturally. Allow me to proceed. Some weeks before contacting my Order and coming to see me, she'd come across some documents belonging to her husband. They caused her a great deal of distress. They implicated him in serious criminal activities."

"Did she tell you how she stumbled onto them?"

"She did. He'd been working late in his study at home. He received a telephone call to a crisis meeting at his office in the city. Not *that* unusual. It had happened before. His business dealings cover a wide range. Problems crop up that require consultations with senior staff, high-level decisions to be taken. Instead of locking his papers, as usual, in the strong room safe, he'd put them in his desk drawer to save time."

"You're saying she rifled through his desk. Why would she do that?"

"She says she suspected him of having an affair. That's why he'd gone out so late." Noticing Standish's face, he said, "Yes, it doesn't quite add up, does it?"

"Sounds a bit glib."

"I thought so too, but let's reserve judgement. Anyway, among the papers was confirmation from a Cayman Islands bank of the transfer of twenty million American dollars to the account of an Arab businessman in Malta. There was a covering letter in English that referred to payments being authorised quarterly

42

for the 'movement of cargos' from the Libyan port of Zuwara to Italy and for 'the provision of protective equipment'."

"And she put two and two together."

"She's an intelligent woman. There seemed little doubt to her that the Arab was funding the transportation of refugees and what else we can only guess at. 'Protective equipment'. Arms? But that isn't all. The letter referred to similar accounts set up in the French and German capitals."

"A criminal conspiracy," murmured Standish, Glendower's briefing receiving confirmation.

"The letter mentioned a 'contact' in the British Cabinet Office. No name, of course."

"The 'contact's' function?"

"Not explained."

"Did she say who the letter was from?"

"In fact, she did. She made a note of all the names she could and passed them to me. It was signed by someone called Jawali."

"A thorough lady. Quite a haul, all said. Did she say whether her husband guessed his desk had been gone through?"

"She doesn't think so. But I get the impression they keep their distance. She's horrified at what she's found out. And disgusted with the man she's been married to for nearly forty years."

"Well she might be, poor woman. It's quite a burden to carry."

"We'll give her whatever support we can. If only the opportunity to share a terrible secret. I have a final crumb for you."

Standish looked surprised. "Not something else up your sleeve, Antonio?"

"Maybe not so much, but you never know. Among the papers was a printed-out e-mail. From an Arab called...I have his name here..." He reached into his inside pocket and took out a small notebook. "Raschid Al-Azhar, to an address in Paris. She was struck by it. A discerning woman. It mentioned an Italian, possibly a Sicilian, who seemed to have a key role in some part of the operation. Not very clear what it was. A Luca Galiano. The name rang a distant bell with me. There may be absolutely no connection but I somehow recall a couple of years back that there was storm of protest in Sicily over the proposed sale by the Galiano family of a painting by Caravaggio. It had been commissioned by an ancestor of the present baron and had remained with the family ever since, although on permanent loan to a gallery in Palermo. The buyer was a Far-eastern financier who obviously would have taken it out of the country. According to our more sensational press, threats were made to the family and the picture was withdrawn from sale. I stress there may be nothing in it, but perhaps worth a second look.

And there you have it, the sum total of my knowledge of the matter." Marcetti sat back, tossed off the remainder of his wine and waited.

"There is one thing you haven't told me."

"And that is?"

"Why you decided to take me into your confidence. Make no mistake, Antonio, I know the value of what you have told me. I'm also aware of the responsibility you've put on my shoulders. But I've got to ask you this: Do I have exclusive rights to it?"

"Why do you feel you need to ask?"

"Rumour has it you intend to make all or some of it public knowledge. Is this a tactic on your part? Do you still intend to pursue it? With respect, you're not known for abandoning a cause."

"Milo, please. You think I would walk into that kind of trap? My detractors would love me to, I grant you. They've tossed me a bait and hover like wolves to see if I take it. Does that answer your question?"

"Only time will tell."

"I learned from the Patriarch you were anxious to speak with me. Your diplomatic role is a useful device but I guess it doesn't reflect the whole truth. I told you he's a discerning man, no? I wouldn't dream of pressing you on that. Nor, I imagine, would you respond if I did! So, frankly, I don't think you should feel you have to press me. Let the rumours burn out. They always do in the long run. I recognise there is too much at stake. From now on, I remain in the background."

"Forgive me, I intend no disrespect, but the words 'Marcetti' and 'background' do not sit easily side by side!"

For a moment, Standish thought he'd overstepped the mark but Marcetti merely shrugged, "Within the bounds of my priestly vows, I offer you whatever service I can." He rose from the table. "Come, His Grace's coffee pot will be growing cold and tomorrow, we all face a long day!"

* * *

Venice
8 April

It was the ringing of the telephone that roused Lavinia Dyer as she dozed on the sofa in her hotel suite. Early evening dozes were rarely her thing. They had become more frequent of late. Glancing at her watch, she saw that the time was approaching 7.15.

"Lavinia Dyer."

"Miss Dyer forgive me for disturbing you. This is Milo Standish. I was wondering if there was any possibility you could spare me a few moments of your time this evening."

"Mr Standish. Good evening. Well, I'm sure I could. I had planned to dine here in the hotel. Perhaps after that?"

"In which case, if it wouldn't be a terrific bore, I wonder if you would perhaps consider changing your plans and join me for dinner."

Dyer hesitated, "How kind...I would be delighted."

"Splendid! May I collect you from the hotel lobby at, say, 8.00 p.m.?"

"I look forward to it."

"Till eight o'clock then."

It was a few minutes after eight when Dyer stepped out of the elevator. Milo Standish was seated on a settee speaking into his mobile, a newspaper on the seat beside him.

"I have to go; my guest has arrived. See you. Oh! Ravi, tell Julia I'll come straight to the office from the airport. If I'm going to be late, I'll call her. But it's the weekend; she's not to wait…I know you will. That's what makes coming home worthwhile."

He got up and held out his hand.

"This is most kind of you, Mr Standish."

"Not at all; it's my pleasure. Please, can we be relaxed enough tonight to be Lavinia and Milo? If you don't think that too forward of me—I know we haven't been long acquainted."

Dyer laughed, "Of course it's not. It will be a very welcome change. It's been a rather formal few days."

"I've taken the liberty of booking us a table at Da Mario's. I don't know if you're familiar with it. It's a short walk from here. Quite small and informal. You eat whatever the Nonna has decided to cook!"

"It sounds wonderful."

"Then please, let's go. It's a fine evening and for a change, the city's remarkably quiet."

The little canal-side restaurant held only eight tables, with two already occupied. Standish and Dyer were conducted to a quiet corner by the window.

"Ideal for discreet conversation," ventured Dyer with raised eyebrows.

"I'd better come clean, that's partly why I chose this place."

"And the other part?"

Standish laughed, "The food, of course. So, let's forget everything else for the time being. I don't think you are going to be disappointed." She wasn't. The Nonna sailed forth from her kitchen, queen of her *domaine*, certain of the reception she would receive and, with all the confident dignity of her years, announced the dishes she was cooking that evening. It was a bravura performance. Soon the reality proved as truly a revelation as the recital of the menu. *Spaghetti alle cozze* followed by veal with fennel, garlic and pancetta and a *torta di cioccolato* as dessert.

"Well," said a very contented Lavinia Dyer over their coffee, "that was quite an experience. This is another Venetian treasure to add to my list. You obviously know the city of old. A regular visitor?"

"Not as often as I would like. But even we poor diplomats have to escape sometimes!"

"It's strange how foreigners think of it as a place to escape to; I suspect most Venetians these days think of it as a place to escape from."

"Surely all our native cities are like that—New York, for example? Don't you think of it as a place to escape from whenever possible? I know I do London. The place, at least."

Dyer looked serious for a moment. "I suppose so. Though like you, I imagine, one spends less and less time at one's home base and more and more on the road. I've reached an age when I would like to reverse that."

"Settle down? Yes, an enticing thought."

"And an elusive one," observed Dyer, "but nothing wrong in chasing dreams."

"And what dreams do you chase?"

"Mostly personal, I suppose. Not many career ones anymore."

"And yet, maybe, one of those you have realised this week. Father Marcetti?"

"Ah! I wondered when we would get around to that subject!"

"Do you mind?"

"I don't think I've got much to contribute."

"Nevertheless, I'd be fascinated to hear your impression."

"For what it's worth, the interview—if you can call it that—lasted all of half an hour, if that. Barely time for the civilities. Most of it taken up with my trying to divert him from the topic of Casamassa's new paintings. He'd been advised by the police not to venture out even with an escort because of the potential threat of an attempt on his life. Because of 'some nonsense on the train from Rome'. His words, not mine. I expect you knew about that?"

"I had heard something."

"So, no visits to the gallery or anywhere else. To be honest, I don't believe he was the least bit interested in the pictures; he just wanted to make sure that he controlled the agenda. He fended off my questions about the migrant crisis and to crown it all, claimed that his recent pronouncements were merely paper talk! Just as the business on the train had been blown out of all proportion. An over-excited student hell-bent on a publicity stunt! He knew all about students' pranks and this was not something to be taken seriously."

Standish raised his eyebrows but said nothing.

"What I find interesting is that it was he who returned to the topic. It seemed to me that his disclaimer was a tactic to keep the matter alive. I've come across that often enough in the past not to recognise the ploy. An interviewee will stress how trivial something is, dismiss it out of hand, but is actually drawing attention to it. The man has skills in manipulation. Perhaps it shows how well it found its mark. I don't believe he's the sort to lay a trap and then walk into it himself, unless he knows exactly what he's doing. Too skilled for that! I'm not sure what to make of it. All in all, Milo, I judge this to be one of my less successful interviews." She laughed. "Probably because I didn't control it."

"In your terms, I can understand it wouldn't measure up to what you were hoping for. In fact, I think you've put your finger on something significant. Exactly how to interpret it, I'm not sure as yet. I don't think your instincts are mistaken. The abortive attempt on the train may have scared him; it's certainly set him thinking."

"To me, it doesn't quite add up."

"In what way?"

"Well, the youth is said to have been of 'Middle Eastern' or North African origin. According to Seiler, *Reuters* reported the *carabinieri* as saying that he accused Marcetti, as a Christian, of being an 'enemy' of his people. How they know that I'm not sure. In all the circumstances, fair enough one might think, but Marcetti has spoken very strongly and publicly of compassion towards Muslim sensitivities, even the need for understanding why some Muslims feel driven to *jihad*. Not exactly a widely shared view in the West! In fact, it's upset a lot of people. OK, to Muslim extremists he still represents the 'wrong' side, but he sees Islam in a sympathetic light. Not quite what you'd describe as an ambassador for the faith, but not an obvious prime target either."

"I agree with your analysis so far. Where's it led you?"

"To conflicting views of the man. On the one hand, he's a very smooth operator. Media savvy, he's had lots of experience there. This is not a man easily tripped up by interviewers! But behind the public mask, I feel that there's a sensitivity about him. Almost a vulnerability. It makes him an appealing figure, but perhaps that's what he wants us to see."

"So you're left with a question mark."

"And a simple question. Who would want Marcetti to be silenced?"

"And the answer?"

Dyer paused, gazing out of the window at a gondola full of excited Eastern tourists passing under the bridge. "Those who are most afraid of him."

"And who do you think that might be?"

"The politicians."

It was Milo Standish's turn to keep silent.

Dyer continued, "If I may, I've another question for you."

"Go ahead."

"What exactly is your interest in this guy? Why, Milo, are we having this conversation?"

"Two questions, one answer. As I was attending the Installation, my ambassador asked me to form an impression of the priest. The UK Government would like to know whom it may have to deal with. Rumours of his possible revelations have created a whole new ball game. Incidentally, how long will you be staying in Venice?"

"I'm here on holiday for another couple of weeks or so but if the paper thinks I should stay on for professional reasons, it could be extended."

"I have to go away but I'd like to speak with you again before you go back to the States."

Lavinia Dyer smiled, "That could count as professional reasons."

"Splendid! I think it's time for another *grappa*!"

* * *

Milan
10 April

She skipped along at her mother's side as they wandered through the shopping mall, sometimes holding her hand and sometimes breaking away to stand entranced at a shop window. She had never seen such sights before. It didn't seem to matter what the shop was selling—clothes, toiletries, televisions—it was the abundance that held her spellbound. Best of all was the shop selling toys. At this window, she pressed her nose to the glass and was for a moment lost in the wonder of it all. The teddy bears were cute but the dolls were her favourite, so well-dressed, bright frocks with a hint of knicker showing beneath, long hair, blonde and flowing, and the make-up so real! At the centre of one window was a doll's house, four floors high—yes, really, *four* floors. Each room furnished to perfection with minute inhabitants engaged in all their daily tasks: Making beds, sweeping a floor, baking in the kitchen and, of course, there were the men, reclining in a well-stocked library, reading and ignoring the womenfolk.

"Ayesha, come along," her mother spoke in a foreign tongue, somewhere Middle Eastern and adjusted her headscarf. Her eyes had caught a window stocked with exotic fabrics in every colour under the sun and she hastened across the mall, leaving Ayesha to her contemplation of the doll's house. As she turned to go inside, a young bearded man wearing a backpack collided with her. The girl with him was clasping a plastic carrier bag to her chest and stopped in her tracks for a brief moment and then headed into the toyshop. An apology leapt to the lips of Ayesha's mother but the youth merely glared, ignored her and, quickening his pace, hurried along the mall in the direction of the crowded café at the end. A middle-aged woman following behind reached out to steady Ayesha's mother as she was whipped around by the sudden force of the youth's collision. Her north Italian accent was difficult for a stranger to understand.

"*Boh!* Young people, no manners these days, are you all right?"

"*Si, grazie, grazie molto,*" Ayesha's mother stammered the few words of Italian she knew. She looked over her shoulder towards the toyshop where Ayesha still stood enthralled.

"Ayesha!" she called out, "wait there, I'm going in here." The child smiled and waved, seeing her mother disappear into the fabric shop and turned back to her doll's house.

Afterwards, she couldn't remember how long she had been looking at the fabrics, choosing one, then discarding it in favour of another—really, the colours and the softness of the materials made choice so difficult. This one perhaps for curtains for their one bedroom and this would make Ayesha a beautiful frock for her grandmother's birthday party, seventy years old next month and still a stranger in a strange land. The blast, when it came, rocked the very foundations of the store, coursing down the shopping mall from the direction of the café. The window dissolved into millions of tiny fragments and for a few seconds, there was total silence. Then someone screamed. A single scream in the silence. She tried to pick herself up for the force of the blast had thrown her among the heaps of fabric rolls. Of the shop assistants she could see none. Then as she stumbled towards the shattered door and looked across the wrecked mall, bodies strewn everywhere, a second explosion came. She saw a child in front of the toyshop picked up and hurled into the air like a rag doll, clothes and hair on fire.

* * *

Villa San Vibio
11 April

Luca Galiano stood at one of the tall windows in the main salon of the villa at San Vibio. Before him, the wooded landscape was darkening as the spring sunshine dropped behind a bank of orange- and red-tinted clouds above the black western hills. At this time of year, twilight seemed to linger a little longer in this part of the peninsular, whereas in midsummer, the transition from daylight to darkness was almost instantaneous. Behind him a log fire crackled in the massive stone fireplace lit an hour since by Gino. A reassuring sound, a feeling of having retreated a lifetime away from a Sicilian farmstead and even further from a Sicilian beach. The past few days had gone a small way towards restoring a badly shaken confidence, though the memory of the events on the beach recurred at odd moments during the day and were never far off from his nightmares—constant reminders of the fragility of existence, his as much as anyone's. At those times, the face of the child haunted him, the look of surprise when he was made to kneel beside the body of his mother. And then afterwards, the terrifying silence.

Today's television news had been dominated by a terrorist bombing, reminding the world how easily the delicate balance between sanity and madness could tip from one day to the next. This time, they had struck at a shopping precinct out in the suburbs of Milan. Eleven dead, 44 injured, some life-threatening and among the dead, three children, the youngest seven years old. Newscasters reported that the police and local politicians were suggesting that the bombers might have come from the Soldiers of the Caliphate. The attacks had all the hallmarks of extreme Islamist terrorism, though so far, no group had claimed responsibility. Little doubt that the Middle Eastern war had once again come right to Europe's doorstep. Galiano felt sick; how far was he personally involved in the deaths of children and the maiming of innocent lives, some destined to add to the fatality statistics, some marked down for permanent disfigurement and disability? He had never considered himself an evil man. But his involvement with the Arab Al-Azhar called that into question.

Blackmail, spelt out in uncompromising terms in a Maltese hotel, had been their trump card. Exposure as a suspected paedophile meant not only lasting disgrace but even worse at the hands of the arcane confraternities of Enna. He had had no choice in the matter. A burgeoning bank account in Malta blunted the reality of the kind of person he had become. There came a time, sooner or later, when nothing could protect a man from himself. Better to shut one's eyes and pretend that nothing had changed, but everything had changed. He was no longer in control of his life. He had traded it for hard currency and made a Faustian pact with the Devil. And the Devil would claim him when the pact was concluded. Who could tell when that might be?

As he brooded on these things, his eye caught two beams of light moving steadily up the long drive from the country road to the villa. It was a rough surface untended for a long time, so the vehicle made no pretence of hurrying. Eventually, it turned into the courtyard of the villa on the far side of the house. No one knew he was here, casual visitors unknown and in any event would never be admitted. Instantly panic surged. He had a revolver in the desk drawer of his study, but that was on the far side of the entrance hall and as for other firearms, all were locked away in the gunroom safe, equally inaccessible from where he was. Then the sound of a woman's voice, enquiring, somewhat high-pitched in tone. As he moved to the salon's double doors, they opened and an embarrassed Gino hovered outside.

"Signor forgive me. Signorina Pellestri insisted."

"That's all right, Gino, thank you." A gasp of relief, but how had she known he would be there? Laura Pellestri only visited when specifically requested.

"*Dio*, I thought my welcome might have been a little warmer. Don't look so worried, *caro*, I called the Villa Galiano. They said you had left unexpectedly on Good Friday evening. That seemed odd. So, I took a chance and lucky me, here you are!" She flung her arms around his neck and ignoring the servant's evident embarrassment, pressed her very shapely body into his—a gesture rather more disconcerting than her unscheduled arrival—despite the anticipation of a pleasure he didn't imagine would be long deferred.

"Thank you, Gino. Everything's fine," he said over her shoulder. "Would you ask Maria to set dinner for two? A table in here tonight, I think."

"And I," said Laura Pellestri, "need a hot bath and a long cool drink, for a start," as the doors closed, "then you may take care of my other needs. Maria's dinner can wait till later. So! Tell me, *caro*, why this sudden visit to your hideaway? At this time of year, I thought your confraternity had first claim on your presence at all those long and tedious rituals."

Much later as they lay curled around each other, Galiano said, "When are you going to tell me the real reason for this visit? What has happened? We both know you never telephoned the Villa Galiano nor would the staff there have told you anything even if you had. In any case, they have no knowledge of this place. So…?"

"Let us just say it was a woman's intuition, *caro*, a woman's intuition."

Galiano freed himself, got up and lit a cigarette from a pack on the bedside table.

"I'm going to dress," he said briefly and went into his dressing room next door, calling out, "And you, my dear, had better put some clothes on too; even the long-suffering Gino and Maria can only take so much!"

Next morning, he rose soon after seven, leaving Laura fast asleep. Wandering downstairs, he could hear the sound of voices coming from the kitchen where Maria and Gino were already busy with the work of the day. Opening the heavy oak door into the courtyard, he paused for a moment to inhale the crisp early morning air, a ritual he always enjoyed at San Vibio, and then crossed to where Laura's Lamborghini was parked somewhat erratically. Laura Pellestri might be a whore but she was one with high-class tastes and, he knew to his cost, a high-class bank balance to indulge them. Typically, the car was unlocked, the keys still in the ignition; at San Vibio, she could never be persuaded of the need for security. Climbing into the driver's seat, he switched on the in-car *telefonino*. There was one message. A man's voice he didn't recognise, "Call me as soon as you get this." Nothing more.

Retracing his steps to the house, Galiano closed and locked the massive doors and entered the small library to the left of the entrance hall, which doubled as his study and office. Seating himself at the desk in the centre of the room for some time, he was lost in thought. First, there was Laura's unscheduled visit and an explanation that was no explanation at all. Someone else knew he was at San Vibio and probably that person had arranged for Laura Pellestri to turn up out of the blue, something that had never happened before; indeed, it would have been unthinkable, given that his comings and goings were always unknown in advance even to the staff. His privacy had hitherto been safeguarded by the unpredictability of his arrangements. Visiting girlfriends, any of whom could have compromised themselves through indiscretion, were strictly and discreetly monitored. They arrived and departed quite alone. And then there was Laura herself, this time an almost imperceptible difference in manner, less relaxed, evasive, reluctant to answer his queries. And what about the message? That compounded his worries. She was being required to report back the time of her arrival at San Vibio. Why? And the big question, to whom? Someone connected to the Sicilian operation, Al-Azhar or one of his associates? He unlocked his desk to take out and check the gun. But the drawer was empty.

Galiano breakfasted alone at a table set by the windows of the salon, open to the terrace on this mild spring morning with a thin mist slowly clearing from the valley below as the early morning sun climbed over the hills. He was served by Gino, seemingly restored after the embarrassment of last night's unexpected visitor. Preoccupied by the missing gun, he wracked his brains to think how long it had been since he had seen it there. Certainly not over the last few days and only he had access to his desk, which was kept locked at all times. He was reluctant to question his staff whom he trusted absolutely.

"Gino," he asked as the man appeared, "has Signorina Pellestri been taken breakfast?"

"*Si*, Barone. Maria took a tray up to her about half an hour ago. She was still asleep."

"Thank you, Gino. I shall go up shortly and discuss our plans for the day. In the past few weeks since I was last here, have there been any unexpected callers at the house?"

The man thought for a moment, "No signor, not unexpected, only the official from the timber company. You'd arranged for them to inspect the plantation of stone pines on the east boundary when you were last here. I was out when he arrived, so Maria showed him into the library. He said they would be sending you a report."

"Yes, it was waiting for me." He had no recollection of having seen a report but decided not to say so.

Pouring himself another cup of coffee, Galiano lit a cigarette and walked out onto the terrace. The spring day was too good to waste idling in the house and Laura Pellestri was unlikely to appear for at least another hour. He would take a walk down to the lake and go up to see her when he got back. Hopefully, that would go some way towards calming his nerves and maybe then he could broach the subject of the car phone message.

The gardens of the Villa San Vibio had, in their heyday more than a century ago, been quite impressive for a small hunting lodge hidden away in the relatively unknown Calabrian countryside. A series of formal parterres had been planted with sweet box, in the centre of which had stood massive and elaborate stone jardinières surrounded by orange and lemon trees. These formed terraces that stretched from the garden front of the villa to the ornamental lake at the bottom, in the middle of which had been the great fountain sculpture of Venus and her handmaidens. However, they had never recovered from the depredations of the Second World War; looting and vandalism had wreaked havoc leaving behind a sad scene of desolation and his elderly relative had had little interest in the restoration of the property. For Luca Galiano, it had never been more than an occasional retreat and two elderly servants could do little except maintain a basic level of upkeep. He walked around the ornamental lake and paused for a few minutes to take stock. It was still early and it seemed a good idea to take advantage of the bright morning to take another look at the stone-pine plantation, which he was considering having felled. The timber would fetch an attractive price. Eventually climbing the stone steps back up to the terrace, he glanced up at the windows of his bedroom suite and was surprised to see them still closed and shuttered.

When he entered the house, there was still no sign of Laura Pellestri. The distant sound of a radio came from the kitchen. He was halfway up the broad marble staircase when the screaming began.

Luca Galiano gazed with horror at the scene that greeted his eyes. Maria, the housekeeper, was crouched in the doorway to his bedroom and as he approached the long corridor from the top of the great staircase, her screams started to metamorphose into something closer to uncontrollable and hysterical sobbing. The headless corpse of a naked woman lay across the canopied bed in a welter of blood. Galiano couldn't see what had happened to the head. Grabbing the elderly housekeeper by the shoulders, he dragged her into the corridor and leaning over the balustrade, shouted for her husband. But Gino was too far away to hear so taking out his *telefonino*, he called him up. The servant answered immediately from the kitchen telephone.

"Signor?"

"Come upstairs! There's been an accident."

Within minutes of Galiano's gruesome discovery, the sound of motor vehicles filled the villa courtyard. He and Gino had managed between them to half-carry and half-drag the collapsed Maria to the couple's room in the servants' wing of the house. Leaving Gino with his wife, Galiano raced down the main staircase to the entrance hall as hammering started on the outside doors. A *commissario* of police with several officers behind him stood waiting.

"Signore, we have received a telephone call about an incident at this address."

Galiano stared at him, speechless. "Come in. But…it's only just been discovered. No one from here has called yet. We're all in a state of shock. Excuse me, officer, if I seem confused. What's happened is terrible; my housekeeper found the body, but…how could you know?"

"We received a call at the Questura at 7.40 this morning, reporting that a murder had taken place at the Villa San Vibio. You will appreciate it took some time to assemble the Scene of Crime team and drive here."

"But my housekeeper took our female guest her breakfast in bed at about 9.00 a.m.—if that's who it is upstairs, I can only assume, you see…it must be her; there's no one else, I mean…she was alive and well."

"Please signor, first if we may see the crime scene. If you would be good enough to show us."

The police spent the rest of the day swarming over the villa and the estate. There was little doubt that the body was that of Laura Pellestri. Galiano identified a distinguishing tattoo of a rose above the left breast. The body had eventually been removed and taken to the police morgue in Cosenza to await further identification. A woman police doctor attending the elderly servants administered a sedative to a deeply traumatised Maria. At her suggestion, it was agreed that the couple would leave the villa that night and be taken into protective custody. It was Galiano's belief that they would be unlikely ever to return to San Vibio. Lengthy statements had been taken by the *commissario* in charge of the investigation, both from himself and Gino; Maria, not being able to handle detailed questioning, would be interviewed the following day. She had merely confirmed the time she took up the breakfast tray and found Laura asleep and then the time she returned to check whether she had awakened, approximately an hour later.

With police permission, Galiano would be leaving the villa later the next day for his home in Sicily where he would hold himself available for further questioning when required. For the time being, a police presence would remain behind at the villa to continue a thorough forensic examination of house and grounds. No murder weapon had so far been recovered but in the course of an initial search, a revolver was found under the front passenger seat of Laura Pellestri's Lamborghini. It was loaded with the chamber full. Galiano identified it as the one missing from his desk drawer. Attached to it was a very ordinary luggage label that bore the words, *For Laura Pellestri from Omar Wazir*.

In the long run, the identity of the assassin was destined to remain unknown. However, the mystery of the corpse's missing head did not remain unsolved. The head turned up.

Chapter Three

Paris, Bois de Boulogne
17 April

The mansion on the Boulevard Maurice Barres, at the edge of the Seventeenth Arrondissement, overlooked the northerly part of the Bois de Boulogne. Built in the latter years of the nineteenth century, its modest but well-wooded garden ensured a degree of privacy from passers-by. From neighbours on either side, there was no problem. They also welcomed protection from prying eyes. This was not an area of the city where the residents encouraged curiosity, especially from each other. Across the boulevard lay the Jardin d'Acclimatation, hidden within its own wooded surroundings, much visited by tourists but closed at this time of the evening. So apart from passing traffic, an atmosphere of quietness had descended on the area. Signs of the affluence of the mansion's occupants were the three-berth underground garage and, if one could have seen it, the rooftop open air swimming pool. Pale blue painted shutters, always kept closed, adorned the windows facing the street on all three floors. Like most of the residences around the Bois de Boulogne, every effort was made to hold *hoi polloi* firmly at bay. Inside, the basement of the mansion, or at any rate a substantial part of it, was accessed by a concealed door in the bookshelves of the ground floor library. To anyone entering it for the first time, it would have been a revelation. A battery of computers was sited along two walls with a number of black leather revolving chairs in front of them. In the middle of the room, a large square glass-topped table housed maps of the continent of Europe and the Mediterranean seaboard. It did not require much imagination to see that this was a major communications centre, not simply an area designed for the convenience and amusement of members of a family.

A young man was seated in one of the chairs, tapping at the keyboard in front of him. Familiar with the necessary protocols, he was intent on retrieving the latest e-mail message from a sender whom he knew was based in the city of Raqqa in northern Syria. There was a clear urgency to the message on the screen, a requirement for immediate confirmation and response. That was way above his grade. He picked up the iPhone that lay on the desk beside him.

A few moments later, the door behind him opened and a tall grey-haired man entered the computer suite. Omar Wazir peered briefly over the youth's shoulder at the screen in front of him and then took the chair alongside. He opened up the computer facing him and entered his password. There followed a lengthy exchange of communications with the Syrian correspondent, referred to as 'The Believer'. Eventually, he signed off and sat back. The youth turned and looked at him enquiringly.

"What now?" he asked.

"Now we move to the next phase."

"And that is…?"

"Appropriation. The time has come to broaden the scope of the campaign. The Caliphate wishes to acquire some notable examples of Western art."

"To teach the infidels another lesson."

"In part. To deprive them of their heritage undermines the very foundations of their society. And for our holy cause, it guarantees a necessary income."

The youth sniggered. "What they call, laughing all the way to the bank!"

"You have adopted too many of their vulgarities. Learn to think and speak at all times like a true member of the Faith—with dignity." The youth, flushed with embarrassment, turned back to his computer screen. Wazir continued, "Send a message to Raschid Al-Azhar. We need to meet."

"He is to come here?"

"No, of course not. Don't be foolish. You know well that is something I never permit."

"I apologise. Where this time?"

"Marrakech. The Garden of Paradise. As usual, after midday prayers. You will come with me. In four days. He is to confirm."

* * *

Venice
17 April

The events that took place at the Villa San Vibio initially received only the most cursory attention in the Italian press. The property was said to belong to an elderly citizen currently in residential care and suffering from an advanced form of Alzheimer's disease. Press speculation came down in favour of the widely held view that the remote villa, unoccupied for some years, had been broken into and taken over by a group of young people whose drunken celebrations had got out of hand, resulting in a young female partygoer falling from a balcony onto the terrace below and sustaining a broken neck. A somewhat wry explanation in view of the actual facts. The subsequent police statement made it amply clear that a tragic accident had taken place as a result of the excessive consumption of alcohol taken with more than just recreational drugs. Having questioned all the witnesses, they stated that no other person was being sought in connection with the incident. The presiding judge ruled 'death by misadventure' and ordered the case closed. The lips of the Italian justice system remained tightly sealed.

There seemed little doubt to Efrem Seiler of *Reuters* in a conversation with the New York journalist, Lavinia Dyer, that the recent terrorist outrage in Milan had resulted in a new and hastily cobbled together strategy to contain rising public concern. Combined with the fact that the whole of the Italian peninsula was, according to certain sections of the Press, 'swarming with migrants arriving daily in their hundreds from North Africa', tensions in the country were running high. Such measures as were being taken, in the opinion of the two journalists, were scarcely likely to alleviate fears among the general population. Highly confidential missives from the Ministry of Justice to local police chiefs demanded a total clampdown in respect of the reporting of serious crimes of the type that had occurred at the Villa San Vibio. Missives so confidential that, in the usual way in which things happened in the Republic, their content was already becoming common knowledge! And if it was thought for a single moment that a blanket of silence would thereby descend on the country, the authorities had badly miscalculated and, almost instantly and inevitably, the press made hay. "*Crime at Country Villa, Police coverup* and *Identity of Villa Victim revealed.*" No mention, however, was made of the state of the deceased's body.

"Well, there you are," said Seiler, "the usual government fuck-up. Nothing changes in this country. To cap it all, one of *Reuters'* Middle East correspondents claims that the Soldiers of the Caliphate are threatening a campaign of decapitations on the streets of every European capital, starting here."

"I wonder what our Dominican friend will have to say about that now that he's safely back in Rome," said Dyer.

"A spokesperson for the Order of Preachers said he left the following day on a pastoral visit to its houses in Paris, Berlin and London. Not wasting any time, is he? Perhaps canvassing support for his future election as Master General."

"Perhaps. Interesting itinerary, though."

"Why so?"

Dyer merely shrugged.

"When do you go back to the States?"

"I'm not sure. I have some loose ends to tie up here first."

* * *

London, Residence of the Papal Nuncio
18 April

"I was speaking to the Master General the other day," said the Nuncio. "He and your friend, the Patriarch of Venice, have been getting their heads together."

"Excellency?"

"People are worried about you, Antonio. That incident on the train. I know you've tried to shrug it off, make light of it."

"A stupid escapade. Student antics."

"We both know better than that. It seems to me you've seriously rattled the bars of someone's cage."

"Over the years, Excellency, I've grown accustomed to upsetting people. It's inevitable with the kind of work I do."

"That's all very well, and I beg to differ. I'm sure you've received threats from time to time. All of us in high-profile positions run the risk. We're no strangers to violent dissent. But you were a hair's breadth from an attempt on your life. No, hear me out. Don't try and play it down, Antonio. It's gone well beyond that. The Master General is anxious for your safety and, I might add, the reputation of the Dominican Order."

"Johann is a far from well man. He's concerned about the future and takes everything to heart. I'm sorry about that. It's certainly not my intention to add to his anxieties. But neither can I give up what I am doing."

"The ultimate sanction on your activity lies with the Order. Forgive me for being so frank. Whether you continue with this very controversial campaign will in the end depend on the General Chapter. Draw back while you have a choice."

Marcetti lowered his head and had nothing to say in reply.

"OK, tell me I'm interfering. I can only speak as a friend."

"Excellency, someone in this country is spending staggering amounts of money for very twisted and evil ends. The net result will bring misery and death down on possibly hundreds of thousands of lives. It is part of a Europe-wide conspiracy. If it succeeds, it is likely to plunge the entire continent into a conflict that will make the last two World Wars seem nothing by comparison."

"Do you know who this person is?"

"I believe so."

"Then surely you have a duty to go to the appropriate authorities."

"Some of the 'appropriate authorities' might very well be implicated. This goes deep. Very deep indeed, to the heart of the British Establishment."

"And you think by publicly shaming the British Government you might…shake the tree and see what falls out."

"At one time, I did think it might persuade the British Government to shake the tree themselves. And that other governments involved might follow suit. I'm by no means sure now that that would be the case. For the moment, Excellency, I have decided to abandon that course of action."

"Antonio, I'm much relieved to hear you say that."

"But only to follow another one."

The Nuncio raised his eyebrows and looked at the other man enquiringly.

"When the time is right, I intend to confront the individual concerned, face to face."

"I would most strongly counsel you against that. You are not trained or equipped for that sort of thing. Leave that to others whose work it is. You are a priest, not a spy!"

"I believe I could intervene in a manner that is entirely consistent with my vocation."

There was a silence in the room broken only by the ticking of a grandfather clock. After a few moments came a knock at the study door and a young man entered, carrying a tray set with afternoon tea. He placed it on a table in the bay window between two armchairs.

"Thank you, William," said the Nuncio. "Come and join me, Antonio."

* * *

London
19 April

The taxi ride from the airport into town was slow and miserable. A steady drizzle and streets clogged with traffic. The cab driver was taciturn and morose, for once disinclined to conversation, as if he too had caught the prevailing mood of the weather. *London on a spring evening!* Standish asked to be dropped in Bessborough Gardens, a short walk across the bridge to HQ. Tonight, a wet walk. The only things to look forward to were to collect Ravi from the office and then home to Pimlico and supper *à deux*. On Cromwell Road, they got stuck for ten minutes, nothing moving one way or the other, and again on Chelsea Embankment. When they started to move again, his mobile rang.

"Ravi!"

"Hi, where are you?"

"In the taxi, it's been slow; we've been stuck in traffic. Heading for the bridge now."

"Can we meet in the pub first, before the office?"

"Sure. Everything all right?"

"Tell you when I see you. Usual place."

Usual place meant a tiny tucked away pub in Kennington, a five-minute walk from the office. A place for a conversation that wouldn't be bugged!

"Change of plan, driver; would you mind dropping me at The Oval?"

"No problem, gov."

Sharma arrived first and when Standish walked in, he was seated at a corner table in an empty bar. Greetings in public were restrained though the delight at seeing each other was evident. The couple were familiar customers; Sean, the barman, came over with two half pints of beer. "Good journey, Milo?" he asked. "Ravi said you'd been away."

"Great, thanks. Apart from the drive back into town." Another customer came in and Sean left them to it.

"You OK?" asked Standish.

"Fine."

"You sounded worried."

"Thought it better to talk here. Received an e-mail yesterday, sender untraceable, could be a scam, I'm not sure. Here, let me show you." He opened up his iPad, retrieved his messages and passed it to Standish. Standish studied it, re-reading it several times and passed the device back.

"What do you reckon, Milo? Have we struck gold or is someone chucking sand in our eyes?"

"It's precise. I wonder if it's too precise. Let's think about it. What exactly have we got?"

"Someone claiming that they've hacked into an e-mail sent from an unknown IP address in Syria to an unidentified server in France…"

"Which they have forwarded to you. For whatever reason, the hacker believes that you should know about this, presumably because of your connection to the Intelligence Service in this country. So, they must know, or guess, that we're involved."

"They're offering us a golden egg. It looks almost too good to be true."

"I agree. Therefore, extreme caution. Whoever's posing as our benefactor is either of a very inventive mind and is laughing up their sleeve or has hit upon a priceless seam. If it's the latter, then he or she has hacked into a potential fortune. They'll wait for our reaction before making another move. And that move could well be a demand for a large slice of the cake."

"Where do we go from here?"

"We ask ourselves, first of all, why you? Why has it come to you rather than direct to the agency via a secure connection?"

"I've been thinking about that."

"Come up with anything?"

"It's somebody who knows me."

"Hm."

"More importantly, it's somebody who wants to make sure we take it seriously."

"Meaning?"

"They were afraid it might be ignored as a scam."

"True. The Service is always a target for scammers. But then, so could you be."

"I don't know why but I have a feeling that it's personal, in a particular way."

"That's what worries me. Being compromised. It's a danger we all face."

"Easier to deal with, though, if it's anticipated."

"We need to go through your list of possible candidates."

"Let's do that later. Leaving it aside for a moment, what do you think the target is likely to be?"

"If it's genuine…OK, let's assume for now it is…The target will be a location where they can apply the greatest pressure. Hence, where a heist might be most easily pulled off, somewhere they'll have an inside contact." He went thoughtful.

"I'm not sure I follow you."

"The Caliphate has got its fingers in a lot of pies in the West. I was going to brief you about Venice after I'd talked to the Chief. Perhaps now, the sooner the better. But I prefer to do it at home. The office can wait till morning."

* * *

The Garden of Paradise, Marrakech
21 April

"Salaam Alaykum."

"Wa-Alaykum salaam."

"I bring you greetings from the Believer."

Raschid Al-Azhar bowed his head in acknowledgment. He had joined two men who were already seated at a table in a shady corner of the garden. Close by a fountain splashing into a bowl the colour of lapis lazuli, the only sound in an oasis of peace, apart from the chirping of a songbird in the branches of the overhanging Judas tree. Glasses of tea had been brought out and the garden was now deserted; the group of three could speak freely without the intrusion of outsiders.

"All is well? And at the farm?"

"All is well. Eight of our soldiers still await their instructions. The rest have been dispatched."

"The operation is on schedule then."

"It is."

"Have you any further news of the contingent that was brought over via Lampedusa last month?"

"Two have already accomplished their mission in Milan and joined our martyrs in Paradise. This you will know."

"They will be received with joy. What else?"

"The execution at the Villa San Vibio. It was carried out by an experienced soldier, a former bodyguard to Gaddafi. A notable recruit to the army of the Caliphate."

"You did well. The Believer commends you."

"I shall now disperse our remaining *jihadis*."

"Keep four of them back. They'll be needed."

"You have something planned?"

"That is what we are here to discuss. What of the Sicilian; he continues to cooperate?"

"Since the loss of his mistress, he looks over his shoulder. That is what I want. But I am watching him all the same."

"You have concerns?"

"There was a minor problem when our present cohort of *jihadis* landed."

"I hear one of them got out of hand. It was the fault of the Sicilian?"

"Partly. He was warned to get our soldiers away before the refugees disembarked."

"Even so, your man overreacted. That is always dangerous."

"He has been infiltrated."

"So, a problem still."

"The Sicilian was careless, but he did not betray our cause. One of the refugees reported the deaths of the woman and child."

"A lesson learned; I trust."

"The Sicilian's whore paid the price for his negligence."

"Let us move on. The Believer has decided that the Western campaign must be extended. A new front is to be opened up. The Caliphate has set its sights on the appropriation of works of art."

Al-Azhar raised his eyebrows. "A surprising choice. Given what is forbidden by our Faith."

"There is a ready market for it in the East. What is degenerate to us is valued elsewhere."

"Have you a target in mind?"

"The first target is Palermo."

"In particular?"

"The Gallery of Fine Art houses the Galiano Picture Collection. From masters of the Renaissance down to the French Impressionists. On permanent loan from the family."

"The family can be persuaded to surrender it?" He laughed.

"Galiano's the legal owner. He can be persuaded; he has no choice in the matter. That'll be your task."

"There are buyers in mind?"

"Naturally. One of our arms suppliers is known to be a collector of Western art. When he knows what's on offer, he will be unable to resist. My nephew and I leave for Sicily tonight. We shall inspect the collection and forward the details to Manila."

"Manila?"

"Yes, that is our prospective client."

"That is good. He is highly regarded. I spoke to the Iranians about Manila's next shipment. They're willing to act as intermediaries. But they don't come cheap."

"Then we'd better make sure that we have something to sell."

"This operation will require careful preparation."

"That is what the Caliphate keeps you to do."

"If possible, we need a contact inside the gallery."

"Excellent, Raschid. We shall give that careful consideration on our visit. A possible candidate might emerge."

"What is the timescale?"

"We're approaching the summer season when visitor numbers to the gallery increase. That always complicates things. I would like to accomplish this mission as soon as feasible. I'll be in touch when we're back in Paris. And you?"

"I return to the farm. I have left Karim in charge."

"Barakallah Fik."

* * *

Venice
23 April

One of the loose ends Lavinia Dyer had mentioned to Seiler came in the form of a meeting with Milo Standish, newly arrived back from a visit to London. At Standish's request, they met over dinner in his hotel just off the Zattere in the Dorsoduro area of the city.

"I chose this place because the hotel's quiet just now and this dining room is large enough to avoid eavesdroppers."

"You sounded quite urgent on the telephone."

"Yes, well, events are moving rather swiftly," said Standish. "I expect you have been keeping up with the Italian press in the last few days. Perhaps even reading between the lines!"

"Efrem Seiler has made sure of that!"

"I'd be grateful for your forbearance, Lavinia. What I have to tell you this evening is for your ears only. Seiler can't be part of this."

"You can trust me on that."

"Thank you. If there is any hesitation on my part, it's only my reluctance to involve you in something from which you may prefer to distance yourself. You won't be surprised that this goes back to our last conversation."

"Please go on."

"I have been asked by my government to look into Antonio Marcetti's allegations that people traffickers have been receiving substantial funds from British and other European states. We're trying to find his sources. What does he actually know and how? What's his agenda? More to the point, what's the real agenda of the financial backers? My guess is that it is political. A process of destabilisation. Then the moneymen move in. The ground all nicely prepared. *Look how we can bail you out.* And the smart money is on the political Far Right."

"History repeating itself?" ventured Dyer.

"We're told that history doesn't repeat itself. I'm sure that's right. But neither do we seem to learn from the lessons of the past. The migration crisis is the cynical face of the Far Right's agenda. It's the sting in the tail that provides justification for a new kind of fascism. Among the migrants arriving here in Italy are so-called Soldiers of the Caliphate—trained *jihadis*—fresh from camps in Libya. And not just here, they're being infiltrated across the EU. Scores of radicalised young Britons left the UK in recent months. Some are now returning home, trained by the Caliphate in Syria and Libya, ready to carry out acts of terror on our streets. You'll have read the recent threat the Caliphate has made about decapitations."

Dyer nodded in reply.

"Well, the threat's already been carried out here in Italy. Not on the streets of Rome, but in a remote Calabrian hunting lodge."

"I've read the reports. Discussed them the other day with Seiler. Difficult to know what's true and what isn't."

"I'll give you the facts as I know them. The lodge's owner is a Sicilian in the pay of the Caliphate and suspected of talking too much about the murders of some migrants. You'll know that the media's been full of it."

"I've seen it. What in God's name was the reason?"

"No one knows, Lavinia. The Sicilian watched it happen, along with a crowd of terrified refugees. His job was to pick up a group of trained *jihadis*. He's in it up to his neck but it's not likely the leak came from him. He gets very well paid to keep his mouth shut. He'll be trying to distance himself from the killings. Plenty of witnesses who could testify against him in the future. Someone has used those deaths to set him up. Now his girlfriend has been found decapitated in a bedroom at his villa. A rather powerful way of keeping him on course, wouldn't you say? The police have tried to cover it up. But nothing remains secret in this country for long."

"Seiler said that there's an official press blackout on the story. Not that that means very much."

"No, but the Caliphate will use it to their advantage. It's either payback time or a weapon of terror to be applied when they see fit. Cross the line and this is how it ends. Silence bought…and paid for. And there could be another reason. The Caliphate needs funds."

"Sounds to me they've already got their hands on a pretty good source of cash."

"It's only as good as it lasts. We know very little about it up to now. But if Marcetti's claims are true, there's a criminal syndicate in the West bankrolling the traffickers, and if that's the case, there's another agenda at work. Someone wants to see the continent flooded with refugees and provoking a right-wing backlash. Right-wing groups don't work totally in isolation from one another. The bankrollers are the lynchpin and with the fear of *jihadi* terror on the streets, the Far Right's got the media where it wants them. Public opinion is swinging in its direction. Take the UK. There's a groundswell in favour of tighter border controls and a halt to immigration. The Caliphate knows that if we cut off its sources of funding, one of its principal means for infiltration dries up. Borders are locked down, the migrant flow decreases. Fortress Europe. Not as impossible as one might imagine. The Nazis managed it in the Second World War."

Standish paused to refill their glasses, glancing at a very pensive Dyer. "Lavinia, I'm not scaremongering. There's a terrible reality to this. And it's being played out on the streets. The Milan bombing last week was a pure terror exercise. So, the Caliphate will be doing two things. One, putting pressure on their bankers until the penny drops that the fountain's dried up; that'll only happen if we get to the moneymen and remove them from the picture. Secondly, terrorists are always interested in alternative sources of income. Remember, they're fighting on two fronts. What they believed was an alliance of interests, they are coming to realise it never was."

"So where do they find new money?"

"Works of art. Think of what's been happening in Syria. They're not destroying everything. They know there's a black market for ancient artefacts."

"They've smashed a good many to smithereens in full view of the watching world."

"To make a religious point. And they know it very conveniently raises the value on what survives. There are always buyers with flexible consciences who won't ask questions."

"What makes you think the Caliphate may be interested in Western art?"

"We've received a tip-off. An anonymous source, so far unverifiable, but we're taking it seriously. It's telling us that our cultural heritage is vulnerable. The Galiano family in Sicily are the owners of a very considerable art collection. Luca Galiano owns San Vibio and a sizable chunk of the province of Enna. You see the connection? Galiano's not cash-rich; everything is tied up in land and art. But he needs ready cash, so he was ripe for burning by Caliphate agents."

"I wonder how they managed it."

"Blackmail. The word is…young teenage boys. True or not, who knows? Most likely a setup. But it worked and he's on the payroll. A few years ago, he needed cash and tried to sell a Caravaggio, on loan to a gallery in Palermo. There was a *very* public outcry and all hell broke loose! Mafia threats and God knows what else. The Sicilians were not prepared to see their national treasures disappear abroad. He withdrew the sale. Now the Caliphate has got him where it wants. The message is clear enough. 'We'll take your art collection and in return, we'll probably let you live. Unlike your girlfriend!'"

"Nothing could be sold on the open market for obvious reasons," said Dyer.

"That's no problem. They're not interested in the open market. They sell to very private buyers. No shortage of customers there, especially in the Far East."

"Casamassa would no doubt be able to tell us something about that," observed Dyer. "The art world is well-informed on these matters," she added dryly.

"We'd like to get any information we can on who the potential buyers might be."

"We're entering a very dangerous world, Milo. Most professionals would steer a wide berth around this. Matteo, I don't know. I think he's too careful to put his head on this particular block."

"At the moment, we wouldn't be asking him to; that might come later."

"Meaning?"

"In any potential transaction, both parties would need an intermediary. An expert on hand to verify the authenticity of the product and set a value on it."

"Are you serious? That would mean someone, a reputable figure in the art world, representing the interests of terrorists and art thieves. No one would do it."

"It may be possible. Knowing what's at stake, someone might."

"With a view to what?" asked Dyer.

"Exposing terrorist agents working in the west. For example, who recruited Galiano? Who's handling the *jihadis* being brought over from Libya? There must be a team behind all that. Whoever's running the operation, knows who's bankrolling it and how the funds are being distributed." Standish paused, looking thoughtful. "You do realise, Lavinia, that in telling you this, I'm—in effect—drawing you into a very dangerous world. The British Secret Intelligence Service is not acting alone. I am already talking to our Italian counterparts. Cooperation is in both our interests. International intelligence is a secret society. Not everyone is comfortable in crossing that threshold. If you would prefer me to stop at this point, now is the time to say so. Nothing I've said so far could compromise you; some of it you've probably already pieced together for yourself."

"I suppose I'd like to know why you have gone as far as you have."

"Alright. You are an investigative journalist with an international reputation. You have an expertise in global communications. Your network of contacts worldwide must be second to none. Many of them, I suspect, out of the public eye. Both intelligence services would find such knowledge invaluable at this time. I personally would like to draw on that expertise and knowledge, if you are willing to share it."

"Have you anything specific in mind, Milo?"

And with that question, Milo Standish noticeably relaxed and proceeded to outline exactly what he had in mind.

* * *

London
30 April

The room was in semi-darkness. The two men who sat facing each other on either side of the empty fireplace were lit only by the distant glow from a single lamp at the opposite end. It was barely enough to make out each other's features. But they had met before in this same place and knew each other well enough. Friends they were not, but more than casual acquaintances. Their relationship was defined strictly in professional and clandestine terms. To have known each other more intimately would have threatened the sanctity and secrecy of their discussions. Thus, the distance they maintained was ultimately their sole protection. The nature of their business precluded closeness but at the same time bound them together in a union that would endure only as long as their common interest endured. Once that was severed, so would end their relationship and at least one of them was well aware that their individual futures would not survive the dissolution.

"Where do you go from here?" asked the first man.

"To visit the others," replied the second.

"You bear the same message you brought to me?"

"It is the same for all."

"They will not be pleased."

"I am not here to please. Simply to convey a message."

The first man smiled. "The privileges and perils of a messenger!"

The second man shrugged, "I am not affected by these matters. Shoot the messenger and you shoot yourselves, or perhaps something else."

The first man drew in a sharp intake of breath. "I have seen the reports," he said. "Was it not excessive?"

"Excessive?"

"The girlfriend. She was not involved."

"She was a warning. He was a fool. The Caliphate will not tolerate fools."

"Nevertheless…"

"I shall convey your sentiments."

"No, please," he intervened, "it was not a criticism. Merely a passing observation."

"Then you should confine yourself to other concerns. You are making the transfers as agreed?"

"Of course, as agreed."

"The routes remain the same?"

"We vary them. Never the same twice running. I keep them constantly under review."

"That is prudent."

"So, our masters are satisfied with progress?"

"You will be left in no doubt if the level of satisfaction drops."

"I trust they appreciate the delicate nature of the alliance we have."

"There is no alliance. You are all businessmen of international standing and indecent amounts of wealth. You have chosen to fund global terrorism in anticipation of increasing your wealth even further. One word from the Believer and you lose everything. *Everything!* That does not constitute an alliance. An alliance implies a balance of power. But this power resides wholly in the Caliphate and it is absolute. Remember, it is the Sword of Islam that hangs over your head—on a very fine thread!" He laughed but there was a chill in his laughter. The first man stiffened, grasping the arms of his chair but remained silent.

"I return to the central point of the message I brought today. It is also a warning. None of you should be so reckless as to entertain any notion that you might take advantage of the situation to pursue a private agenda."

"A private agenda?"

"Other than that of expanding the boundaries of your financial empires, a long-term aim that the Caliphate has recognised as valid within certain defined limits."

"There is no such agenda. Nor do I think that the limits of the long-term outcome have ever been defined."

"They will be made perfectly clear at the appropriate time."

"We wish only to safeguard our futures."

"The West is finished."

"We accept that. You have said it yourself many times. We are all agreed that it is to the East that the world now looks. That is where our future lies also. It is our 'indecent wealth', as you put it, which will make that future a reality."

"Then you must make sure that there is no deviation from the terms of the agreement."

"There will not be. We wish only to lead the world into a new era."

"And so you shall! As long as you keep your heads!"

Long after the second man had left, the first man remained in his seat staring into the empty fireplace. He replayed the conversation in his mind over and over again. He tried to recall every gesture, every nuance. It was important to remember all the details of their exchange, the nature of the questions, the reaction of the other man to his answers. The exercise left him feeling depressed and strangely disoriented. Had his reassurances been sufficient? What message would be taken back? As to the reason for the visit, had some intimation of their private agenda somehow been leaked? Was it a random guess or was the messenger on a fishing expedition? If so, what had instigated it? It had always been his belief that their political ambitions could not remain shrouded in secrecy for long. However, it was inconceivable that any of his associates had allowed the true nature of their activities to slip through the tight net of security with which they had surrounded themselves. But moving vast sums of money around the world was fraught with danger. Many intermediaries were involved at every stage of the operation. A margin of error was unavoidable and hence, there was always the possibility of carelessness or even betrayal. He would look to his own organisation. There must be no question of a breach there. It was time for some very serious housekeeping. Meanwhile, there were his associates to consider. They should be warned of what to expect. He picked up his mobile phone and made a call.

* * *

"Pronto."

"May I speak to Father Marcetti, please?"

"May I ask who is calling?"

A slight hesitancy. *"Rosamund Cross."*

"Uno momento, Signora."

This time, a longish pause and then, "Signora Cross? This is Father Bonifacio."

"I was hoping Father Antonio might be available."

"Alas, Signora, he is not here. Father Antonio is visiting some of our Study Centres in northern Europe. We do not expect him back in Rome until the end of the week. Is there any way in which I might be of assistance?"

"I am coming to Rome next week and had been hoping to see Father Antonio. It was…is…quite important. Could you let him know that I have been in touch?"

"Of course, Signora. I shall endeavour to contact him myself and pass on your message. Meanwhile, if there is…" The line suddenly went dead. Father Bonifacio turned to his companion and shrugged.

* * *

Enna
12/13 April

Galiano's return to his home in Enna had been greeted with customary insouciance by his household staff. Used to his sudden departures and equally unscheduled reappearances, daily life at the Villa Galiano had continued with the same routine as normal. Enquiries as to his wellbeing had been few. Mostly from the Confraternity. Luca Galiano had learnt of late to distance himself as far as possible from social contacts. He was not a man innately inclined towards friendship. Even his casual intimacies with the opposite sex required little emotional investment. By their very nature, they were transient. A basic need fulfilled. Basic needs were easily accommodated by a man who travelled much and had the means to indulge his sexual adventures, however exotic, at a safe distance from the domestic scene. Not that sex with Laura Pellestri could be described as *exotic*, though she had been the first to lead him by the hand into areas in which hitherto he had been less than a novice. Martina's conventionality from their wedding night onwards had proved ineluctable. The gift of San Vibio after ten years of sterile marriage had been a life-changer. He was generally regarded by his contemporaries as a conventional man, according to the accepted standards of Sicilian manhood. One night in a Maltese hotel bedroom had changed all that. Looking back, he had little recollection of what, if anything, had actually happened. But the evidence was there in black and white. *Believe what we are telling you and accept the consequences. Or not, it's up to you.* Plead innocence and pay the price. Not that it mattered to his tormentors, one way or the other. A price still had to be paid. In personal terms, it could not have been higher. A future consigned into the hands of agents of the so-called Soldiers of the Caliphate. The reward: The staggering sum of one million euros, just for starters.

It had been a nervous and unsettling drive back. The memory of the horror he had left behind affected him to such an extent that he had been compelled twice to stop the car and throw up in a roadside lay-by. Once, another motorist approached him with a kind enquiry as to whether he needed help, even offering a bottle of mineral water, which was gratefully accepted. He went over and over the events. Somehow, they had got to Laura Pellestri. Given her his gun with a message from 'Omar Wazir'. Who was Omar Wazir and what was her connection to him? Had she been ordered to kill her lover? Then why had she been butchered instead? It was better to try to block out the past two days by concentrating on the task in hand—to get back to Enna in one piece.

Towards San Giovanni, a light misty drizzle settled in and the queue of vehicles waiting for the ferry crossing thinned out. Even so, late in the evening, there was a crop of tourist caravans making for the southern Sicilian beach resorts, their inhabitants looking tired and subdued. The mood matched his own; the lights on the car decks casting a pallid glow on proceedings as deckhands directed the flow making sure that all available parking space was utilised. He switched off the engine, rested his head on the back of the seat and unscrewed the bottled water. This time, he would take the more direct route to Enna. Disembarkation seemed to take forever. The driver of the car in front had wandered off, holding up the entire deck. Then at last, he was on the road. Familiar as he was with it, there was almost a feeling that he was making this journey for the first time. In a sense, he was. Nothing would ever be the same again, the future a blank canvas, the paintbrush in hands other than his own.

On the large round table in the centre of the villa's entrance hall lay the accumulated mail from his absence. All things being considered little enough for a man of his station. Collecting it all together and sending old Seppi off to his bed, he settled himself in a chair by the window in the library and despite the lateness of the hour, proceeded to sort through it. A number of pressing enquiries emanated from the Confraternity of the Most Holy Shroud, requesting an immediate response upon receipt. That he had expected. Beyond that, the occasional social invitations to dinner or the marriage of a friend's daughter, or the usual round of charitable functions requiring patronage and, naturally, financial support. And a letter from the director of the art gallery in Palermo that housed the family's art collection, informing him that an art historian was coming to view it for a prestigious American publication currently in preparation. The black border on one envelope denoted a bereavement notification and this he placed to one side to be dealt with last of all, in no hurry to embrace more bad news.

Enquiries from his children were infrequent. His son, Lorenzo, in Milan had telephoned to say he had failed to elicit a response from his father's mobile phone. Members of staff tended to treat Lorenzo with a degree of benign neglect, part of the inevitable fabric of the place, not to be approached with anything like friendship. This was all in marked contrast to his elder sister, Catarina, the darling of the family. Surprisingly, in the circumstances, the siblings enjoyed a remarkably close relationship. Assured that his father, as far as was known, was in the best of health and possibly in an area where a mobile signal was unreliable, he left a message asking to be contacted as soon as…yes, it *was* urgent, he needed to speak personally, he would shortly be leaving for the United States, please convey to my father etc., etc. Galiano's relationship with his son had over the years been volatile. There was nothing to complain about the boy's progress through university, able but not outstanding, and the job in Milan in the lucrative field of financial management seemed to have placed him in an advantageous position for future advancement. It also carried an income that his father would have regarded as staggering had he known what it was. Travel to all parts of the globe at company expense was inevitable and Lorenzo knew full well how to exploit the advantages of family background. Trying his son's number with no result, he left a message.

Glancing again at the bereavement letter, Galiano pushed it one side. Tomorrow would be time enough for that. Well! Perhaps better to get it over and done with after all.

Picking up the black-bordered envelope addressed to 'Barone Luca Galiano, Villa Galiano, Enna', he opened it. His mouth went dry and a wave of dizziness swept over him. It slipped from his fingers and fluttered to the floor. For a time, he sat like one paralysed, his breathing wrenched out of him in short gasps. Eventually, he recovered his calm and reaching down, picked it up and read it again.

'It is with great regret that the recent passing of Signorina Laura Pellestri has been announced. A Requiem Mass will be celebrated for the Repose of her Immortal Soul on the forthcoming Feast of the Ascension in the Cathedral of Enna at 2300 hours. Your attendance is required.'

Nothing more.

The eastern sky was already beginning to lighten when he at last dropped off into a thin and troubled doze and then in no time at all, the first shafts of sunlight penetrating the slatted shutters of his bedroom windows brought him back to life again. To face another day, another page in the chapter of his history. It was a journey that was inevitable and one he must accomplish alone. He lay quite still for a few moments and then did a very unaccustomed thing— he began spontaneously to weep. But for whom or for what was he weeping? Something had brought into his mind the words of a poem, often quoted by his English mother when her children were out of sorts. 'This is the land of lost content; I see it shining plain'. Had he ever really known content? For a brief moment, when his daughter had been born, the promise of life realised in this exquisite child, his own creation. But by the time Lorenzo came along, the promise, unaccountably, seemed to have faded. Odd, considering how much a male child was prized in Sicilian society and how enthusiastically the birth of a son had been greeted by the whole community.

Showered and dressed, he made his way downstairs in search of breakfast. Already, the staff was up and about the daily tasks of the house. Seppi met him at the foot of the staircase.

"*Buon giorno*, Seppi. What have you there?"

The houseman was clutching in his arms a large brown-paper box, which he deposited with a thud on the hall table.

"*Buon giorno*, Barone. This has just been delivered. It comes from Count Lipari's vineyard; his label is here on the box."

"Ah! Yes, it will be his gift of last year's special vintages, he promised to send some over when they were ready. Excellent. Is the driver still here?"

"No signor. He left immediately. A new man, I think, I didn't recognise him."

"I'll call the Count. Take it to the library please, Seppi, I 'll open it there."

The houseman manhandled the package onto a low carved chest and fetching a knife from his desk, Galiano set to work while the old fellow shuffled off. The brown paper came away easily enough, revealing underneath a layer of what looked and felt like oilcloth secured all around with heavy tape. It took some removing and then more tape held the lid of the box in place. As he opened it up, a strong chemical smell mingled with something indefinable emanated from the package. Removing several layers of a thick type of tissue paper inside, Luca Galiano found himself gazing into the glazed and sightless eyes of Laura Pellestri.

* * *

London/Rome
1st week of May

The private executive Lear Jet, conveying Rosamund Cross to Rome's Ciampino Airport, had been delayed in taking off from Farnborough due to the late arrival of its passenger whose chauffeur-driven Bentley had been seriously held up in the rush of traffic leaving town. As a consequence, it had missed its slot and the pilot was forced to adopt a revised flight plan. To its passenger, this was of little significance. Whatever the hour, she would be met at her destination by limousine and taken to her hotel in one of the most exclusive areas of Rome close to the Spanish Steps. Over the years, the spring season had always been a delight to her, the classic time to be back in her favourite city. Like everywhere else these days, it already overflowed with tourists among whom she most decidedly refused to number herself. On this occasion, however, she was filled with apprehension that marred the prospect of a few days in the Eternal City. Never before had Andrew questioned her so closely about her proposed itinerary, even asking the names of the fashion houses she would be visiting and what other plans she had for her visit. How would she spend her evenings? With friends, what friends? Andrew Cross was not the kind of man who could make a question sound casual or convey the impression he was at all interested in what his wife actually did with her time. For him, simple dialogue took on the trappings of an inquisition; subtlety an art he had learned to practice only when negotiating financial deals. Then, he could be very subtle indeed.

But something had changed in recent weeks. An unaccustomed interest in the mundane affairs of his family and especially of his wife. In the normal course of events, their daily lives followed different trajectories, crossing only when social expectations required their joint participation. In those respects, Rosamund was a dutiful spouse, at her husband's side when needed and presenting a public image of a stable and supportive partner. She imagined that like most businessmen of his age, he had had his fair share of extra marital relationships but if so, these had never impinged on the outward harmony of home life. He always had a restless nature but she supposed that all billionaires were restless; how else did they keep a grip on so much money? Indeed, how

72

else did they make so much money in the first place? Putting off her customary post-Easter trip till the beginning of May had proved a further complication. Why the delay? She had some items on order that would not be ready until then—the delay her fault because she had changed her mind. Rosamund Cross sighed, rang for the cabin attendant and asked for coffee to be brought.

Later in her Rome hotel suite, she called the headquarters of the Order of Preachers. A meeting was arranged for 11.00 a.m. the following day, a meeting Rosamund Cross would never attend.

* * *

Palermo

They made an interesting and handsome couple. The tall woman in a white trouser suit, sunhat and dark glasses and the young man dark-haired and athletic in smart jeans and a pink polo shirt at her side. They might be mother and son, possibly British or North American, embarking on a tour of European galleries and museums, part of a young man's education, maybe a post-graduation holiday in celebration of academic success. But the impression they gave, the impression they intended to give, to the casual observer was some way from the truth. Lucy Black and Vassilio Pritsi were on a wholly different mission. The young man, a few years older than his appearance suggested, was already an acknowledged specialist in Renaissance art and his companion, although well-versed in the subject, was not a specialist. But both had been carefully groomed in the task they were about to perform.

Arriving at the gallery in Palermo, they had been courteously conducted to a small waiting area outside the office of the Director by a middle-aged female secretary, who was more than a little taken by the sight of the handsome young art historian. It wasn't every day her job was enlivened by such a prospect. Visiting academics seemed to be a dry bunch on the whole but this one was certainly something to talk about over lunch. After an interval of a few minutes, the door opposite opened and Claudio Melzi emerged from his room. A small, diffident-looking man in his early sixties, bald with a fringe of longish grey hair, Melzi was dressed in a trim dark blue suit, white shirt and bow tie. His somewhat abstracted air to those who knew him better concealed a very shrewd operator.

"Dr Black, and Dr Pritsi, I presume. Welcome, welcome! I'm delighted to meet you both, please come in." To his secretary, "Signora Bertelli, would you please come in and take notes? Professor Casamassa has, of course, written to introduce you and tell me a little about the reasons for your visit." He swept the pair into his office. The room was a surprise: Large, high-ceilinged, raftered and wholly painted a dazzling white, one wall accommodated floor-to-ceiling white-painted bookshelves and a window that overlooked the rear of the building. At the other end, two tall windows looked out over the piazza; the other two walls were filled with bright modernist paintings. In the centre of the room, a large glass table served as a desk. Melzi conducted his guests to armchairs on either side of an ornate fireplace and took his place in a third, his secretary just behind him.

"This is, of course, Dr Melzi, just an initial visit," Pritsi began, "to obtain an overview of the Galiano Collection. I am here on behalf of the Ministry of Culture, which is backing the exhibition of items from the collection to tour some of our major art galleries. Dr Black represents the American publisher, Actaeon, which will feature pictures from the collection in a forthcoming publication."

"Your publishing house, Dr Black, is well-known. It features prominently among my reference books here. And, of course, it is always a pleasure to welcome the Ministry to the gallery. When I heard of your visit, Dr Pritsi, I was delighted to know that our Culture Ministry was enthusiastically supporting this initiative. We are honoured to think some of our pictures will be viewed by greater numbers of our citizens." Melzi beamed cherubically.

"We would like to see the range of pictures from the Collection on show in the gallery," Pritsi continued. "And make a preliminary assessment of which artists might be selected to feature both in the exhibition and the publication. Clearly, it's impossible to include everything but if possible, perhaps we could also view any that are not currently on display or are with restorers."

"I can make arrangements for both those requests if you are able to return. I imagine, like myself, your time is limited. Tomorrow afternoon, perhaps?"

"Thank you. Perhaps, I might explain the overall timetable." The young art historian took a sheet of paper from the manila folder he was carrying. "If all goes well, Director, we would like to arrange a second visit as soon as possible with our photographer. Professor Casamassa from Venice will also be with us. His role, together with yourself, is to advice on which works might be selected for the travelling exhibition. We shall probably need to come on more than one occasion. To begin with, to look at the selected paintings and discuss with you the requirements for photographing them. I shall, of course, be with the photographer at all times. Pictures currently on show would be photographed in situ. Any others would naturally require special arrangements. The actual photography would have to be done when the gallery is closed to visitors. I know you are more familiar with the procedure than I am, Dottore!"

Melzi smiled indulgently at the young man. "It is always helpful to rehearse the arrangements. I have already written to Baron Luca Galiano in Enna. He is the present head and representative of the family. He is yet to reply to my letter."

"Do you anticipate any difficulty in that area?" queried Black.

"Not especially. Though he is not the easiest person in the world to tie down. However, it has always been understood that the gallery has full responsibility for day-to-day decisions regarding the collection and I don't believe that this proposal transgresses that understanding. The collection has been with us for almost twenty years. It was the father of Luca Galiano who took the decision to transfer it on permanent loan to the gallery. He felt strongly that his fellow citizens should have equal access to enjoying this unique heritage. Hitherto, they had been more or less hidden away on various family properties. I believe that he would have approved the plan to photograph and publish the collection, or at least as much of it as is viable in the circumstances. Wider knowledge can only be of benefit to the art world and future artists in the long run."

"Forgive me, but if I might intervene at this point, Director," said Black. "Proposals of this nature, and I can only speak for the publication, inevitably give rise to other considerations, particularly matters relating to security. Publication of a little-known private collection, however exclusively marketed, will arouse attention worldwide. That has implications of which you will already be fully aware."

"Yes, it has been at the forefront of my mind. The Galiano family in the person of Baron Luca will certainly seek assurances that the gallery's security system is equal to the increased public interest and the increased risk that goes with it. However, Dr Pritsi will, I am sure, confirm that it is kept under constant review by our Ministry of Culture."

"And, in any case," added Pritsi, "as far as the exhibition goes, the Ministry will be underwriting the insurance costs."

Black raised her eyebrows and looked at Pritsi. As if on cue, the young art historian passed Melzi a sheet of typescript from his folder. "Director, these are the suggestions for covering advertising. As you see, this will appear in the relevant journals and on the art pages of all leading newspapers approximately a year in advance, if our schedule goes according to plan, and then followed up some three months prior to publication date. However, we would like to put out a flier in the next few weeks to kindle interest. Professor Casamassa has generously offered to exhibit some paintings at his gallery in Venice for the summer season as a precursor—at very short notice—with your agreement and that of the Galiano family."

"Most generous; I am sure it can be arranged."

"It will soon become known that items from the Galiano Collection are about to reach a wider public," added Black. "That would be enough to excite an unhealthy interest from someone wishing to exploit the situation. I say this, Dr Melzi, not to cause undue alarm but that we should all be aware that in this day and age, our cultural heritage is constantly under threat."

"Your admonition is well made and timely, Dr Black, and the sooner I can speak to Baron Galiano and offer reassurances, the better."

"At some point," Black continued, "we would like to meet with the Baron and obtain background for the book. Family history, when and by whom the collection was acquired. That sort of thing."

Melzi frowned, "That may be more difficult than you imagine. The Galiano Collection is shrouded in mystery! Remember, colleagues, this is Sicily. There is a natural reluctance to enquire too closely into the origin of things. There is much concealment here. We have always been a closed society. Between you and me, not all the Baron's forebears were…well, as particular as he. It would be indiscreet to delve too much into family connections. The acquisition of some of the pictures was—how shall I say—to be diplomatic, a little controversial. *Piano*, dottori, *piano,* yes, indeed, this is Sicily." He got up from his chair and clapped his hands in almost childish delight. "But, please, let us take some coffee now and then I'll escort you on a personal tour around the Galiano Collection."

It was some time later, as they got into their hired car, that Pritsi smiled at his older companion, "Well, Lavinia, until tomorrow. I think we've brought it off so far, don't you?"

* * *

The City of Enna
The Feast of the Ascension, 14 May

From dawn and throughout the morning, masses in celebration of the Ascension of Our Lord had been said in all the churches of the city of Enna. Early masses seemed to be most popular with the elderly who liked to get their religious obligations over and done with for the day. After all, they were already up and about on this fine spring morning, no lying abed which their grandchildren's generation seemed to think the more proper course while the generation in between was far too busy making a living! Also, early masses were conducted without undue ceremonial, said rather than sung and therefore concluded all the sooner. The notable exception was the Duomo where at midday, High Mass presided over by the Bishop of the Diocese of Enna was celebrated with great pomp and circumstance, crowded with a transient congregation of visitors, some no doubt there by conviction but most simply to savour the spectacle and listen to the choral splendours—just another event on the tourist trail.

When Luca Galiano arrived at the Great West door shortly before the appointed hour of that same day, the celebrations were long over and the visitors had departed. A smaller door to the right of the main doors was slightly ajar. The vast interior of the building, dimly lit by the few remaining sanctuary lamps still burning, was heavy with the incense that had suffused it during high mass when it had issued forth in great clouds from the silver censers swung by the altar boys. Dipping his fingers in the holy water stoop by the door by habit and making the sign of the cross, Galiano cautiously made his way down the central aisle of the nave towards the High Altar. At first, he thought he was alone and the place deserted but as he drew nearer, he became aware of a shadowy group over to his left in one of the small side chapels of the cathedral. He could make out two figures and the merest outline of a third behind. One of them stepped forward and Galiano recognised the commander of the Soldiers of the Caliphate, Raschid Al-Azhar.

"Welcome, Barone to our commemoration. I see you are empty-handed. I had thought Signorina Pellestri might have been joining us for her Requiem! No matter! We shall proceed without her," he laughed and the great cathedral seemed to laugh back. A second figure then moved out of the shadows and stood beside him. "Allow me to introduce General Jawali who trains our freedom fighters in Libya. He has honoured us with his presence tonight." The tall white-bearded figure stared at Galiano but said nothing. Al-Azhar continued, "You must forgive my little ruse to get you here tonight. It was a necessary preliminary to our gathering. But perhaps the gift was appreciated, no? A reunion of lovers! A present from the Caliphate! The death of Signorina Pellestri is a reminder that our masters do not tolerate disloyalty and indiscretion."

"There was neither on my part," said Galiano.

"Believe me, Barone, if there had been, you would not be standing here now. But we are not here to lament the death of one of your mistresses. I have no doubt she was instantly replaceable."

Galiano reached out and grasped the back of a chair as a wave of nausea swept over him. "She had a family, a child."

"One of your bastards?"

"No, not mine. She married very young. It did not last but there is a child."

"Collateral damage, a casualty of the war," snapped Al-Azhar. "And better off without that whore of a mother."

"My God! What kind of people are you?"

"In our Islamic State, our women give themselves to our warriors out of duty, not from some perverted kind of pleasure." It was the general who spoke, his voice so soft Galiano could scarcely hear the words. "We are people with a divine mission. To destroy your corrupt Western society and replace it with a caliphate, which will purge this evil from the face of the earth." His voice rose as he turned and gesticulated with both arms outstretched, encompassing the vastness of the basilica around them. The third figure in the shadows of the chapel seemed to stir a little at these words but remained silent and invisible.

Al-Azhar spoke again, "Allah be praised! Now let us get down to business! Your pathetic sentimentality has no place here. You have rendered some small service to our mission, not without benefit to yourself. Your continued survival depends on your continued cooperation. The time has come for a further demonstration of your goodwill."

"What more can you demand of me?"

"Oh! Your commitment, Barone, has only just begun! Your family possesses the finest art collection in Sicily, indeed, one of the finest in Italy," he smiled. "You are about to make a generous gesture and present it to the Caliphate. We need funds to advance our cause. Already, buyers are lining up, salivating at the prospect of acquiring some of the finest examples of Western degeneracy anywhere in the world."

"It is impossible! The collection is no longer in my keeping."

"You are a fool! Do not think to dissemble with us. The pictures may not be in your custody, of that we are aware, but they are still in your ownership. The only matter to be discussed today is the manner in which ownership will be transferred. And that has been already decided. Your futile attempt to sell a

Caravaggio a few years ago is evidence enough that a more robust approach is required."

"Robust?"

"Items from the Collection are about to be photographed for a forthcoming book. Subsequently, a number of items will go on tour to several Italian galleries, as the Director's letter made clear to you. Yes, Barone, don't look so surprised we know about that too. This affords us the perfect opportunity to gain access to the gallery and decide what we wish to take. We shall take what we want. *InshAllah!* Details of how do not concern you. All that is required of you is to ensure that the process is allowed to take place without interference on your part. The director, Melzi, and his staff will be taken care of."

"There must be no violence."

"MUST! Do you dare to make conditions? Do you forget who you are dealing with? We shall determine who lives and who dies in our sacred cause. How many demonstrations of our power do you need? The Pellestri whore was not enough?"

"I was only trying to protect the innocent."

"There are no innocents. You are all guilty of blasphemy," intervened Jawali. "And by the words of the Prophet—peace be upon Him—you all stand condemned. You along with all the others. Your life hangs by the merest thread. Enough of this! The time for talking is past."

Al-Azhar took a step forward. "You will inform Melzi of your full support for the project, requesting only to be present when the collection is to be photographed. Our source will let us know when and *you will* be there, Galiano."

"As you wish."

"No, as we command." Jawali's voice was soft again but dark with menace.

"Don't worry; you will receive your usual fee…for the loss this time of your pictures!" Al-Azhar's sarcasm was palpable. "Though I have no doubt the loss will be felt more by your compatriots than by yourself. You have shown scant respect for your inheritance in any case. It is time it passed into other hands. I trust your regrets will be accepted as genuine. The people of Sicily are well-known for exacting their own retribution!"

It was not until Galiano had left the cathedral that the third figure emerged from the shadowy depths of the chapel and joined the other two.

"You heard everything?" asked Al-Azhar. "The words of a frightened man."

"Frightened, yes," said Omar Wazir, "but like all his kind, also greedy!"

* * *

Rome

A crowd had gathered on the pavement at the foot of the Spanish Steps. Others jostled on the Steps above for a better look while those passing along the Piazza di Spagna stopped in their tracks and a group around the Fontana della Barcaccia broke off to crane and see what was the cause of all the interest. As always at this time of year, tubs of bright pink azaleas covered the Steps, a traditional celebration of Roman springtime. A few of the staff from Babington's tearooms had come to the door to see what all the fuss was about. At the sound of the approaching ambulance's siren, some of the crowd drew back to make room for the inevitable paramedics revealing the body of a woman lying in a foetal position. Some signs of life seemed to issue from the twitching form. Two *carabinieri* ran up and began to clear the onlookers away.

"What happened?" A middle-aged English tourist, a scared-looking wife clutching his arm, accosted a youth who merely shrugged and walked on with his arm around his girlfriend. Hearing him, another tourist, an American this time, stopped.

"I watched her coming down the steps. I don't know why but she caught the eye, among all this crowd she seemed kinda different, smart looking, if you know what I mean, an Eytalian I expect. Somehow, she stood out, probably not on holiday like us, too smart for that," he laughed, "then suddenly she staggered and fell, rolling down the last few steps. Heart attack, I expect. God, you never know when it's coming, do you! Back home I said to Ellie, you never what's around the corner, Ellie, let's go see Rome while we still can. Where you folks from?"

"England."

"I guessed you were Brits. Where exactly?"

"Manchester."

"Manchester! You don't say. Ellie, do yer hear that? They're from Manchester. Our Josh's wife's folks are from Manchester. Kinda small world, isn't it? Perhaps you know them."

But they didn't and with the excitement of the moment passing, they said cheerio and went on their way. Meanwhile, the paramedics were bent over the patient ascertaining that vital signs were still present. A drip was attached and the twitching body carefully lifted onto a stretcher. Then, in what seemed like no time at all, the ambulance—siren sounding once again—moved off heading for the Mater Dei hospital. It was later announced on the local news that the patient, a 57-year-old Englishwoman, who had been admitted with a suspected heart attack, had died. Relatives were being informed.

Bonifacio tore along the corridor, almost slipping on the polished parquet floor. Arriving breathless at the Order's library doors, he burst in, causing a ripple of alarm to the half-dozen brothers and novices seated at tables around the room and standing before the shelves. Spotting Marcetti seated by a window with a book open before him, he hurried over.

"Antonio, come quickly, the Master is asking for you. A message from Mater Dei. About the visitor you're expecting. I took it myself. There's been some kind of accident. Come!"

The Master rose from his chair and came around to the front of his desk as Marcetti entered the room after knocking. "Antonio, come in and sit down. I'm afraid I have some grave news. Your penitent Signora Cross died in the Mater

Dei this morning. She had been taken by ambulance from the Spanish Steps where she apparently collapsed. I know you had been expecting to see her today."

"Bonifacio said an accident…"

"No, not quite. And not a heart attack either, which they thought at first. Though there was, I understand from the medical director, heart failure and the collapse of all bodily systems. She briefly regained consciousness and was able to tell them that she had been on her way here to meet with you when she experienced a sharp pain in her leg. Nothing more, she said nothing more before lapsing into unconsciousness again."

"Has there been any contact with her family? She has—had—a husband and two children."

"A number for Signor Cross was found on her *telefonino*. Dr Riccardi has already been in touch. I know her meetings with you were…highly confidential. I have to ask you this, Antonio—was her husband aware of them? It is possible that that knowledge has been passed on. Unwittingly. I trust it does not present a problem for you."

"No, Master, not now."

Chapter Four

Venice

The flight from Palermo landed at Marco Polo Airport right on time. Collecting her case from baggage reclaim, Lavinia Dyer headed through the main concourse and out towards the *vaporetto* station, an easy walk with wheeled luggage. Venice—late spring verging on early summer. Coaches coming and going, crowds of tourists standing around, new arrivals eager for their first glimpse of the lagoon, departures sorry to leave but anxious to get the homeward journey started, the airport responding with an air of resignation to the thousand demands being made upon it. *And what next*, thought Dyer. A mission accomplished, amusing looking back; she'd never before played the role of someone else, at any rate not since the days of the school play! Lucy Black—indeed, was there such a person? Standish had assured her everything checked out with the publishing house. Who was the real Lucy Black and what did she look like? *She came and went. But nobody remembers her.* Still, the satisfaction of a modest contribution, not to put it too highly. Now, she thought, report back to Standish and soon no doubt, high time to think about returning home! She couldn't stay indefinitely. The last few days had an air of unreality, actually all of it, come to think, since the day Ferdy Keymer had walked into her office and made a smart remark or two.

And there he was, Milo Standish, just off the *vaporetto* and looking around as if in search of someone. Too kind, but then how did he know her time of arrival? The departure time from Palermo had been brought forward, a last-minute decision. Pritsi had been worried about the photography, said he wanted to return to the gallery for a further briefing with Melzi 'to tie up a couple of loose ends'. *Loose ends—there were likely to be plenty of those before they were done.* She raised her arm to attract his attention but at that precise moment, he turned away. Too far away to call out, Lavinia checked, uncertain and suddenly unsure. Standish started to move, he'd seen someone, someone he'd really come to meet. Dyer watched as a young dark-skinned man emerged from the crowd on the quayside, carrying luggage. They embraced, seemed pleased to see each other, and Standish took him by the arm and led him apart. The conversation earnest and serious, the young man explaining something and then shaking his head, Standish still holding on to his arm and reluctant to let go while he explained something. Then the young man nodding assent to whatever it was the older man was saying and laughing. Dyer was fascinated by the scene, all too aware that at that precise moment, she stood alone; for a minute, there was no one around her and she was open to being caught out staring. The *vaporetto* was about to leave so she hurried over and walked on board as the gate began to close. Moving to the other side of the deck, she could still see Standish but this time, he was on his own, his companion out of view. No, there he was, trailing a suitcase and running for the *vaporetto*, but too late. As the boat pulled away from the quay, Dyer watched as he turned around to call out something to Standish. But Standish didn't hear as he crossed the road, heading for the airport terminal.

Well, what to make of that? Hardly a covert meeting, in full public gaze, yet with something of the clandestine about it despite the obvious warmth between the two. The young man himself chimed with a description from an earlier conversation. In the restaurant was it, after her abortive interview with Marcetti? The youth on the Rome-Venice train. She tried to recall what Standish had said at the time but the details slipped away. Probably not the same individual at all, this one older than she imagined. She remembered a vague description and being surprised at the youth's reported remarks, his apparent hostility towards the Catholic cleric, a cleric who had always spoken up in support of persecuted Muslim migrants. None of it made sense unless it was intended as a threat to secure Marcetti's silence. As far as she could remember, Standish had been reticent, perhaps knowing more than he was willing to share. Yet this meeting was not something she felt she should mention when they met later for dinner. If Standish wanted to say anything, it was up to him. Relax, she told herself, enjoy the journey. Out of the wind, the sun was warm on her face, the motion of the boat seductive on a comparatively calm lagoon. She felt a gentle tug on her coat and looked down at a small boy of maybe five or six who had slid off his seat and onto his mother's lap, leaving the space for her. "*Grazie*," she smiled and was rewarded with a shy "*prego*".

Soon, they were entering the Grand Canal and passing the Santa Lucia *ferrovia*. *Almost home*, she found herself thinking. But it wasn't home; it simply felt like it with the comforting glow of familiarity. The Number One deposited her at the Accademia stop, a few minutes' walk from her hotel. On the way, she had to pass Da Gino's. Stopping for a coffee was like checking whether all was well with the neighbours.

"*Buon giorno*, Dotoressa, macchiato?"

"*Grazie*, Marco." Really home at last!

Dyer hadn't settled into her hotel room more than a few minutes when her mobile rang. Vassilio Pritsi sounded agitated, "Lavinia!"

"Vassilio? Where are you?"

"In Palermo, at the hotel. There's been a problem!"

"What's happened?"

"It's Melzi. He's had a stroke. I got to the Gallery and the ambulance was just taking him away. His secretary said he was showing some people around when he suddenly collapsed with a pain in his leg. I don't know how serious it is yet. I'll stay till tomorrow to see how things are and maybe get the afternoon flight."

"Vassilio, call me and let me know before you leave. We may have to re-plan the whole timetable. I'll let Milo know when I see him this evening."

Standish's and Dyer's evening was destined to be tense before it started. The large dining room of the hotel off the Zattere was crowded and noisy. The hotel had filled up with a fresh crop of visitors, all of whom seemed to want to eat at the same time, a fair percentage of them teenagers and younger children whose conversations were conducted at several decibels above the average. An air of high-octane excitement and confusion pervaded the place as guests milled around finding tables and harassed staff coped with orders coming from all directions. A distracted maître d', profuse with apologies, suggested that the signor and signora might wish to return to the cocktail bar until things quietened down and he would try to find a table away from the general hubbub—*some hope of that.* At least the cocktail bar allowed for more or less normal conversation.

"I'm afraid we should have gone somewhere else," said Standish. "Well, you're back. I checked the flight this afternoon from Palermo, but I missed you."

"That was kind of you, Milo. You had a wasted journey."

"Not really, I was there anyway. I trust you're no worse for your brief spell as Dr Black!"

"As you can see. The actress returns."

"You know, Lavinia, we're very grateful."

"I still don't fully understand the need for the subterfuge. Anyway, it may all prove to have been a waste of time and effort…"

"No, really I…"

"Milo, you haven't heard. Vassilio called before I left to come here. Melzi had a stroke earlier today while showing some party around the gallery. Vassilio's staying on until tomorrow to try and find out how serious it is."

"Oh God! Bad news. We could do without this." He paused to take a drink, looking thoughtful. "I'm not sure where it leaves our plans. It'll be up to the trustees and the Ministry of Culture to decide if the exhibition and photography should go ahead in Melzi's absence. In a small gallery like that, I doubt his deputy would have that kind of authority. If he has one."

"We only met an assistant, more a secretary really. I didn't get the impression she had much of a say."

"We *have* to get the Galiano Collection recorded as soon as possible. It's almost inconceivable it's never been properly done."

"From what Melzi told us, perhaps nòt such a surprise. The Collection's history is murky to say the least. Like much of the family's history, I gather."

"Lavinia, I've taken the liberty of asking Matteo Casamassa to join us for coffee after dinner…I know, I know. Apologies. I really don't want to embarrass you but at some point in the not too distant future, he's going to become key to this entire operation. I want him to hear from you how things worked out. Impressions of the setup…especially now that this has happened. He'll need to know if Pritsi can handle this."

83

"I suppose this means that you're aware of our history. Why am I not surprised?" Standish had the grace to look embarrassed. *Well, almost.* "At least while you're here, there'll be safety in numbers! Perhaps you had better do me the courtesy of explaining exactly how he fits into all this, given that I have no choice in the matter," observed Dyer a trifle tartly. And Standish did just that, leaving out this detail and that—not a man to show all his hand at one go.

Dinner, when it came, proved better than expected given the chaos in the restaurant. True to his word, the maître d' had found a place at the back of the room well away from the large family tables. *A table of discretion, suitable for confidences.* But with silent agreement, discussion was suspended for the duration of the meal. Monkfish cutlets with peppers followed by pears cooked in wine with yoghurt and a very decent vintage from the Veneto. Then eventually coffee, taken back in the cocktail bar. No sign of Casamassa when they sat down in button-back armchairs in a quiet and comfortable corner, the coffee tray already waiting for them. Standish ordered two cognacs and the bar waiter returned with them and poured the coffee. Small talk was beginning to wind down when Casamassa turned up.

"I am so sorry if I've kept you waiting. Hell of a day! Alarms went off. Absolute mayhem. Visitors rushing for the exits, thinking the place was about to burn to the ground. Then the *carabinieri* swarming all over. An American tourist accusing a group from Japan of getting too close and trying to touch one of the new pictures, preparing to fight the Second World War all over again!" Dyer smirked and Standish tried to look suitably sympathetic.

Casamassa laughed. "All said and done, I suppose a fairly normal day in the life of an art gallery!" Tension relaxed and Standish signalled the bar waiter. Casamassa asked for a grappa.

"I think," said Standish, "Lavinia wants to bring you up to date. It's been a hell of a day all around."

The briefing complete, a pessimistic silence settled on the three of them. Casamassa shook his head and waved the bar waiter over, as if to say, *words fail me, we might as well drink.* Then, decisions to be taken, arguments for and against, looked at first this way and then that way.

Standish summed up, "One way or another, Melzi's out of it. But we go ahead as planned. With maximum publicity for the exhibition and the photographing of the Collection. We want it as widely known as possible that this is a major piece of Italian and Sicilian heritage and it's staying where it belongs. But we're going to need your help, Matteo. Pressure on the authorities to allow these projects to go forward. We have to get the Minister of Culture behind this."

Casamassa nodded but said nothing.

"I agree with Milo," said Dyer. "It should be stressed that the Director had been committed to the project and believed he could bring the Galiano family along with him. We've come so far it would be criminal to risk the Collection falling into the wrong hands by pulling out now."

"Has anyone actually spoken to Galiano himself?" Casamassa asked.

"Melzi told us he had written but hadn't received a response. He assumed it would be positive."

"Let's hope so; the Ministry won't proceed on the basis of assumption alone. The gallery will need to secure a written agreement. If one's not forthcoming, I'm not quite sure who'll do that now. It's likely the Ministry will want to put in an acting Director. That's a point I can raise with the minister tomorrow."

"Galiano's got rather a lot on his plate at the moment but he mustn't slip through our fingers." Standish was grim-faced. "I gather the police are keen to bring him in—they're lining up a string of offences—but I'm told they're prepared to hold off till this is over. Always assuming his Caliphate masters haven't got to him first. At the moment, we need him in place. He can lead us to some very important people. After that, well...maybe it's better left to his paymasters. A brutal conclusion. Either way, I don't rate his chances!"

Casamassa got to his feet. "Milo, Lavinia, you must excuse me; it's late and tomorrow I'm expected in Rome. A conference. The Minister will be attending in the afternoon. So, an opportunity. Milo, if you think of anything else, I should know, call me. I'll be leaving home at seven."

After he had left, Lavinia Dyer breathed a sigh of relief—the evening had concluded without complication. As she stood, Standish also got to his feet.

"Let me see you back to your hotel."

"Milo thanks, but I'm literally just around the corner at the Americana."

"I insist, it's late. And I'm desperate for a breath of air."

"Milo, just now...you meant what you said about Galiano."

"In particular?"

"What could happen to him?"

"It's the reality of what he's chosen."

"But if he was set up. With the threat of blackmail. I mean, how many of us...?"

"Lavinia, I know. We could all find ourselves there. Perhaps, in a way, some of us have. We... Let's talk about it again. Believe me, Lavinia, I'm not as hard as you might think. I've learnt there is always a price we have to pay to keep faith with ourselves. Galiano chose not to pay that price. He may have to pay a higher one. If we can save him from the hands of the Caliphate, we'll try." *But I'm not making any promises.*

As they passed through reception, Dyer noticed a young Indian man leaning against the counter chatting to a young female member of staff. He half turned to glance at them, rather too nonchalantly. The young man from the airport. However, there was no sign of recognition between him and Standish. Total strangers!

At 7.45 a.m., Dyer was finishing her breakfast at a table near the window of the Americana Hotel, watching a barge laden with fruits and vegetables make its way slowly along the Rio di San Vio. There was much shouting and laughter between the bargees and a hotel porter waiting for the delivery. Already along the Fondamenta Bragadin, the daily routine was under way. A young woman with a child skipping by her side stopped to speak to a white-haired grandmother, exchanging the gossip of the moment. Two schoolchildren came by, one holding a book open and explaining something important to her friend. A young woman in jeans and T-shirt recognised one the bargees, called out to him and got a cheeky answer in response. The porter laughed and received a filthy look for his pains. This was the Venice she loved and missed in New York. Sunlight on the canal and on the blushing pink houses opposite. A life unchanged in centuries doing what it had always done, all too soon to be overrun once more by the invaders of the twenty-first century. Invading her life too, for her mobile shrilled out, demanding instant attention.

"Hello."

"Lavinia, it's Vassilio."

"Vassilio, what news?"

"The worst…Melzi died last night in hospital. Never regained consciousness after they admitted him. Medics seem to be playing it a bit close to their chests, about the actual cause that is. I spoke to a young doctor who hinted that they think he might have been *poisoned*. But vague. *Deliberately* vague. Doesn't make sense. They know more than they're prepared to own up to. I'll be back in Venice this afternoon. I'll see you at the hotel later."

Milo Standish paced the hotel bedroom. Mobile telephone in one hand, he brushed back hair from his eyes with the other. He knew the call couldn't be long in coming. He was also certain he knew what it would be. Melzi's collapse and the reason for it—*a pain in the leg*—sounded ominously like that of the billionaire's wife, Rosamund Cross, a report of which Glendower had passed to him in London. *Just thought it might be of passing interest!* Glendower was not one to waste time, aware that he had little time left to waste. For a while, he'd had had his sights on Cross, a name on his watchlist. And not the only one. *Too much money and hand in glove with all the right people, hence, gets around a lot and you'd never know where next.* Glendower, laconic as ever, was good at reading between the lines.

"Come back to bed; it's early!"

"It's nearly 8 o'clock."

"Early!"

He laughed. "Haven't you had enough of me?"

"You underestimate yourself."

"And you are a very cheeky boy!"

"I can't bear you walking about naked. It's very unsettling."

Placing his mobile on the bedside table, Standish climbed back into bed. "Yes, I can see that."

Further unsettlement was, however, to be deferred. The mobile rang out. Standish relinquished hold and turned around to pick it up.

"I didn't expect it to be you…No, it's fine. I was waiting for another call… Yes, he's OK. He's with me now. You sound anxious. What's happened?"

There was a long pause while Standish listened.

"I see. Look…don't do anything yet. I'll talk to Ravi and get back to you…I will." He put the mobile down.

"That was Julia. The office is in a panic. They think they've lost contact with Khalil. Have you heard from him?"

"Not since Bologna. But I haven't really been expecting to."

"He was due to report in when he got back to Paris. But nothing. Yet."

"Just keeping a low profile, hopefully."

"The hacked e-mail, you don't think…"

"I've asked myself that question. But no, I don't think Khalil would have the skills to do it. His sister, Amina, has. She's a genius with computers, works as a programmer. But not Khalil. Anyway, he'd have come back in triumph with it. Loves a drama."

"He went way beyond his remit on the train. That business with the knife was never part of it. A verbal threat, he was told. Sound menacing. Frighten the man. What would he have done if the conductor hadn't chanced along and disturbed him?"

"With Khalil, you never know."

"Don't tell me. We both had our doubts."

"He gets carried away. Always has."

"An operational risk, yes. You said so at the time. Well…where were we?"

"Here."

And the phone had the temerity to ring again. *Ah! Lavinia.*

* * *

Enna

Luca Galiano was counting the cost. A call from the Palermo gallery. The Director's secretary with the worst possible news. The Caliphate had not wasted time. There was no doubt in his mind. This was not natural causes. An obstacle was out of the way. And there was nothing he could do, no one he could turn to. His instinct was to run but he could think of nowhere to run to. His paymasters' reach extended into the deepest recesses known to humanity. If they knew he was running, even *thinking* of running, their wrath would be boundless and their retribution total. The headless body of Laura Pellestri lying on his bed haunted him, but the eyes gazing up at him from that box, sightless but somehow seeing into the depths of his soul, drove him to despair. At least her human remains were now reunited. The Cosenza police came and took the head away. A funeral could now take place. Her family was not only stricken with grief but confused. Too many questions and no answers. An orphan child to be cared for, who never would know, could never be allowed to know, the truth.

A frightened man is an unpredictable man. An unpredictable man is liable to panic. Galiano was frightened but not stupid. He paced up and down the library, trying to weigh his choices in the scales of what was possible. But they seemed hopelessly balanced against him. From time to time, a member of his staff looked in, offering refreshment of one kind or another but everything was refused with a polite shake of the head. Cigarette smoke hung heavy on the air. As one was finished, another was lit from its butt. The late spring day declined into evening. What broke the chain reaction was a call on his mobile from Lorenzo, complaining, "Why can I never get hold of you?"

"I had to go away."

"You've got your mobile, but I can never get through."

"Sometimes there's no signal. Anyway, business complications."

"Always reasons."

"Well, you know how it is. You're no different. I thought you were in the States."

"I would be but the people over there have postponed it. Problem with computer hacking. Some fifteen-year-old kid, tired of playing with himself and looking for something else to do. Next thing he knows, he's into Pentagon defence contracts. All hell breaks out and the White House's shitting itself!"

"So's he, I imagine."

"Serves him right, the silly prick. But Papa, I need to talk to you about something. I keep getting calls from this bloke who says he's a journalist but won't say who he's working for. Of course, he may be freelance."

"What's he want?"

"Rabbiting on about the family art collection. Says he hears it's coming on the market and can I give any details. Papa, what the hell's going on? Are you trying to sell?"

A long silence.

"Papa, are you there?"

"Lorenzo, I'd rather not discuss this over the phone."

"You *are* trying to sell."

"I didn't say that. It's…it's…more complicated than that."

"Well, what am I supposed to say?"

"What are you telling him?"

"That I know nothing about it. What else can I say? I *do* know nothing. Papa, you have to let me know what it's all about. You owe me that at least."

"You won't have heard; Claudio Melzi died. Two days ago, following a stroke."

"Who's he?"

"Director of the Palermo Gallery."

"So, how does that affect things? These calls have been going on for weeks."

"It complicates things. I can't explain at the moment."

"I've got a few days to spare. I'm flying down. I'll pick up a car at the airport."

"No, Lorenzo, hold on…Lorenzo? Lorenzo! Damnation!"

Lorenzo Galiano was puzzled. Over the years, his father's behaviour had often seemed strange to him. Secretive certainly, at times even verging on the bizarre. His sudden absences and as sudden reappearances never explained, never accounted for. But equally strange was the apparent lack of curiosity on the part of the rest of the family. His mother in particular fended off his questions about his father's whereabouts. "Papa's very busy; he has to travel much to take care of the family's interests. You'll realise when you're older how great the responsibilities are for a family like ours. One day, it will be your responsibility too." But papa never explained himself, never took his son and heir on one side to show him what was in store. In fact, the opposite. He once asked his English grandmother why papa never discussed anything with him, but she had little light to shed. "You must do well at your studies and learn to support yourself. The estate will no longer be able to maintain you and your wife and children. Those days are past. Every generation must learn to stand on its own two feet."

This did not accord well with the young Galiano's hopes for the future. But notwithstanding, he was no slouch. A promising career and an aristocratic name was the perfect combination for the restoration of the family's fortunes. Perhaps once again, the Galiano name could achieve some standing. But now, from the sound of it, his father might be planning to throw it all away for some short-term advantage. But what? And more to the point, why? Did his father have some grand scheme in mind? Lorenzo did not associate his father with grand schemes. He had to find out before some irredeemable folly was committed. He booked his flight, kissed his pouting girlfriend, *not enough, cara, what about this then?* Less than a minute later, he had her in bed. Lorenzo's quick solution to most personal problems. He, in a hurry; she, wanting to linger over the preliminaries. He knew how to deal with that.

* * *

Palermo

The telephone in the back office was ringing. Old Sergio shuffled through the garage. On the wrong side of seventy with a shock of unruly white hair and the distinct bulbous nose of a lifetime drinker, his old blue overalls still contrived to make him look like a worker. In fact, arthritis had put a stop to that years ago. Two of the firm's removal vans stood idle, one was being serviced, a third one hired out on a job somewhere. *These days*, grumbling to himself, *that passes for busy*. Pushing open the door, the phone went on ringing from under a heap of paperwork that cascaded to the floor as he rummaged around for it.

"*Pronto.*" A pause as Sergio tried to make out what the caller wanted. Couldn't quite sort out the accent.

"Yes...yes, hold on. You should speak to Nico. Hold on, hold on!" He slammed the phone down on the desk and bawled from the doorway, "Nico! Phone for you!"

"Who is it?" He slid out on a trolley from under one of the vans, spanner in his hand, face streaked with engine oil. "Who is it, papa?"

"Ach! Some foreigner."

Nico scrambled to his feet and made for the office, wiping his hands on a bit of rag.

"*Pronto...si signor*. This is Nico... Yes, we would be pleased to assist... We have three vans in the fleet. Two three and a half tons and one five-tonner... What will you be needing? We offer a discreet and efficient service." *So discreet in fact that our vans are unmarked. You can't be too careful for some customers.* "OK. To go where? *Si, va bene*, but we must know pick-up point and destination...and date when you need it. *Pronto*?... Are you still there?" The caller had rung off and Nico was left holding a dead receiver.

"Who was it? What did he want?" asked the old man.

"*Dio*! Some fool just wasting time. If he rings back, tell him to piss off. Well, perhaps better call me first and I'll tell him to piss off."

Nico picked up his spanner, got back on his trolley and disappeared from view under the van. Old Sergio, muttering to himself, slammed shut the office door hard, causing the building to shake. From under the van a curse from Nico.

"I'm going to Giorgio's for the coffee," the old man barked.

"Holy Mother be praised, it's not before time!"

"I can't do everything here."

"No papa, I don't know how I'd manage without you," Nico laughed.

The old chap stepped out of the small door in the garage's sliding doors, letting it swing to behind him, then shuffled off down the street to Giorgio's open-fronted coffee bar. Two workers in overalls lounged against the counter outside, familiar greetings and a good-natured pat on the back from one of them. Inside the tiny smoke-filled space, EU regulations politely ignored, more greetings hailed Sergio as he slapped his euros on the greasy counter.

"*Giorno*, Sergio, *come sta*?"

"*Va bene*."

"How's the transport business today?" from Giorgio.

"Business...what business?"

"Oh, come on, can't be that bad. You had a customer waiting outside when I got here this morning, not even 7 o'clock."

"Well, he wasn't there when I turned up. Wha'd he look like?"

"Office type, suit, foreign-looking. I mean, not one of us. Anyway, never seen him around here before."

"And probably never see him again."

"Tell Nico to let me know if he wants to go to the match tomorrow night."

"Oh, he'll go."

"About that guy this morning. Say to Nico. Seemed odd the way he was hanging around. At that time. Wondered if he was 'family'."

One of the others guffawed, "At that time of day! Too early for them!"

Sergio snorted, "Not much 'family' business here."

Giorgio shrugged, "You'd never know." He put the lids on two polystyrene cups and passed them over the counter. "Watch your step, they're hot."

"*Grazie*, Giorgio, *ciao*."

"Ciao, Sergio."

* * *

Mestre
3 June

The Consular Service of the British Foreign and Commonwealth Office maintained a local facility to serve the needs of visitors to Venice. No longer in the city itself, it was based in the Piazzale Donatori di Sangue close to the commercial centre of the town of Mestre on the mainland, managed by a small office staff and an Honorary Consul. A room was set aside for interviews and meetings, with DVD equipment set up and a screen at one end. On this particular afternoon, it hosted Milo Standish and his junior colleague from London, Ravi Sharma. Standish had arranged the venue with the agreement of the Consul for a meeting with a member of the Italian Government's foreign intelligence service, known as AISE *(Agenzia informazioni e sicurezza esterna)*. It was AISE which had requested the meeting in order to discuss 'certain matters of joint interest'. Cooperation between the two services was essential in an operation that spanned the concerns of both the UK and the Republic of Italy. Italy, anxious to get its hands on those behind the smuggling of migrants into Sicily; Britain, to nail her fellow countryman who was funding the entire disgusting business. Both countries were desperate to prevent the sales of priceless works of art to anonymous buyers, almost certainly poised in the Far East ready to scoop the sale of the century! The two British intelligence officers, very clear about the agenda were, however, in for one or two surprises.

A knock on the door and a young male clerk announced the visitor. Alessandro Menotti, for all the world, resembled a prize fighter. Of less than average height and stocky build with thick black hair and in his late fifties, his pugnacious face broke into a wreath of smiles as Standish came around the table to greet him.

"Milo! *Dio*, it's good to see you again. How do you manage never to age? Don't tell me, it must be love, you lucky man!"

"Sandro. You're incorrigible! And looking pretty good yourself. Meet my colleague from London, Ravi Sharma. Alessandro Menotti, doyen of Italian Intelligence."

"Mother of God, Milo, is the British Intelligence Service recruiting children now! Ravi, apologies, apologies, take no notice of this old fool. I am charmed to meet you. It's good to see some young blood in the service. And I hope you are a good influence on this reprobate."

Sharma laughed, "I couldn't possibly comment!"

Another knock and the clerk came back in carrying a tray of coffee and a plate of pastries, which Standish acknowledged with a smile.

Menotti opened his briefcase and took out several DVDs. "Perhaps while we have coffee, you'd like to look at these."

"Ravi, would you?" Standish passed them over.

"First of all," said Menotti, "we've got hold of the CCTV footage from the entrance foyer of the Palermo gallery. You'll notice from the date at the top of the screen that this relates to the week in which Director Melzi was taken ill and admitted to hospital with a suspected stroke. I think, Milo, you expressed a particular interest in this one. So, let's run it please, Ravi."

To begin with, a fairly normal week in the life of the gallery. Visitors coming in twos and threes at a time, a couple of parties of schoolchildren shepherded by harassed teachers, a group of American alumni and the inevitable Japanese clearly unhappy to be parted from their cameras for which the janitor handed tickets for reclaim at the end of the tour. Finally, the crucial day itself. Typical morning, then the gallery closed for lunch. Mid-afternoon and an outside camera picked up Melzi himself as he appeared at the top of the entrance steps, dapper and smiling, ready to welcome a group of about two dozen or so alighting from their tour bus. A grey-haired woman in her fifties, in charge of the party, shaking Melzi by the hand and then beckoning the others to follow her up the steps and into the entrance atrium.

Sharma craned forward in his chair, scrutinising as group members briefly came into view of the two static cameras placed halfway down the atrium, one pointing towards the entrance doors, the other to the interior of the building. The group milled around waiting to be organised, some of them looking at a stand at one side with visitor information laid out. Sharma's attention was caught by a youth in jeans and T-shirt hanging back, slightly distancing himself from the rest.

"There! Milo, look, at the rear of the group on the left, back towards the camera, wait for it, he's turning, there!" he yelled. "My God, it's Khalil! Unmistakable, clear as day."

"Khalil. Yes, no doubt at all."

Led by Melzi and ushered forward by their tour guide, the group passed out of camera range into the gallery itself. The disc came to an end.

"I'm afraid that's it," said Menotti, "only a couple more cameras in the gallery and both apparently out of order! Bloody typical! So, where do we go from here? All this tells us is that that guy was there on the day Melzi collapsed and subsequently died. What's his history?"

"We recruited him last year for a special operation. To be more accurate, I recruited him," said Standish.

"At my suggestion and with my help," added Sharma.

"Before we watch the other disc, perhaps you'd better fill me in a little," said Menotti gently.

"Let me, Milo, I've known him a long time." Sharma leaned forward against the table; hands clasped in front of him. "Khalil Khourasan. Twenty years of age. At school with my younger brother, Sanjeev, and a very good friend. Like the Khourasans, we were Muslims too. So, the two families visited and the men attended the same mosque. Khalil was a bright boy. Very clever at school, got a place at the London School of Economics to read politics. Two years and dropped out, end of summer term last year, said he wanted a gap year and would go back to studying later. We were looking for someone for a job. Short-term, time limited, just a bit of surveillance. I said to Milo, I would vouch for him, maybe we could use him, give him something to do. Something that would stretch him a bit, calm him down. That was the main thing against him but I thought we could handle it. He was inclined to get over-excited about things…"

"What sort of things?" asked Menotti.

"Oh, you know issues, rights and wrongs, state of society. Khalil would sort it out, put it right. Solve the problems of the world. Well, this operation came up…"

"My brainchild," said Standish. "You're aware of some of the background, Sandro?" Menotti nodded.

"Fr. Antonio Marcetti, Dominican friar and to say the least, general disturber of the peace…"

"Pain in the arse," said Menotti, "been giving us headaches for years."

"Has been threatening to tell the world that the British establishment, maybe even the government itself, was bankrolling Libyan people traffickers. My orders from on high. Shut him up! And find out who's throwing money around. So, one very small part of the plan was to confront Marcetti. Khalil seemed the obvious choice. He'd been shadowing Marcetti on his visits to London, so he knew what he looked like. The job was to threaten him, but verbal threats only, NO rough stuff. Just enough to scare him witless, if anything could. Anyway, worth a try."

"And it worked, Milo," Menotti pointed out. "He's shut the hell up…so far."

"Nearly didn't work. Khalil went way over the top. Fortunately got stopped before committing actual murder. And then went quiet and disappeared. Until now."

"Let's take a look at the other disc," said Menotti. Sharma fed the disc into the machine.

"Not so good, this one. CCTV bottom left of the Spanish Steps in Rome and directed diagonally up to the church. This one covers the day we're interested in, 6 a.m. to midday."

One of the most popular tourist spots in Rome, it was decked in its traditional springtime flowers. Crowded with tourists most of the time. So much coming and going. Impossible to pick out a single individual of interest. They ran through it, then again and again. Each time, they studied with care the disturbance over on the left-hand side as a woman appeared to trip and fall. A passer-by, a middle-aged woman, reached out to try and grab her. Too late. She was on the ground, twitching. The crowd around her fanned out. Nothing more. Then Sharma peered closely up at the screen.

"What is it, Ravi?"

"Nothing, really. Just looking at someone disappearing behind one of those damn plants." He laughed. "Perfect cover. Look, Milo. I'll run it again…

There, young, male, could be Arab, carrying a plastic bag. Now almost at the top of the Steps. I wouldn't put my money on it, but…maybe I just might!"

"Maybe."

"And just maybe," said Menotti, "I can help. There's one more to look at for that day. At the top of the Steps, another CCTV, filming people entering the church of Trinita dei Monti. This we got from the church authorities, with a bit of a struggle! Perhaps a long shot. It operates from 9 a.m. Please, Ravi."

The screen lit up again. Several worshippers leaving the church after an early mass, the camera catching them from behind. Then tourists in ones and twos. Few and far between at that time of morning.

"Ravi," said Menotti, "I think we can speed it up. We'll pick it up at about 10 a.m."

More visitors to the church now. 10 o'clock, 10.15, 10.30. A family group of four, parents and two young children. Then from behind them, someone in a hurry, pushing their way past, seemingly not aware of the CCTV. The full-length figure of Khalil Khourasan filled the screen. In a second, he had disappeared inside the church. For a few minutes, the three intelligence officers stared at the screen in silence. Then Sharma leaned forward and switched it off.

"Your boy's been getting around," said Menotti.

Later, Standish escorted his Italian colleague down to where a taxi was waiting outside the consulate to take him to his train. He was returning to Rome that evening. Talk had been muted after the revelations of the DVD. One or two areas of mutual interest were identified where interagency cooperation would be essential. Menotti, supportive and sympathetic, offered his help in trying to track Khourasan down. Another priority for the British service. There was little more to say. They shook hands on the pavement and Standish opened the rear passenger door.

"Milo…that's a good young man you have there."

"Yes, I think so."

"I, umm…it's nothing really. None of my business. Just wanted to say, thank God for some things in life. Look out for each other. *Ciao*."

"*Ciao*, Sandro."

The taxi pulled away from the kerb and Standish watched it until it was lost in the traffic.

Chapter Five

Venice

Ravi Sharma wandered along the Zattere, hands thrust deep in trouser pockets, head slightly down, and a troubled expression on his face. A breeze from off the Giudecca canal blew his long dark hair across a face fringed with a day's growth of beard.

He seemed oblivious to passers-by: An assortment of Venetians hurrying home from work, day tourists gathering by the *vaporetto* stop heading for Piazzale Roma and the coaches waiting to collect them. Those who were staying over inspected menus deciding which restaurant would be lucky enough to receive the benefit of their custom that evening! He had refused all offers of company from Standish. Nothing Standish had been able to say had shaken him from the belief that the Khalil Khourasan disaster, *there really is no other name for it, Milo*, had largely been of his making.

"I'm the senior officer by a long chalk, Ravi. It was down to me and I decided we should use him."

"But only because I suggested it. I practically grew up with him, for God's sake. I knew what he could be like. He's five years younger, yes, but we kids did everything together. He was the only boy in a family of girls, so he spent half his life with my brothers and me. For a time, I even thought he quite fancied me! But that was only because I was like an elder brother."

"All we actually know at this moment is that Khalil was present at two locations when an individual collapsed and subsequently died. Yes, Ravi, don't look like that…I know. There are coincidences and coincidences."

"And this is one too far!"

"OK. Let's go over the background."

"Milo, please, give me half an hour to go and clear my head. Half an hour, I promise, then we'll talk."

"Would you like me to come too?"

"No. I'm fine."

"All right. I've got some calls to make. One thing we have to think about is whether we want to remain staying in the hotel while we plan the next phase."

"What have you got in mind?"

"We could take one of their small service apartments. Give ourselves some breathing space. And easier for meetings."

"Sounds good to me…there…I'll be back soon."

At the bridge over the Rio di San Vio, Sharma paused, leaned against the stone parapet and stared out across the canal to the Church of the Redentore on the island of Giudecca, its façade now lit. Further over to his left, the Isola di San Giorgio with its little community of monks was similarly illuminated. Venice was gradually settling into its evening routine, bringing with it a sense of calm, almost saying, *don't worry, some things never change!* Lost in thought, he didn't notice a couple of visitors who had come out of the Americana Hotel and were making their way down to the Zattere. Lavinia Dyer and Vassilio Pritsi were out for evening drinks and dinner. Passing behind him on the bridge, Lavinia checked for a second, noticing the same young man who kept turning up at the edges of her life. Perhaps the time had come to ask Milo Standish a question or two. Still, she supposed it was none of her business. By the end of the week, she should be back in New York, a prospect of mixed feelings.

When Sharma walked into their room, Standish was on his mobile.

"I'm glad you agree, Chief. As long as key members of the operation are here, it makes sense. We want to avoid any sign in Palermo that anything unusual is happening. A very low profile...Pritsi's found a photographer, Erik Seth, a Swede living in the States, who has quite a reputation in the art world. We'll bring him here first for briefing as soon as possible, and with any luck, by the end of next week if his schedule permits...if all goes well. Menotti's leaning hard on the Ministry to get the Gallery's security sorted out. It's in a bit of a mess; he says the non-functioning cameras had been disconnected the night before the attack on Melzi! Yes...careful planning...all right, I'll be in touch. Look after yourself." He rang off.

"The boss?"

"Yep!"

"What's he saying about Khalil?"

"Very little, but then I've told him very little. He's got enough to contend with just now."

"I suppose there'll have to be an internal inquiry."

"Don't let's jump the gun. We'll conduct our own inquiry first. But Ravi, we're doing nothing till we've had dinner."

"I'm not very hungry tonight."

"OK, room service, we'll get them to send something up. I could kill for a drink!"

Later, they sat together over a bottle of wine, a tray of sandwiches between them more or less demolished, Sharma discovering he was hungrier than he thought. He was flicking through the hotel's brochure of service flats.

"I've checked with reception, there's one available right away if we want it," said Standish. "We could move in tomorrow morning after breakfast. They're next door, part of the hotel so we can use all its facilities."

"I think we should go for it. How long do we need it for?"

"At least a fortnight. It's difficult to know the exact timing. All depends on the photographer. I'll call down to tell them." He got up and went over to the internal telephone.

"That's done. Now, we have to talk about Khalil."

Sharma sighed. "OK, I'll start. I've been thinking it over. Last summer…the beginning of June, he finished his second year. Everything seemed normal. He announced he was going off to Paris to visit his uncle and aunt. Salim Khourasan is his father's elder brother. The Khourasan boys had mixed parentage—Syrian father, Italian mother, she was a Catholic, Khalil's grandmother, that is. Planned to stay a couple of weeks and wanted Sanjeev to go with him. But Sanj had a holiday job helping Dad and needed the money. In the event, Khalil was away practically the whole summer vacation. He came back to London, third week in September, I suppose. That's when we noticed a difference. Sanj pointed it out first. Said Khalil seemed to have changed but couldn't explain exactly in what way. Anyway, we boys all went out one night and that's when Khalil told us he wasn't going back to LSE. Needed a gap year! Had no plans, or so he claimed. Then he began to go on about Syria, how awful things were and it came out that his uncle, Salim, had taken him over there a few weeks before, to Damascus I think, supposedly to visit other family members, he didn't say who. They were there only a few days and it wasn't clear who they saw or what they did. Whatever happened, it made an impression on Khalil. None of us could persuade him to go back to university and he just seemed to be hanging around at a loose end. His parents, you can imagine, were crazy with worry. Kept asking him his plans and getting nowhere. That's when I stepped in and you know the rest."

Standish was thoughtful, twirling the stem of his wine glass around between his fingers.

"First time I met him was in that coffee bar in the bookshop. You brought him in, made it look accidental. Chatted about everything and nothing. I remember him saying he wished he'd had a year off after school. Seen a bit more of life before university. Told us about going to Syria, quite liked the idea of having been in a 'war zone'. Typical youthful exuberance! And nothing wrong with that. I doubt he'd been exposed to any real danger, though what he saw must have been quite a shock for a British boy. Suddenly faced with a civil war and family all over the place. What came out later during his training was a genuine thirst for action. Didn't balk at the idea of taking risks. Bravado, yes, but looking back, more than that, a need to prove himself. Did we miss something there? Obviously, we didn't tell him the whole story, only as much as we thought he should know. Marcetti wasn't even a name to him. Just someone we wanted to keep tabs on while he was in the country. Did we present Marcetti as a threat to Muslims? If there was a weakness, that was it. Of course, he wasn't; he was a threat to Britain or at least to the British government. We needed Marcetti to be scared, to believe his life was in danger, *so Father, keep your mouth shut.* I was to engineer a meeting with him, which I did here in Venice a couple of days later. I waited for him to bring up the train incident, but he didn't. When Lavinia Dyer interviewed him the day after, he was laughing it off or putting on a show of pretending to."

"Was there another way we could have done it?"

"It's easy with hindsight to think like that. At the time, we go for a practical solution without too many obvious drawbacks." He smiled ruefully. "In the field, we operate under a variety of constraints and often don't have much room for manoeuvre. We had a newly elected government, convinced it was poised on the brink of scandal. *Still* convinced. And it's probably right. The FO's in a permanent state of panic. At any moment, it might all burst open. It's our job to respond to that sort of pressure and, in a measured way, I believe we did."

"I keep asking myself what more I could have done, what more could I have told you?"

"Ravi, you've nothing to blame yourself for. We covered every outcome we could think of: We got him to sign the Official Secrets Act, we warned him he was likely to be bound by it for the foreseeable future. I hinted that if this went well, we might use him again, but I tried to impress upon him he should finish his degree. *In any case, no promises.* We have to move on. We'll keep Khalil in our sights, Sandro will too. We haven't heard the last of him. But he mustn't become a distraction. He's part of the picture but he's not the whole picture. Sooner or later, we'll pick him up. By the way, one question still needs answering. It's been bothering me. If the internal cameras in the gallery were disabled, why didn't they fix the entrance ones too? Lack of opportunity? Suggests to me it was done during opening hours. If so, by whom? Interesting, and maybe a break for us."

"How do you mean?"

"Do the Soldiers of the Caliphate have someone on the inside? Tomorrow afternoon, I'm calling Lavinia Dyer and Pritsi to a briefing. Bring them up to speed. See what they think about it. Lavinia Dyer has her wits about her. She's a useful asset if I can persuade her to stay on. We'll meet in the apartment. You look exhausted. Why don't you turn in? Tomorrow's going to be another busy day."

"I think I might."

"I shan't be far behind you, need to make a couple more calls first."

"I'll still be awake." But he wasn't. When Standish got into bed, Ravi Sharma was curled up and in a deep sleep.

* * *

Enna
5 June

Lorenzo Galiano drove into the courtyard of the family villa in Enna; his father's car was parked outside. He sprang out, ran up the steps and pushed open the inner glass doors from the vestibule into the main hall. Making straight for the library, he found the door locked, hammered on it and called out. No response. So, go to the centre of life. He made for the kitchen situated at the back of the house, reached by a long corridor that led past the dining room, serving pantry and the villa's innumerable domestic offices. Sounds of activity came from the cavernous room at the end. Busy at one of the sinks, Anna, cook and long-standing member of the household, turned to see who'd come in.

"*Dio Mio*! Lorenzo! It's you, what's happened?"

"Nothing's happened. I live here. Or used to. It's been so long you've probably forgotten me. *Come sta*?"

"Forgotten you, could I forget the pain in my neck?" she grumbled, then looked him over and laughed, drying her hands. Of all the staff, Anna had been his favourite as a boy, always to be relied upon to slip him and Catarina a treat when they escaped their mother's notice and crept like a couple of conspirators into her domain. He hugged her, then held her at arm's length.

"Let's look at you, you old moan. Well, not too many signs of wear and tear, all things considered."

"Ah, *piccolo*, if only that were true. I should've given up working years ago! Seventy-three at last count…yes, really. And you. Let's see. A bit pinched and too thin."

"Too much work, a lot of drinking and way, way too much sex!"

"You're a dreadful boy. But lucky, eh?" A knowing smile. "Are you going to marry the girl?"

"Which one?"

"Lorenzo!"

"Come on, *cara,* you know there's never been anyone but you."

"Sit down; you're like a tiresome child! When did you last eat?"

"Some garbage on the plane."

"There's wine over there, pour yourself a glass…and a small one for me. I've got some fresh pasta. And this morning, I made pastries." She fetched a plate from the dresser and doled out a generous helping from a saucepan on the stove.

"Where's papa?"

"Where indeed."

"What does that mean?"

"Eat first, it'll get cold."

"Come and sit with me. I want to talk to you."

Anna settled her large plump frame at the table opposite him with a sigh of relief. Good these days to take the weight off one's feet given the chance. She studied him for a moment, wondering where the conversation was going to begin; even more, where it might end.

"What's been going on, Anna? I couldn't get any sense out of my father on the telephone. That's why I landed down here. Is he in trouble?"

"You know your father. Left hand and right hand complete strangers. Do you think he tells us anything?"

"He never tells anyone anything."

"No, he never does, never has. Even your poor mother lived by guesswork. Him disappearing all the time, her worried sick at first, then learning to let it wash over her. She had her hands full, what with the house and you two kids. Then later, her illness. We all watched her fading away. Though to be fair, he *was* distraught. For a time at least, he stayed at home, then as it went on and on, he began to slip off again."

"Where did he go to?"

"Why, that place of his, up in Calabria."

"What place?"

"You know, his bolt hole."

"I don't know of any 'bolt hole'. Who knew about this?"

"Well, *piccolo*, I suppose everyone here knew and nobody knew. Who could say anything? That's what it's like on this damned island. *Omertá!*"

"But how did people find out?"

"Oh, Lorenzo *mio*, how does anyone find out these things in Sicily? Someone talks, whispers go around, an old wife tells her man, he tells his friends, nudges in the bar, finger against the nose, perhaps the clan gets to hear. The men are worse than the women. Soon everyone knows, but mouths are as tight shut as…you get the idea!"

"What's this place called?"

"Don't ask me. Word is it belonged to your great-grandmother's family; they came from Naples. Those were the days when Naples and Sicily were all one kingdom. Bit of history I do know. My mother used to say…"

"It's unbelievable. I remember he was always going away. Family and estate business, all we were told. I wonder when he was last there."

"Now there I may be able to help."

"Go on…"

"Something happened…during this year's Holy Week ceremonies, the Good Friday procession to be exact. It was his place, be yours one day, to lead his Confraternity…"

"That dismal bunch of farts."

"Be quiet and listen. They'd entered the Duomo and taken their hoods off. Then, old Massimo Serra, according to his misery of a wife, said your father told him to take over, he had to leave. They all thought he was ill. Seppi told us he got back here, white as a sheet, asked him to bring the car around, left ten minutes later. Didn't appear again for a couple of weeks."

"So how do you know where he'd been?"

"Stands to reason. The bolt hole. It's where he always went when there was trouble. And there's more…"

It was clear to Lorenzo that staff at the villa had for years known a good deal more about his father's comings and goings than the baron ever realised.

Anna's story was far from finished. Rumours had been rife in the city, *who knows where they started*. It was the baron's 'bolt hole,' the scene, that is, of an unfortunate accident sometime after Easter. A drugged-up girl fell from a balcony onto the terrace and broke her neck. *Serve her right for being so stupid*. Only one problem, according to the gossips, someone's mother-in-law's brother had a girlfriend whose father knew someone who had worked on the estate years ago and could swear to it that there were no balconies on that side of the villa! "Could've been a window, I suppose, but you don't generally fall out of windows unless you're pushed." Though what experience Anna had had of defenestration wasn't clear. Still, no one was quite sure if it was the same place. Calabria, what can you expect up there, drugs and all kinds of crime. You know what they say, still run by the 'Ndrangheta'! No, Anna couldn't remember the name now. Others said, if it was in the papers it had to be true, *people's faith in the press was touching, no?* One thing was certain: Lorenzo's father had been away from Enna at the time, so putting two and two together didn't take a genius. Of course, one never knows, the whole thing could just be a story. But when the baron came back to Enna, he was badly shaken, that much you could have seen for yourself. And then there was the business of the crate of wine from Count Lipari, except it wasn't.

"Wasn't what?" asked Lorenzo.

"Wasn't from the Count and probably wasn't wine."

"Well, what was it, for God's sake?"

"You'll have to ask Seppi. Your father locked it in the wine cellar, kept the key and last week police from Cosenza came and took it away. Our Lady Mother be thanked. Seppi said it stank to high heaven!"

"Jesu-Maria, this bloody place has gone mad!"

"Now, *piccolo…*"

Somewhere in the villa, the distant sound of a door slamming.

"I'm going to find my father."

Father and son met in the entrance hall. Greetings were cursory and on the chilly side of cool.

"So you're here."

"As you see, and I'm not leaving until we've talked. I don't care how long it takes."

"Please yourself…We'd better go into the library."

He unlocked the door, let them in and then locked the door again behind them.

"What's all that about?"

"I don't want us to be disturbed. You have to understand one thing, Lorenzo, what I have to say to you could be very dangerous for you, for me, for all of us in this house."

"Papa, what the hell have you got into?"

"For once in your life, shut up and listen."

Lorenzo shook his head, walked over to the long sofa in the window and threw himself down at one end. Luca leant for a moment against the massive stone chimney piece and studied the portrait of his father hanging above it.

"Last year, the estate had serious financial worries. It began to look as if selling property might be the only solution. Your grandfather used to say that once you start down that road, there's no turning back. I met some businessmen in Malta. One of them came up with an investment plan which offered a possible way out of our difficulties. I signed up and found out, too late, that they were crooked. Tried to manoeuvre myself out of it, found my life threatened. Now they want some of the pictures from the art collection. That's it. That's the situation today."

"Are they Italian, Sicilian?"

"Arab."

"*Oddio!*"

"Before you say it, police is not an option. They made sure of that."

"And what about the rest of the story?"

"There is no 'rest'. That's the whole story."

"Come on, papa, there seem to be rumours flying around all over the place. I didn't come down from Milan for half a tale."

"Then go back to fucking Milan if you don't like it!" Galiano shouted.

A long hostile silence. Lorenzo leant back staring at the ceiling; Luca bleak, defeated, seemed to have shrunk into himself, his eyes fixed on some indeterminate spot on the carpet. The only sound was the ticking of the clock on the desk at the other end of the room. Eventually…

"There's no point in going on like this. Either you trust me or you don't. I thought I might be able to help in some way."

"Too late for that. Not your fault. Go back to your life, Lorenzo."

Luca walked to the door, unlocked it and left.

* * *

Palermo

A hired car pulled into the public parking space outside the gallery. A man and a woman got out and stood for a moment looking at the classical façade with its handsome Doric columns. At its centre was a pediment adorned with a panoply of gods and goddesses, blackened with the grime of passing centuries but apparently unfazed by the less than pristine appearance they presented to visitors. Not that most visitors spent much time pondering the divine cavortings. Dotoressa Francesca Paso was accompanied by the distinguished Renaissance art historian, Professor Matteo Casamassa of Venice. The Italian Ministry of Culture had deemed it prudent that the dotoressa, recently appointed to the acting directorship of the Palermo Gallery of Fine Art, would be thus escorted on her first visit to Sicily. It was not, however, simply a question of professional courtesy. Behind the Ministry's politesse lay a carefully planned strategy, devised and then refined by Sandro Menotti and Milo Standish and sold to the Ministry in the time-honoured manner of pulling strings. These strings had been pulled from a very lofty height indeed.

A succession of meetings had taken place over a period of ten days in the Venetian apartment to which Standish and Sharma had moved. Planning the next phase of the operation, to be known as Operation Persephone, required the input of certain key individuals. To begin with, it became clear that for the time

102

being, they had lost the assistance of Lavinia Dyer. To her obvious annoyance, pressures back in the New York Times office required her immediate presence. Though in her considered view, quietly conveyed to Standish, Ferdy Keymer needed to be convinced that a 'story' of manifestly international importance was about to be played out on the island of Sicily. There was concern among the British and Italian intelligence officers that Vassilio Pritsi would be less convincing on his own without Dyer there to hold his hand. Ravi Sharma, with the suspicion of a grin and no serious intent, offered to do that on her behalf, to which Standish—to Sharma's surprise and slight irritation—readily agreed. Sharma would proceed forthwith to Palermo to 'prepare the ground', find appropriate accommodation for the team and assess how cooperative the gallery staff would prove to be. Pritsi and the photographer Seth would follow in two days. Standish and Menotti would fly down at the beginning of the following week and, if all went well, Dyer would join them as soon as she could extricate herself from Keymer's dithering. It was agreed, after some dissent from Casamassa, who was brought in again at the later stages of planning, that Erik Seth would only be told at this point that the Galiano paintings, all of which he was being asked to photograph, might become the focus of criminal interest. Finally, and rather more to Casamassa's taste, it was confided that the Italian Minister of Culture had specifically requested that he be asked to accompany the new Acting Director to her appointment and, by the way, would he graciously consider doing something for television on the subject of this unique example of Italian heritage. The professor was prevailed upon without further demur. It was agreed, however, that he would not at this stage make any announcement as to which paintings had been selected for summer exhibition at his Venetian gallery. There was no point in giving too much away so early in the planned operation. These were temporary arrangements in an emergency situation, not at all the manner in which art gallery business was usually carried out.

The new Acting Director was more than she seemed on initial appraisal. Cool, blonde, efficient-looking, mid-thirties, Francesca Paso had joined the Intelligence Service as its specialist in Fine Art investigations. Her ability to assess situations and act without hesitation frequently disconcerted her colleagues, though the hostility that this sometimes engendered left her remarkably unmoved. Matteo Casamassa, if not actually disconcerted by a powerful younger woman, was cautious to a degree in her company, even solicitous in an understated way. The Lothario in him for once was notable by its absence! That hinted at the other reason for not putting a foot wrong. Professor Casamassa's television interview and presentation to RAI on the Galiano Collection would be introduced by the Acting Director, with a contribution from the Collection's current legal owner, Baron Luca Galiano, if he could be persuaded. The overall plan to raise the profile of the pictures and ensure maximum public interest was beginning to fall into place; at any rate, the foundations were being laid. Italians took their art very seriously, Sicilians even jealously. *There was no way the Caravaggio debacle was going to happen again in a hurry!*

The female receptionist looked up and smiled as the two visitors approached her desk, ready to sell them a couple of tickets until Casamassa politely indicated their wish to speak to the director's personal assistant—they had an appointment. A flicker of surprise and a request for names, and then Signora Bertelli was informed that she had two visitors. Sara Bertelli, for once, wasted no time in coming down to reception; you didn't keep the new acting director waiting. At first sight, a comfortable-looking woman in her fifties, round-faced with dark greying hair and a contrived smile, today the normally trim tailored suit seemed to hang a little languidly, the usually bright observant eyes were lacklustre and the cool personal assistant manner so carefully cultivated over the years, hesitant—one might almost say caught off balance. It occurred to the keen-eyed receptionist, who took rather an interest in these matters, that the reason for these changes might somehow be explained by the presence of a previous visitor to the gallery who even now materialised at the top of the staircase leading to the director's office. His arrival an hour or so earlier had clearly been neither foreseen nor welcomed by Signora Bertelli. But introductions complete, she swept her two guests up the staircase, smiled a little nervously towards her earlier visitor and proceeded along the corridor to the director's office.

"A busy time for you, signora," remarked Paso, "and in such distressing circumstances. Our sincere condolences on the sad loss of Dr Melzi. It must have been a great shock for you."

"I had worked for him for over ten years. He was a great man and a good friend. And a wonderful director of this gallery."

"I would be very happy to chat to Professor Casamassa for a few minutes if you would like to take leave of your visitor."

"Oh…no…thank you. Mr Husseini wants to look around the gallery on his own. He is a journalist, an arts critic for an Egyptian newspaper. I understand this is his first visit to our gallery and I was explaining a little of our history and how the collections were acquired and built up."

"Indeed."

"Maybe, Dr Paso, you would like to make his acquaintance?"

"Well, I'm sure our paths will cross when Professor Casamassa and I take our own tour of the building. Incidentally, Signora, have the security people from the Ministry been in touch with you yet?"

"They started work yesterday. Seem to be all over the building."

"I'll take the opportunity to meet them while we're here today. Incidentally, I shall officially take up my duties tomorrow morning."

"I'll make sure all the staff is made aware of that."

A knock on the door and one of the male porters came in carrying a tray with coffee cups and a white porcelain pot of steaming coffee.

"Excellent," said Paso, "most kind of you. Matteo…?"

They took their seats in the white leather and chrome armchairs and the porter handed around the coffee. Bertelli sat on the edge of her chair, glancing anxiously towards the door from time to time.

"Signora, I don't wish to take up your time this afternoon. You have much to do. Please feel free to leave us to our own devices. You and I will catch up with one another in the morning."

"Thank you. Dr Paso." A look of profound relief. "Let me know if there is anything you require. My office is the room on the right of the waiting area and my extension is marked on the telephone keypad on Dr Mel...on your desk."

As the door closed behind her, Casamassa started to say something but Paso signalled silence. She smiled and raised her eyebrows. Getting up, she wandered over to a window overlooking the rear courtyard of the building. An electrician's van was parked there, its rear doors open. After a moment or two, she turned round.

"What do you make of all that, Matteo?"

"Anxious. Perhaps to be expected."

"Under a lot of stress. More to it than just grief, though that's only natural. The sudden death was obviously a shock."

"I wonder about their relationship."

"Hm. We shall see. Something else too, I think. Let's have a look around. I wouldn't mind bumping into that journalist chap again. We might make some discreet enquiries in that direction. I'll call Sandro Menotti later."

As the pair emerged from Melzi's office, Paso noticed the door to Bertelli's room was slightly ajar. Instinct told her that their departure was being listened for. She ignored it. They made their way downstairs, collected a guidebook from reception and entered the first great gallery. A handful of visitors were being shepherded safely around a ladder where an electrician was engaged in fitting wiring for the new CCTV system. A young worker in blue overalls was watching out for his colleague. Casamassa glanced at him as they passed by; almost a sign of recognition but Ravi Sharma's face remained impassive. On to the next room where a sign over the entrance announced that the pictures were all part of the Galiano Collection. There was only one visitor at that moment, the journalist, Husseini, studying a group of three French Impressionist paintings. He looked around and Paso nodded.

"I understand from Signora Bertelli you are a first-time visitor to the gallery," she said casually as she approached him.

"I am," he replied briefly.

"I'm Francesca Paso, the new acting director. A newcomer like yourself. I hope you are enjoying the collections. As yet, I am not myself familiar with them. But a journey of discovery is itself a pleasure, is it not? Is there any school of artists you are particularly interested in?"

For a moment, he seemed nonplussed by her question and looked around the room as if trying to make up his mind.

"Not particularly."

"As our guidebooks tell us…" noticing he was clutching one, "the paintings in this room, and the next two, form the famous Galiano Collection. They were lent to this gallery by the present Baron Galiano's father on a permanent loan basis so that the whole community could have access to them. The people of Sicily are very proud of this part of their national heritage."

"No doubt."

"Some of them will shortly be photographed for a prestigious American arts publication. Coming out, I think, early next year. Your readers would perhaps like to know about it."

"Yes, probably."

"Well, Mr…?"

"Husseini, Mohammed Husseini."

"Enjoy the rest of your tour, Mr Husseini. I'm sure we shall meet again."

"Thank you."

An apparently incurious journalist, a characteristic Paso found a contradiction in terms, especially in a journalist visiting an art gallery who claimed to be an art critic.

Chapter Six

Enna
6 June

From where he had parked his car just outside the city limits, Galiano had a panoramic view of the surrounding countryside. It was not a good day for sightseeing. A heavy grey sky was reflected in the cold grey waters of Lake Pergusa, the wind whipping the surface into tiny flecks of white. One or two brave souls in sailing boats were struggling with the contrary gusts that hurled themselves down from the hills in unpredictable directions. Usually, the parking lot would be overflowing with tourist cars and caravans. But not today; the sudden rain showers had discouraged all but a handful. A family of four trudged by, misery on the faces of the grown-ups, disappointment on the children. *We went to Enna for the day, but it rained.* His confrontation with Lorenzo had been a rare but bruising event. Rare because they had successfully avoided each other in recent years. Lorenzo, now an infrequent visitor, had shown little enthusiasm for either family or estate since settling in Milan, as much his fault as his son's. As a young man growing up, he'd never talked to him about his inheritance, explained how things worked or discussed the practical aspects of running a landed property in the twenty-first century. 'Too late now' he'd told him; it had always been too late. It had been Martina who'd taken the children to the gallery in Palermo to view their grandfather's donation. He couldn't remember whether he had even asked them what they thought about it on their return. Last night, they'd eaten together in silence, like a monk's refectory. Seppi had served them, but the poor old man had been uncomfortable and awkward. Luca had picked at his food and Lorenzo had flipped through the pages of a paperback. He'd left the table before Lorenzo had even finished. Family life!

'Rumours flying around all over the place.' Yes, of course, why hadn't he seen that coming? This was Sicily after all. *Omertá* didn't stop the whispers, the knowing looks, raised eyebrows, the hand over the mouth. How far had the innuendos gone? Who knew what had really happened at San Vibio? Who saw what was happening under their very noses? His staff, for a start. Then there was the farm at Altrabia. A terrorist's hideaway. Had that bullying bastard, Al-Azhar, got his gang of murderers out of it by now? They could hardly have escaped notice. His mobile shrilled, bringing him back with a start—the villa landline.

"Yes?"

"Papa."

"Lorenzo, you still here?"

A pause while Lorenzo ignored the question.

"Papa, the director of the gallery called, twice. She's…something Paso…I think that's it. Seems anxious for you to see the new security system being installed. Wants to reassure you. The Collection's going to be photographed, but I expect you knew that already. Someone's writing a book about it. Anyway, she said she'd be there all day."

"I think I'll drive over now."

"Papa, please can I come with you…please?"

Another pause. Lorenzo held his breath; he could almost hear his father thinking.

"I'll pick you up in ten minutes."

So, a small breakthrough. *Don't put too much on it*, Lorenzo told himself. Just a beginning, maybe not even quite that, more the beginning of a beginning.

* * *

Palermo
Sicily, 11 June

It was generally agreed by the British and Italian intelligence communities—Standish and Sharma for the former and Menotti and Paso for the home team—that the initial phase of Operation Persephone had been launched successfully. The first key element was the installation of a new security system in the Palermo Gallery. This had been accomplished in record time. It was a source of wonder to the inquisitive receptionist that workmen from the mainland—the firm was based in Naples—could achieve so much in so short a time. Her fellow Sicilians would have carried out the job with altogether less urgency but perhaps more sociability. The Neapolitans got on with it, assiduously avoiding all local contact. Erik Seth had arrived, accompanied not only by Pritsi but by an alarming amount of photographic equipment, to be housed in a storeroom adjacent to the Collection, most of which Sharma found himself lugging there on his own.

A producer from RAI met with Casamassa and Paso in the latter's office, together with a young arts programme presenter; the latter so impressed with the elegance of the surroundings that she wanted to use it to conduct the interview part of the package. They would then be filmed descending the grand staircase and entering the first room that housed the Collection. At this point, the Acting Director would make a short introduction to the pictures explaining how they came to be on permanent loan. This would all take place the evening before Seth was to begin his photographic session. The finished programme was scheduled to be shown a month later on nationwide television. It was still hoped that Baron Galiano, who had so far declined to participate, might have a change of mind. Paso had found him difficult and somewhat monosyllabic, showing signs of stress manifested by an apparent inability to concentrate on the conversation and anxious to leave the gallery as soon as possible. On the other hand, his son, Lorenzo, proved an engaging personality, keen to learn all he could about the Collection, though strains in the relationship between father and son were all too evident. Privately, she thought it a pity he couldn't take his father's place before the cameras—altogether a more congenial subject and she determined to bend her mind towards the fulfilment of that possibility, though the prospects were not bright and time was short. So, phase two of Persephone was set to begin.

* * *

Rome

Antonio Marcetti was about to launch an operation of his own. The death of his 'client', Rosamund Cross, had at first been a shock, then a passing sadness and ultimately a sense of anger that would rapidly turn to outrage. To begin with, he was determined to search for an answer to what might be an impossible question—he had never before balked at impossible questions. It was to the Mater Dei hospital he turned, he was no stranger there. Members of the Order were regular visitors to the sick within its doors; many had had recourse to the knowledge and skill of its medical staff for their own problems. They were a familiar sight and generally welcomed. Marcetti had one contact on its staff of particular value. A sixty-year-old surgeon whose marriage had broken down after he had confessed to his wife of thirty years to a gay affair and then rather dramatically and publicly 'come out', the object of his desire being a twenty-five-year-old plumber, whom many thought had an eye to the main chance. The wife had responded with venom that Marcetti imagined had been lying dormant for half a lifetime. His intervention with the hospital's medical director and the board saved the surgeon's job, if not his face, which to all intents and purposes was now beyond saving. Thereafter, the poor man was securely in the friar's debt. The time had come, Marcetti felt, to realise his investment.

The body of Rosamund Cross had been recovered by her husband and flown back to the UK, where a memorial mass in London had been attended by the good and the great, two bishops and an abbot being among the featured participants. A handsome donation had subsequently been received by the Mater Dei for 'services rendered at a very distressing time'. Marcetti wanted a small service to be rendered to himself for which a personal visit was necessary. An appointment was made and the contact provided with an outline, verbally, of the information being sought. It was really quite simple. What was the actual cause of Rosamund Cross's death? The answer was startling. She died of a rarely known poison administered intravenously into the leg. Medical records, of course, told another tale, as did the death certificate signed and attested by the senior consultant physician to the hospital. So the record was false? Not exactly, she did die of heart failure but there was no mention of what had caused the heart to fail in an otherwise healthy woman.

London
17 June

The next stage of Marcetti's plan came to fruition through the fortunate occurrence of a visit to the London headquarters of the Order, deputising for the Master General who had become unexpectedly indisposed. A telephone call to the head office of the Cross Organisation secured the appointment he was seeking with surprising ease.

The confidential private secretary tapped on the panelled door, listened for a moment, his ear close to it, then went in. Andrew Cross was seated behind a decidedly modest desk in a room which, from its proportions and standard of furnishings, might have accommodated an employee well down in the chain of command, some stage below what was usually termed 'middle management'. The walls covered in a typist grade paper were devoid of pictures with the single exception of a standard print of Canaletto's *View of Greenwich from the River Thames* behind the desk. But it was into these somewhat less than salubrious surroundings that Marcetti was duly conducted. Afterwards, he wondered whether the billionaire had chosen this particular setting for his visitor's benefit and that elsewhere in the building there was an executive suite in which more elevated callers were entertained in a style befitting their status. Probably not, this kind of eccentric behaviour was well known to occur among some members of the English ruling class who liked to maintain the fiction of being ordinary. Normal civilities concluded Marcetti was invited to sit, hospitality offered and declined.

The conversation began with pleasantries. Cross was keen to demonstrate knowledge of the Dominican Order, the intellectual work it was engaged in through its study centres, especially in the undeveloped world. To Marcetti, the apparent interest was a little too glib. No more than small talk really. An Englishman's way of charming a foreigner. *Show you've taken the trouble to get the background.* A softening up for the hidden agenda, cut and thrust waiting just around the corner.

"I'm grateful for your visit, Father. My wife valued your ministrations."

"They were little enough, Mr Cross. But my Order was happy to be able to offer pastoral care. The cause of her death was a shock to us all."

"She had had a problem with her health for some time."

"Indeed...I never had any intimation of that."

"The Mater Dei hospital would not have known about it."

"So, her medical advisors here in London were satisfied by the hospital report and the contents of the death certificate? I assume it was passed on to them."

"Why does this interest you so, Father Marcetti? It occurs to me that this is not a normal part of a priest's role as spiritual advisor. Are you not in danger of trespassing on ground where you are not wanted?"

"An unexpected death is always of concern."

110

"Would the Master General countenance these enquiries into matters clearly outside your remit?"

"He would want to be reassured that everything was done at the Mater Dei in a competent and professional manner."

"Do you have reason to doubt that?"

"Only what arises from the confidences your wife shared with me. She was a devout and loyal Catholic."

"Devout, certainly." A slight lift of the eyebrows. "You mentioned in your letter of condolence that she was greatly relieved to be able to share 'the burdens of conscience'. I think that is how you put it. I was unaware, of course, that my wife's conscience was so heavily burdened. I was wondering if you would be able, now that she has passed away, to enlighten me further on this matter. I would not like to think that Rosamund died with a great sorrow on her mind."

"My discussions with your wife were conducted under conditions comparable to the seal of confession."

"Comparable, yes, but not identical."

"Some of our conversations were part of a penitential exercise. Others took place under the seal of priestly confidentiality."

"But that is not the same as confession."

"The effect is the same."

"Your church, in certain circumstances, would not forbid you to divulge such matters."

"The church would expect me to uphold the obligations of my priesthood."

"And if your silence placed in jeopardy the safety of others?"

"It would be my responsibility as a priest to determine that."

"Tell me, Father, how do you set about making that determination?"

"All human lives are sacrosanct, that is the central tenet of our practice."

"Some possibly more sacrosanct than others? Given the early history of your Order, perhaps little has changed." Words tinged with sarcasm.

"God does not make such distinctions."

"But you, I suspect, do. You argue, Father Marcetti, more as a Jesuit than a Dominican."

"You are familiar with Jesuits?"

"I was educated by them. I recognise their casuistry. I hadn't appreciated that it had infected the Order of Preachers to quite the same extent. So where do we go from here?"

"I think I have made my position quite plain, Mr Cross. My silence protects not only your late wife but you also. Any matters concerning you personally of which she may have spoken are equally under the seal of priestly confidentiality."

"I don't wish to cast doubts on the integrity of your intentions, Father, but I have to tell you, I am not reassured as to the integrity of your silence."

For a few minutes, Marcetti said nothing. When he began to speak, his voice was so quiet that Cross leaned forward a little, straining to hear.

"It is not my silence that matters in the end, but the silence of God and I do not believe that God will keep silent. None of us can know how or when He will speak out. But the cries of those who suffer will be heard, of that there is no doubt. What happens then is out of all our hands, it is out of my hands, it is out of your hands, it is even out of God's hands, for He will have set the wheels of destiny in motion—that is His nature. He cannot act against His own nature. You and those who are involved with you in this evil will ultimately be powerless to stop it. You will be destroyed because you will have destroyed yourselves. I will pray for you, Mr Cross, but I greatly fear my prayers will be of no avail."

He got to his feet, turned and walked out of the room.

Cross sat for a long time staring into the middle distance. He picked up his iPhone and called a number.

"This is Andrew Cross. I need to speak to Omar Wazir."

* * *

Palermo

From the top of the steps, Ravi Sharma watched the last of RAI Television's vans leave the front courtyard of the Palermo gallery. Standing close by was a smartly besuited Lorenzo Galiano whose contribution had been to answer a couple of questions on the grandfather benefactor he himself had never personally known. No matter. A brief, tetchy moment with his father had eventually evolved into something more constructive and elicited sufficient background information to lend a little family colour to the proceedings and that's really all the programme makers were bothered about. "It adds to the authenticity," the presenter assured him. Lorenzo's satisfaction at being involved was evident. Paso came up and shook his hand.

"Thank you for your input. They think it went well." She nodded to the group on the steps above them—Casamassa with the RAI presenter and the arts series producer.

"Hope your father will be pleased with the result when it's shown next month."

"I've learned not to hope for too much."

"You were great. They said you're a natural with the camera. He should be proud."

The day before the filming, father and son had again faced each other after an 'urgent' telephone call from Paso expressing distress that the project might fall apart without some family input. From her convincing performance, one might have suspected a theatrical background! Lorenzo determined that if it had to be a stand-off, then the risk was worth it.

"Tell me about my grandfather."

"There's nothing to tell."

"What sort of a man was he?"

"Conscientious, conservative. Everything always the same. Same routine every day, every week, every year. Never varied. My mother, too."

"How did you get on?"

"With him, fine at a distance, didn't really see him on his own, always people around. So, he was careful what he said."

"Your mother?"

"My mother was wary. A foreigner marrying into a Sicilian family, and English too. It was felt to be odd."

"Why was that?"

"Questions. You've never shown any interest before."

"I think it's time I did. I'm nearly thirty, papa, and I know nothing of my own family."

"More my fault than yours, I suppose. Your grandmother, English, a difficult race at the best of times and English Catholics more so. Years of persecution made them cagey, suspicious, always on the lookout, but tough— my God, were they tough. Like my mother, a bough that would never break, not even bend."

"But they accepted her, the Sicilians?"

"Don't think it went down too well with the locals, to begin with. She made herself fit in and it worked out in the long run."

"Did you get on with her?"

"Seemed to. She talked about her family. How, after years of persecution, they learned to live looking over their shoulders. At one time, their priests were hounded, forever on the run, but your grandmother's family hid them and kept them safe. But in spite of everything, she was proud of her culture."

"Yes, she introduced me to English literature."

"As she did me: Shakespeare, Milton, Housman, all the poets. Bought volumes for me. I have them still in the library here."

"Did you visit her family in England?"

"Once or twice. She grew apart from them after her marriage so the chance to go didn't come up much. An only child as well, unusual for Catholics. Then the older generation died out, so that was it."

Lorenzo had let him go on, didn't want it to stop. They talked about Catarina, her American husband and growing family. A grandchild he had never seen, another on the way. It was the longest conversation with his father that Lorenzo could remember. Afterwards, Luca seemed to retreat within himself again. He reluctantly agreed to Lorenzo taking a limited part in the film, knew he couldn't really prevent it. If he'd said no, Lorenzo would've gone anyway. He perhaps regretted letting his guard slip and wandered out onto the terrace, lost in thought, staring out at the landscape. Lorenzo, watching him from the library window, realised he wouldn't find the answers he was looking for before the time came for him to leave.

He had called his office in Milan, checking on schedules. No change in the situation in Washington. Pentagon boffins were still wrestling with hacked computers. The hacker's parents were kicking up a fuss, claiming an innocent child was being victimised by the repressive state. The innocent child had now been released back into their custody. His computer impounded he had presumably returned to his former more harmless pastime of self-abuse. The office thought it might be appropriate for Signor Galiano to take advantage of the lull and enjoy some annual leave. It suited Lorenzo but the girlfriend was going to prove a trifle trickier.

For the duration of Operation Persephone, the team had taken the tenancy of a quietly situated villa close to the town of Aspra on the coast of northern Sicily. Its proximity to Palermo meant it was easy to monitor day-by-day developments while keeping the team's profile as low as possible. In particular, it was important to follow Seth's progress closely. They were expecting him to work to a tight timescale and the photographer was not kindly disposed to being hurried. "I don't just take snaps. This is a serious art form." It was clear that this was not going to be concluded quickly; Seth estimated it would take at least four days to complete the whole assignment. There were thirty pictures on display and a further eleven either with the restorers or in store. Casamassa and Pritsi would make an initial selection of twelve pictures for the Actaeon publication, though it was more than likely that this number would be reduced to a final choice of eight by the publishers themselves. The team had received welcome news that Lavinia Dyer, once more adopting the persona of Dr Lucy Black, would be returning in a few days, ostensibly to represent the interests of Actaeon but in reality to represent the interests of the world's press. Ferdy Keymer had given way in the face of achieving an old-fashioned scoop.

As parts of the gallery were still open to the public, the movement of people around the building was being scrutinised by Ravi Sharma on the CCTV monitor and to his intense irritation, Signora Bertelli constantly dropped by on one pretext or another. When Paso called in to check how he was doing, Sharma took the opportunity to comment on the fact. The visits promptly stopped. Standish kept in touch with Sharma every hour and reported everything back to Sandro Menotti. By the early evening of day two, Seth had completed the majority of the pictures in the second room and was pleased with his own progress, thinking he might be finished by day three if they were prepared to work late both nights. Sharma relayed this back.

Casamassa had already made his selection of the four pictures he wanted to exhibit in Venice, comprising Old Masters of the Renaissance and including the Caravaggio, a choice not wholly approved by Pritsi on behalf of the democratically-minded Ministry of Culture whose preference was to let the public have access to a cross-section of artists and periods represented in the Collection.

"Impossible," said the learned professor, "the Ministry knows perfectly well, *you* know perfectly well, that would be utterly inappropriate for my gallery." Pritsi made a mental note of the emphasis applied to the word 'my'. That was, perhaps, an argument for another day—one he would happily pass over to his superiors. As the photographing of each of the selected canvasses was completed, gallery staff removed them to the storeroom where they were wrapped up and cosseted like the vulnerable elderly, which was, of course, exactly what they were.

"It's going ahead of plan," said Standish to Menotti. "I think we should go over tomorrow evening. Hold their hands a bit."

"Fine. I've got the *carabinieri* patrolling tonight. But nothing to report. I've checked up on that journalist guy Francesca was interested in. Curious, but none of the Egyptian press people have heard of him. She said it confirms what she thought. Would you ask Ravi to keep an eye out? Francesca says there's been no further sight of him. She's questioned Bertelli about him. Interesting reaction, Milo. Bertelli came over vague, couldn't remember when he first made contact. Thought Dr Melzi would have known all about it. Francesca got the impression Bertelli's scared of him."

"I have a gut feeling he fits in somewhere, but God knows where."

* * *

The following day, things were going quite well but then the schedule slipped. Some of the special lighting kept shorting. Electricians brought in to help were puzzled until one of them discovered that junction boxes had been tampered with, but no one could say how. Sharma reported to Standish and told him he was taking up position in the basement where the boxes were located. Paso would take over the CCTV monitor. Seth was working hard to complete but had lost precious time; it might be a very late night.

Later that evening, certain events were taking place in another part of the city. Above the sliding doors of the garage, a board proclaimed 'Pozzi's Removals' and underneath, the legend, 'Any Time Any Place' was difficult to make out through the accumulated layers of dirt. At one time, old Sergio would clean it with a bucket and brush but not anymore. "If you think I'm going up that fucking ladder at my age, you've got another thing coming!" So, time and grime worked their inexorable way to anonymity. Over the board, a row of small square windows equally succumbing to the passage of time dimly showed a light burning in the garage. A deserted street. Business premises packed up and closed for the day. What little lighting there was barely penetrating the solid darkness that fell over this rundown commercial area of the city. A car appeared at the far end moving slowly down the street until it reached the Pozzi place. It came to a stop opposite the garage and sat there, engine idling. Inside sat four figures, obscure in the darkness. The driver, smoking, lowered his window from time to time to let the smoke out and flick his ash. There seemed to be no conversation. Like the other three, the passenger in the front seat wore dark clothing with his face partly hidden behind a scarf, a light grey woollen hat on his head pulled down to just above his eyes made him stand out from the others. One of the men in the back seat looked at his watch and said something, at which grey hat laughed. Another ten minutes passed. Then the rear doors opened and the two passengers got out, followed by the one in front. He seemed to be youngest of the group, moved more agilely, was noticeably slimmer. On closer inspection, really just a boy.

115

One of the older men and the boy crossed the street to the small door of the garage, a signal and the third one joined them. The driver stayed behind the wheel. Gently, one of them pushed at the small door and found it gave a little under pressure. He nodded to the youth, again pushed and listened, easing it open, looked inside and around the garage but couldn't see anyone. He stepped in followed by the youth. All three dark blue removal vans were parked inside. He walked over to one of the two smaller ones, patted the engine hood, which was still warm, went around to the side and looked in the cab. The keys were in the ignition. Reaching in through the open window, he switched it on and looked at the petrol gauge. There was the sound of a door opening with a creak. Old Sergio stood in the office doorway peering about him myopically. He saw customers, a bit late in the day, but you can't turn business away.

"Si signori?"

"You are the owner?"

"My son…my son's the owner. Nico!"

"Yes, papa, I'm nearly finished," Nico shouted back from the office.

"A customer!" the old man bawled back.

"What…?" he came up behind his father and stopped when he saw they had company.

"How can I help you gentlemen?"

The words were scarcely out of his mouth when Nico found himself looking at the barrel of a revolver, pointed not at himself but at his father's chest.

"You drive these vans?"

Of course, he fucking drives them, thought old Sergio.

"Si."

"We need this one," nodding to the van on his left.

"I'll need to check it."

"Don't bother."

"But signor, it may need filling up."

"Don't waste my time; it's three quarters full, enough for my purpose. Get in."

He turned to the youth, "Open the doors."

The youth ran to the double doors and started to roll one back. The third man slipped through the opening and helped with the other one. As the doors slid apart, the man with the gun turned to Sergio.

"Into the office."

The old chap, shaking like a leaf, shuffled in followed by the gunman who snatched at the telephone and ripped its connection from the wall.

"Sit in that chair and don't move."

Returning to the van, he climbed in beside Nico, said something and the engine started up, faded. Nico tried again and the second time, it came to life. Slowly, the vehicle began to edge forward towards the entrance. Leaning out of the passenger door, the gunman called to the youth.

"Close the doors behind us. Lock them if you can." Nodding back towards the office, "Keep him quiet and follow in the car."

Nico's mind worked overtime as he drove the van through the back streets of the city towards the centre. Directions given by the passenger were clipped and brief, the accent strange, hard to place. It was a humid, still night; sweat was running down his face and neck, clouding his eyes like tears, soaking the hairs on his chest and running down his back. At last, they turned into a *calle*, office buildings on one side, on the other loomed the rear of a huge block.

"Slow down!" he was told. They came to a pair of cast iron gates, already open and leading into a courtyard. "Pull in here and turn the van around ready for driving out, there's plenty of room." As Nico was making the manoeuvre, the figure of a woman appeared for a moment in the headlights. She looked scared and slightly wild, clutching a bunch of keys, unsure what to do next.

"Pull over some more, leave room for a car to get in. Stay in the cab till I tell you to get out and give me the ignition key." Flashing a revolver in the woman's direction, he snarled, "Get inside and keep your mouth shut." Gesturing to Nico, "Out! Open the rear doors." Nico folded the doors back against the sides of the van and secured them. Another man appeared in the doorway—tall, grey-haired, casually dressed in sweater and chinos. *He didn't really look like one of the others*, Nico thought, *out of place here*. He hesitated, looked at Nico, turned and followed the woman. She led the way up a stone staircase with iron railings to the first floor of the building. Nico heard the man say something but couldn't make out what it was—a cultured voice though and Sicilian. Nico started to follow when a door on his right opened slowly. The gunman behind him moved to one side into the shadow of the stairs as Ravi Sharma started to come out into the corridor. A hand shot out, caught him on the side of the head with the gun and Sharma crumpled instantly.

"In here, drag this bastard in as well. Keep quiet else neither of you will leave this room alive."

The door was pulled shut and Nico heard bolts shot into place. It was pitch black inside and as far as he could tell, it was windowless, but he heard the sound of another vehicle being driven into the yard and then footsteps outside the door and a foreign voice speaking into a mobile. A few minutes later, Nico was lying beside the unconscious man, bound and gagged.

* * *

At 9 p.m., Francesca Paso made a call from her office in the Palermo Gallery to a restaurant in the centre of the city, a recommendation from her secretary, Sara Bertelli. An order was placed for food to be delivered to the gallery for the team that, on Seth's latest prediction, was likely to be working until well into the small hours. Little over an hour later, a delivery van drew up outside the main entrance and a girl and boy got out, each carrying a large box. They were met at the main entrance doors by Ravi Sharma. Paso decreed a break for everyone, Bertelli was asked to set out the meal in the director's office and by 10.30, the team had assembled. Seth had been reluctant to break off but was clearly famished and looking close to exhaustion. There was a nervous tension in the air. Casamassa was uncommunicative for once, lost in thought, as though he was in another world. Pritsi was pacing up and down the office like a caged lion, food in hand. Bertelli took hers over to a chair by the rear window, trying hard not to look as if she were keeping watch. Paso, chatting quietly to Sharma, was not missing a trick, aware of everything going on around her. An hour or so previously, she'd received a message from Menotti that they were on their way. In less than half an hour, they were all making their way back to their various workstations. There was still no sign of the intelligence men.

Standish and Menotti had left the villa in Aspra shortly after ten and were driving the few kilometres into the city to join the team. "We'll take a break for food when you arrive," said Paso. "We can all gather in my office."

"Better," said Menotti, "we check around the building while you're eating. We'll get something after that."

Traffic on the coastal highway had been relatively light until they reached Fiume-Eleutherio with its view across the sands to the Tyrrhenian Sea. Up ahead was a build-up of cars and caravans into the outskirts of Palermo and the distant prospect of blue flashing lights. "What the devil…" said Menotti who was driving. He made a call on the in-car phone, listened a moment, then said, "Bugger, pile up in front; everything's at a standstill. We'll need to wait until we come to a halt and then turn back the way we've come. We can weave our way around this but it's going to take a lot longer. If I'm clever, I'll hit the autostrada if I can find it from here—this isn't my territory."

"I'll call and let them know," replied Standish. A long pause. "Ravi's not picking up. I expect he's out of range somewhere in the building."

Let's hope so, thought Menotti. He tried calling Paso with the same result. The stream of vehicles slowed and eventually came to a halt, people getting out for a better view of what was happening. Menotti pulled their car across the road, reversed and set off again, foot down hard as the car raced back in the direction of Aspra.

"Sat Nav's going to be useless. I'll have to trust my own instincts," said Menotti. There were twists and turns as he tried to keep as parallel a course with their previous route as possible. Cul-de-sacs, one-way streets going in the wrong direction, streets that led them back the way they'd already come, streets that led them nowhere at all. Eventually, Menotti found a sign for Contrada di Simone and the autostrada. It had been an hour and a half before they pulled into the forecourt of the gallery.

The front façade of the building, normally illuminated, was in darkness, the interior likewise. "This doesn't look right," said Menotti. One half of the great front doors was slightly ajar. Standish looked at Menotti who indicated that they should draw back. The two men moved along the colonnade keeping to the wall of the building until the portico ended. Menotti leaned close whispered, "I'll take the front, you work round to the back. I'll give you fifteen minutes before I go in. It's quite a long way around. Don't know what you'll find. There'll probably be gates leading into the rear yard and a service entrance. Take care, Milo."

Standish nodded, checked the time by his watch, and said, "And you." He headed across the forecourt keeping to the shadow of the buildings on his left-hand side. Reaching the street that ran in front of the gallery, he turned left letting the shadows of the trees along the avenue offer some cover from the lights of passing traffic. Then, again to his left was a narrow *calle* barely illuminated, just a streetlamp at each end. He quickened his pace and was startled for a moment as a street cat hissed and darted in front of him. At the end, another *calle* ran parallel to the main street. He took a left once more, completing the circuit of the complex of buildings. A cautious approach now— this street was more brightly lit and as ill luck would have it, there was overhead lighting outside the entrance gates. A car came along from behind him but passed by without slowing. Staying close to the wall, Standish peered into the gloom of the rear yard of the gallery. Parked inside was a dark-coloured furniture van drawn up close to the service entrance and beside it, bonnet pointing to the exit a black sedan car, empty of occupants.

Standish crept low around the front of the van seeking the protection of the shadows on its left-hand side, pausing to check the time. Eight minutes since he'd left Menotti. Reaching the rear of the van, he crouched low against the back wheels, listening and waiting. The rear doors had been opened and fastened back. Not a sound to be heard so he edged around until he was able to peer inside. As far as he could make out, a number of large packages were stacked along the right-hand side. The metal door of the gallery's service entrance had been left open, the only light coming from somewhere above a flight of stone stairs with iron railings that wound upwards on his left. Immediately on his right, a wooden door was bolted top and bottom on the outside. Gently easing the bolts back, he tried the handle and luckily the door swung inwards with a slight creak. From inside came a muffled sound of groaning. Taking a flashlight from his pocket, Standish switched it on and shone the beam around the room. It lit up two figures lying a few feet apart, one gagged with silver tape, arms and legs similarly bound and tightly secured. The other figure was unbound and unmoving. Ravi Sharma was unconscious.

Menotti gently pushed at the door and slipped inside. It was almost pitch black, impossible to make anything out. He moved forward, his right hand holding his revolver by his side, aware that the intense silence somehow vibrated with the lack of sound. Then the door behind him slammed shut and as he whipped around, the entrance foyer flooded with light.

"Throw down your weapon!" And as if to emphasise the point, there was a zipping sound as the stone-flagged floor spat twice at his feet. "On your knees, lie down facing the floor!" Menotti heard footsteps crossing behind him and turned his head a little to risk a sideways look. He saw at least two or three figures in black wearing head masks. "Face the floor." He got a savage kick to the side of his head, then, "hands behind you!" He was handcuffed, sticky tape put across the mouth and a black hood was pulled over of his head, then there was more tape binding his ankles together. Apart from the one voice, the rest were silent. He strained every muscle of his hearing to detect what sounds he could make out. Then he found himself being dragged across the floor, lifting his head as much as possible to avoid it hitting the stone paving. Then the sound of a gun being fired, no silencer this time and a searing pain in his right side. There was the roar of a voice in Arabic, "Cursed fool!" "I swear by Allah, it just went off." The sound of someone smacked across the face. He heard a door being opened and knew he was being dragged inside. Then silence again. Close to him, he heard a muffled sound. Someone struggling to breathe? Or was it himself? He closed his eyes beneath the hood and tried to double over to contain the pain. He felt a stickiness and fainted.

Stooping down, Standish felt for a pulse and noted that it was steady. He gingerly checked Sharma's eyelids and touched the bruise on the hairline on the right side of his forehead. He resisted the temptation to move him to a more comfortable position so that nothing looked disturbed. The other man presented more of a problem. Nico's eyes followed every movement and his muffled protests became more agitated. Finally, Standish knelt beside him and whispered into his ear, "Police. For God's sake, keep quiet and give nothing away. Understand?" Nico nodded vigorously. Standish removed the tape from his mouth. "Do you work here?"

"That's my furniture van out there." Standish nodded, understanding.

"Please help us by going along with what they want. We'll have you covered and we'll stick close behind you. We need to find out where they're going."

"I think they plan to drive it themselves. Heard one of them say that some bloke would guide them."

"OK, they may just leave you here. I'll be back. Sorry I have to put the gag on again."

"*Va bene*. Who's this guy?"

"It's OK, he's one of us. Keep an eye on him, though there's not much that you can do."

Standish moved to the door, listened and slipped outside, drew the door closed and bolted it once more. As he crept to the bottom of the stairs, he heard sounds of voices above him and footsteps beginning to descend. On his right was a door, pray God it wasn't locked. It wasn't. He looked into a long passage that appeared to run through to the front of the building. It seemed to be used as a repository for broken items of furniture and old picture frames. Against the wall on the left-hand side was an old *armadio* minus its doors but deep enough to let Standish crouch out of sight. Two voices, maybe three, receded as they passed through and out of the service door into the yard. He crept up to the door, listened again and hearing nothing, opened it a crack in time to hear the service door open again and two men speaking in Arabic. He drew the door closed but kept one hand on the latch with the other drawing out his revolver. The bolts on the circuit room were slammed back. It was difficult to work out exactly what was happening, to piece together the terrorists' movements. There were sounds now of more voices and footsteps racing down the stone stairs, then suddenly the outer service door was slammed and silence descended.

Standish waited—impatient and worried—then could wait no longer. He slipped out and down to the circuit room. This time, the door was wide open and he could see Ravi Sharma still lying unmoving on the floor. There was no sign of the other man. The service door had not been closed properly and had come open just a crack. Outside in the yard, the figure of a young man bound and gagged was being hauled into the furniture van, the rear doors were shut with a clang and then it started up. The clutch screamed then engaged and the vehicle lumbered to the gates and out onto the *calle*. Standish could still hear it when it reached the end of the street and turned onto one of the main highways through the city. Easing open the service door further, Standish looked out at a deserted yard. The car too had gone; the sound of its departure cloaked by the sound of Pozzi's Removals.

Chapter Seven

Palermo
24 June

In Lavinia Dyer's view, somewhat jaundiced in the circumstances, it was hard to escape the conclusion that inclement weather was pursuing her around the globe. She had left New York-Kennedy on a wet and blustery day and her arrival at Rome's Fiumicino was in much the same vein. That at least could have been avoided had she not agreed to the paper's request—conveyed in terms verging on obsequiousness by Ferdy Keymer—to a meeting with a representative of the Osservatore Vaticano on his commission to write a series of articles for the *New York Times* on the Pontificate of Pope Francis. With muttered remarks about 'doing your own dirty work', she nevertheless agreed. It meant a delay of twenty-four hours before she could continue her onward journey to Palermo. She found the gentleman in question weaselly and conceited, though no doubt fully possessed of the appropriate journalistic credentials for the task in question. So it was at last with considerable relief when her plane touched down at Palermo's Falcone-Borsellino airport. The taxi deposited her in the street at the front of the Palermo gallery where she was greeted with a scene of horror. With mounting apprehension, she got out of the taxi and stood looking about her.

The forecourt was full of police vehicles and *carabinieri* officers, two ambulances with flashing lights, one just pulling away, the other being loaded with a stretcher, three fire tenders lined up at the foot of the steps. The police had erected barriers and the media had already started to gather, at least one television crew and a group of reporters with cameras. A woman officer approached her, asking for her name and, realising she had an American on her hands, for her passport as well. Milo Standish was sitting on the front steps looking dazed and exhausted when he spotted her. He came down, greeted her with a kiss and confirmed her identity.

"Lavinia, this isn't the kind of welcome you were expecting."

"Milo, what's happened?"

"As you can see, there's been quite a lot going on. Let's go inside. We can't talk here; we'll go up to Francesca's office." He took her arm. "I'm afraid you're going to have to prepare yourself for some bad news."

He guided her up the steps into the building. Inside was a scene of chaos: Items of furniture smashed, two women trying to clean up an indefinable mess on the floor of the foyer, the air acrid with the smell of smoke and chemicals.

Francesca Paso came out of her office to greet them, looking glad to see a female colleague, an air of warmth between the two women.

"Lavinia, what a welcome back. Come and sit down, I've sent for some coffee. Milo, you too, for heaven's sake, you look all in. The police have just taken Bertelli away. They found her cowering in a storeroom, a quivering mass, spilling her heart out to them. Now we know why we were always one step behind. As yet, we don't know why she did it." For all her usual calmness, Paso was voluble, white-faced, for once working hard at keeping control.

"I expect they had something on her, some means of coercion," said Standish. "At a shrewd guess, some pressure on the family."

"We'll find out soon enough. The officer in charge is a Commissario Leone. He's being as helpful as he can."

"Let's hope he can provide a lead or two; we're going to need all the help we can get." He slumped in a chair opposite Dyer.

"Milo, fill Lavinia in, will you?"

"Lavinia, I'm sorry. There's no easy way. We've two fatalities. Pritsi and Seth. Shot by the terrorists. They never stood a chance. Just mown down."

Dyer stared at him. Her face registered nothing. She got up out of her chair, didn't seem to know why and sat down again. He made to go across to her but Paso got up first, walked over, crouching by her side.

"You OK?"

Dyer looked at her and nodded. She put a hand on one of Paso's resting on the arm of the chair.

"We've got to find those bastards," she said almost under her breath, "find them and stop them."

"I know," said Paso.

"Vassilio…just a kid. You know, Erik Seth was said to be the most talented art photographer alive." She got up and walked over to the front window. The forecourt was still a hive of activity, but quiet—everyone moving about almost mechanically—flashes from the press cameras behind the police cordon. She turned back to the room.

"So…tell me about the rest."

"Sandro's been taken to hospital, shot on the right side and lost a lot of blood but not on the danger list. Matteo's there too, shot in the arm and knocked about a bit, quite lucky actually, could have been a lot worse. He tried to stand up to them. Sandro heard him calling them 'vandals'! Don't know how he got away with it. Sandro thought they would kill him."

Dyer shook her head, "Matteo, gentleman to the last."

"Ravi's in hospital too, a mild concussion but he'll be fine. Then, of course, there's the collateral damage."

"Do you really want to be bothered with it, Lavinia?"

"Tell me."

"Francesca."

"The pictures in the storeroom that were crated up ready for Venice have gone and six other paintings, Impressionists for the most part. When the attack came, I was in the upstairs storeroom checking the pictures that had been packed. One of the janitors, Lotty, was with me. Once I worked out what was going on, I told her not to panic. 'Panic?' she said, 'what the hell for?' She grabbed me, pushed me into the little room the cleaners use for their stuff, no more than a large cupboard really. We emerged, two cleaning ladies with buckets and mops, me decked out in blue overalls and hair tied up in an old scarf. Two of the jihadis came in and were quite surprised to see us, asked what the f…we were doing. Lotty said what the f…did they think we were doing, posing for photographs? The younger one started to throw his weight around. Swore a lot, threatened to rape me. Unzipped his trousers and took it out. Lotty told me afterwards that she nearly fell around laughing at a sight that wouldn't have brought a smile to the face of a gnat! Instead, she confined herself to telling the youth to 'put that trinket away'. And believe it or not, he did! Though for a very ugly moment, I wondered what was going to happen next."

Despite everything, Dyer was forced to laugh. "Thank God for the Lottys of this world."

"One in a million. She seemed to have no fear at all. She even complained when they dragged us downstairs and made us carry out the smaller pictures from the first gallery. You know, in a peculiar way, I think the brutes were almost scared of her. I think it saved our lives."

"By the sound of it," said Standish, "they had every right to be."

"They're not used to having a woman stand up to them," said Dyer.

"Thank God they put you in the room with Sandro. What you were able to do for him certainly saved his life."

"I've got a lot of things to blame myself for, Milo."

"I don't see what more you could have done."

"Well, for one thing, when I went upstairs to the storeroom, I'd left my revolver down here in the office in my jacket. A stupid mistake."

"Not necessarily, Francesca. If they'd searched you and found it…a different ending to the story."

She shrugged, "Maybe. What now, where do we go from here?"

* * *

From the far end of the *calle* where his café was, Giorgio could see that a group of customers were gathered outside waiting for him to open. It was already past seven-thirty and he would normally have been there to look after the first batch of workers wanting breakfast before starting the early shift. One of them saw him, told the others and a mocking cheer went up. Teresa had been the cause of this morning's lateness. It was unusual for her to make demands on him first thing in the morning. She was a night-time girl, every night in fact and not just once. Sometimes it was more than a hardworking man could cope with. But Giorgio was not one for complaints. At fifty-two, you were glad for what you could get, especially with a girlfriend of twenty-nine. But this morning! When her head disappeared beneath the duvet, he knew there was trouble afoot. Mind you, last night he'd been out late with the boys and when

124

he'd got home, she was fast asleep in bed for once. So he'd slipped under the duvet quiet as you like so as not to wake her.

Passing Pozzi's garage, he noticed the padlock on the main doors hanging from the latch but unfastened. Not like Nico. He stopped and pushed at the small door, which was locked from the inside. Looking up at the windows above the doors, he thought he could see a light, dim behind the dirt, difficult to make out. Odd! He shouted down the street to the waiting group, "Have you seen Nico or Sergio?" No, no one had.

"Come on!" someone yelled. "It's late. Where've yer been?"

He thought he heard Teresa's name and laughter broke out. He hesitated, unhooked the padlock and started to slide open one of the doors. A couple of his customers outside the café sauntered down the street to the garage. Giorgio stepped inside and noticed one of the vans was out and there was no sign of life. He called out the two men's names. No response but saw a light was on in the office and walked over. The two from the café came into the garage.

"Everything ok, Giorgio?" one called.

"No one here," he said and opened the office door.

They heard him cry out, a strangled sound and an oath.

"Jesu-Maria!" he backed out, leant against the wall and vomited.

One of the others peered in. "Fucking hell!"

"Police, call the police," gasped Giorgio. One of them took his mobile out and dialled the emergency number.

Pozzi's garage was thus a second major crime scene and what had been discovered was not long in being reported in all the media. And in the way in which these things come out, in no time at all connections were being drawn with last night's vicious attack on the Palermo Gallery of Fine Art and the theft of extremely valuable paintings. Over the course of a few hours, death had stalked the city and the city, no stranger to death throughout its long history, was traumatised. In time, bit by bit, details leaked out. The disappearance of one of Pozzi's removal vans linked the two events in the minds of the investigating officers and provided the press with ample scope for speculation. Nico inevitably became the central figure in the police hunt for the killers, though no one really believed Nico himself to be a suspect. At last it emerged, though not for public consumption, that the decapitation of old Sergio Pozzi had been, one might say, only half successful.

* * *

Altrabia
25 June

Altrabia, one of the numerous farmsteads on the Galiano estates, was remotely situated in the central highlands of the island. Its surrounding land no longer in use for arable farming, the farmhouse itself had remained unoccupied for years since the last peasant farmer died there alone in the 1970s. True, a group of hippies had squatted there a decade later but the estate manager and a few farmworkers had turned up and seen them off after a fire was started in one of the outbuildings visible from miles around. After that, the old farmhouse quietly slid into decay, occasional hikers its only visitors. Too far out of the way to be useful for storage, its surrounding acres had long since become unproductive and more or less been abandoned to the flora and fauna of the region. Then in the summer of 2014, new residents moved in. With them came an air of secrecy that surpassed anything to which even the island of Sicily was accustomed. Al-Azhar, the Caliphate commander in the Southern Mediterranean, ensured that a strict guard-watch was maintained over the approaches. If a casual passer-by wandered too close—a rare occurrence—a polite warning would be given that the area was being used by the military and was off-limits. Even the local population seemed to swallow this version of the actual facts without question. Sicilians had learnt over centuries not only to keep their mouths shut, but also not to go where they were not wanted.

Nico Pozzi's unmarked furniture van had rocked and rumbled its way over miles of rough roads and rougher farm tracks until it came to a creaking stop in the cobbled courtyard. Parked in front was an ex-army transport vehicle, the one that had been used to bring the jihadis up from the coast. Alongside it was a black sedan Fiat. Dawn was breaking and an early morning mist rose from the valley bottom bringing the surrounding hills into hazy relief. It promised another day of enervating heat, when early morning and evening were the best times to get anything done and midday was a time of lassitude and retreat. Al-Azhar was a satisfied man, more than that could never be said of him, a sense of purpose on his battle-scarred and hardened face. The will of Allah, all praise to Him, had prevailed and the contents of Pozzi's removal van were the living proof of that. The Caliphate was potentially richer by hundreds of millions of dollars. Buyers of western art in the Far East would probably scheme and plot to outbid each other, even kill if necessary. To the cause of international jihadism, it mattered not a whit if they cut each other's throats over it. His task now was to ensure that the pictures were lodged in a place of safety and security where, if need be, buyers could gather and haggle in peace.

He confronted an exhausted, haggard-looking Galiano, a defeated man with an uncertain future. Luca Galiano was a man betrayed by his own existence. Betrayed by what he was now coming to realise was a love he had never been able to show, had perhaps never wanted to show, for his son. Lorenzo, gagged and bound, had been thrown onto his side on the van floor, every bone and muscle in his body aching, his arms bruised and head knocked almost senseless. At long last, the rear doors opened and he was greeted by the sight of his father and another man peering in.

"Get my son out of that bloody van," Galiano said with uncharacteristic force.

"There's more valuable cargo to worry about," snarled Al-Azhar. Turning to a youth behind him, he said, "Get him out!"

Lorenzo was dragged feet first to the doors and then allowed to lower himself painfully to the ground.

"Release him," snapped Al-Azhar and the youth snatched the tape from Lorenzo's mouth, causing him to gasp with the pain of it. Taking out a vicious-looking knife from the waistband of his trousers, he cut the tape from his hands and feet.

"So, papa, a nice welcome for your son."

The youth reached out and smacked him across the face. Lorenzo felt his lip crack and tasted blood.

"Enough!" barked Al-Azhar. "I'll tell you when that is required. Now leave us. Get the hell into the house and stay there!"

The subdued youth slunk off sullenly towards the farmhouse.

"Let me explain to you both," continued the commander, "what is going to happen next. Shortly, the contents of this van will be transferred to another vehicle. They will be taken to a place of security pending their sale. Silence!" as Lorenzo started to say something. "You have no voice in this, either of you. You, young man, will accompany the pictures on that journey as a pledge of their safety. After that, if Allah so wills it, you may be released. You, Barone, will be driven from here back to your house in Enna where you will await further instructions. And now you may enjoy each other's company until time of departure." He turned on his heel and strode off towards the farmhouse.

"We seem to be in this together, whatever it is."

"That wasn't my wish. Now you know why I wanted you out of it. Why did you have to involve yourself?"

"Because you're my father and because you were in trouble. It's what fathers and sons do. It's a flesh and blood thing. Did your father never tell you that?"

"My father never told me anything. Look where it's landed you."

"Well, we still have a chance to do better."

"Do you really imagine we can do anything against this lot," he dropped his voice, "this gang of murderers?"

He walked over to a low crumbling stone wall behind them, once part of a pen for farm animals, and leant against it, looking down and scuffing his feet on the ground where bits of stone and mortar lay around. For all the world, to Lorenzo, he looked at that moment like a lost and desolate schoolboy. He wandered over and sat on the wall next to Luca.

"I don't know how long we've got, but don't let's waste it in recriminations. They're letting you back home for the moment. It may be a chance, a slight chance, to do something, get some help."

"Not with you as a hostage. Why do you think they're taking you? I won't risk…" he broke off.

There was the sound of someone's footsteps from behind the van and a figure appeared, a middle-aged man in blue overalls smeared with engine oil. Hesitating when he saw them, he looked behind him, then walked over, casual but eyes wary. Pale-looking, tired and rubbing at his wrists.

"You're the one they call the Barone?" he asked in a low voice, a mumble. "I'm Nico. I drove the van here. They took it from my garage, forced me to drive to that gallery place, then here. There's not much time. They were talking as we came here in a foreign language; I didn't understand but caught a few names. That chief one was on his mobile. No! Shh...listen. He kept mentioning a name, Calderari. Several times he said it. Calderari."

"Calderari, *l'ombelico di Sicilia*, the navel of Sicily," said Galiano.

"Yes, Calderari, you know, papa, it's where the Lantes had an airstrip. They sold it to a guy who wanted to set up a small private flying club. I don't remember what happened."

"It's a possibility...they could be intending to use it. Fly the pictures out of the country. I don't know what kind of aircraft you'd need or what could land there."

"Nothing too large; it was made just to take light aircraft. It's worth a try. Why else would they be interested in a place like Calderari? There's nothing else there. Try and get hold of Francesca Paso. She's the only contact we have and she seems to have a lot of pull."

"Let's hope I leave first. I daren't use a mobile here."

"They took mine and smashed it," said Lorenzo.

"Mine too," said Nico. "They leave nothing to chance..." his voice trailed off as they heard the farmhouse door open. Quick thinking, Nico promptly sat down, back to the wall, head on his crossed arms. Al-Azhar came around the van, looked over towards them briefly, then climbed into the back of the military truck, emerging a few moments later.

"Lorenzo, get on your feet; you'll be needed to transfer the pictures. Into the house. If you're lucky, they may give you something to eat."

"I'm not hungry."

"Go! Damn you to hell! I don't care if you starve to death."

Lorenzo got up and disappeared around the van. The sound of the farmhouse door opening and closing was heard.

"You, van driver, you help as well. Galiano, you're leaving in five minutes," he turned on his heel and made for the house.

* * *

Palermo

The message received by Francesca Paso came from a mobile to one of the gallery's landlines. The voice, indistinct and muffled, was probably being disguised, she thought, by the simple device of a handkerchief over the mouthpiece. It was impossible to identify, that not surprisingly being the point of the subterfuge. Nevertheless, the import of the message was clear and in less than a minute, it had been relayed to a villa on the north coast near the village of Aspra where it received immediate attention. Standish's contact at intelligence headquarters in Rome acted promptly on the information. In the absence of the hospitalised Menotti, Paso herself had for the time being been placed in charge of the fieldwork side of the ongoing operation. It was her decision to conduct things from her base in the Palermo gallery, which remained closed to the public to allow Commissario Leone and his forensic team to continue the work of investigation and analysis at an uncontaminated site. Only staff members present at the time of the attack were to report for duty and thus be available as and when required by the investigating officers. The only exception being the gallery's perceptive and always alert receptionist, who—Paso decided—could play a useful role in fending off the innumerable enquiries from the public and especially the media, a role the said lady clearly relished and undertook with admirable efficiency and evident enjoyment.

The late Dr Melzi's secretary and self-appointed personal assistant, Sarah Bertelli, remained in police custody. But the canary had fallen silent, her present mental state a cause of some concern. Leone was convinced that at the very least, members of Bertelli's family were being threatened by the 'criminal organisation' behind the attack. It was not beyond the bounds of possibility that actual kidnap might be playing a part; Leone's staff were on familiar territory there. So, two junior members of the team were following up and tracking members of the family. But it was a lengthy business as relatives were scattered all over Sicily and even the mainland, and in the nature of the enquiry, discretion was vital. "Concentrate on the kids," he told them, "they're the ones most at risk."

He was seriously considering releasing Bertelli but keeping a tail in place. This ploy might, he hoped, achieve two outcomes: One, reduce the level of threat if she was no longer perceived to be a 'person of interest' and second, raise the hope that a lead may come up if Bertelli were to be contacted by those threatening her. Though nothing could be guaranteed, there was an outside chance the terrorists might try to find out what discussions had taken place between her and the police. Naturally, whenever he suggested a surveillance operation, his senior managers either muttered about dwindling resources or quite suddenly became unavailable. All around, it was a delicate moment in the progress of the affair. A time, Leone knew from experience, when it was of prime importance to hold one's nerve.

Priority had also to be given to set up an operation to prevent valuable art works from being spirited out of Sicily; once that happened, the possibility of recovery was virtually non-existent. But the message had also hinted at the taking of a hostage, specific details were not given and the line had been abruptly cut. Educated guesswork was required here and Francesca Paso excelled at that. At the top of her hostage shortlist was Lorenzo Galiano. He had not been seen since Milo Standish had witnessed him being dragged into the back of Pozzi's removal van on the night of the attack. On Paso's list, his father ran him a poor second. As a hostage, Lorenzo was the most valuable commodity going. Hostage takers always, by preference, went for youth. By far, the greatest pressure was that of time. In brief, the window of opportunity for a rescue attempt was very small. It needed the combined resources of intelligence agencies, police and the military. The latter, under the command of a colonel of military intelligence, were to be sent in two helicopters;

authorisation and orders down the line were translated into action with a speed that amazed Paso. "What on earth did you say to them, Milo?" she asked.

"Oh, I just appealed to their sense of patriotism," he said off-handedly.

Standish was worried that once again a lack of intelligence information could compromise the outcome of the operation. Identification of Calderari, *l'ombelico di Sicilia,* as the most viable collection point for the smuggling of the paintings out of the country was based on the indistinct and imprecise tip-off of an anonymous caller. He was inclined to accept Paso's assertion that the content of the message was, in all likelihood, genuine, though deliberate deception could not be ruled out. If, as Paso believed on rather scanty evidence, it originated from the Galiano household, therefore either father or son, the odds were broadly even as to which one, though logic and recent experience were weighted in favour of the son. The father was altogether a poor candidate for the display of moral courage required for such an action. In this conclusion, the intelligence officers were in for a surprise.

Calculating a timescale, therefore, for the movement of the goods to the pick-up point was virtually impossible. To be blunt, no one knew precisely from where they were coming. A map obtained from the Commune of Enna showed the location of Galiano properties in the area. Even this was wildly out of date though it did indicate that the family estates were less extensive than had originally been imagined. So, it was on the basis of a balance of probabilities that three properties were pinpointed. Santa Rosa, Costiforte and Altrabia all lay some thirty kilometres or so south, southwest and north of the town of Enna. Standish was inclined to reject Altrabia as too inaccessible for the terrorists' purposes. Sharma and Paso disagreed. The jihadis who had been infiltrated into the island from Zuwara needed to be contained somewhere well out of sight. Altrabia was perfect for this and known not to be farmed, though they conceded that it was a much less convenient venue for the interim storage of the stolen paintings, which the thieves would be keen to move on as soon as possible without attracting attention. Pozzi's removal van had to be within easy striking distance of Calderari. It was a cumbersome vehicle and on the kinds of roads that surrounded Calderari, it would barely be capable of reaching speeds of more than thirty or forty kilometres per hour at best.

Paso got in touch with Commissario Carlo Leone, spent a moment trying to persuade him, then urgently requested that a police helicopter be employed to patrol the area around the three properties in the hope of spotting the van either still at its present location or, with a stroke of luck, *en route* to the Calderari airstrip. Forward thinking as always, the commissario was able to tell her that he was already ahead of her and had needed no persuasion either as to the logic of the request or its urgency. His seniors, however, had thought otherwise. It was a large area to cover, the day was getting on, hadn't he heard there was a crisis down at Lampedusa, resources…resources…etc., etc. Carlo Leone was generally a patient man. Generally. Not one to bang the desk, unless…the son of a prominent Sicilian citizen was being held hostage while millions of euros worth of Sicilian heritage was being abducted from the country. They caved in, albeit with bad grace. Such is the premium, remarked Paso, set on the preservation of official reputations. Those official reputations were, along with the intelligence team, blissfully unaware that the much discussed Pozzi's removal van was playing no part whatsoever in the transportation of either art or hostage.

Eventually, reports were to come in from police HQ that the helicopter had failed in its mission to spot the removal van. There was a very simple and rather obvious reason for this. The van could not be seen because it was no longer visible from the air. Nico's final orders had been to drive it into the shell of the old burnt-out barn where, among the charred timbers, its black-painted roof blended into its surroundings. The mutilated body of a man in an oil-smeared boiler suit would not be discovered for several days.

The range of the police helicopter covered a radius of approximately thirty kilometres from the centre of the town of Enna; cars, caravans, motorcycles and clearly marked commercial vehicles abounded. A dark blue unmarked furniture van was not among them. In the vicinity of the old farmstead of Altrabia, a military transport truck had been spotted on the road travelling south to Enna. A radio check to police HQ in Enna elicited the totally erroneous intelligence that the military had been carrying out exercises in the region whereupon interest in the truck faded. Meanwhile, the military wing of the operation was faring even worse. One of the two UH-1N Huey helicopters was grounded with mechanical problems, the other had been diverted at short notice to the island of Lampedusa where a new migrant crisis was erupting after a dingy had sunk a few miles offshore with large potential loss of life and a search for survivors was underway. The news could hardly be worse and the intelligence team at Aspra was in low spirits.

"Maybe," said Ravi Sharma, "we're wrong about Calderari. It's all based on very tentative evidence."

"Yes, but Francesca says the caller referred to *L'ombelico di Sicilia*, the navel of Sicily. The airstrip at Calderari's the nearest to it. Inconclusive, I know. Who was the caller and how did *he* know, if it was a 'he'? We're not even sure of that. Whoever it was knew something of the area. What else do we have to go on?" Standish sounded pessimistic.

"Ninety-five per cent waiting, you told us in training, for five per cent action. I'd settle for one per cent right now," said Sharma ruefully.

Standish's mobile rang. "It's Leone," he said.

"Carlo, any news? Nothing," he rung off. And the waiting went on. And on.

It was much later in the evening of that long hot day that a result, if that was what it could be called, was finally delivered by a subdued Carlo Leone. In default of the police helicopter having come up with anything of interest and in view of the failure of the military response, a police SUV had been dispatched from Enna to the Calderari airfield. All was quiet, the airfield deserted apart from a couple of small private aircraft parked on grass close to the runway. Darkness had fallen and a search of the area took some time but at length, the discovery was made of a military transport truck parked behind a disused farm building some distance away. Leone wanted to know if it could have been the same one spotted earlier from the helicopter. Quite possibly, he was told, and someone somewhere had been in error—there had been no military exercises in the region within living memory. 'And while you're on, Commissario, we found fragments of a substance on the floor of the truck which forensics think is called *gesso*. Does that mean anything to you?' Leone swore and called on the name of the divinity. The birds had well and truly flown. But how and, above all, where? Because of the migrant crisis at Lampedusa, aircraft had been flying backwards and forwards all over the place. Nothing could have been easier than for one more to slip through the military observation net, headed for God knows where.

Among the members of the team gathered at Aspra, options were endlessly debated. At one time, there was almost a consensus in favour of North Africa, and that probably meant Libya: A country riven with internecine upheaval, where international jihadism found a ready breeding ground for recruitment, where effective surveillance could not be guaranteed and control of what came and went was non-existent. A vast country, a desert state on the edge of Sub-Saharan Africa. Reliable intelligence was almost impossible to come by. Lavinia Dyer headed the opposition to that idea. Who in their right mind would be prepared to send experts to travel to Libya to authenticate paintings and negotiate terms for their purchase? Kidnap and ransom par for the course. Even more, it would be madness to commit such valuable commodities to the risks of a violently unstable environment. So where? The arguments went backwards and forwards. Most European countries exercised tight controls about what entered and left their airspace. Discussion covered practically the whole of the Mediterranean basin, anywhere an aircraft could fly to from the navel of Sicily and that meant literally *anywhere*. It didn't, however, seem probable that the Caliphate high command would countenance the paintings being passed outside the sphere of their control. The outlook for the missing paintings, said Sharma, even more for the missing hostage was on the downside of dismal.

But if Ravi Sharma had remembered all his training, he would have recalled something else he and his fellow recruits had been told. That once in a while, something totally unexpected turns up out of the blue. Usually out of character with how the normal course of events in an intelligence operation was expected to unravel. It was fully twenty-four hours after the discovery of the empty truck and the team was sitting around morosely with a last drink before retiring to bed. Soon after midnight, Standish's mobile rang.

"Milo, it's Carlo. Have you got a spare guest room at the villa? Is it made up and ready? Great, I'll be with you in an hour. You've got a guest."

And so, it was that forty-five minutes later, Carlo Leone appeared with the guest in tow. Paso had opened the door to them. For a moment, she stood there dumbstruck.

"Do we get to come in?" asked Leone with a laugh.

An exhausted but smiling young man followed them into the house. Lorenzo Galiano was finally among people he had come to regard as friends.

Paso and Sharma, discovering it was some time since he had eaten, disappeared into the villa kitchen to produce food for the unexpected guest.

"It was the commander who let me go. 'While you're alive,' he said, 'you're the guarantee of your father's cooperation. And we still need him. Soon his usefulness will be over. Then you will live your life looking over your shoulder. Believe me, we shall be there.'" Lorenzo, recalling the words, shivered involuntarily. "Not much of a prospect, is it?" he said.

"Lorenzo," said Paso, "listen to me. The fight against terrorism, of one kind or another, will go on. It is the nature of our world. It's never been any different. If I could promise you freedom from threat, I would. But we all live under the same threat. What ultimately can bring it to an end, I don't know. I don't think you'll find anyone in this room who does. But I do know, in fact I passionately believe, that we have to go on trying. You've had a terrible time. Use it to help us. We need to debrief you as thoroughly as possible. Every last detail you can remember—sights, sounds, smells—nothing will be unimportant or too trivial. Milo and Ravi will tell you that without intelligence, we can go nowhere. Give us everything you've got. I'm sorry; it will be a long and tiring process."

"We'll give you all the help we can," said Sharma. "You'll experience moments of amazing clarity when the tiniest details will come to you. That's what we need. You'll also misremember, sometimes obvious facts will evade you. At times like that, don't worry. It's a normal part of the process."

"There's quite a lot we can do to help you unlock it," Paso added. "Trigger memories and so on. Milo will take you through the main narrative. But not tonight and not until you're rested. Now, time for bed, you're all in."

* * *

The initial debriefing of Lorenzo took place over the next three days and then Standish was summoned back to London for his own debriefing of Operation Persephone; Sharma was to be called later. Paso and Sharma were to take over Lorenzo but would employ a less formal technique. Sharma took the young man, close to himself in age, for long walks along the Tyrrhenian coast, dropping into bars and cafes here and there, often talking about things quite unrelated to the operation. He found him easy company; they were the same age—give or take—though from very different backgrounds and with different life experiences. The laddish young man about town shone through Lorenzo's accounts of an endless stream of girls, so Sharma marvelled that someone who had spent so much time on sex had been able to devote any time at all at forging a successful career in high finance. On Sharma's part, his personal life was more muted in tone. He felt there was a tacit acknowledgment between them of his own sexuality. Nothing said in so many words but an understanding with which both men were comfortable and if Lorenzo was aware of his companion's relationship with Milo Standish, it didn't come up. Sometimes they would have a laugh if one of them caught sight of a good-looking girl or boy. A degree of good-natured mutual teasing helped foster a relaxed atmosphere. Afterwards, Sharma admitted to his intelligence colleagues that he feared there was little he had gleaned that would add to the store of knowledge being built up about jihadi activity.

"Don't disparage what you've learnt," Paso remarked encouragingly. "What seems next to nothing now may well prove useful later."

"He speaks about his father all the time. Mostly in terms of disappointment but I think the fact that it comes up so often shows a real affection underneath, frustrated though by Luca's lack of response. And lack of openness."

"Hardly surprising," said Paso, "given the mess he's got himself and the family into."

"Lorenzo thinks he was forced into it. Something happened out of his control, not just greed. You know Milo's theory about the blackmail?"

"It's become more than a theory, Ravi. About underage boys. Ask Lavinia; I think Milo's spoken to her about it."

"Lorenzo certainly doesn't know anything about that. If he did, it would have come up. He's not shy to talk about things. I've found him very open. Especially about his girlfriends! Like father, like son. Luca had a string of mistresses."

"Hm. Not the cheapest of hobbies. No wonder he needed money. Has he said anything about the jihadi youth?"

They were sitting in the villa's salon. It was a hot sultry night; windows open to the terrace that faced across the gardens looking out to sea. Lorenzo, tired tonight, had gone to bed early and Lavinia Dyer had taken herself off to her room to work on her account of the attack on the gallery.

"Not very much," Sharma said in answer to her question. "A very general description that could fit anyone about the same age. Brutal in manner, he said, and uncouth, but uncouth in a deliberate kind of way. I asked him what he meant. But all he could say was that he thought the youth was better educated than he wanted to seem. He spoke Arabic but probably not very fluently. Though Lorenzo admits he's no judge. He doesn't understand the language himself. I suppose the little he's told me, Francesca, ties in with what you've said. No names ever mentioned. I know some of us are thinking the same thing. Khalil Khourasan. Could it be him? I don't know; there's nothing to go on and what little we've got doesn't chime with the Khalil I remember."

"The Khalil you remember," said Paso gently, "doesn't exist anymore. Khalil was radicalised. The whole point of that is to produce a totally different person, one even his own family wouldn't recognise."

"I guess you're right. I wonder what Milo will have to tell us when he comes back tomorrow."

"I haven't come back empty-handed, but I've got less than I hoped. God, the flight was tedious—delays for this, that and the other. Security seemed tighter this time. Everyone was irritable, losing baggage and kids complaining about the heat." Milo stretched and threw himself into an armchair in the salon. Sharma put a Campari and soda into his hands.

"Thank you. I've been looking forward to this for hours," he smiled at him.

Lavinia also accepted a drink from Sharma. "We're glad you're back; we're dying to hear how it went. Francesca's taken Lorenzo out shopping. He wanted a few things. Poor boy landed up here with nothing."

"I'll tell you what I can while they're out and you can bring Francesca up to date later. Before anything else, Ravi, the Chief's had to give up and go back into hospital. Not looking good, I'm afraid. I saw him briefly. Very poorly. My heart went out to him. He's got no family and in the nature of things, few friends. Still, battling on. And naturally wanted to know everything. That's what keeps him going. Of course, while he's out of it, the vultures have started to gather. I hardly need to tell you but I'm sure you can guess who's leading the pack, baying for blood! The minister was surprisingly helpful. But basically, the guy knows bugger all. And one thing more, you're not being called back yet, at least until the next phase is over. Now, the operational review. We'd admitted the failures of Persephone and that took the wind out their sails. Found it difficult to accept that the lack of pre-operational intelligence was down to lack of resources. And when they did come around to it, naturally the Italians got it all in the neck. Some truth in that but as you know, not wholly fair. I won't have Sandro and Francesca thinking they let us down. By the way, how is Sandro?"

"Out of hospital. He's fine, gone home to recoup a bit. And fall out with his bosses, so he says. You know Sandro; he'll be back when he can."

"Our stake in it was just as important, with a British national on the loose, murdering left, right and centre. That's the British priority now. We have to find Khalil Khourasan."

Later in their room, Standish asked, "Ravi, have you had any luck with Lorenzo? Does he remember anything that can help us?"

"Nothing definite. But a jihadi youth keeps cropping up in the various accounts. I know it could be anyone, but I've got an instinct…and Francesca seems to agree."

"Hold on to it. Whoever it is, he could give us the clue we need. I didn't mention it downstairs earlier but there's a lot of concern in London that events here have conspired to distract us from trying to identify the money man behind this affair. Peter's had his theories and you know how sharp he can be. The videos of the CCTV we watched with Sandro would confirm one of them but they need to be a hell of a lot more conclusive than that. In legal terms, the evidence is entirely circumstantial. London's demanding more. I'm going to have to try and get to the Dominican again. Well, my dear Ravi, it's been too long."

"I've been waiting to hear you say that."

"I think I'll take a shower," said Standish, "wash the journey off a bit."

"Wouldn't it be better to shower afterwards?" enquired Ravi. "Save time now."

* * *

135

Dyer had wired her report of the Palermo robbery. Keymer liked the local colour that she had given it and wanted more on the tie-up with the Soldiers of the Caliphate and the vulnerability of artworks generally to terrorism. He'd then turned to her interview with the journalist from Osservatore Vaticano and couldn't quite get off the subject, Dyer felt. Not sure why. Another of Keymer's hidden agendas.

"I tell you, Ferdy, the guy's a weasel. You may think he's going to dish the dirt on the Vatican, but he's a weasel, a conceited, over-opinionated weasel! And I don't understand what the big deal is. The world's falling apart and you get knicker-twisted over some grubby goings-on in the Holy See. What's it all about? Who the hell's leaning on you? No one's leaning? That's what you say, Ferdy…Why *are* the Catholic hierarchy over there winding on about the church's reputation? They're struggling to keep the faithful onboard. Ferdy, don't make me laugh, I bet the money still rolls in.

"They wouldn't just happen to be trying to divert attention from some of their own problems by any chance. Bishops falling by the wayside…Oh! Now I get it. That's it, isn't it? Bloody hell, how did you get mixed up in all this? You wife's *what*? Christ, Ferdy, if you'll forgive the expression. Well, this creep from Osservatore may know, or think he knows, what he's talking about; some of it may even be true but if I were his boss, he'd be reporting on what good Catholic mothers give their kids for breakfast. Yes, I know I *said* he was well-qualified, he's been at Osservatore long enough, he must have learnt something. If you don't believe me, send Gerda over; she had a lot of contact with that lot when she was with *Reuters*, she'll know straightaway and she'll agree with me…so you don't like what he's done. Ferdy, he knows if he spills too many beans, he can kiss his pension goodbye, that's still how things work in the Holy See. Well…perhaps there aren't that many beans to spill. Francis is the new broom, he's aware of what's been lurking in the Vatican's dirty corners. Probably that's why he moved into St Martha's House so that he could keep an eye on what they were all up to.

"I can't get more worked up about it than that. I only saw him to oblige you as I was *en route* anyway. You might be generous enough to say thank you. As it is, I got here after the attack was over, and a pretty bloody affair it was. I suppose I was lucky not to get caught up in it. But I feel real bad for the others. Get a statement from Actaeon about Erik Seth. He was the best art photographer in the world, it's the least they can do…Yes, well, I'm feeling quite cut up about Vassilio Pritsi. Amazing young man, already high up in the Ministry of Culture here. Quite an achievement at his age. Those two are a big loss to the art world. Even Casamassa took a bullet in the arm; apparently Matteo was amazing, lucky to escape with his life…

"No, I'm not, don't be so bloody cheeky. OK Ferdy…watch this space."

* * *

The next day was bright and breezy. The Tyrrhenian Sea was grey-green, white-flecked and with enough swell to bring one or two hopeful youths with surfboards to try their luck. But too tame for proper surfing—a coastline not noted for it—fun for learners and no danger of being caught by the undertow. Very young children floated in on diminutive boards with squeals of delight. Older ones gave up with shrugs that said 'it's hopeless', kicked a football about for a while and then threw themselves down on a sandy bit of beach to soak in the sun and talk about whatever teenagers talk about. Ravi Sharma leant on the rails of the balcony of his and Standish's room and surveyed the scene with a mixture of resignation and restlessness. The failure of Operation Persephone had created a kind of limbo in the progress of his life. Ninety-five per cent hanging around. He had begun to wonder, was it enough for a life? Milo had come back from London with orders to continue the hunt for Khalil Khourasan. He knew it had to be, Khalil was a suspected terrorist killer. Khalil, friend of his youth, close enough to be a brother, he and Sanjeev had shared everything with him. They'd laughed, they'd cried, they'd cursed, they'd celebrated together the milestones of their lives. Sharma had no appetite for what he knew lay ahead. He'd begun to doubt whether his relationship with Milo Standish could see him through this crisis. For a time, he'd wondered whether British Intelligence would eventually lose interest if Khalil kept out of the country. Small chance of that. Khalil was the link to everything else.

Chapter Eight

Rome
2 July

It was a sultry summer's day in Rome. Members of the Provincial Chapter of the Order of Preachers had been meeting all morning. Items of general business had been dealt with and attention turned to more pastoral matters. In particular, the Master wished to raise an issue in respect of a member of the order where there was a need for consultation. He took pains to assure his colleagues that this was just a question of an individual's safety and therefore, a matter of brotherly concern. An issue, he said, to which this Chapter was no stranger. It had been at the forefront of their minds more than once in the past, but he sought guidance on how to proceed further in the matter. One or two older members shifted awkwardly in their seats—they suspected what was coming. They must all, the Master continued, have experienced a deep sense of anxiety that the life of a member of the Order had been seriously threatened. He was, of course, referring to their esteemed and greatly loved brother, Antonio Marcetti. Threatened, not this time, by negative comment in the media or vague insinuations; the press had always been sharply divided in their opinions depending on whom you read. This time, the threat arose from an actual incident that had occurred in a public space. Potentially, there might have been serious consequences for other members of the travelling public. Happily, that did not arise because of timely intervention by an official of the railways, to whom the Order was indebted. Had that official not been on hand, there is no telling what might have taken place on board that train on that day. To state it plainly, a young man, a fellow traveller, had threatened to take the life of Father Antonio, as far as can be gathered, on account of his public pronouncements about the flow of migrants into Europe from the Middle East and North Africa."

"We have been here many times before, Master," remarked an elderly friar, "and it seems to me that our advice to Father Antonio has been consistently ignored."

"I agree," commented another, "and this time, I think a line has been crossed."

"You have the authority, Master, backed by this council to place our brother under a vow of silence in respect of promulgating his personal views to members of the media," continued the first speaker.

"May I offer an alternative view?" The speaker was one of the younger and newer friars to sit on the Provincial Chapter.

"Please speak, Ambrose."

"I am puzzled by the details of this incident."

"In what way, Father?"

"In all his publicly expressed views, Antonio has made it very clear that he has enormous sympathy for the plight of migrants who are fleeing persecution and death in their own lands to seek a better life for themselves and their families in the west. That's a view that none of us here would, I imagine, wish to challenge. In which case, why would a person from the migrant community feel in any way threatened by Antonio's public statements?"

"If," intervened another of the younger friars, "the youth did come from the migrant community."

"Exactly," said Ambrose. "There is no logic in how the incident has been reported in the media. It seems to me more likely that the threat would have emanated from the ranks of those who, as Antonio has claimed, are funding the illegal trafficking of human beings. He has quite strongly asserted he would be prepared to name names."

"It's absurd!" expostulated the elderly friar. "Where does he get all this information from?"

"Antonio has built up many contacts over a long period of time. Networking, they call it these days."

"Networking! Dangerous backstreet gossip!"

The Master coughed discreetly.

"I venture to suggest yet another possibility," continued Ambrose. "The countries where these financial backers are based will surely be very concerned to prevent this from becoming public knowledge. It doesn't take much to imagine the political consequences of having prominent citizens accused of participation in a people-smuggling operation, proven or not."

"If what I think you're suggesting could be the case, Ambrose, we are getting into very deep waters. Too deep for this council or indeed for our Order. I appreciate all your opinions, brothers, and thank you for your wisdom but I must bring us back to the only issue that directly concerns us. How to protect a member of our community and safeguard members of the public. I shall speak to Antonio and I bid us all to call to mind that there is a time to speak out and a time to keep silence. This chapter is concluded. The Grace of Our Lord…"

"It won't work," remarked the elderly friar to the colleague sitting alongside him. "He's not taken any notice before."

"This time he has to, brother, else we might all become the targets of extremism."

"Well, this Order's no stranger to that. We invented it."

Master's Study

"So you should know, Antonio, that your brothers are concerned about your safety and," he added, "the safety of this Order." The Master stood at the window of his study overlooking the courtyard. "Incidents of that kind are not what this Order is about. I'm not requesting you; I'm now requiring you to desist from making any public statements at all on this particular topic, and maybe it's better for the time being on any other matter. You are under obedience; you will understand what that means and all it implies."

Leaving the Master, Marcetti went down to the gardens where he made for a quiet, private arbour, a favoured place for reflection and, for once, unoccupied. He knew that what had just happened heralded a great change in his life, one forced upon him but strangely, not unwelcome. He was tired of confrontation, of fighting for good causes, tired of challenging the privileged, of being seen as the champion of the oppressed. Half a lifetime spent in conflict. It had drained his spirit and sapped his mental energies. 'Burnt out' was the expression used by the pundits these days. Appropriate now that his Order had finally extinguished the flame that had burned as long as he could remember. More and more, his mind had begun to turn to the place where he was born, where he, a son of the soil, was now a stranger. For generations, his family had been subsistence farmers in the impoverished southern province of Calabria, never stirring beyond the confines of their village. He'd been the first to break free, noticed by the village schoolmaster for his quick wit and sharp mind and recommended to the old parish priest who dropped by one day with the enlightened bishop of the remote southern diocese. He was taken out of class and, to his delight and the relief of his parents, asked if he'd like to study at the secondary school up in Cosenza. After that, there was no looking back. His future seemed to be mapped out. He couldn't remember when the idea of priesthood first came up. Later in life, when he was occasionally asked how it had come about—people always wanted to know how and why—he used to reply that it seemed a good idea at the time. An answer that amused some and infuriated others! Perhaps the time was approaching when he needed to return to his roots, spend time with his family. Take an interest in the younger, growing generation. He would seek permission to spend time away from this place and try to rediscover his native origins. But first, there were loose ends to be tied up.

He knew whom he had to talk to, the question was how. He listed the options in his mind. One name stood out. The American journalist who'd interviewed him in Venice after the Installation of the Patriarch. He hadn't been very co-operative—evasive, to put it mildly. But if anyone could, she would have the means of contacting British Intelligence. She could be the route to Milo Standish. He flicked open his mobile to check whether he had the number she had given him. A simple message to set up a meeting. The Order had forbidden him to speak out publicly. This meeting would be private, discreet, wouldn't contravene the vow of obedience he was under. And once he'd done it, the book could be closed forever on a most troubling chapter in his priestly life. At least, that was what he believed. He needed a secure line. A public payphone or better still, a private telephone. Where? He had it. Father Paulo, the little flat next to St Callixtus Church where Paulo said mass. And he could check over the church's suitability for a meeting. Across the river in Trastavere. Marcetti got up, went to his room in the house, changed into civilian clothes and slipped out of a back door unnoticed.

Paulo woke with a start in his chair by the glass door that opened onto the miniscule balcony outside his living room. The doorbell had rung several times before he collected himself and muttering, struggled up to answer it.

"Antonio, what a surprise, come in, come in, I was just saying my Daily Office, I'll make us coffee...no, no, I want some too. Yes, of course, these mobile gadgets are so unreliable; use my telephone, over there on the desk."

So, by this somewhat devious route, Milo Standish, lounging on the terrace of the villa in Aspra, was informed of the meeting proposed between himself and Father Antonio Marcetti of the Order of Preachers. Confirmation of his attendance was to be provided by a message to be left for Father Antonio at the headquarters in Rome which read, *please thank Father Antonio for his mass for our beloved sister, Rosamund.* Father Bonifacio, answering the telephone, dutifully conveyed the message word for word.

* * *

The Church of St Callixtus I, Pope and Former Slave 9 July

You wouldn't have found it on any of the usual tourist maps of the city of Rome. Hidden away in one of the less fashionable areas south of Vatican City, removed from those parts now favoured by the upwardly mobile, St Callixtus was, nevertheless, ancient and rumoured to be late 10th century on a 3rd century foundation—though that had been disputed. The half-dozen or so faithful who attended mass regularly couldn't have cared less about architectural exactitude. It was here, always had been and so were they. Father Paulo, parish priest— looked eighty but was probably ten years older—dutifully said mass, well, more accurately stumbled through it, at 8 o'clock on Sundays and half past seven in the week for holy days of obligation. Days when you were expected— no, not expected—*required* to attend. At St Callixtus, they included an array of saints many of which, on account of their legendary origin, no longer featured in the Church's calendar. But so what? Let them demote all the saints in heaven if they wanted to; the faithful of St Callixtus prayed to the saints they'd always prayed to and always would. '*Noantri*', the residents had once been known as, 'we others', distinct from the metropolitan, cosmopolitan elites that seemed to take over the Queen of Cities, the latest version of the barbarian invasions that had descended on her from time immemorial. The seven hills had always held a peculiar fascination for outsiders, since Romulus and Remus had been suckled by the she-wolf; she, no doubt to her surprise, found she had a child on her hands with fratricidal tendencies. But Fate had been played out to its inevitable conclusion. Roma became Roma, not Rema.

Standish's directions to the venue chosen by Marcetti had proved confusing. Wrong turns, sometimes up blind alleys, no one could help. 'St Callixtus?' A shake of the head and a shrug. *Not around here, mate, try... Have you got the name right?* Always, there would be a tourist looking for somewhere that didn't exist. But then he turned a corner, stepped around a pile of rubbish left in the street and there it was. Small, grey stone, tucked into the corner of a tiny square, blending into the dilapidated buildings around it, stonework streaked where runnels of dirty water had run down for years. The small-paned windows were covered in rusty wire mesh, probably put there in the Second World War, now a sort of protection against youthful hooliganism. Though if youth even knew of its existence, it would be a miracle.

The double doors bleached by the sun looked firmly closed. Standish pushed at one of them and it swung open with a series of creaks. Stepping inside from the sunlight, he could at first make nothing out in the gloom. Then gradually, the interior began to take shape. A single aisle with chairs on either side led up to the high altar. A flickering red lamp hung suspended from the ceiling. The altar reredos pretended to be baroque but did not quite make it. At its centre was a sorrowful Crucifixus with a coy Madonna and a very effeminate St John. Something stirred, the shape of a figure kneeling at a wooden prie-dieu in front of a small side altar on the right. Standish walked halfway down the aisle and then sat in the centre of a row on the left-hand side. For a few minutes nothing happened, then the figure rose, stood for a moment, made the sign of the cross and came over to where Standish was sitting, taking a chair a few places away from him.

"A little different from the Patriarch's dining room. I'm sorry to drag you all the way from London for this." He looked around him.

"I wasn't in London, nearer at hand when your message reached me, but still a journey and, I hope, a journey of discovery," said Standish.

"I've known this church since I was a student at the Angelicum. The priest who's here, retired now, was here then. The congregation's smaller and forty years older," he smiled. "St Callixtus. Have you heard of him? St Callixtus I, Pope and former slave, of humble background. As a young man, he was accused of mishandling some funds he'd been entrusted with. He was condemned to work in the mines. For reasons not entirely clear, Marcia, the wife of the emperor, intervened on his behalf and he was released. She believed in his innocence and had been impressed, I think, that the Christian community had rallied around. Thus, began his career in the Church, which led to the Throne of Peter. From slave to Pope. Not bad, eh? Indulge me a little longer, Milo, if you would. The real story begins now. As Pope, Callixtus was very tolerant towards sinners. Very understanding and forgiving. Lax, his great opponent Hippolytus said, but he was a real reactionary. Father Paulo told me the story when I first came here, a green country boy bewildered by the big city. I've never forgotten it."

"I was wondering, why here?" said Standish.

"Not just nostalgia nor on a whim. Were you followed?"

"I don't think so. If I had been, they must have been as confused as I was."

Marcetti laughed. "Now you understand my directions!"

"Why the subterfuge, Antonio?"

"To avoid compromising you and myself."

"I was pleased to get your message and anxious to see you. When we met in Venice, you promised your help, within the limitations of your office, you said."

"That remains the case."

"I would like to find out how far those limits extend."

"Not as far as you would like, Milo. But perhaps further than you expect."

"I'm here today at your invitation. I'd like to believe that you and I have a common purpose in mind."

"That is why I invited you."

"Then let me tell you how things stand at present. Since we last spoke in Venice, events have moved on. There have been a number of deaths connected to the investigation I am conducting on behalf of the British Government. We don't believe they were accidental, though in two instances, prima facie evidence might suggest that. It is possible that a British national working with the so-called Soldiers of the Caliphate is directly responsible. I've been given the job of tracking this person down. At least four of the deaths are those of Italian citizens and took place on Italian soil. Technically, therefore, a matter for the Italian authorities. The other death, a British woman, also occurred on Italian soil, wife of a prominent British businessman, a well-known philanthropist—again a case for the police here. However, we have reached an accommodation with our Italian colleagues.

My service is to be given a free hand to pursue the British suspect in return for passing on to our Italian counterparts any information we receive that might assist the search for works of art stolen recently from a gallery in Palermo. Paintings worth many millions of dollars, now in the hands of an international terrorist organisation of which the suspect is a part. That is where you may be able to help."

"I don't understand. Why would this suspect be of any interest to me especially? Notwithstanding that he may be a killer who should be brought to justice."

"You could identify him; we believe you know him—that is to say, you have met him."

"How is that possible?"

"On the morning express from Roma to Venezia. He left the train at Bologna."

For a long moment, Marcetti was silent.

"How do you make the link between those deaths and that bothersome youth?"

143

"More than 'bothersome', Antonio; he threatened to kill you. Only the arrival of the conductor prevented it."

"You think he would have carried out his threat?"

"I have no doubt about it."

"What makes you so certain?"

"We know him too."

Marcetti said nothing, waiting for Standish to continue.

"At the time he confronted you on the train, he was a member of British Intelligence."

Watching Marcetti's face, Standish knew a connection had been made, a corner had been turned. One of those moments in life when one would like to retrace steps but knows it isn't possible. Whatever happened next was inexorable.

"Acting with your authority and...under your orders." A statement, not a question.

"Up to a point. He exceeded the remit he was given."

"Ah! British diplomatic speak. Forgive me, Milo, but please don't insult my intelligence." He was angry now, turned away, stared at the altar and shook his head. "If I were a lesser man than I believe myself to be, I would ask for an explanation."

"I'd like to give one anyway. An explanation in part, not an apology."

"Do I have a choice?"

"You can always get up and leave."

Nothing happened; the friar continued to stare at the altar. He shook his head again as if to say, little chance of help from that direction.

Standish resumed, "Consider the context for a moment. You're a prominent member of the Dominican Order. You have a reputation, built up over a lifetime of devoting yourself to high-profile populist causes. You have been supported by your co-religionists, both your superiors in the Order and in the wider church. It's no secret you have the respect and admiration of Pope Francis. Earlier this year, you made a very public pronouncement to the effect that certain European member states were guilty of financing the trafficking of migrant people from North Africa and the Middle East. Your claim, at least as it has been reported, is that the purpose of this operation is to establish a long-term strategy for the subversion of the liberal democracies in order to bring the political far right into prominence. I presume I needn't elaborate." He paused, Marcetti shifted in his chair and turned to look at him.

"The British Government took the view that such disclosures would be a serious threat to political stability across the continent, perhaps even to public order. All this is known to you, Antonio, my apologies for labouring the details. Hardly surprising, therefore, that a premium should be set on securing your silence."

"By assassination!"

"By no means. It was decided that you could be intimidated into silence, at the very least to encourage you to stop and think. Had you considered the

144

implications of going public? There was a political naivety in what you were doing. All very well for a first-century desert prophet, a less appropriate approach for a monastic in a twenty-first century global society. The youth on the train was meant to remind you that our words have consequences far beyond the histrionics of the moment."

"Is that answer meant to satisfy me?"

"It is the only answer I have."

"And you still feel you have the right to ask for my help?"

"The right, no, the need can scarcely be overstated. It was expressly my plan and mine alone. I take full responsibility for what happened. That is the reason I shall go beyond my own remit now and tell you one thing more. I trust you will keep it within the bounds of confidentiality that we share. For your protection, the youth's name is Khourasan, Khalil Khourasan, a Syrian Muslim whom we believe was radicalised by his uncle on a visit to Damascus. He is being urgently sought by my agency. You never heard me say that, just as this conversation has never taken place."

After this exchange, Standish could not have said how much time elapsed. He was conscious only of his own breathing and the beating of his heart. He stared in front of him, focussing on the reredos behind the altar: The dying Christus, eyes closed, no longer engaged with this world, the absurdly young Madonna not seeming to be part of the scene at all, and the young man, lost, bewildered.

"I believe you are an honourable man, Milo, working for a not very honourable profession."

"If we do nothing, a great many deaths will follow. Deaths are recorded every day. Lampedusa again, you will have heard. How many this time? Hundreds. It's become commonplace. I'm told the Aegean Sea is littered with the corpses of the drowned, washed up on holiday beaches," Standish paused.

Marcetti got to his feet, walked into the aisle, genuflected to the altar and turned back towards Standish. Reaching into his jacket pocket, he took out a buff-coloured envelope, held it out to the British spy, seemed to hesitate and then placed it carefully on the chair beside Standish.

"Go with God, Milo."

He walked out of the church.

Standish didn't move. Then he glanced down at the envelope, saw his name handwritten on the front, stared at it and picked it up. For a moment he did nothing, turning it over in his hands, thinking about the conversation. There was finality about it, yet strangely it didn't feel incomplete. They would probably never speak to each other again but might never need to. He slit the envelope open with his finger.

Inside were two papers, each carefully folded. The first one was a photocopy of a death certificate for one Rosamund Cross, lately a patient in the Mater Dei Hospital, Rome, attesting to the fact that the said person had died in the hospital—cause of death, heart failure. The second was a cutting evidently taken from a medical journal concerning a poisonous substance which, if injected into the human body, resulted in death within thirty to sixty minutes from heart failure.

"Even in the Republic of Italy, we're disposed to take the falsifying of medical records seriously." Menotti and Standish sat together at an outside table at the Ristorante Horatio in Trastavere under the shade of a vine-covered pergola. White-coated waiters flitted between tables that were filled to capacity in one of the best-known restaurants of the area. They had managed to secure a table at the edge of the terrace and well to the back, giving space enough for private conversation.

"You'll be happy to leave it in my hands?" He dropped a buff-coloured envelope into the briefcase at the side of his chair.

"Of course, Sandro, all we have to agree on is the timing. I don't want my guy to do a runner if he's warned by someone in the Mater Dei. Marcetti didn't say how he got the information, so we have to assume there's someone on the inside. Maybe not involved themselves—owing a favour…you know how these things work. If that's the case…I'll leave it to you."

Menotti nodded, "More useful left where they are. What are your plans for the London end?"

"Not my problem, thank God. I'll let the politicians and lawyers worry about that. Shrewd guess, they'll try to cover it up. Last thing they'll want is a public trial. A pillar of the establishment. Can you imagine it? They'll try to immobilise him somehow. How do you immobilise a billionaire?"

"They could do worse than throw the bastard to the Caliphate! They'd come up with something imaginative!"

"When a government's been badly hurt, they're not inclined to be too finicky. But I doubt they'd go that far."

"Well, Milo, keep your distance. If your people are anything like mine, they'll try to stick your hands in the dirty water."

The two men fell silent while the waiter placed espressos in front of them.

"*Grazie.*"

"*Prego.*"

Menotti leaned back in his chair, stirring sugar into his coffee.

"How's the team doing?"

"Keen to get you back."

"In a few days, I hope. Usual fight on my hands. Question, how many intelligence officers does it take to find ten stolen paintings? Answer, too many!"

Standish laughed. "Then don't tell them what I tell our trainees. The job's always ninety-five per cent waiting. What Ravi calls 'hanging about'!"

"*Dio mio*! We'd all be out of work! Have you made any headway with Khalil Khourasan?"

"A couple of leads but nothing very substantial. Ravi's convinced he's the youth who was with the group at Altrabia, based largely on what Lorenzo says. Francesca's hunch is that it was Khalil that night in the gallery. The one who threatened to rape her, probably the one who shot you."

"I wouldn't mind getting my hands on that little bastard. Don't worry, he's all yours."

"So Sandro, what's your guess, where are the pictures now?"

Menotti shook his head. "What's that saying you have, how long is a piece of string? Does that make sense? Not in Italy at any rate and not yet hanging, I think, on some billionaire's wall. I've had an expert go out to Calderari to examine the tyre marks on the runway. Incredible what they can come up with. She said she found one set of very heavy treads. Probably some kind of small transport. Not quite what you'd expect at a private flying club and the club itself confirms that. But I suppose that only confirms what we already knew. There was a hell of a lot of stuff flying around the south of Sicily that night after the Lampedusa crisis. We'll look at the reports of the incident. Something may turn up."

"Unlikely the jihadis have that sort of transport themselves. Hired it in, I would guess. I'll try a contact I've got, ask around. Names come up from time to time."

"I'd be grateful for any help, Milo. When do you go back to Aspra?"

"Tonight. There's an evening flight from Fiumicino."

"They'll be glad to see you. How's Ravi since the robbery, no ill effects?"

"No, thank God. But bored, could do with a bit of action! As we all could. By the way, how long have we got before your people want to pick up Galiano?"

"They've been asked to hold off until we give them the nod. From what we know of him, I can't see there's much danger of him running off. The guy's got nowhere to hide. The real risk is that the Caliphate might decide to go for him first. Which I imagine they will as soon as they judge that he's of no further use. Then he becomes a liability for them. Knows too much. Frankly, once we take him in, he's a liability for us too; they'll try to get to him one way or another wherever we keep him and that puts other people at risk too."

"Confirms what Lorenzo told us. I feel sorry for that kid. His future's on hold. He feels he'll never break free from the mess his fathers landed him in! I don't see how much use Galiano can be to them now; Altrabia's been blown and they've got their hands on the art. What else is there? Sure, as hell they're not going to go on paying him. For what? The terrorists don't pay for silence, they have other means."

"Hmm...perhaps I should just go for it and take him in. Hide him somewhere and try to keep him out if their hands, if I can. Easier said than done, though."

"It's probably safer all around if he's on the loose, if you can keep an eye on him."

"That's my problem."

"If it would help, Sandro, I could let you have Ravi for a while."

"Would you really? That would be fantastic. There's no one I'd rather have."

"Call it interagency cooperation! That should bring a smile to the faces of our elders and betters!"

Menotti laughed, "If anything can. I've been thinking about this. The way I see it, Milo, there are two options to monitor what's going on at the villa in Enna. There's just a single access to the place, so a work gang down the street, digging up the water mains. Advantage is it keeps three or four agents on site most of the time, but less viable at night unless a real emergency can be staged. Trouble is, takes a lot of setting up, is very expensive and the Commune has to play ball. DIS is inclined to be reluctant to push local authorities too hard unless it's a major crisis involving the public, which isn't the case. The alternative is to put a couple of night watchmen at a nearby location with a view of the villa. In which case, Ravi's role could be to liaise between them and us. He'd have the freedom to move around and be ready to intervene if necessary."

"He'd relish the opportunity, Sandro. I know he feels he needs a chance to make up for what happened to him at the gallery, though that was no fault of his."

"OK, we'll go for the second option. I need forty-eight hours to set it up."

"Leave it with me, I'll talk to him tonight. You can brief him when you come and we'll tie up the details between us."

Chapter Nine

The Republic of Malta

Sanny Darmanin had his fingers in more pies than the average pastry chef could cook in a lifetime. A large proportion of the pies were connected one way or another with transport, or more accurately, transportation. Sanny specialised in moving things. Usually inanimate, but occasionally of the human variety. He had, for example, overseen the delivery of a coachload of Libyan schoolchildren to a jihadi training camp in the desert. A school outing that was destined to last an unspecified length of time and was more for recreation than education. But human transportation did not come up very often and when it did, it was inclined to be expensive. Darmanin was not a man greatly troubled about the dictates of conscience; what was written in the credit columns of his ledger counted for more than what might one day be found in the recesses of his soul. He had acquired his reputation for the safe conveyance of *objets de vertue*, especially where the *objet* was what an art dealer might describe as high worth. For Darmanin's line of business, you would search the trade directories in vain. All was done by word of mouth and with the assistance of modern technology. Though it would be fair to say that he placed more reliance on the technology of his office landline than on the fickleness of satellites. But even Sanny Darmanin would concede that one had to move with the times and when it came to a question of handling large sums of money, it was better to bite the bullet. Consequently, his briefcase with its resident laptop kept him up to date with his accounts in Cyprus and never left his side, even in bed.

His appointments system was both complex and old-fashioned. A call would be made to the landline containing a coded message naming time and venue for a meeting. How the system got set up in the first place was a mystery. But if Darmanin's order book, which didn't actually exist, was anything to go by, business was brisk. One might wonder how he managed to achieve so much in the space of a mere twenty-four hours. The answer would be the magical modern word, 'networking'. He was such a prolific networker that you might think he'd invented it and the net spread far wider than the island of Malta. Top-grade information flowed in and out of Darmanin's office. The robbery, for example, at the Palermo gallery was being discussed before the goods had even arrived at Altrabia. For the good and the not-so-good, he was a gem. But entrepreneurs of such gem-like quality could not be expected to have all work and no play. And Sanny Darmanin liked to play with little things.

The girl opened her eyes and rolled over onto her side. Sanny Darmanin was stretched out naked on his stomach, face buried in the pillow. She traced her forefinger down from the nape of his neck along the line of his spine until it came to rest at the cleft of his buttocks. Darmanin muttered something into the pillow.

"Filthy beast," she said but did it anyway. Groping for her, his hand stroked the top of her thigh, working its way over and up to her corresponding place.

"You're a dirty little monster," she said, but made no attempt to stop him. Then she rolled again onto her back so that his hand was forced to find somewhere else.

"Umm…nice for a change," she murmured, "but not like the real thing."

So, the real thing again.

"Sanny, when are you going to take me away as you promised?"

She lay on her front watching him pull on his pants and then a pair of khaki chinos and a yellow and white striped top. He stuffed his feet into a pair of navy deck shoes.

"Soon, my angel, very soon."

"You always say that. Or you say when you're older." She pouted, brushed back her dark hair from her eyes. "That'll be ages," she raised her voice. "I can't wait so long. I can't."

"Hush! Everybody in the street will hear."

"I don't care, I want everybody to hear. I want everybody to know you're my lover."

"If you carry on like that, I soon won't be. They'll find out and take you away."

"Take *me* away! Take you away, you mean."

She was truculent now, beating her legs up and down on the bed.

"How many others like me have you got?"

Sanny whipped around to face her. "Shut up, you little bitch. Do you really think anyone will believe you? I've seen that Nadaro boy hanging around you. How often has he had it up?"

"It's so small you wouldn't notice. Not like you," she laughed.

Darmanin sighed, "Get dressed, it's time you went back to school."

When he got back to his office from the bar down the street, the telephone was ringing. He could hear it as he climbed the stone stairs to the second floor. The office, though that was an elevated description of the room, was more of a rendezvous place than a business centre. In place of a desk was a double bed, covers tangled now and less than pristine. On one side of the bed was a small white-painted table, on the other a metal-framed kitchen chair next to a grey metal filing cabinet. The telephone was in an alcove of the single window that overlooked the narrow dusty alley in downtown Valletta. The building had been there since the days of the Knights and no doubt the self-same room had served the self-same purpose for most of that time. From the peeling cream-painted walls, the smell of sex seemed to permeate the whole place. Darmanin picked up.

"Transport Solutions."

"Café Ritter, 6 p.m."

"Alright."

The bar down at the waterfront overlooked part of the Grand Harbour. Darmanin sauntered up, hands in pockets. One of the tables outside was already occupied. A dark-haired, bearded man, slimly built, somewhere in his early sixties, wearing a plain white shirt and dark blue trousers. Their eyes met; the man nodded. Darmanin stood in the open doorway.

"Ali," he called, "beer please."

He sat down opposite the man.

"The packages are safe?" the stranger asked.

"Need you ask?"

"I want to be sure."

"That's what you pay for. I assume you're here to tell me payment will be made."

"In part."

"In part why you're here or to tell me you're paying in part?" Darmanin laughed nervously.

"Do you doubt my word?"

"My friend, I doubt everyone's word."

The stranger turned to look out over the road towards the Grand Harbour.

"In the first place, I am not your friend, merely a business associate. Secondly, your doubts don't interest me."

In the silence that followed, Darmanin shifted in his seat uncomfortably.

"You have more business for me?"

Ali came out with a glass of beer. He placed it on the table in front of Darmanin.

"Something outside your normal line."

"Would you care to elaborate?"

"Let us say there's a human factor."

"That could be expensive."

The man shrugged, "Everything is negotiable."

"Except risk. Human factors are generally high risk. That carries a high premium."

"It's all a question of degree."

"Exactly so and I have to be the judge of that."

He picked up his glass, had a drink, put it down and wiped his mouth with the back of his hand. The stranger had a look of disgust on his face he made no attempt to conceal but Darmanin appeared not to notice.

"So," he asked, "what's the risk this time?"

"My client has an interest...in young people."

"Ah," said Darmanin, "a social reformer. Most commendable. Has he a preference?"

"Usually no, willingness is all."

Darmanin picked up his glass again, thought for a moment and put it down without drinking.

"I think I might be able to accommodate his particular tastes."

"Excellent."

"What's the timetable?"

"He is due to arrive here quite soon to inspect some acquisitions he is making."

"It seems to tie in very neatly."

"That is my impression," said the stranger.

He finished his drink, stood up, nodded to Darmanin and walked off towards the harbour. Darmanin sat on drinking his beer and drumming his fingers on the table. He smiled to himself. Very soon, a certain young lady of his acquaintance would realise her dream of a lifetime.

* * *

Milan

Throwing his bag onto the back seat of the taxi, he climbed in after it and gave the driver his address.

"Come far, signor?"

"Palermo."

"Never been," said the driver. Lorenzo didn't answer and the driver left it at that.

Lorenzo gazed out at the wet streets. A steady rain reflected back the street lighting, enhancing the vibrancy of the city's nightlife. It felt good to be back, really like coming home. He felt comfortable in the familiarity around him. Thoughts of the last couple of weeks chased around his head. A kaleidoscope of events, sad not to have seen his father before leaving. Not thought to be a good idea by his new colleagues, as he regarded the team, to risk going back to Enna. Terrorists running around, his father hopelessly compromised. He knew now with the certainty that came from ties of blood that Luca wanted to reject the allegiance into which he had been dragged and consign it to some deep recess where it could no longer demand anything further of him, but Lorenzo also knew his father's ties to the Caliphate would not be disposed of so easily.

As he got out of the taxi, he looked up at the windows of the apartment. Sixth floor. No sign of life, windows were dark. He'd called from the airport, receiving what he felt was a fairly tepid response. Women. You never knew where you were with them. Blowing hot and cold or, this time, just tepid. In the foyer, he nodded to a middle-aged couple he recognised, leaving for a night out. He'd bumped into them once or twice in a swishy restaurant that he occasionally took Lisa to. The husband, he thought, was a commercial lawyer. They were never seen around at weekends, which were spent at their country place near Lake Maggiore. Other people's lives, he thought, as the lift took him up to the sixth floor, what would they have made of the last couple of weeks of his? Thoughts of his father wandering around lost in his own home in Enna.

Hanging on by a thread. How long before the thread snapped? The lift door slid open and he turned right towards the door of his apartment. It was open. The sound of music was playing softly in the background and standing there in the hallway—Lisa. He stepped inside, dropped his bag on the floor and she was in his arms before he knew it. He kicked the door shut with his foot. Still mouth to mouth, she drew him into the living room, lit only by candles on the glass-topped coffee table. Then through the living room and into the bedroom beyond. Her hands had pushed the jacket off his shoulders and were tearing at the buttons of his shirt, which also fell to the floor. He realised that under the cotton shift that she was wearing, she was naked. They'd reached the end of the bed, she pushed him down and suddenly his jeans and pants were gone; she lifted her arms and the shift went too. She was kneeling on the floor in front of him. It all seemed too soon, too quick, so he grabbed hold of her, pulled her up, rolled over and on top, slowing the pace.

Eventually, side by side, he turned to face her. "*Buona sera*, Signorina di Vallo."

She smiled, buried her face in his neck.

"I thought we were never going to speak again! Would it be impertinent of me to ask how you've been?"

"Oh Lorenzo, I've been desperate for you."

"Now what, I wonder, could be the reason for that?"

"Not just this, everything."

"You mean more than just sex. You were in such a hurry. I thought it would all be over before it'd begun. Usually, you're the one to take things slowly."

"I feel safe when you're inside me."

"I feel safe too, Lisa."

"It's been horrid while you've been away. Did you enjoy yourself, have fun? You didn't fall out with your father, did you?"

"So many questions."

"But you don't tell me anything."

"I've hardly had time to draw breath," he said laughing. "And no. It was no fun. As for papa, you know what he's like, just as I've always told you. A bit of this and a bit of that. Mostly that."

"The news has been full of that robbery in Palermo. They said it was something to do with the Galiano family."

"It was our pictures they took. Loaned by my grandfather."

"Will the police get them back?"

"I don't know, Lisa. No one has any idea where they might be. Not in Italy now, that's for sure."

She was quiet for a moment. "A man kept calling."

"Calling here? What man?"

"On the telephone. Lots of times, I can't remember how many. He eventually gave me his name. I wrote it down somewhere. At first, he was quite charming and then…I don't know…a bit sinister somehow."

"Did he threaten you?"

"No, why would he do that?"

"Don't know, Lisa. These weirdos. You can never tell. What did he want?"

"That's the funny thing."

"What?"

"He never once said what it was he wanted. Just kept asking about you. How was your work? When were you going to America? How long would you be in Enna? On and on. Leading nowhere. I got fed up and called the telephone people one time. They said there was nothing they could do because he hadn't been abusive or anything like that. Then the calls stopped. That was it."

"I wonder if it was the same journalist guy who kept calling me before I left. That one rabbitted on about the pictures. Were we thinking of selling them? Bloody cheek. I nearly told him to piss off. Can you find that name for me?"

"I'll get it."

She slipped out of the bed. Her nakedness shimmered in the candlelight from the living room, flickering on her bare flesh. She was gone a few minutes. Lorenzo propped himself up on the pillows and made himself comfortable. When she came back into the room, she had a glass of champagne in each hand and was clutching a piece of paper torn from the telephone notepad. Lorenzo switched on the lamp on his side of the bed. She held out a glass, gave him the note and saw what she'd been missing. She slipped back into bed sipping her champagne, her other hand wandering. Lorenzo read the name—Husseini—and a mobile number. Putting down his glass on the table, he got out of bed and rummaged through the pockets of his crumpled jacket. Taking out his mobile, he dialled the number on the note.

"Not in use," he said as he got back into bed.

"Is this ever going down?" she asked.

"Not while you're doing that."

On a table on the villa terrace, Ravi's mobile was ringing. He was busy with one of his usual early evening tasks, the preparation of the team's pre-dinner drinks.

"Milo, get that for me."

"Hi, Lorenzo. How's it going? Safely home, I hope…all well?

He listened for a few minutes.

"I hope she wasn't frightened. Right…what did you say…Husseini?"

He raised his eyebrows at Paso sitting opposite.

"I'm not sure what it means. Give me the number you tried…say that again? I see. Lorenzo, if he calls again, try to keep the conversation going. See if you can pick up any clues, references to anything specific. If he wants to meet you, agree, but with several days' notice and a city centre location. Somewhere busy. You make the conditions or tell him there's nothing doing. Then let us know immediately and we'll be there. Do you think you can do it? Great. Thanks for everything. *Ciao*…

"So, the mysterious Mr Husseini. Been pestering his girlfriend while he's been away."

"Crops up all over the place," said Paso.

"Seems to have some sort of watching brief. Keeping his fingers on the pulse. Wish I knew where he fitted in."

"Perhaps that's it. Just there to muddy the waters. Divert our attention. Why don't we give Carlo Leone a call, see if the police got anything more out of Bertelli? She's the most direct link we've got to him."

Leone wasn't available but when Menotti returned the next day to join the team in Aspra again, he had spoken to the commissario to update himself and had been told that Bertelli was no longer being held in custody. She had been released through the efforts of a very persistent lawyer, conditional on residing at home. Leone was doing his best to keep tabs on her but surveillance was low-level. Lavinia came up with the suggestion that Dr Lucy Black might drop in to see Bertelli, a courtesy call really, commiserate, express concern, offer help. Was there anything the signora needed? The Palermo forensics team were expecting to finish up at the gallery next day and Paso was keen to get back and let it reopen to the public, though the Galiano Collection would remain closed for the time being. Paso was interested to see if the mysterious Mr Husseini would turn up again, though it was generally considered unlikely.

That evening, Milo and Ravi had bedtime conversation.

"How do you feel about going tomorrow?"

"Relieved to be doing something at last. A bit excited, I suppose."

"It may mean more hanging about, waiting to see if anything happens."

"But at least there'll be some point to it. Trying to keep up with the unpredictable baron. It's a pity I couldn't stay in the house."

"Too risky all around. And Francesca's right, Galiano wouldn't wear it. He's like a frightened rabbit. The business with Lorenzo shook him. He knows he's the key to his son's survival. The man's never had much honour, but at least he's trying to show some backbone."

"I wish I knew my way around Enna but I'm a complete stranger."

"All the better; that's your cover. You're a student on summer vac. You might even find one or two others to mingle with."

"Don't you think I look too old?"

Standish laughed, "Fishing for compliments! No, seriously, it's fine. You're studying architectural history. It was your subject anyway, so you'll know what you're talking about. And don't worry; we've squared it back in London with UCL if anyone tries to check. I don't think this mission will last that long, Ravi. Sandro's laid on a Fiat Uno for you and you've got the address of the student hotel where you will be staying. Call me twice a day. I just need to know that you're OK. Now then…why does this bloody phone always go off when we're…"

"It's a text," said Ravi picking it up. *From the Abbess.*

Milo sat up in bed, alert. They read it together,

Re: Your enquiry about the delivery of altar vestments. Brother Damian has received them.

"That's it!" said Milo. "I knew it; he was my first choice. It had to be him."

"Brother Damian, isn't he the Malta connection? We've come across his name before."

"Exactly. Brother Damian. Sanny Darmanin. A nasty piece of work. Now we're really getting somewhere. It makes sense. It makes perfect sense. Malta is where it all began for Galiano. The boy in the hotel. Darmanin almost certainly set that up. He knows the kind of kids that would do it. Malta—so that's where the stolen art ended up. And still is; I would stake my life on it. Darmanin would never let it out of his grasp until the deal was done."

"The Abbess has come up trumps again."

"Our contact in the European underworld. Has never let us down. Her information's always reliable. God bless her."

"Is it really a woman?"

"They say so. I've no idea. Peter Glendower once told me never to get on the wrong side of her. And I wouldn't want to. She's pure gold."

"A boost for Sandro."

"Yes, he deserves a break."

"If it rings again in the middle, let's leave it."

This time it didn't, which was just as well, for the middle went on quite a long time.

"Signora Bertelli?"

"Si."

"*Buon Giorno*. This is Lucy Black speaking. You may remember I came to the gallery a few weeks ago with Dr Pritsi to see the late Dr Melzi."

"Yes. What is it you want?"

"I hope I'm not intruding, signora, But I wanted to say how very sorry I was to learn of Dr Melzi's passing."

There was silence at the other end of the telephone.

"I know what a horrible experience you've had since then. It must have been a dreadful few weeks."

Again, no response.

"Signora?"

"Yes."

"I was wondering, as I'm in Palermo again for a few days, if I might come and see you."

"What for?"

"No particular reason. Just perhaps to be a friendly face."

"Well...I don't know."

"I thought, Signora Bertelli, it might be a break for you, if I were to call and take you out to lunch. A change of scene?"

"Yes, well, that would be welcome. You get tired of looking at the same walls all the time."

"That's what I thought. Would tomorrow be convenient? I have some free time and planned to do shopping in the morning."

"Yes, thank you."

"Should I pick you up about 1 p.m.? There's a nice not-too-busy place near the harbour. Are you easy to find?"

Lavinia spent the morning shopping in the centre of town. Mostly personal items but she looked for a twenty-first birthday present for a goddaughter back home. Twenty-one still seemed the magical age even though eighteen was more of a turning point these days. What had she done for the eighteenth? Only three years ago but she struggled to remember. There certainly had been dinner in a smart place and tickets for Cary and her friends to a pop concert. She felt out of touch with what young people liked these days. She hesitated over a number of things, all of which could be found in any decent store in the world. She'd hoped for something Sicilian, at very least Italian, but clean out of ideas, she settled for a pearl and gold bracelet based on an Etruscan design in the end. Were the Etruscans in Sicily? She didn't think so and it didn't matter.

Bertelli's apartment was on the second floor of a newly built block south of the city centre. Lavinia parked in the private area behind the flats. Walking across to the rear entrance, she noticed she was being watched by the two occupants of a black BMW. They were still there when she came down a few minutes later with Sara Bertelli. Leone's surveillance team? Not exactly inconspicuous. Driving out of the gateway, she could see the BMW in her rear mirror reversing out of its space and sure enough, it kept a couple of places behind all the way to the harbour-side restaurant. As Lavinia parked across the road, it drove on and disappeared.

At first, Bertelli seemed unsettled and ill at ease, but Dr Lucy Black kept the conversation light and inconsequential. *The problems of shopping for presents for young people these days who seemed to have everything.* As Bertelli relaxed, she became more talkative. *New York must be a wonderful place, did Dr Black live in the city itself, she would love to go there one day.* From time to time when the restaurant door opened and new customers came in, she was jumpy, looking around to see who it was. Then as the place thinned out and became quieter, the pressure lifted, talk turned to family and Lavinia knew she was reaching a defining moment in their conversation. She mentioned the pleasure there must be in buying for grandchildren and Bertelli's eyes filled with tears.

Lavinia leaned forward, patting her on the arm.

"What is it, Sara? Anything I can help with?"

She shook her head, bit her bottom lip and fixed her eyes on the plate in front of her. Lavinia dismissed the waiter with a shake of the head as he came to the table to enquire if there was anything else they would like. It was that moment in a conversation when one knew that a turning point had been reached. Tempting to go for it but better to wait.

"They've been threatened. Their lives. Because of me." She stopped, looking as though she knew she had said too much. Lavinia held her breath, continuing to wait.

"I don't...I... How much do you know, Dr Black?"

Lavinia reached out and covered Bertelli's hand with her own. She felt Bertelli stiffen instinctively.

"Pretty well everything, Sara."

"I thought so. I don't know why...just felt you knew more than you were saying. How do you...? I think it's time I went." She started to gather up her handbag.

"Before you do, let me tell you a couple of things. I work with people who are trying to help you, for a start. We understand the pressure you've been under. We know you're not to blame for anything you've done. The people you got involved with are evil—I don't need to tell you that, you've found it out for yourself in the most horrible way possible. But your grandchildren will be safe, they're under police protection. The threat will go away because you're no longer of any use to these terrorists. Let's have another coffee."

She turned to signal the waiter who stood at the bar with his back to their table. At that moment, the door of the restaurant crashed open. A man stood there, a gun in his hand. For a moment, the restaurant was totally silent, people's conversation frozen in mid-sentence, then someone gave a scream that was cut off suddenly. As Lavinia turned back to the table to try and grab Bertelli and pull her down to the floor, a shot rang out, then two more. Something hit the edge of her outstretched hand. Bertelli slumped forward onto the red-checked tablecloth with a dark hole in the side of her head. At the foot of the bar, the waiter lay sprawled on his back, a growing crimson patch in the centre of his chest and an offended look on his face.

Paramedics administered first aid to Lavinia and then led her, protesting it was just a scratch, to the waiting ambulance. Others went their rounds of the customers in the restaurant checking for injuries and a policewoman dealt with shocked questions. Someone had heard the word 'Mafia' uttered by one of the restaurant staff and this prompted a flood of tears. Lavinia identified herself to one of the paramedics and asked to speak to the senior police officer in charge.

Later, right hand bound up, she lay on a recliner on the villa terrace. Carlo Leone, sitting opposite, poured another cup of tea from the villa's silver samovar, added lemon and passed it to Paso who took it and placed it on a small table beside her chair. Lavinia smiled her thanks.

"It begins to look as if our terrorists are using local hoods to do their dirty work," ventured Leone. "Descriptions we're getting of the gunman vary quite a bit, as you might expect, but they don't fit the *jihadi* mould."

"I'd go along with that," said Lavinia. "I wish I'd been able to get the number of the car, Carlo, but I didn't get a decent look at it."

"I doubt it would have helped us much. Probably stolen. That would be their style."

"To be honest, when I first saw them in the apartment car park, I thought they might be yours."

"Unfortunately, small chance of that. It took all my efforts to get a patrol car to call once a day and check whether she was there. Mind you, city hall's really shaken up now, after the gallery. It'll all take its toll on tourism, that's what is upsetting them."

"What do the *jihadis* think she could have told us that we didn't already know?" asked Menotti. "She wasn't the only one who could have identified Husseini. At least four of us have seen him. He's got to be the key to it somewhere. Bertelli never initiated contact with him; he was always the one to reach her when they needed information. Why take her out? She was redundant."

"We could be barking up the wrong tree," said Paso. "Maybe they weren't trying to keep her quiet. It was just a message, a warning. They're telling us they've finished here, they've got what they wanted for now, they're clearing up and getting out. Dealing with any loose ends before they go."

"Who is next on the loose ends list?" asked Standish.

"Galiano?"

"I'll let Ravi know when he calls in," said Standish. "He can brief the night-watchmen too, Sandro. We don't want them walking into the middle of a Mafia gunfight."

"What about your police colleagues, Carlo?" asked Menotti. "Can we rely on cooperation if and when it's needed? In the event of a problem, I'd like to know that backup would be there, but with great respect, the last thing we want is the local force crawling all over the operation."

"I agree with you. Don't worry, I'll handle it. I'll go down myself. Easier to explain it that way and I can see how the land lies."

And a few more odds and ends tidied up the discussion.

* * *

Malta

The narrowness of some of the alleys in the old towns and villages of Malta testified to the fact that they dated from the period when the Knights of St John of Jerusalem held the island against Arab invasion. The story goes that they were so designed to make it impossible for an enemy to wield his long sword in combat with an assailant. It was, perhaps, a partly romantic notion but one that bore a certain practical logic. More cogently narrow streets rendered it difficult for horses to gain access, enabling the population to have time to retreat to the safety of the citadel or some other fortification. And the narrow streets afforded another kind of protection, which might, all along, have been the real reason for their dimensions. They prevented the full heat of the sun from penetrating the houses there. Consequently, the sun never stole into Sanny Darmanin's business centre. No doubt the outside coolness of the alley counteracted the heat all too often being generated inside the room. The shadows in the alley

159

were deep in contrast to the dazzling brightness beyond and anyone walking from one end to the other would stop and blink on entering and, for a moment, see nothing until their eyes grew accustomed to the inner gloom.

Darmanin found that this happened every time he entered the alley, but so familiar was he with his surroundings that it never caused his footsteps to falter. This afternoon was no different, or maybe it was. As he strode out of the glare into the darkness, a sixth sense checked his stride and instinctively he felt that he was not alone. Something stirred in the shadows of a doorway to his right a few doors down from his own entrance. Squinting, he peered in but at first glance could make nothing out. Then as he went to pass on, a hand shot out and grabbed at the loose shirt he was wearing. He was dragged into the doorway and before he could draw breath, a knee crashed into his groin. With a scream of agony, he doubled up and collapsed to the ground. His assailant said nothing. Eyes screwed up and head between his knees, the pain was unendurable and even breathing seemed beyond him. How long he stayed like that he couldn't have said but when he eventually forced himself to open his eyes, he was quite alone. He leaned back against the wall and drew his knees up to his chin, the pain between his legs unabated, a feeling of nausea sweeping over him.

For several days following the assault, Darmanin avoided going to the office altogether. But that couldn't continue indefinitely. So a change of routine was called for. He discovered that if he entered the alley from the opposite direction, he could do so from a street already shaded from the sun thus giving his eyes time to become accustomed to the shadows. It meant the inconvenience of a rather longer walk and because the alley didn't run straight, it was impossible to see what might lie at the further end near his own doorway. But by and large, a more comfortable experience. Also, inside his shirt, strapped to his body with a belt, he carried a sheathed knife. Not that he had any intention of using it—never had and in fact, was not at all sure he would have the courage to do so if required—but the knowledge that it was there gave him confidence. There was a confrontation with the girl on the occasion of her next visit. She usually came two or three times a week, had been twice and he wasn't there. She demanded to know why. She'd had to make do with Nadaro and that wasn't the same thing at all. There was something about the way she spoke that caused Darmanin to suspect that the Nadaro youth might not have been unconnected with the incident that had taken place. He knew him to be a vicious little bastard and it was quite within his capabilities. When he told her that their assignations would have to cease for a while, she became hysterical. A screaming match ensued and the sound of windows in the alley being slammed shut was heard. Efforts to calm her down only prevailed when he told her plans were being made for her future happiness. Naturally, not a word was mentioned that he himself would be playing only a subsidiary role in these long-term arrangements. But the promise of dreams about to be fulfilled induced a temporary serenity. When and where, were questions he could not presently specify, but the day was just around the corner. No, she need do nothing herself in preparation. In fact, it was vital to carry on her daily life in a perfectly normal manner. When the time arrived, she would come to the office as usual at her lunch break and further instructions would await her. That would be her last day on the island of Malta. So reassured was the girl that she lost no time in showing her gratitude.

Chapter Ten

Enna

The sky was overcast, the air heavy and humid, threatening a downpour. The main highway was busy with local and tourist traffic in both directions. Ravi followed the signs for *centro*. Some way ahead of him, he spotted two girl hitchhikers with backpacks, trudging uphill to the city centre, students like himself, probably making the most of the summer vacation to hitchhike around Europe. Ravi caught up with them, slowed and came to a stop, greeted them with a cheerful '*buon giorno*'. Attractive girls in their late teens, both fair-haired and sun-tanned, Ravi guessed Scandinavian. Not much room in the Uno but they crammed their backpacks and themselves into the little car. Speaking English, in which both girls seemed pretty fluent, they fell into easy-going chat and he soon learned that they were from Estonia and were at university there—one doing sociology and the other engineering. Yes, they were planning to stay in Enna a couple of days and then go on to the southern coast of the island. After that, who knows? Wherever the inclination took them though the general plan was to work their way up to Italy, finishing in Venice. What about him? Much the same, nothing hard and fast. Architectural history, at uni in London. Just about to start his post-grad year. Afterwards? He laughed. Not much of a plan there either as yet. Perhaps try to get into an architect's practice, would quite like to specialise in restoration work. He discovered that they were booked into the same student hotel, at least that's what it called itself! Just behind the cathedral. Anyway, a good location, very central. Turned out to be clean and comfortable and with their arrival, the hotel was for the moment full. Booked into their rooms, they agreed to meet shortly in the lobby and make an initial assault on sightseeing. Ravi suggested that they tackle first the Duomo, the cathedral, then a bar for lunch.

During daytime, Ravi felt his cover would be secure as long as he could merge into student company, and the two Estonian girls were perfect for this. Apart from the terrorists, the only person who might recognise him was the man he was there to watch—Luca Galiano, who had no idea he was being shadowed. The girls, Adela and Sophie, were full of the news of a Mafia shooting in Palermo. Not concerned for their own safety but intrigued that incidents of that kind still occurred. Along with many people, Mafia activity was thought to be a thing of the past. Ravi had received the barest outline of it from Standish the night before, not wanting to go into details on the mobile. Consequently, he was reticent on the subject and the girls jokingly thought that a typical boyish reaction. True to his promise to Standish, he called twice a day, literally a few words, having agreed in advance that they would not use the call-in to discuss details of business so as to maintain security as far as possible. At times, he felt a bit left out of the main action, not that there was any main action just then, but he liked to be part of the team's discussions. And to tell the truth, he was soon beginning to tire of the girls' company. By and large, their interests and his did not much coincide. Conversation became tedious and he was conscious that the age difference between them, though only a few years, showed how quickly young people grew apart once they went into working life.

But cover required him to play along for as long as the two Estonians remained in Enna. That proved mercifully short. After a couple of days, Sophie announced that it was time to move on. Adela was downcast, clearly sorry to be losing Ravi's company. The more serious of the two, she had been genuinely interested in what he had to say on his subject and even more in Ravi himself. No stranger to female attraction, Ravi knew when he was being pursued, however gently—excuses to stand close, exchange of looks and hesitant, or not-so-hesitant casual touches. Once even snatching a goodnight kiss and obviously hoping for more. All part of the job and by no means the most unpleasant part. But a relief when it came to an end. On the third morning, they said their farewells with hugs all around and from Adela, a somewhat lingering kiss. In the hotel, the company changed frequently—most of the students staying no more than a night or two, Enna worth a visit but a time-limited one.

Perched on the edge of the high escarpment on which the city was built, the Villa Galiano presented a number of surveillance problems. Unobserved access from the centre of the city was difficult, there was one way in and one way out, but the great advantage of that meant anyone leaving the villa was equally easy to spot. Menotti had secured the use of a one-room flat over a bar at the end of the street. Visually, it could have been better but had the advantage of plenty of comings and goings below to deflect attention and Ravi could drop in without raising suspicion. He made a habit of calling in to see the watchers once a day at different times, finding the elder of the two taciturn, the younger closer to himself in age more forthcoming and willing to chat. They had nothing to report. The only callers at the villa were one or two members of the staff; of the baron himself—not a sign.

The governing council of the Confraternity of the Holy Shroud met monthly in a handsome chamber attached to the Church of St Joseph of Aramathea. The association of the Confraternity with the saint was too obvious to require explanation. At least to a good Catholic who knew his scriptures. Back in the early nineteenth century, a pious parishioner, said to be of a collateral branch of the barons Galiano, had bequeathed generous funds for the building of a meeting place attached to the church where male members of the ancient society could assemble to discuss whatever it was male members of ancient societies liked to discuss in the absence of their wives—not always, it was said, related to the business of the Confraternity. So they assembled, they conferred, they deliberated, they even gossiped to their hearts' content. To be fair, first and foremost, they liked to talk about the Shroud, the burial cloth of Our Lord, miraculously preserved over the centuries and now housed, and venerated, in its own chapel in the Cathedral of Turin. Pilgrimages from Enna were organised from time to time when the Shroud was exposed to public display, talks were given by the cognoscenti, masses were said, devotions were paid and donations received for the care of the terminally ill.

At one end of the long-panelled council chamber, facing the visitor on entering, hung a life-size reproduction of the holy relic itself. Arresting in its stark portrayal of the Crucifixus, it was an image of death bearing all the marks of the Passion. A few years back, the present Baron Galiano had provided funds for its proper illumination, which created a dramatic effect, providing old Massimo Serra had remembered to switch it on. From time to time, excitement mounted in the Confraternity when the hierarchy of the Catholic Church was disposed to make encouraging statements about the genuineness of the relic. Similarly, despondency, which had been known to turn to fury, resulted from the merest suggestion that the object of their devotion might have been a fake. As for putting this to the test by snipping off bits of the fabric for carbon dating, the less said about that the better. *Just another example of the atheism into which the modern age had collapsed!*

Prevailing scholarly opinion, that the Holy Shroud was actually a cunning artifice devised by over-zealous Templar Knights in the fourteenth century, reduced certain members of the confraternity in Enna to a state of near apoplexy. *But opinions are opinions, however spurious, and we don't have to have truck with them.* A more immediate concern was the recent curious behaviour of their patron who had abandoned the leadership of the Good Friday procession for reasons he, and presumably the Almighty, alone knew. An invitation to the said gentleman to offer an explanation of this deeply distressing interruption of a centuries-old tradition, after prolonged discussion, was put to the vote and unanimously rejected. A more dignified course of action was approved whereby a fellow member of the council would approach the patron and enquire, with a certain delicacy, if all were well and could his fraternal colleagues offer any support. And who better to discharge this duty than their most respected brother, Signor Massimo Serra, on whose unsuspecting elderly shoulders had fallen the responsibility of taking over the leading role at the Good Friday cathedral mass. A task Signora Serra had not ceased talking about virtually since the moment Luca Galiano had bolted. In his working life, Serra had been a senior official in the Commune's administration department which placed Signora Serra, at least in her own estimation, well up the scale of social standing in the community, certainly in a position where she expected her opinions to be taken seriously. Not that her views on the Galiano family were broadcast to more than a small circle of intimates. But that was enough to ensure widespread dissemination. The present baron's lifestyle scarcely bore scrutiny. *You heard about that business at the villa in Calabria. Well, Calabria—what else can you expect up there?*

In the middle of the afternoon of Ravi's fourth day in Enna, he was about to leave the watchers' post when a car drove along the street through the entrance gates of the Villa Galiano and drew up in front of the *porte cochere*. It seemed an age before the car door opened and an elderly man climbed slowly out. He made his way up the steps to the main door and reached out to pull on the metal chain that hung on the right-hand side. After a wait of several minutes, the door was opened and he was admitted.

"Put out a trace on the registration," said Ravi. "What do we know of him?" Retired local authority civil servant, married to Teresia Monti, six children, member of Governing Council of the Confraternity of the Holy Shroud, all-round worthy citizen of the city of Enna and loyal subject of the Republic. Hence, of passing interest only. And the watching and the waiting, the 'hanging around', went on. But not for long.

* * *

Malta
Late July

The *Aphrodite,* registered in Manila, gleaming white from stem to stern, lay at anchor a nautical mile outside the Grand Harbour of Valletta. Mid-July and mid-morning, there was a burning sun in a cloudless sky. For once, Homer's legendary 'wine-dark sea' was turned into an azure lake with barely a white-flecked ripple to disturb its surface. It was a fine time of year for cruising and the Mediterranean was a cruiser's paradise. Yachts of all sizes and degrees of splendour peppered the sea around the island of Malta and filled up all the available space within the harbour. Aboard the *Aphrodite* human activity was kept to an absolute minimum. Such work as was needed was carried out in well-nigh total silence by a Filipino crew kitted out in white t-shirts and shorts and soft-soled deck shoes. Orders were few; crewmen knew what was expected of them, but when necessary, they were conveyed in sign language, so the whole scene on this summer's day with silent forms moving around the decks was faintly reminiscent of a ghost ship. Not, however, in performance. Capable of a cruise speed of twenty-four knots, the diesel-electric powered vessel and its crew of thirty-six had two helipads, fore and aft, its tenders stored in two garages in the stern that opened through doors on each side of the hull, a below-deck parking space for two cars, a gymnasium and two swimming pools, one exclusive to the owner's private deck. It was around this pool that a group of five young teenagers, two boys and three girls, lay on sun loungers in various stages of undress. Conversation was muted. It was not by any means a scene of joyous holidaymaking. On the contrary, looks exchanged among the group were furtive, perhaps apprehensive or just resigned. From time to time, one or two slid into the pool, swam around a little in a desultory manner and then climbed out. An onlooker trying to sum up the atmosphere would describe it as one of pervasive boredom. On the fore deck, a helicopter was parked, dark blue with a surrounding silver stripe, ready for the owner's pleasure or, maybe, business. Frequently, the two were intertwined. Whatever it was today, it was not long delayed. The young people sat up and looked at one another as the sound of the helicopter's rotors came suddenly to life. One youth tried to balance on his sun-lounger to peer over the protective decking but found it too high, wobbled and toppled over causing a rare burst of laughter from the others, which was soon suppressed. Several minutes later, the helicopter lifted off. The young people shaded their eyes to watch as it hovered over the yacht, swung away doing a circuit around the vessel before heading off in the direction of the island. Its departure seemed to ease the tension around the pool a little, at least until the cabin door to the upper sun lounge opened. Heads turned to look at the figure of a grey-haired woman who stood studying the scene.

"Get dressed," she rapped out. "It's time for your lunch."

Hastily, they pulled on shorts and T-shirts and filed into the sun lounge. Meanwhile, on board the helicopter, Maxim Zamorra, billionaire owner of the *Aphrodite* and arms dealer, smiled. The day ahead looked promising. He was about to increase his considerable art collection, a source of pride and entirely private enjoyment, and he had been told that a further, unnamed, acquisition would greatly add to the pleasure of his forthcoming Mediterranean cruise.

* * *

Enna

28 July

The absence of the last two remaining members of staff somehow rendered the Villa Galiano lifeless. Yet somewhere, there was life in the place, of a sort. Ravi Sharma felt alone but knew he wasn't. An empty house was an empty house and instinctively one sensed it to be such. This was different. Lifeless, but not devoid of human existence. As soon as Khalil Khourasan had been spotted entering the bar below the watchers' post, an SMS was sent to Sharma. He in turn knew exactly what he had to do and the *commissario* of police received a request. Anna the cook and Seppi the houseman had been detained for their own protection and to ensure that they didn't try to return to their place of work, which was now classified a grade 'A' terrorist location. With the Enna police thus alerted and dispersed accordingly—though to judge from the deserted air around the villa, it could not be said that there was a single officer anywhere near—the operation was set to begin. Did it have a name? Well, not as such. In retrospect, younger members of the force would refer to it by a variety of names, all their own invention, and designed mainly to impress the opposite sex. Ravi Sharma had his own reasons for wishing it to remain anonymous. So, just *the operation*.

He had, of course, tried to prepare himself for this precise moment. What would be his first words to Khalil? The boy he'd grown up with and shared all the experiences of childhood and adolescence.

166

"*Hi, Khalil, how's it going? Fancy meeting like this.*" Probably not. "*Let's talk.*" No, the time for talking was long past. Well, no doubt something would occur on the spur of the moment. Training hadn't covered this; hadn't it foreseen the possibility of old friends meeting in such circumstances? Presumably not. The much-vaunted rulebook for agents of British Intelligence needed an extra chapter. After it was all over, he'd offer to write it. That would make Milo smile. So exactly *what* was he expecting to happen? For Khalil to raise his hands and 'come quietly'? Some chance of that. The operation was all Khalil—he was the focal point, the only one of the terrorists so far to have been identified within the city. Perhaps there were others, waiting, undercover. But it was Khalil who was destined to be the star of this particular show. It didn't seem fair that the ones responsible for radicalisation were beyond reach. Salim, the uncle, a resident of Paris, orchestrating death for a cause. A cause that wanted human existence to start over again from the beginning on a blank page. For Ravi Sharma, the very idea of a cause would have to bear a certain nobility of aim, maybe a simplistic view, he would readily have admitted. Hard to imagine how the *Caliphate* would qualify. Where was the nobility in annihilation? Then there was Al-Azhar, the jihadi commander, whose voice he'd heard but whose face he'd never seen, the agent of annihilation. Passing shadows with a terrifying corporeal reality.

He inched his way along the passage from the villa's kitchen towards the entrance hall. Coming to the open double doors of the dining salon, he paused, crouched down and tried to peer into the room. With little natural light and the shutters closed, he dimly made out the vast table that ran down the centre of the room. Listening intently, he heard only the ticking of a clock somewhere at the far end. Playing safe, he crawled past, standing again when he reached the far wall. Reaching the entrance hall, he paused again. A row of marble pillars separated the hall from the passage. In front of the pillars, left and right of the central archway, were two statues—marked on a plan that Lorenzo Galiano had drawn up for the intelligence team as Persephone on his right and Demeter over to the left. Persephone, a demure figure, was clutching her robe to her youthful form, almost embarrassed to be seen in her vulnerability by everyone who arrived at the villa. It would be difficult to hazard a guess at which precise point in her life the sculptor had intended to portray her. Was it before her rape by Pluto? Before listening to his blandishments and with maidenly virtue, declining the invitation? An invitation? *Accompany me to the dark chamber of my desires; yield yourself there to the promise of eternal ecstasy.* Hard to believe that Pluto was capable of such politeness. What he wanted, he took there and then. If the artist had captured her at the exact moment before her descent to the underworld, it was at her most unsuspecting, still believing perhaps, that no meant no. Demeter, on the other hand, was insouciant. No mother wishes to believe ill is about to befall her daughter, clearly her outrage not yet manifest.

Sharma moved slowly through the archway and into the hall. The air around him seemed to vibrate with silence. Some instinct made him reach for the gun tucked into the waistband of his trousers underneath his loose shirt. Then the library door opened. A figure came out. The figure of a man, macabre in appearance, bloodstained and smiling. Sharma stared—if he had any words, they were stuck in his throat—he could only stand and gape. Khalil Khourasan took a step forward and stopped. His eyes glowed with excitement and his whole face seemed radiated with the pleasure of greeting a close friend absent for too long, reunited at last. Except Sharma knew that Khourasan wasn't seeing him at all, hadn't even registered his friend's presence. In his right hand, he clutched a curved knife, twelve or maybe eighteen inches long. In his left, an appalling object. Sharma, aware of it, couldn't take his eyes off Khourasan's smiling face. Then he found a voice, but not his, more a stranger's.

"Khalil."

Khourasan turned towards the statue of Persephone as if she had been the one who had spoken. In a single movement, he hurled the object in his left hand across the stone floor towards it. As the severed head of Luca Galiano rolled over the floor, it left a slight trail of blood in its wake and came to rest at the feet of the statue. On the face of Demeter, there was the trace of a smile of satisfaction as if to say, "Persephone, now you have your revenge." Khourasan took another step forward towards Sharma, his left arm still raised as though in salute.

"Khalil, stop!"

But if he heard, he paid no regard.

"Khalil, it's me, Ravi."

Still he advanced. Sharma raised his gun and couldn't pull the trigger. Khourasan seemed to realise nothing was going to happen, lowered his arm and continued moving forward. He pointed the knife at the figure in front of him, made a circle with it in the air and nodded. Sharma fired once, then again and again. The knife in Khourasan's hand clattered to the floor. He looked down at his chest, surprised at what he saw. He was no more than five or six feet away from Sharma. Then slowly, he crumbled at the knees and sank to the ground falling forward on his face, his outstretched arm and bloody fingers centimetres from the tip of Sharma's shoe. In a final effort, he twisted his head to one side; the smile had never left his face.

Ravi felt a presence behind him but hadn't heard a sound. He stiffened, still holding the gun, finger still on the trigger. Arms encircled his body and the gun was gently removed from his grasp. Unresisting, his head went back, resting on a shoulder that was only too familiar.

"Ravi, it's over. Time to go."

* * *

Malta
30 July

The tiny airstrip a mile from the town of Rabat was situated on land owned by the Alquemada family since the fifteenth century. The Villa Bugja, begun in the late 1700s and extended a century later, was still inhabited by the current *Marchese* and his young family. The Alquemadas were pillars of Maltese society. Tino, thirty-something, tall and athletic, was the head of the family. His wife, a doctor and daughter of doctors, had given up a medical career to marry and have children. Tino's mother, the sixty-year-old dowager *Marchesa*, was an outstanding example of Christian piety whose charitable efforts on behalf of abused and neglected children had earned Papal commendations and recognition from human rights groups. For some years, she had lived in the large top-floor apartment of a late nineteenth-century building overlooking St Paul's Bay. A second family palazzo of staggering proportions and even greater antiquity sat mouldering away within the old walled city of Mdina, occupied by Alquemada's ancient step-grandmother, widow and second wife of his now long-deceased grandfather.

Alquemada's business interests were wide and varied, outwardly respectable, some even laudable. Closer scrutiny would have revealed a tendency to flirt with individuals whose professional reputations were embedded in enterprises of more than passing concern to law enforcement agencies worldwide. But then these days, who couldn't say that? Lucky and rare, the businessman whose friends' hands were whiter than snow, indeed whose own hands were... But there it goes—big business ventures call for big stakes. 'Money making' is 'risk taking', as Alquemada's late father used to say. One such venture, high in the league tables of risk, the young *Marchese* had entered into with the Philippine arms dealer, Maxim Zamorra, which was why the latter's blue and silver helicopter was about to land on the Alquemada airstrip.

As Zamorra descended the steps, an aide stood at the bottom waiting to welcome the billionaire. A brief handshake, then a short journey by car to the villa. If one was to pass him in the street, and it is most unlikely one would ever do so, Maxim Zamorra would fail to attract attention. A plain-looking man, heavy features, late sixties, middle height, average build, grey hair, his appearance was distinguished by a right eye with a drooping eyelid that was the result of a youthful brush with the leader of a rival street gang. The gang leader had come off worse, far worse—he hadn't survived the encounter. That fact together with the drooping eyelid had served only to enhance Zamorra's reputation as a man who knew what he wanted and was not to be deterred. Lunch took place on a covered terrace overlooking the formal garden of parterres and fountains, orange and lemon trees and stone urns—a scene of Arcadian charm. It was strictly an *en famille* affair. And the guest, though duly charmed, was not the sort of man to allow himself to show it too much. The boy from the back streets of Manila had learnt a thing or two on his way up. The meal concluded, the two men withdrew to a quiet and cool loggia for coffee and conversation.

"Are we ready to proceed with authentication?" asked the billionaire.

"The expert arrived in Malta yesterday. The morning has been spent in examining the items and I am expecting a verdict later this afternoon."

"You're sure you have complete confidence?"

"I don't foresee any problems, Maxim. The provenance is unquestionable. What is more, they have remained in the same hands since the moment they were removed from the gallery and transferred to the air transport in Sicily. Their arrival here was overseen by our local agent whom I know well and trust implicitly. He supervised their transfer to Mdina. Members of my own staff have looked after them since then."

"This so-called expert…what do we know?"

"The best there is. One of the world's leading authorities and we're lucky to have secured his services."

"How much does he know of the…circumstances?"

"He knows only that the Galiano family, the legal owners of the pictures, wish to make a private sale under terms of the greatest secrecy, given public sensitivities about national heritage. He is aware of the need for discretion. This is not the first time for him."

"For which, no doubt, he will be well remunerated."

"Naturally."

"These Galianos…how well do you know them?"

"Hardly at all. The present head of the family has some business interests here. He cooperated with the arrangements."

"All well and good, providing he keeps his mouth shut."

"I believe that has been taken care of."

Zamorra waved a hand in the air as if flicking away a fly.

"You're sending them out by air freight. Not on your yacht?" enquired Alquemada.

"Less risky in the long run and, naturally, quicker. With fragile items like these, one needs to get them into the right environment with as little delay as possible. They're destined for my private island. I hope you and your wife will come out and see them in situ."

"Thank you. More than likely, I shall be on my own."

"I see. As you please."

"What is the schedule for your stay in Malta?"

"Once the pictures have been passed as authentic, I wish to view them for myself. Unfortunately, that cannot be today. Tonight, I'm entertaining some international businessmen for dinner on the yacht. I shall return here by helicopter tomorrow morning at 11 o'clock. Please make sure that you are available to take me to the palazzo for the viewing. I know I can rely on you to ensure maximum security for that visit."

Alquemada inclined his head.

"Your agent…I can't recall his name…has, I believe, a gift for me."

"Darmanin, yes. I do know about it. The gift will be delivered to the *Aphrodite* immediately prior to your departure. Darmanin has all that in hand."

"Excellent, Tino, we await only the expert's call."

"There are one or two other business matters I rather wanted your advice on."

"Please, whatever I can do. Your father was kind enough to take me into his confidence; it would be a pleasure to do the same for his son."

The call came as they took a stroll through the gardens. Alquemada listened for a few minutes, then slipped the phone back into his pocket. Zamorra looked at him enquiringly and Alquemada smiled.

"All completed. They are in total agreement. The paintings are authentic works from the hands of the artists. They were particularly excited by the Caravaggio. A little-known work executed by the master during his sojourn in Sicily in flight from his accusers. He had been thought to have committed murder. Congratulations, Maxim."

"You said 'they'. I don't understand. I thought there was only one expert."

"My fault. A small deception on my part. I knew you'd need to be one hundred per cent certain, so I called in a friend on my own initiative from the Prado. He'd done work for the family before. They knew each other by repute, so I made sure they examined the works separately. No collusion. They were only allowed to confer after forming their independent conclusions. It's a triumph, Maxim."

"You're a very clever fellow, Tino. Incidentally, what would you have done if it had gone the other way? Or if they had failed to agree? Would you have told me?"

Alquemada hesitated for a fraction of a second, perhaps a fraction too long.

"Of course."

Zamorra laughed. Not that clever, then.

* * *

Palermo
31 July

"This is Mr Robinson from London," said Milo Standish. A man in his late fifties and carrying too much weight for his less-than-average height turned from looking out of the window as Ravi Sharma came into the room. Hands in his trouser pockets, the jacket of his dark brown checked suit was buttoned and straining across an ample stomach. His flushed, moon-like face smiled briefly and he pushed his spectacles back onto the bridge of his nose and sniffed audibly. Removing a hand from his trousers, he reached out to shake Sharma's.

"I hear congratulations are in order," he said.

Sharma said nothing and shook hands briefly.

"Why don't we all sit?" said Standish.

Robinson sighed as he sat down, unbuttoning his jacket and his creased open-necked shirt seemed to take over the strain. Sharma found himself wondering if its buttons would withstand the pressure.

"Mr Robinson has come to see us," said Standish somewhat unnecessarily. Unusually, he seemed lost for words. "That is to say, he has come to…"

"Review the situation," broke in Robinson.

"What situation would that be?" asked Sharma.

"Oh, just in general, in general," continued Robinson.

Standish looked uncomfortable—very unlike him—and found the ceiling of the salon of abiding interest. Sharma thought he had never seen him look so out of sorts. But then, after a moment, Standish gathered himself, sat upright in his chair and very obviously took command of the situation.

"Mr Robinson, why don't you start by setting out your agenda?"

"Agenda?" Robinson looked startled, as if the word carried some closet meaning he hadn't thought of.

"Yes, tell us exactly why you've come and what it is you would like to know."

"More a case of what London would like to know," said Robinson defensively.

"And what is it that they don't know already?"

"Ah...well...I suppose...the circumstances of the death of the terrorist, Khourasan. It was thought, that is to say, it was *hoped*, that it would have been possible to take him alive for questioning. London feels there is much he could have told us about the terrorist network he was involved with. Other key players, for example, and where they might be hiding out. That sort of thing."

Sharma was thinking he made it sound like *Butch Cassidy and the Sundance Kid.*

"Questions we would all like the answers to, Mr Robinson," he said.

"If Khourasan were alive to provide this information, I doubt very much whether he would do so and Ravi Sharma most certainly wouldn't be, alive that is," put in Standish.

"Quite," said Robinson, "quite."

"Would you like a blow-by-blow account of what happened?" asked Sharma somewhat disingenuously.

"Yes, well, that might be helpful."

So, Ravi Sharma began from the moment the call came from Menotti's night-watchmen to say Khalil Khourasan had entered the bar below their post. He told his story simply, carefully, detail by detail, omitting only an account of his own innermost thoughts as the operation progressed. It was the most factual, unemotional description of an operation Standish had ever heard. When it was over, the three men sat in silence.

"Well, there we are then," said Robinson at length. "As I was saying...there we are. Time I was leaving."

"No questions, Mr Robinson?" enquired Sharma.

"Er...not at this stage."

"Mr Sharma and I will be taking a break before returning to London," said Standish in a tone of voice that brooked no contradiction.

"An excellent idea. London, er...advocates it." *Actually, London bloody well insists on it.* "Take all the time you need. There's no need to hurry back. Where are you thinking of vacationing?"

"We rather fancy Malta," replied Milo Standish.

They got up and as he reached the door, Robinson turned round.

"By the way, I forgot to say, Sir Peter Glendower passed away the day before yesterday. Most unfortunate."

Standish looked at him as if he couldn't quite believe what Robinson had said.

"Unfortunate? Yes. And sad, I would have thought. Above all, very sad." There was an edge to Standish's voice.

"Quite," said Robinson.

"You'll let me know the arrangements?"

"No arrangements, by request."

By whose request was not clarified and before Standish had time to ask, Robinson had gone.

* * *

31 July

"So, we're all set then," said Sandro Menotti. "Malta it is. Great news about you and Ravi."

"And London none the wiser. In fact, London is as happy as sand boys. Obviously, we're not welcome home yet."

"Nice to be loved, isn't it?"

"Has its upside, that's for sure."

"You're not worried? Dirty work behind your backs."

"Let's face it, Sandro, there's always dirty work behind our backs. Sometimes, it's just better not to know about it."

"Much the same at my place, I can tell you. What we call the 'office boys' elbowing for position. Most of them know nothing about the field. Think it's where you put cows to graze."

Standish laughed, "I must tell Ravi."

"Is he getting over the Khourasan business? Quite a trauma."

"I think so. Haven't really got him to talk about it yet. He'll do that in his own time. Knows he's got to. I suppose I've been lucky; I've never had to face a friend in a situation like that."

"Few of us have, thank God."

"A colleague, once. But we'd seen it coming for a long time. And anyway, it's not the same as a friend you've grown up with."

"He's a tough kid, Milo. If anyone can cope, he will."

"I know. He's looking forward to helping out with the Malta thing. So am I."

"Well, thanks to you, we've got a lead to follow up. Sanny Darmanin?"

"His name's cropped up a few times, but just on the periphery of things. Calls his business Transport Solutions, that's what rang a bell with me. Started out as just a useful contact for small-time hoods who needed to move stuff along, then got a bit more ambitious—guns, drugs and possibly, kids. According to the Abbess, he's become a very nasty piece of work indeed."

"And looks as though he may have graduated to the premier league if he's got into bed with the *Caliphate*. Moving top-notch stolen art demands a degree of professionalism. Got to know what you're doing, or no buyer would look twice at it."

"He's got to have a contact in Malta if that's where the artworks are stashed."

"Their intelligence people have instructed Customs to keep an eye out for any small air freight carriers coming in. There's only been one. A consignment of medical supplies sent by the Order of St John here in Italy for a charity working in Somalia. They hadn't any concerns about it. Often happens. The Order's well known and respected. Does it all the time."

"All the same, why send it via Malta?"

"The charity it's going to is run by the mother of a Maltese aristocrat, Sylvia Alquemada, best friends with the Holy Father. I know, I know, Milo. You don't like the sound of it." He laughed. "Anglo-Saxon scepticism?"

"Probably, Sandro."

"Don't worry, I'll follow it up. I don't much like the sound of it either. The other thing I want to know is who is the buyer?"

"Or buyers. Could be more than one. We're looking at a lot of money."

"Yes. I asked our friend Casamassa about that. He reckons over half a billion euros on the open market. A lot less, of course, on the black market. Opinions differ. Some say as little as ten per cent, others would go as high as fifty. Who can tell?"

"Small change for a billionaire, Sandro, in any case."

"No one's going to buy without inspecting first and getting authentication. Could be a problem for them, finding an expert willing to do it."

"There's always an impoverished academic who can be suborned into making a few extra bob."

"A few 'bob'?"

"Sorry, an expression. Old English money. Let's say a handy little packet of euros!"

Menotti laughed.

"So, for a few 'bob', our billionaire, whoever he is, gets them authenticated, then he has to come and see for himself to make sure that he's spent the money well. Maybe there we have a chance. He flies in or sails in. Whichever it is, we have to know about it. Our Maltese friends will help us there."

"Nothing much can be done unless you catch him with his hands on them, so to speak."

"Wherever they have got them hidden, they'll have to be moved sooner or later. So we watch and wait."

"There's Darmanin, don't forget. They won't go anywhere until he's been paid. He'll see to that. He'll watch them like a hawk and if we can keep tabs on him, he'll lead us right to them."

"We're going to need all the team on this."

"Ravi and I are ready as soon as you give the word. Lavinia too."

"Right, Milo. It is, as you British say, game on!"

Chapter Eleven

Rome
2 August

Early mass in the conventual church of the Order of Preachers was over and the friars filed out, making their way to the refectory for breakfast. There was always a handful of visitors cutting across the court to the gate that led out to the street. The Order encouraged visitors to attend its services, one way to open up to the world and dispel some of the myths about the monastic life. Today's batch was regulars mostly but including one or two tourists; the first mass of Sunday was less popular than the High mass later in the morning. The air was humid, the sky cloudy with a light drizzle on and off. One of the visitors hung back from the rest. Small, thin, with a pale heavily lined face, an inconspicuous man, weedy, not someone you would look at twice in passing. Despite the haggard appearance, probably not much beyond the late thirties—difficult to guess with such a man. Hands thrust deep into the pockets of a gabardine coat with the collar turned up, he wore dark grey trousers and trainers that had seen better days. Rain had soaked his hair into lank strands that hung down in front of his eyes, so a casual glance might have suggested just another down and out, looking for something to turn up. But the fellow was on the lookout for one of the members of the Order, scrutinising their faces as they passed by. One or two shot him an enquiring look before heading off for other duties elsewhere.

Among these was Antonio Marcetti, not bound for breakfast but intent on another commitment in his schedule. When in Rome on Sunday mornings, he said mass for the Little Sisters of the Charity of St Mary Magdalene in a room that served as a humble chapel in their house a few blocks away from the Dominicans. The Little Sisters were a safe house for a small number of abused women who had had to leave their matrimonial homes and, in most cases, abandon their children. It was a duty Marcetti valued in giving him the opportunity to be in touch with people in desperate need of protection and for their part, the women were glad of the friar's ministry among them. After mass, he would stay and have breakfast with them and let them talk if they wanted to.

Accosted as he hurried out, Marcetti stopped and looked askance at the stranger before him.

"Father Marcetti," the man said, "I have a message for you."

"For me?"

"For you, Father."

"And it is…?"

"A bereavement notice."

Marcetti stared at the man, "Who are you?"

"Just a messenger. Though not an angelic one."

"My friend, I regret I haven't time for these games."

"No games, Father Marcetti."

"Then, please state your business and let me be on my way. I'm already a little late."

"My master says this to you. The dead have cried out and have been heard, as you foretold. God will not be silent."

The cadence of his words caused Marcetti to step back in surprise.

"Perhaps you had better tell me your master's name."

"He is known by many names. He said you would understand the message."

"I do not understand."

"That is all I can tell you. He says you and he are destined to meet soon."

"And this so-called bereavement notice?"

"It is for the one who will destroy himself, as you have predicted."

Again, the words resonated with Marcetti. His own words, uttered all too recently, coming back to him, scarcely out of his mouth. London, the city. The financial heart of everything. The place where money seemed to leach out of the very paving stones. A meeting in a dingy office with a powerful and dangerous man, a man whose cold fury he had felt burning into his back as he had left that room. Cross. Was something about to happen to Cross?

"You say I am to meet with this master of yours. When will this be and where?"

"That is not for me to say. You will know when the time comes."

"Tell him I am waiting."

It was much later when he left the refectory after lunch that the Master caught up with him.

"Antonio, a minute of your time, if I may. It's cleared up a bit. Shall we take a stroll in the garden?"

As they walked, the Master began, "I've been approached by your friend, the Patriarch of Venice, for assistance with a plan he is forming later this summer. He tells me he has been presented with the opportunity to open up discussions with the head of an Islamic foundation. A man of some distinction, I gather, who is interested in exploring the possibility of an inter-faith dialogue between a group of young Muslims and a similar group of young Christians. To examine areas of common interest between the two faiths, such as the welfare of refugees who've been forced to seek shelter in the West. A relevant and pressing topic for all of us. Giancarlo says it's an opportunity to identify issues where there could be a crossover between ourselves and Islam. He's specifically asked for your assistance with this—at least in the early stages of planning—and he's asked me to sound you out before making a formal request to the Order. How does it strike you, Antonio?"

"Initially favourably but with reservations, Master, an ambitious plan. The scope sounds a little vague at this stage."

"I agree. But I'm sure Giancarlo will clarify that. That's where you'd be able to help. You hesitate, Antonio?"

"Only that I am constrained by the vow of silence the Order has placed upon me."

"I don't see a problem, providing it's made clear that your input is purely a matter between you and the Patriarch. He has said that this is a private initiative and he is keen to keep it such. The media is to have no part in it, at least at this juncture. It would raise a storm of controversy that would be anything but helpful at such an early stage.

"Then I'll be happy to give what help I can."

"I'll let him know you're interested and he can make the arrangements. Just let me know when you plan to be away."

* * *

Palazzo Alquemada, Mdina
3 August

Pausing at the corner, he fumbled for his cigarettes and flicking his lighter several times, dropped the large iron key in his hand with a clang. It echoed all around the *calle*.

"Shit," he said, picking it up and continuing along the stone wall to an arched doorway, he fitted the key into the lock of one of the iron-studded doors. It turned with ease; he'd made sure of that at the start of this business—oiling it and working it until it operated like new. He lifted the latch and pushed the door open. Once inside, he closed it carefully and relocked it with a loud metallic sound. Looking around the courtyard, all was quiet. The guards would be with their charges on the far side. At least that's where they should be, waiting his arrival and instructions for the next and most important phase of the contract. Once the items had been dispatched to their new owner, all that remained was the safe delivery of the special consignment. A potential problem off his hands and an additional fat fee into his Cyprus account. It was all working out as he had hoped and planned. This decaying and miserable ruin of a place would see the successful crowning of his latest enterprise. There was no telling what heights he might aspire to after this. Transport Solutions would go viral, a global operation dealing exclusively with the wealthiest and most privileged of clients—*total discretion guaranteed*—and best of all, he would be one of the wealthiest businessmen in the whole of the Republic of Malta.

He stopped to look at the fountain at the centre of the courtyard, crowned with a statue of the goddess Circe, daughter of Helios, distinguished for her magical arts, now silent. Silent these many years. Even the dribbles of water that had leaked from her upturned hands had now dried up. Streaks of rust ran down her legs and over the edges of the cracked stone basin where at one time, the water level had overflowed. The urns in the cloister arches that ran on three sides of the courtyard were empty, some cracked and crumbling. Glancing up, he noticed that all the window shutters had been closed against the midday sun even on the shaded side of the palace. Flaking plaster from the walls of the cloister and on the staircase up to the first floor lay all around.

Reaching the *piano nobile*, he turned left along the wide corridor ignoring the double doors in front of him into the Grand Salon, knowing they were always kept locked from the inside. At the end, he came to the antechamber and in the corner was the smaller door once used by palazzo servants. He listened—not a sound—but he knew she would be there. Quietly opening the door, he slipped inside. There she was at the far end in her wheelchair drawn up to the large recessed window that overlooked the front of the palazzo and the street. The once grand reception room was now sparsely furnished. Along the right-hand side wall on each side of the main doors was a row of fauteuils, the gilt chipped and flaking off, the faded dark green damask threadbare showing the lining beneath, the material hanging in shreds, some of it trailing on the floor. The walls were also dark green silk, stained, bespattered with candle grease and God knows what else. There were large darker rectangular areas where portraits had once hung, the candelabra brackets each side of them long since gone. In places, the silk paper had peeled away and hung down. Down the centre of the salon, a series of four huge chandeliers were draped in white covers—unlit for a generation or more. Between the windows on the left-hand side, there were gilt-framed peer glasses, still surviving but cracked now and pocked and hung over two white marble-topped rococo side tables. To describe the scene as one of faded grandeur would be a gross understatement. Despite the dry stillness of the atmosphere, he shivered involuntarily.

As he passed through to the far end, she saw him. She turned in her chair and glared. Usually, she never addressed so much as a word to him. But this time, her croaking voice cut through the stagnant air.

"You again! Why have you come back to my house? You, and the others."

"The others are here because they have to be. You should be glad of company in this decaying heap. No one would come out of choice."

"Not them, you fool boy."

"Who then?" he snarled.

"Not those who came yesterday either."

"You're rambling, old woman."

"Don't 'old woman' me!" she barked. "This is my house, show some respect."

"Shut up! You old hag. What 'others' are you talking about?"

She turned to stare out of the window.

He went and stood in front of her chair, persisting, because she saw and heard everything that went on in the house.

"What are you saying? Who else is here? Tell me!"

"You'll find out soon enough."

"You're crazy, you demented old fool."

"Yes, no doubt I am. Crazy. But *you* are the fool."

179

He kicked out at her wheelchair. She gave a little laugh and went back to staring out of the window.

He walked away towards the doors at the end of the salon and stopped and listened for voices. He thought he heard a faint sound and bent close to the join in the two doors. Nothing. Were those bastards asleep? He turned back to look at the old woman. She was still staring out of the window and he thought he heard her mutter something to herself but couldn't catch it. She seemed unaware that he was still there. Mad old bitch. But was she? Not as mad as all that. Not at all. She missed nothing. He supposed a servant, carer, whatever, would come eventually and wheel her away. Watch while she ate next to nothing, put her to bed and next morning, the routine would start all over again.

Again, that faint noise, but he couldn't be sure it came from the room beyond the doors. Was the old woman muttering again? He reached out, gently took hold of one of the heavy bronze door handles, eased it down and pulled the door towards himself. He'd catch those idle fuckers out. Give them hell. It opened without a sound. The chamber beyond was in total darkness. He knew where to locate the light switch that would turn on the single chandelier, just inside the door to the right. Stepping forward, he felt around the edge of the doorframe and his hand came into contact with the metal switch. He flicked it down, but nothing happened. He started to step back into the Grand Salon but as he did so, there was a loud clatter and the shutters of the room's only window were thrown open. Dull evening light streaming through revealed two figures, one each side of the window. The one on the left stepped forward.

"Mr Darmanin, I assume, of Transport Solutions. Allow me to introduce myself. Raschid Al-Azhar. My associate," turning to the other man, "Mr Husseini. It would be best, I think, if you were to close that door. We do not wish to disturb the *Marchesa* further. So…you are no doubt surprised. Let me explain. I represent the vendors in this matter. Mr Husseini, the interests of the purchaser. He will have some questions to ask you."

Darmanin was in a daze. Events had taken a turn for which he was not at all prepared.

"Yes…that is…no problem." He looked around the room.

"Where are the guards?" he asked.

"Dismissed."

"Dismissed? Who dismissed them?"

"The Marchese Alquemada."

"Why? What for?"

"There was no point in their being here."

"I don't understand. What's going on?"

A suddenly white-faced Darmanin felt panic rising within him.

"They had nothing to guard…of any value, that is."

"These paintings…?"

"Ah…yes…the paintings… These paintings here I assume you are referring to. Worthless. According to the experts. Worthless copies. In other words, Mr

Darmanin, forgeries, fakes. Not even well-executed. On some, they said, the paint scarcely dry more than a day or two."

Darmanin gasped. His head swam.

"It's not possible…it's not possible." His voice rose and shook.

"Oh," said Al-Azhar, "it's perfectly possible. And it's perfectly possible that you can assist in this matter." His voice was rich with sarcasm and venom.

"I don't see how; I don't know any more…I don't know what I can do." Darmanin was frantic now, looking back to the door he'd come in by as if weighing his chances of flight.

"Don't even think it," said Al-Azhar and Darmanin found himself looking down the barrel of a revolver that had somehow magically appeared in the commander's hand.

"Get that chair, put it here and sit!"

Al-Azhar placed himself directly in front of him.

"Where are the originals, Mr Darmanin?"

"I don't know what you're talking about. I really don't know. They came here to Malta. That's all I can tell you."

"No, Mr Darmanin. You are going to tell me a great deal more than that."

"I can't tell you what I don't know, for God's sake."

"For your own sake, Mr Darmanin, believe me. God has very little to do with this. Let me make things easier for you. Let us go back to the beginning. You were contacted by an agent of Mr Husseini's client, the purchaser. A contract was discussed, agreed and drawn up. All very proper. How am I doing so far?"

Darmanin mumbled incoherently and Al-Azhar took it as an answer and continued, "Tell us the terms of that contract. What exactly did you agree to?"

Darmanin looked up, the misery on his face slightly evaporated.

"I was to supply a transport plane to collect freight from this airfield in Sicily. Calderari, it was called. To be flown here to a private airfield belonging to Marchese Alquemada. It was all arranged. Contacts of mine had made the arrangements. The contents would be unloaded into an ambulance supplied by my company and brought here. An expert would come and examine the pictures. Zamorra, the buyer, was to come and inspect them. Then they would go back to the airfield and be flown out of Malta. I don't know where. God knows, I've no idea. It wasn't discussed with me, it wasn't my business," his voice hesitated and trailed off.

"So far, so good. You see how easy it is when you cooperate. Please continue."

"Maltese customs were informed that a consignment of medical supplies had been flown in from Sicily for onward transmission to Somalia in the Horn of Africa. The freight carriers were acting for the Order of St John. Given the Order's connection with Malta, that information wasn't challenged. A mission of mercy. For the starving."

"Very convenient, to use the starving people of Somalia to cover your tracks. Imaginative."

"We had to think of something."

"Indeed. So, Mr Darmanin, my next question to you is this. Where was the exchange made? Where did your transport aircraft go when it took off from the Calderari airstrip in Sicily?"

"It came here. It flew directly here."

"It cannot have! You're a liar!"

"I tell you it did; that's all I know."

"And what happened then? Were these forgeries *run up* here, is that what you want us to believe?" Al-Azhar shouted. He turned and walked over to where the paintings lay stacked against the wall. He whipped back towards his victim.

"We have plenty of time, though shortly my patience will start to wear thin. Think over what you have said. And what you haven't told us."

"I've told you everything."

"Listen very carefully. Mr Husseini here is an expert himself. In extracting information from unwilling individuals who think they can pull the wool over our eyes."

"I did everything I was asked. Please, believe me." He was pleading now, frantic. "Including Zamorra's special request," he added.

"Ah! So there is more."

"Tell us about this 'special request'," Husseini said.

"Zamorra was looking for a young person to accompany him on his Mediterranean cruise. His yacht, the *Aphrodite*, is anchored outside the Grand Harbour. You know what his preferences are."

Al-Azhar and Husseini looked at each other. Darmanin continued, "No business of mine. Surely you were…"

"Go on."

"I knew of a young lady who'd be willing to join him for this holiday. The holiday of a lifetime."

And then he explained the arrangement.

"This plan for the girl, I take it, is on course?" Husseini asked.

"Yes, yes, I've told her what to do and when. She'll come to my office tomorrow to be collected and I'll take her down to the harbour. She'll go out to the yacht by tender. We couldn't do it before; it was too risky. We had to wait till the *Aphrodite* was ready to sail."

"Mr Zamorra will have some consolation for his pains," Al-Azhar observed dryly.

"Small enough compensation for his loss," Husseini replied.

"When does your contract stipulate you are to be paid?" asked Al-Azhar.

"As soon as the girl boards the yacht."

"Indeed. That, I would think, is now open to considerable doubt."

Darmanin shrank back on the chair, wringing his hands together to disguise how much they were shaking.

Al-Azhar walked back to the window, took his mobile out of his pocket and spoke briefly. Too quietly for Darmanin to hear what was said. Husseini smiled down at him in a way that made shivers run down his spine. Al-Azhar came back, looked at Husseini and nodded.

"What...what happens now?" asked Darmanin.

"A number of things will take place, some of them not very pleasant...for you, that is."

Darmanin felt sick; he clutched the sides of his chair.

"On the other hand..." Al-Azhar paused, "some things will turn out rather well, for these paintings in particular."

"What...do you mean?"

"If it's of any interest to you, Mr Darmanin—though I doubt it is any longer—they will be returned to the Palermo Gallery from which they were stolen."

"They'll know instantly they're fakes."

"No, Mr Darmanin, they'll be delighted to receive back ten genuine paintings, part of the famous Galiano Collection. For that is exactly what these are." He smiled.

Sanny Darmanin looked up at him. He felt a choking in his throat. He couldn't speak. Couldn't work out what was going on. None of it made any sense, except...except maybe it was beginning to. It started to dawn on him that he had, perhaps, walked into the middle of a very clever confidence trick. And he was not going to walk out of it anytime soon. The sound of voices and several footsteps came from behind the double doors. Al-Azhar strode over and opened the doors.

"Inspector Cachia, thank you for being so prompt. Please come in. The gentleman you're looking for, as you see, is here."

The policeman came into the room followed by four officers.

"Darmanin, get up!"

He struggled to his feet, shaking so much that he grabbed hold of the back of the chair for support.

"Handcuff him."

One of the officers stepped forward, seized his hands and forced them behind his back.

Cachia addressed him, "I won't take up the time of these gentlemen now reciting all the charges you're about to face. Suffice it to say that supporting terrorism and the corruption of minors will certainly be prominent among them. You have just enjoyed your last day of freedom for many years, Darmanin." He turned to the two men. "Two of my officers will remain here to guard these paintings. They have been impounded by order of the Supreme Court of Malta. They were brought illegally into the country and therefore, for the time being, remain under our protection. Boys," he said to the two officers, "you'll be relieved by the next shift in four hours." As he prepared to leave, he turned and smiled, "Signor Menotti, on behalf of the government of Malta, I thank you and your British colleague for your assistance with this matter."

The three policemen left with their prisoner between them. The remaining two settled themselves in chairs facing the doors into the Grand Salon and lit up cigarettes. The spies bade them goodnight and followed the others out. The old woman in her wheelchair by the window was no longer there.

* * *

Valletta
4 August

Her excitement had reached fever pitch. So much so she could hardly think about anything else. Starting to do one thing then dropping it for another. Offering to help in the house, unheard of previously. Not needing to be asked twice, a new parental experience. All the family noticed it. Her father thought it was something to do with the boyfriend, though Nadaro hadn't had this effect before and when his name was mentioned she was scornful. Her mother simply ascribed it to age and hormones. She couldn't settle down and to her siblings, she was suddenly unbearably nice. A sure sign something was up. And yesterday after school in the old janitor's room that was no longer used, Nadaro was vouchsafed a few minutes for a bit of fumbling. He was in ecstasy—for ages he'd been ignored and he blamed that old pervert Darmanin. Well, a kick in the balls had sorted that out. Now the passion of his life had come back and she'd got him so worked up, he couldn't hold off long enough.

Now it was lunchtime. Sanny had warned her that this might be it. For her, that was enough, perhaps at last the moment had arrived, the gates of paradise were about to be flung wide open. She entered the tiny alley that led to the love nest, the place where her desires had been gloriously fulfilled. She was almost breathless as she climbed the stone stairs to the second floor. She opened the door and stepped inside. A man and a woman stood there smiling. She looked around; no sign of Sanny.

"Where's Sa...?"

"He's fine, nothing to worry about. You're to come with us. It's all been arranged. We have a car waiting at the other end of the street."

They walked briskly along the alley, the man following close behind. A white car was parked, engine running, a man in dark glasses behind the wheel. The woman opened the back door and she got in and the woman got in beside her.

"Where're we going?"

"Not far, you'll see."

That was the moment when a slight cloud of doubt first crossed her mind. The woman's accent had a hint of American. But she composed herself and the woman carried on smiling encouragingly. The car wound its way through the back streets of Valletta. Streets she felt she ought to know but she began to feel slightly disoriented. Places that should have been familiar started to seem unfamiliar. But this was what the secret life was like, to throw others off the scent. It wasn't until the car pulled up outside the police station that she felt a real pang of alarm.

"Now dear," said the woman taking hold of her arm in a very firm grip, "come along with me, you're going to meet some people you know."

She squirmed, trying to pull her arm away, but the grip tightened like a vice. Out of the car, up the steps and into the police station, the man following close behind. Along a corridor to a room at the end. The door opened, several people stood around, including her parents. Her mother stepped forward, her eyes full of tears, her father stretched out his hand and took his wife's arm.

"Give it a moment, dear."

The girl turned back to the door but if she was contemplating escape, there was no hope there. The dark-skinned man who had accompanied them stood in front of it, looking serious. From the group of people around her parents, an official-looking woman said, "Why don't we all sit down?" And the girl burst into tears.

* * *

The Grand Harbour, Valletta
5 August

From their vantage point in the Upper Barrakka gardens, they were able to look down over the Grand Harbour. They stood and watched the scene slowly unfold. The motor yacht, *Aphrodite*, anchored in territorial waters, had been escorted by an offshore patrol vessel of the Maltese Navy to a prepared berth within the confines of the inner harbour. On the quay that ran alongside the berth, the flashing lights of police cars and an ambulance were seen. Activity on this scale was rarely seen. It was some time before a motorised passenger gangway was manoeuvred into position against the access door of the yacht. By this time, a group of officials had gathered, waiting to climb the stairs to board. Police uniforms were prominent as well as those of the harbour authorities, Customs and the Financial Security service of the Republic. Several men and women in plainclothes also formed part of the embarking group.

The taller of the two watching men turned to his companion.

"Check the account information again…"

"Still nothing."

"That's it then. A heavy price will be paid for this."

The other man swore.

"Months of fucking time and effort for nothing."

"Calm yourself, Raschid. We need to discover all those responsible and deal with them one by one. You personally will dispose of Menotti and that interfering bastard of a British spy, Standish. They have made us look like fools with their insulting impersonations. Darmanin will prove more difficult. He's in custody. I want him out of the way before he talks any more. The fool will think that the more he tells them, the lighter his sentence will be. And they'll encourage him to think so, even if it isn't true."

"Have no worries; he's a dead man."

"Inshallah!"

"And your plans?"

"Paris, London and then I'll see. There is much to do. The Caliphate gains ground in Syria. Raqqa is now once more established as its capital. I planned to visit and report our successes here in Europe. With these events, that has become more difficult."

They lapsed into silence while they watched the boarding party.

"Zamorra's little harem is about to be broken up," remarked Al-Azhar. "Still, the least of his worries, I guess."

"And he's the least of ours. A corrupter of youth. Deserves all he gets."

"The arms shipment?"

"Delivered. Thanks be to *Allah Ta'ala.* And thanks to our Iranian brothers."

"But the last shipment from this particular dealer?"

"We have others. The Caliphate has many options. Never trust one alone. But the immediate concern is the Englishman, Cross. He has been compromised and endangers us all."

"His wife betrayed him and jeopardised our cause. She's been dealt with."

"Too late, my friend, she'd already talked, the Dominican knows everything. Cross panicked and spoke to his French and German counterparts. The flow of funds has been slowing. It's only a matter of time before it dries up altogether. We can intimidate them, threaten reprisals, but it's no longer enough. They see better and quicker ways of advancing their political agenda."

"Such as?"

"New alliances. Last week, the three of them met in Lisbon with leading members of the American Republican Party. Remember, next year is the American presidential election. They see an opportunity. A right-wing candidate in the White House. It could affect the whole balance of power globally. Especially in Europe. The political right is stirring: AfD in Germany, Marine Le Pen in France, Austria has Hofer bidding for power and Holland's up there with that fascist Wilders. The financiers have denied, of course, that they have a private agenda. But I've known it from the start. That's the reason we have been seeking alternative sources of money. That is why we must make a demonstration of our ability to spread terror throughout the continent."

"That is why you go to London."

"It is, and this time, without my beloved brother in arms, Khalil."

"My heart grieves with you."

"The time for grieving is over. Tears must be translated into action. He was a noble and brave soldier of the caliphate. No uncle could have expected more of his nephew. His reward will be in Paradise, *Inshallah.* His murderer will rot forever in hell."

"Inshallah!"

"Allah wills it so. You have a plan for dealing with your targets?"

"They are as good as dead."

"The young one, Sharma, can wait. He will be mine."

186

The Palazzo Alquemada, Mdina
Evening, 5 August

When they arrived, the Grand Salon was deserted. This time, to their surprise, they'd been able to enter through the main double doors that stood wide open. On every side were signs of activity. A set of stepladders had been placed beneath one of the vast chandeliers, its linen cover removed and lying in a bundle on the floor. The gilt fauteuils had been pulled out from their places against the wall on each side of the doors, one of them stripped of its old rotten fabric, which lay in a heap beside it. Propped against the wall where the sofas had sat for years, paraphernalia for cleaning and decorating was there. Of its usual inhabitant, there was no sign in the room, the window space empty of its wheelchair. Dyer and Sharma stood looking around in fascination. Menotti turned to Standish.

"This is a turn-up. What do you suppose this is all about?"

"A major restoration, by the look of it. I wonder what's inspired it all of a sudden."

"Umm…maybe someone's just been paid. Time for a party. Though why here?"

"The work's barely started…and then ground to a halt!"

"Quite a place!" said Dyer. "I can't imagine doing this up will come cheap."

"If you're in the pocket of a billionaire, it might help," said Menotti.

"I wonder where the old lady's been shifted to," mused Standish.

"Big enough place, no shortage of choice."

"Something's not right."

"What's worrying you, Milo?"

"Look around. It's…like a stage set. As if we were meant to think…all this is for real. That they're just doing the place up."

"Perhaps they just are," said Sharma. "It needs it."

Standish shook his head and walked to the door at the end of the salon. He opened it and for a moment, stood quite still. No police guards, no pictures. The room was empty.

"Surprise number two," he said.

Menotti swore and then pulled his mobile from his pocket as it rang. He listened to the message and called another number.

"Menotti…" he listened again and then laughed, "you had us worried, Inspector. Yes. We're there now…I see…what time's take-off scheduled? OK, I shall be on the flight. See them safe back. Seven in the evening then, I'll be there." He ended the call. "Relax, friends. The pictures were released by judicial order of the Supreme Court this morning. They're on an Italian military transport aircraft at Luqa airport, leaving for Palermo tonight. I shall be on board!" He beamed with obvious delight.

The group wandered back into the Grand Salon, a sense of relief that at last the mission seemed in sight of a successful end. Only Standish looked thoughtful as he surveyed the scene. Ravi Sharma glanced at him. He could tell when Milo had something on his mind.

"A penny for them," he said.

"Half a billion dollars rather."

"Our Arab friends must be smarting. It's a lot of money to let slip through your hands."

"Maybe…" and before he could finish, an old woman in a wheelchair appeared in the doorway of the salon. This time, she was not alone. A grey-haired woman in a nurse's uniform guided her chair.

"You're leaving," she said. Not quite clear whether it was an observation or a request.

"Madame," Menotti moved forward and took her hand. "We cannot thank you enough for your patience. But at last, you will have some peace. The disturbance to your life has been considerable and unpardonable."

"I shall miss the activity. It's been very interesting. Not all the company, though. That revolting little man. I understand he is to receive his just desserts." Her language was old-fashioned, courtly but with a spark of mischief. She may have sat on the sidelines but not much had slipped past those keen eyes and keener hearing for all her eighty odd years.

Menotti indicated the room.

"There will still be some activity. A transformation taking place. No?"

She shook her head a little sadly. "No. This is all illusion, Signor. An illusion created by my step-grandson. Tino tries to be too clever by half. It was meant to deceive you all. But it had a darker purpose."

"Marchesa?"

"There was a conversation here. Tino and… They had come together to inspect the paintings, Tino and the arms dealer. The arms dealer left and then the other one arrived. Oh yes, signor, you all think I sit in that window and hear nothing. Just a mad old mumbling woman. No, no apologies." As Menotti started to protest, she added, "I'm not offended. It suited my purpose. Bertha, wheel me across, we'll continue from my favourite place. The eyes and ears of the world." She gave a croaking laugh. "Not like the monkey, though, 'hear no evil'…I heard it, saw it and once or twice, even spoke it. For purposes of my own. Now, where was I…? I can lose the thread sometimes."

"The conversation," said Menotti gently.

"Ah, yes, that conversation. Tino…such a promising boy when he was younger. Fallen into bad company. Ruined now, like this place." She turned in her chair to take in the room. "Such times we had in those days. When there was a ball, the musicians were seated right here in this window. If I shut my eyes, I believe I can still hear them, the waltzes, the couples swirling round. The men in uniform or white tie. All done and finished… But yes…the conversation, I haven't forgotten. I'll never forget. They stood right there…in that doorway and spoke of murder. They thought I was asleep! Asleep in my chair, but I heard everything. Even my own name. I pretended to wake up and ask the time!" She put her hand out towards Ravi and gave a little laugh. "You wouldn't think this old woman could be an actress, would you? Such an actress."

Ravi crouched down by the side of her chair, his right hand resting on its arm. "*Marchesa*, tell us who the other man was; did you know him?"

"Dear boy. Are you from Malta?"

"No, madam, I'm English, from London."

"But not originally, from the look of you."

"No, my family came from Pakistan."

"Ah…a beautiful country, but sad people."

"Can you help us any further? A name, perhaps. Or what was being planned."

"What was being planned was bloody murder!"

"Did you know the other man?"

"I never knew his name. You must excuse me. I'm very tired. Bertha, take me back."

The group moved to one side as the wheelchair slowly left the room. When they reached the double doors, she signalled the nurse to stop. Without turning around, she said in barely more than a whisper, "You see, Tino couldn't wait. My husband gave me this house for as long as I lived. But he couldn't wait. He planned to fill it with assassins, all meant to look as if they belonged to this…charade!" And the last word she spat out.

"Bertha, I wish never to enter this room again."

The group crossed the courtyard, through the entrance gates and then along the *calle* towards the piazza in front of St Paul's Cathedral. Not a word was spoken. Each was buried in their own thoughts and, truth to tell, shaken by what they had just heard and seen. Coming around the corner and into the piazza where their car was parked, the blue flashing light of a police car seemed to light up the whole square. As they approached the car, the door opened and an officer got out.

"Would one of you gentlemen be Dottore Menotti?"

"Yes, I am."

"I have Inspector Cachia on the phone, sir. He would like to speak to you."

Menotti walked around to the other side and climbed in. He emerged a few minutes later.

"Well, my friends, the evening's surprises continue."

"What now, Sandro?" said Standish.

"Sanny Darmanin was found an hour ago, hanging in his cell."

For a moment, no one said anything, then Standish asked, "Presumed suicide?"

"Presumed. But Cachia is keeping an open mind."

"Interesting."

"The thing is that he would like me to be there. Have a look at the situation."

"You'll go?"

"I think I should. It means missing the flight to Palermo. Damn it."

"I could go with the flight. Both of us, if you wanted."

"Why not me?" said Lavinia. "I can cancel my Rome flight. Change the booking for Kennedy from there. After all, you two are supposed to be on leave."

"That seems hardly fair," said Standish.

"Not a bit. You two have been in the thick of it far more than me. You deserve a break. I'll go. It will be good to see Francesca again."

"I'm very grateful, Lavinia," said Menotti. "Officer, can we take Miss Dyer to Luqa on the way?"

"No problem, sir."

"It means going via the hotel first to collect my luggage."

"It'll be a pleasure, madam."

"Milo, a word in your ear." Menotti took him by the arm and led him aside from the group. "One problem solved but a bigger one unsolved."

Standish looked at him enquiringly.

"It's good of Lavinia to offer to stand in for me on the flight. But you and Ravi, you can't stay here. This operation's blown wide open. Al-Azhar and company are here somewhere, and where they are, you're not safe. This is a small island. Not too many places to hide away."

"Occurred to me too, Sandro. Not exactly ideal for a holiday destination. I haven't said anything to Ravi yet. We have to get out. I thought the Palermo flight might have been an answer."

"Chances are they'll have it covered at the other end. They'd know you'd be back in Sicily as soon as you landed. And so would their Mafia friends."

"Then Lavinia can't go either."

"They won't be expecting her and she's already booked on the Rome flight tonight. The call's out for you, me and Ravi. They'll be looking for us. But in any case, we'll send her undercover as flight crew. I can arrange it."

"You'll brief her?"

"I'll brief her. Where will you two go? No, on second thoughts, don't tell me. Better I don't know."

"You need to look out for yourself. You'll be a prime target while you're here. Someone got to Darmanin. From the inside. They're probably still there."

"Cachia seems to think so too. That's why he wants my help. Try to find the rotten apple."

"Some world we inhabit, eh, Sandro?"

"*Uno bel domani*, my friend, one fine day."

Goodbyes were a somewhat peremptory affair. The team was aware that after weeks together, this marked the break-up of a bond that had first been sealed back in Venice. They'd worked together well as professionals. In the nature of the job, they probably wouldn't get the chance again. But that's how things went. After the police car had driven off, Standish and Sharma wandered over to their own vehicle and sat inside for a moment, neither inclined to say much, thinking over events.

At length, Standish said, "We'll miss Lavinia; she's a remarkable and talented woman."

"We couldn't have managed without her. Her Lucy Black was quite an act!"

"Totally convincing."

"I wonder who the real Lucy Black was. Did she exist?"

"She does now…Ravi, we have something to discuss, urgently."

"What's the matter?"

"You realise we can't stay in Malta. It's become far too dangerous."

"Is that what you and Sandro were talking about?"

"Among other things."

"So, we're on the run?"

"Not the way I'd care to put it. Taking precautionary measures."

"Comes to the same thing."

"Except the initiative's with us."

"Sounds like semantics to me! Sorry, Milo, if I'm sounding cynical."

"Not like you. But you've had a lot on your plate in recent weeks. Time for us both to chill out."

Ravi laughed, "First time I've heard you use that expression. Have you any ideas?"

"One or two. I've got access to a safe house on Corfu. The thing is that if we go for it, it means a complicated journey. We can't just board a plane for Corfu and that's it. Separate travel arrangements for a start. Roundabout route and all that. Preferably different identities. Meet up again when we get there."

"Life isn't simple in this job, is it?"

"Are you up for it?"

"I'm up for anything as long as we stay together."

"Let's get back to the apartment; I've some planning to do."

Ravi drove back to Valletta, in silence for some time, then… "Milo, I want to ask you something. Back there in the palazzo, how did you know that room was a sham?"

"I saw it the minute we walked in. A stage set."

"Tell me why."

"Easy when you work it out. The chandelier with its cover off. Those massive things work on chains. They have to, they're an enormous weight. To clean them or light them, they're lowered to the floor. If the room was being renovated, cleaned, painted and so on, the very last thing you'd do is strip off the protecting covers. That would come at the end."

"And that's it?"

"Not quite. The gilt sofas. The fauteuils, to use the proper name. Restoring them is highly specialised work. Repairing, re-gilding, and the rest, before applying the new fabric. A lot of skilled work and would be carried out in the upholsterer's workshop. Not what we saw. A pathetic attempt to make it look as if restoration work was taking place. Would never happen like that. Clumsy and amateur."

"And the purpose of it all?"

"To get a team of killers into the place under the guise of something else. Do away with the police guards and anyone else in their way. The old Marchesa included. She was mistaken about one thing. It was nothing to do with his wanting the palace. He gets it anyway when she dies. Alquemada knows she doesn't miss a trick. She'd already seen too much. That's what he was afraid of. What she heard, without telling us in so many words, was the planning of her own death. Passed off as collateral damage. Probably, they were hoping that with a bit of luck, we might turn up too. Then they'd remove the pictures in the van, out to Alquemada's airstrip and out of the country."

"But they left it too late."

"Yes, thank God. For once, we were one step ahead. A bit of a fluke actually. The police moved first as soon as the court issued the release order."

"The other man?"

"There I'm not sure. My guess would be either Al-Azhar or possibly Husseini. The enigmatic Mr Husseini. Always part of everything but on the fringes. In the shadows. The big question is that who is the mysterious Mr Husseini?"

"Want to take a guess?"

Milo leaned towards Ravi and whispered a name into his ear. "Now you know another reason to get out of here."

Milo put his iPhone down and sat back. On the pad beside him were the scribbled notes he'd made.

"You've brought your French identity with you?"

"Yes, Jean-Marie Nottin, schoolteacher from Lyons."

"OK. Your route will be Marseilles-Athens-intercity to Igoumenitsa and ferry to Corfu town. Say three days, allowing for hitches. The moment you get dropped off at Luqa, start looking for a tail. There's bound to be a number of swops. You know what to do. You're good at spotting."

"You think they're that sophisticated?"

"They use locals who know the terrain. When you get to Corfu, collect a hire car. People carrier—looks like a family on holiday and plenty of room for kids and kit."

"Where do we meet?"

"Kassiopi. Down at the harbour, there's a shop that sells locally made lace, been there forever, called Stella Stephanos. Noon of the fourth day. If I'm not there and you have to stay overnight, try one of the *pensione* nearby. Plenty of choice. Then noon every day. Don't worry, I'll find you. Don't call unless it's an emergency."

"And your route?"

"From here to Venice, then ferry all the way."

"Straightforward."

"Best way to draw them out. Especially on the boat. The Adriatic's deep, well, deep enough. Remember, I'm Piero Gamberini, a computer programmer from Napoli. Once we get to the house, we can relax; it's very secure and very hidden."

"But sooner or later, we have to go home and it starts all over again."

"That's the nature of the trade we're in."

"What are we going to tell London?"

"We've decided to go island-hopping. They can always reach me. Definitely no itinerary in advance. Any calls you get deflect to me, but they'll leave you alone for now. The office knows how to look after us; Julia will fend off the prying."

"Well, that's it, set to go."

"I need to destroy these notes."

Later, they lay side by side, tired but complete.

"I've been coming to one or two personal decisions." Ravi turned on his side and propped up his head on his elbow. "And they're nothing to do with our earlier discussion. Well, not much."

Milo looked at him enquiringly.

"I'm nearly twenty-six. It's time I left my parents' house. Also, we've got to face the reality of the situation we're in. You're bound to be in line for promotion now."

"I wouldn't bank on it."

"It's a ministerial appointment isn't it?"

"Ultimately, yes."

"Whatever you say, it's bound to be on the cards. Our relationship wouldn't be sustainable. No, let me finish. You know what they're like. Somebody will point it out. We could make an inspired guess who it would be. And let's face it, Milo, they'd be right. We both know it couldn't work on that level. Difficult enough as it is. I think we should anticipate a problem ahead."

"I know we're going to have to be grown up about it sooner or later. But for me, some things aren't negotiable."

"For me, too. That's why I've been thinking. I'd like to leave the Service. My degree's a good one. Good enough to take me further in the academic world, wouldn't you say?"

"Is that really what you'd like?"

"For a while, at any rate. There's a research fellowship coming up at King's in modern migration studies, with a view to a PhD. I'd like to have a shot at it."

"You'd have quite a lot to bring to it, especially after the last few weeks."

"Yes. One way or another."

"You'll still be bound by the Official Secrets Act."

"I realise that. Still, I don't think it'll hold me back."

"No reason at all why it should. It applies mainly to operational matters anyway."

"There've been plenty of those lately! Whatever, a small turning point in life!"

"And you'd leave home?"

"It's time. We could set up home together, properly. If you'd want to, of course."

"You know, I would. I've been thinking of getting a bigger flat. My present one's too small. We'd both need some private space for working. But only if you really want to leave the Service."

"What's it been? Just over four years. Straight down from Cambridge. Pretty green about the gills!"

"Ravi be honest with me. This isn't all about Khalil, is it?"

"No, it isn't. I'm working through that, bit by bit. You've been good enough to let me do it in my own way. This is all about us. I want to spend the rest of my life with you, if you can stand the thought of that!"

Milo said nothing, his actions speaking louder.

* * *

London

6 August

Andrew Cross stood at the window of his office and watched the rain falling steadily. A summer's day in London. In the street six floors below, people scurried about, a sea of umbrellas, which were bright spots on the greyness of the city, the traditional black now rarer than it used to be. In the city, there were always the few diehard traditionalists who eschewed anything other than the formality of the past, but the old bowler hat brigade, once such a common sight, had all but disappeared. Rainbow-coloured umbrellas and more casual dress now. Cross couldn't help feeling a degree of displeasure at the sight. In his own organisation, there was to be no 'dressing down'. The faces too, if one could have seen them from his vantage point, would have likewise reflected the changed complexion of British life. He sighed. The realities of a multicultural society. How he hated that expression. On the desk behind him, the computer screen flickered and bleeped as communications poured in from all corners of the Cross Organisation's worldwide empire. Very few were intended for his personal attention, dealt with by the various departments to which they were directed. But even billionaire businessmen liked to hold on to the fiction that they were keeping their fingers on the pulse. For the Crosses of this world, it was only the big picture that commanded their attention. And the big picture meant the global picture. Money, politics, power—the holy trinity of globalisation. He was part of that indivisible and sacred union as were his associates in Paris and Berlin. He felt things were moving too slowly in Britain, the government less sure-footed, barely acknowledging his own adroit exercise of power play, much of it designed to keep the administration in place and keeping its distance. Promising the earth but struggling to manage their own square foot of turf. Talking endlessly of a referendum on Europe, anything to keep the populace quiet, but too timid for its own good. His colleagues elsewhere seemed to exercise a degree of influence on internal affairs of which he was both admiring and deeply envious. British over-caution could yet cause the whole plan to unravel. It was time to speak again with his contact in the Cabinet Office.

Then there were the threats from within his own organisation. Who to trust, who to watch? In a multinational corporation, impossible to know! Even worse was the betrayal from within his own family. But that had been dealt with, quickly, brutally and as it turned out, not quite cleanly enough. The leak had been plugged, the price a spouse's death, achieved with a fine display of public mourning and truth to tell, private relief. At the beginning, Rosamund had been an adornment to his career—attractive, intelligent, sociable and with an impeccable background. As a wife and mother, she couldn't have been faulted. Gradually, her religion invaded every aspect of their lives, from the bedroom to the boardroom. That damned Dominican presuming to pull the strings of their marriage. Let the Caliphate deal with that. As for his two grown-up children, the loss of their mother had been hard to bear. Nevertheless, there were compensations. In the billionaire's creed, everything could be measured in terms of a balance sheet, even the emotions of offspring. He turned away from the window and looked at his watch. Time to leave for his meeting in the long dark room.

Usually the first to arrive, this time he was awaited. The other man was seated in his usual chair to the left of the empty fireplace.

"You are late, Mr Cross, how unlike you," as Cross took his seat. "Today I do not come as a messenger," he continued.

"You have no message from the Caliphate?"

"Today the Caliphate has no need of a messenger."

Cross looked at him, uncomprehending.

"But for the moment, let that be. We need to consider the present position. The work of the Caliphate has been seriously compromised. Only your contributions to our cause have kept you alive so far. But the schedule of payments has not been adhered to as agreed. What is more, the last transfer of funds to our account showed a marked decrease from what was in the charter drawn up between us. The Caliphate finds that incomprehensible. Either an error has been committed—the fallibility of modern technology, perhaps. Or there is a problem of which you have failed to apprise us..." he paused. "So, I take it from your silence that we can rule out *computer error*." The sarcasm was inescapable.

"You have to understand that what I and my associates negotiated was subject to market forces, to the uncertainties of global economics. There are highs and lows as markets fluctuate. That has an effect and is outside our control."

"That is an insulting answer and you know it! A large proportion of your personal wealth is untouched by such considerations. Do you take us for ignorant peasants with sand between our toes?"

"You fail to understand the complexity of what we have undertaken."

"And you apparently fail to understand that you are not dealing with fools who believe every lie you throw in their faces."

Silence. At length, the other man spoke again, "There is also the question of your late wife. Her revelations to the priest cost her her life."

"The priest gave me assurances that Rosamund's disclosures to him would remain 'under the seal of priestly confidentiality'. That is the most sacred of all trusts for these priests. Whatever my wife revealed to him will die with him."

"You expect the Caliphate to believe what these infidels claim! Infidels who murdered their own co-religionists, who burned them at the stake and then had the hypocrisy to make them saints! You would trust infidels like that!"

Again, silence.

"The priest is no longer of relevance. But the price of your failure has not been fully paid. There is an outstanding balance. The Caliphate feels it must be settled, finally."

"Kill me," said Cross, "and you kill your golden egg."

The other man leaned forward and took a document from the table beside his chair.

"Not quite, Mr Cross. I have here an account in your own words of your dealings with the Caliphate. A confession, in your late wife's parlance, no? How fitting! It details every discussion, every meeting, the financial arrangements made, the names of your associates in France and Germany, negotiations with people traffickers, the meetings you have had with extreme right-wing political groups, even details of your recent meeting with the Americans. And, to crown it all, the name of the contact within the British Government who has proved so useful to your cause. I don't believe anything has been left out. It is the greatest document of betrayal the world has ever seen. I wonder if you'd care to put a financial value on it. What would it be worth to your government alone? To your associates? To your Organisation? I could go on. Now *this* is the Golden Egg!"

Cross sat rigid in his chair. "What do you intend to do with it?" he asked.

"Your deathbed confession? Like all confessions of criminality, I intend you should put your signature to it. That is all that is required; witnesses have already most helpfully countersigned. Unimpeachable witnesses. You will know them when you read it."

"Don't be ridiculous! You can't force me to put my name to that worthless scrap of paper. Who would believe for an instant that it was genuine? A concocted bit of rubbish extracted under duress."

"Did you imagine our conversations in this room were under the 'seal of priestly confidentiality'? Your Catholic faith has led you sadly astray. Every moment, every word, has been filmed and recorded. It is what we might call, supporting evidence of your treachery."

Cross closed his eyes and rested his head on the back of his chair. "So," he said, "you're telling me that this is the end of the road."

"Yes, Mr Cross."

"I will not sign that paper under any circumstances. Do with me what you will."

"Let us not indulge in meaningless melodrama. If you refuse to sign, you will take a little longer to die and it will be considerably more painful. At least have the grace to exit this world with a modicum of dignity."

In his hand, he had a black and gold fountain pen which, as he stood up, he held out to Cross. Cross got up, crossed the space between them and took the pen from the other man. To sign the document, he had to go down on one knee before the low table. It took some time to sign each of the pages. But it was his last symbolic act of submission. As he signed the final page, he heard the words of the other man behind him, "You told me, in the course of one of our discussions, that you would have liked to meet the Prophet Mohammed, peace be upon him. Now you are about to. *Allahu Akbar!*"

Chapter Twelve

Malta
6 August

Milo had one more task to perform before he left Malta. He'd seen Ravi off by taxi from the apartment at 7 o'clock that morning. His own flight to Venice was due to depart from Luqa at 1.50. Shortly after eight, he and Sandro Menotti sat together at a table at the back of a small café across the road from police HQ in Valletta. For Menotti and Joseph Cachia, it had been a long night. And not a productive one. Hours spent searching police staff records including ancillary staff had failed to turn up even the merest hint of a lead. Then shortly before 3 a.m., a call had come through. A call that relegated their current investigation into the death of Darmanin to the category of low priority. Information had been received from Security at Palermo Falcone-Borsellino Airport that military transport flight ZX 962 from Luqa, Malta had failed to show up. It took time to ascertain that the flight having departed on schedule at 7 p.m. the previous evening had, within less than half an hour, disappeared from the radar. In the normal course of events, the flight would take off on an approximately south-easterly heading and therefore, in the general direction of the coastline of Eastern Libya. It would then turn on a north-westerly heading for Punta Raisi and the airport of Palermo. It was not known whether the change to the new heading had taken place. Nothing further had been seen or heard of it. An extensive search was being launched by the Italian authorities.

After Menotti had given the news, the two men sat in stunned silence. There seemed nothing to say.

"There's no point speculating at this stage," said Menotti, stirring his coffee with more than usual vigour and shaking his head, still in disbelief. One unspoken thought in both their minds—Lavinia. He banged his fist on the table and swore, "Why...did I...?"

"Sandro, you can't...don't. We can both torture ourselves."

"I can't help thinking what the options might be. Accident, bomb or hijack. Are there any others?"

"Either way, we'll get to hear soon enough. If there's a chance they've got the pictures again, that could prove a lifesaver, something negotiable. We've just got to hope."

"Fucking pictures! I wish to God... The damned aircraft was on the ground here only a few hours. Guarded night and day. Whatever the outcome, the point is that the bastards got to it. In God's name, how?"

"Maybe there are more rotten apples than we think."

"Ravi get away all right this morning?"

Standish looked at his watch. "Due to take off in half an hour. I'll be glad to see him out of this place." They lapsed into silence once more.

Standish broke the spell. "Incidentally, did Cachia say anything to you about what they're doing with Alquemada? It's possible he may have some answers if they can prise them out of him."

"Not much there yet. The bastard's got plenty to answer for, one way or another. They've sent someone to bring him in for questioning. Good luck to them. Frankly, Milo, I worry that the cops here are struggling to keep up with all this. They're doing a decent job but it's way out of their usual league; in fact, way out of anybody's league.

"And your investigation hasn't come up with an answer yet to Darmanin?"

"Not remotely. Damn it. It has to be an inside job. We've looked at every way an intruder might have got access to the cells. Nothing adds up. I'll say one thing for this lot—security's as tight as a duck's arse."

"Suicide, then."

"Impossible. Strung up with a belt that wasn't his. A very peculiar belt. Exceptionally long, not for a man's trousers, even a bloody big one. Forensics is having a go at deciding what it is. Probably not a belt at all. They think possibly made in Argentina. Why don't they ask His Holiness what he thinks, he's from there! I ask you, Argentina! What the fuck does that tell us? And naturally, no note."

"How long will you stay on?"

"No point in staying. Cachia agrees. I'll fly back to Rome tonight. Francesca's flying back in a day or two. Culture Ministry's putting in another temp as director for the gallery, offering the guy a long-term job if he wants it. She says she'll be glad to hand over and be out of it. Quite cut up about Lavinia."

"Don't suppose you've spoken to Lavinia's boss, Keymer, yet."

"Not yet. Another hell of a job to do. Want to hold off until we get something positive."

Menotti looked tired. He ran his hand through his hair and puffed out his lips. His face was grey, eyes bloodshot, lack of sleep catching up on him. "I know. I know. The best would be that the bloody plane turns up somewhere and we get a ransom demand. Some bargaining chip, eh? A human life and half a billion worth of art."

"Another chance to nail the bastards."

"While we're on the subject, any idea what your lot are doing about Cross?"

"No idea at the moment. Bugger all, I expect. Hoping the Caliphate will do it for them."

"Oh, they'll do it all right. But not while he's delivering the goods."

"I've always wondered what the deal was. I mean, how much and how often? How do billionaires manage these things? Not *direct debit*, that's for sure," he laughed. "Imagine it, Sandro, say a million a month going out of your account."

"If that's what's going out, imagine what must be going in!" Both men laughed at the thought.

After all, if there was really nothing to laugh about in life, you simply had to find something.

Standish leaned over and patted his friend on the arm. "Glendower once said to me that the secret of money laundering was not to be in too much of a hurry. At each stage of the process, you need to let it lie dormant for weeks, preferably months. Passing it slowly around the chain and changing the sequence, relatively modest amounts at a time. At least what they would call modest. Eventually, it lands in the end user's account in a backstreet little bank in a shanty town somewhere."

"A bugger to trace."

* * *

Venice

10 August

Antonio Marcetti was greeted with customary warmth when he arrived at the patriarchal palace in Venice. An internal Alitalia flight had brought him to Marco Polo, thence by private launch—compliments of the archdiocese—to the riva entrance where the Patriarch, Giancarlo di Mario, was waiting.

"Antonio! A pleasure I didn't expect to be renewed quite so soon."

"You must have been very persuasive when you spoke to the Master General. He spared me willingly enough for your sake, but against pressing concerns in the Order. He feels the pressures just now and, I fear, his health suffers."

"You know what we Dominicans are like. We value friendship over more mundane matters. But I'm sorry to hear Johann's not well. You must take him my special greetings. But come, let's take some coffee, unless you'd like to rest first after your journey."

"No, Giancarlo, I don't want to waste a moment of your company. I'll need to be back in Rome in two or three days."

Settled in his study, the Patriarch got immediately down to business. He outlined the nature of the unusual request he'd received from the Islamic Foundation of the Levant.

"I hesitated at first, Antonio, not knowing anything about them or what their credentials might be. There's a professor at Padua who's a Muslim and teaches archaeology. My chaplain told me about her, so I thought it was worth a discreet contact and I put some feelers out. Very helpful. Reassured me that this is a venerable and highly respected centre of Islamic Studies. It has a broad cross-section of Muslim academics representing all aspects of Islamic culture.

For some years now, it has been based in Beirut. Have you ever come across it in your work with the Order's study centres?"

"No. I must confess I don't know anything about it. We could ask Johann if he's familiar with their work."

"I did, and he isn't personally, though he says he's heard that they have quite a formidable reputation for scholarship in the Muslim world. By coincidence, one of their number—an art historian called...let me see...ah! Yes, here it is. Dr Mohammed Husseini. He's in Venice at the moment on a private visit. Telephoned and asked if there was anyone who could speak to him about the mosaics in Santa Maria Assunta on Torcello. I took the liberty of saying that I had a Dominican guest coming to stay who could probably help him. Knew a lot about them. Invited him to dinner tonight but he wasn't able to make it. I felt he seemed a little bit reserved about the proposed study conference. Something in the tone of his voice...anyway, I don't know what it was. At any rate, he seemed keen to speak to you and would like to meet up with you tomorrow in Torcello at the basilica. I suggested the late afternoon, but I promise, I haven't committed you if you're at all reluctant. If you want to go ahead, we're to leave confirmation at the Danielli. That's where he's staying, lucky fellow!"

"Well, perhaps in the interests of interfaith relations, it would be churlish to turn him down. Can you spare me for the afternoon?"

The Patriarch smiled, "I can never spare you, but I think I shall have to make the sacrifice. I thought if you and I meet in the morning, we could make a rough outline of what we see the discussions covering. Location too—we need to think about that quite carefully. I'm not sure how acceptable this place would be perhaps more neutral territory."

The next morning boded fair for Marcetti's return visit to Torcello. Early morning mist cleared from the lagoon and by midday, the sun blazed down. Tourists crowded onto the various *vaporetti*, plying here and there to the islands, the Lido being especially favoured by those who planned a day on the beach. After lunch with Giancarlo, he went up to his room and changed into casual clothes. Deciding to walk for a while, he left the patriarchal palace and wound his way through crowded streets heading in the general direction of the Fondamenta Nuove where he knew he could get a *vaporetto* out to Torcello. He'd only been back once since his first trip in 1975 to lead a party of young Dominican novitiates on a pilgrimage for the Feast of the Assumption. High Mass had been celebrated in the Cathedral of Santa Maria Assunta. *How different*, he thought, *had been their reactions from those of his and Salim's.* Twenty years on, the younger generation seemed much less moved by the experience, took it more in their stride and gave the impression that they'd seen it, done it all before. Perhaps they had or perhaps he was just getting old!

Once he got off the boat, lagoon breezes left behind, the sun hammered down as he ambled along the riva past the familiar landmark of the Ponte di Diavolo and the famous Locanda Cipriani. Tourists were coming and going, day trippers straggled along the pathway in desultory fashion, the heat getting to them and raising a crop of complaints from the children. *When can I have an ice cream, when are we going back on the boat? Can't we stop and have a drink?* So on to the basilica, he smiled to himself when he saw 'Attila's chair', which most definitely wasn't, remembering a conversation all those years ago! Forty years, give or take a week or two. Well, he'd better look for the learned Dr Husseini. Hopefully, the academic would recognise him from the description of what he would be wearing in the message that he'd left at the Danielli. Inside, the basilica was busy and noisy. No longer, he thought, able to impose on its visitors a reverent silence, one of the many changes over the years. A group of ten- or eleven-year-olds scampered around excitedly looking at this and that, while a harassed teacher tried loudly, too loudly, in French to explain something of its history. He heard Attila's name mentioned several times and 'Huns' featured prominently in her story. Only the *hodegetria* remained the same—quiet, composed and apparently unfazed by the racket around her. Finding a seat at the end of one of the pews close to a pillar with an uninterrupted view of the mosaic, he settled down to wait for his guest. Gradually, the spill of visitors thinned, the children were marshalled out and an atmosphere of semi-calm descended on the church. He closed his eyes; was it only a few minutes or longer? When he opened them, he became conscious of a figure standing in the centre aisle opposite to where he was sitting. Startled for a moment, he got hastily to his feet.

"Dr… Good God, can it really be you?"

"As you see."

"I don't understand. I've come here to meet a Dr Husseini."

"You're speaking to him."

"It's *you*?"

"The same. Or if you prefer, I'm sometimes known as Omar Wazir."

"Why the changes of name?"

"You've really no idea?"

"Very little makes sense these days."

"Yet, I think in your heart, you may know very well." He sat down in the pew next to the centre aisle.

"I've learnt not to trust what's in my heart; it's betrayed me too often recently. Nor, for that matter, what's in my head either."

"That's unfortunate. You were always more of a 'heart' man. Led more by feeling than reason, wouldn't you say?"

"At last I've learnt that the heart is an unreliable guide."

"I think it may still tell you something. One more betrayal. Even if you don't want to hear it."

"So, Dr Husseini, tell me what's happened to Salim Khourasan."

"Ah! Salim Khourasan. Wanted on three continents. Mohammed Husseini, Omar Wazir, Vizier of the Caliphate, former Dominican student, former Christian, former friend of Antonio Marcetti."

"Never that!"

"Yes, that too! No going back," he spoke fiercely, his voice rasping.

Looking around, Marcetti was aware that the basilica had emptied of visitors. A janitor hurried up from the back.

"I have to shut the doors now," he said. "When you two gentlemen leave, please pull the side door over there closed. No more visitors can be admitted today. No, it's all right, please stay. The Patriarch telephoned, there's no problem for two scholars. I'll come back later to turn off the lights. *Buona sera*, gentlemen." He shuffled off, leaving them alone.

"Why here?" asked Marcetti. "Where there is so much memory of friendship?"

"Where else could we have met? This is where it all began for me. With her." He made a gesture with his hand towards the mosaic.

"She who shows the way. But not the way you chose, Salim."

"How can you be certain of that?"

"I remember how touchingly you spoke of it. You said you'd first come here as a young teenager with your mother. Even then, it had made an impression."

"Not all first impressions are made to last."

"Nevertheless, it was still with you when we came here together. Why else would you bring me?"

"The lost boy from Calabria. Remember how you hated Venice? You said the richness and the beauty of the city disgusted you. I brought you here and showed you this, and it gave you peace of a kind. A reassurance, I suppose. I can't recall exactly how you put it; you were always better at expressing yourself than I was."

"One thing comes back to me quite clearly; I don't know why it's stayed with me. We were sitting on the grass by Attila's famous stone chair! I made you laugh. I said I couldn't imagine him carting that great thing around with him. We talked about the mosaic of Our Lady. I picked up a note of uncertainty in what you were saying. Something along the lines of it not making sense until you'd been back to see your family in Syria. When you got back for the new semester, everything just went on as normal. Nothing seemed to have changed."

"You'd changed, Antonio. You can't any longer see what was in plain sight then. You'd been home to Calabria. Do you remember? When you got back, you were a soul possessed! Ready to tear the world apart. Anger, burning up everything around you. All the injustices of society, you couldn't stop talking about them. It was as if nobody had ever cared before you. You were going to solve the problems of the world. And whatever stood in your way…you would be the angel of judgement. Do you know what we called you behind your back? Savonarola!"

"I've heard that a few times since."

"If ever anyone had become radicalised, it was you. A radicalised Christian. You Christians don't think in those terms, do you? But, yes, that's what it was…and it was you who turned me."

"I turned *you*?"

"I saw your fury. Felt it. Your total commitment. But you needed the Church and the Order behind you to make you credible. They took some convincing but, in time, you succeeded. That was never destined to be my route to salvation. I was the outsider, the true iconoclast, prepared to pull it all down and start again. The Caliphate provided the means to do it. To build an entirely new world on the ruins of the old. You, believe or not, were the inspiration. Whatever I've achieved has been down to you."

"Don't try to make me complicit."

"But that's just what you are."

They lapsed into a silence that went on so long, Marcetti thought their conversation was at an end. He started to get to his feet but Salim Khourasan spoke again in a voice so quiet Marcetti strained to hear, "If events had turned out differently for us, I had it in mind to take you to Damascus to meet my family. See things for yourself; see the city of Paul's revelation."

"The street called 'Straight'."

"I thought the irony might appeal to you."

"I would have liked to see the actual place of conversion, 'the road to Damascus'."

"There've been many suggested. Impossible to guess. But that is where it all began to make sense to him. And to me."

"Yes, a journey! From persecution to revelation. But what of your journey, Salim?"

"Mohammed, peace be upon him, showed me the way of faith."

"What would your mother have said to that?"

"We shall not speak of her. Allah will be her judge as He judges all."

"From revelation to persecution. No going back from that."

"*Inshallah!*"

The sounds of the outside world failed to intrude on the intensity of the silence within the basilica. The two men sat once more enveloped in their own private thoughts. Marcetti broke the deadlock, "You ordered my death on the train from Rome." A statement of unadulterated fact, not a question. "It made sense as soon as the British spy gave me the name. Khalil Khourasan, son, nephew? At any rate, your flesh and blood, your DNA. When you ordered it, were you remembering the moments of intimacy we had shared? I told you secret things I'd never told anyone. Laid bare my soul to you—more than I ever had to Father Pascal. Joined at the hip he once said we were. He could be dramatic and trite! The British only wanted to frighten me to secure my silence. You wanted my silence because you wanted my soul and you knew it was the only way you would succeed. That was your aim. You ordered the other deaths too."

"Yes, I ordered your death. And the others. Too many now to list. And one fine day, as you Italians say, Allah will doubtless order mine."

"So the Caliphate's way of life is the way of death. No doubt the white-clad virgins who await you in Paradise will stand before you, covered in the blood of the last warrior who entered eternal bliss. That is the salvation you preach.

What a glorious prospect! That is what you claim the merciful Allah promises his faithful. But, Salim, I don't find it in my heart to believe that the Prophet Mohammed was so cruelly deceived. It is you and the fanatics who follow you who have twisted the words of the Almighty. For what appalling ends, only you know."

On the *vaporetto* ploughing its way back across the lagoon to Venice, they stood leaning against the rails, watching the lights flickering on the islands. Only San Michele, the cemetery island, seemed to be shrouded in its own half-light. They stood together as forty years ago, but now apart—the real distance between them that of a lifetime. Everything that could be said had been said. Silence now—no longer the comfortable wordless exchange that characterises friendship—a cold bleak silence of things unresolved. Not, however, the silence of uncertainty. There was a clarity about it that would define the future. When the boat pulled alongside the Fondamenta, both men disembarked. Marcetti turned right heading for San Marco and the residence of the Patriarch. Salim Khourasan turned left towards the Arsenale.

Epilogue

As days morphed into weeks and weeks into months, nothing further was heard of military transport flight ZX 962 from Luqa, Malta to Falcone-Borsellino Airport, Palermo. A combined operation of certain member states of the European Union had launched an extensive airborne and sea search for the missing aircraft. It had proved impossible to establish whether, after take-off, the plane had turned onto its new north-westerly heading or had continued in a south-easterly direction to the eastern Mediterranean. Contact had been lost with the cockpit barely twenty minutes later and there had been no indication from the pilot—an experienced military flier—that there might be a problem. A blanket of silence had descended and a blanket of silence remained.

Two apparently unrelated events, however, occurred over the subsequent fourteen months following the plane's disappearance.

One morning in his office at the Gallery of Renaissance Art in Venice, the Director, Professor Matteo Casamassa, happened to be scrutinising the catalogue of a forthcoming sale in Geneva of Old Master paintings to be held by a prominent international auction house. Listed—and indeed illustrated—was a little-known work by Caravaggio, provenance to be announced later. A pre-sale estimate of between ninety to one hundred million euros was given. The professor's attempts to glean further information on the provenance issue proved fruitless. Whereupon Casamassa determined to attend the sale and view the painting for himself. On arrival, he signed in and amidst much bowing and scraping, was conducted by a junior member of staff to the viewing. On the way, the young gentleman escorting him vouchsafed to the professor the information that one item had, unfortunately, been withdrawn from sale by the proposed vendor, namely *The Robber Barabbas rails at Jesus* by the master Caravaggio.

Not known for his temperate approach to such situations, the professor exploded and demanded to be taken instantly to the Director of the auction house. Apologies were profuse but there was nothing that could be done. Details of the vendor's identity were, regretfully, a strict matter of confidentiality between the individual and the auctioneers. Such considerations, stormed Casamassa, did not apply when the item in question was almost certainly a painting looted by terrorist thieves from the Palermo Gallery of Art in 2015. It was a matter for the police and if the auction house valued its reputation, it would take immediate steps to report the matter. Although obviously nothing was said in so many words, the professor strongly suspected that the vendor had offered a substantial sum of money in compensation for the withdrawal of the painting from the sale. That constituted, in his view, a disgraceful act of unprofessional practice and, in the particular circumstances, the possibility of a criminal offence.

Suffice it to say, an international investigation involving Interpol was set up. The vendor was traced to the address of a lawyer's office in the Swiss town of Lugano. However, no record was found there of the client's name and the investigation stalled. Until, that is, the local police were called in by the law firm to trace a young secretary, an Isabella Reno, who had been taken on a few months before but had not appeared at work for two weeks nor had been in touch with her employers to explain her absence. The head of the firm agreed with his partner that it was a *trifle* odd that the girl's name corresponded to the name of the vendor currently being sought by Interpol.

Enquiries were made and police officers called at an address in the Via Ciseri that the girl had given as the apartment of her parents. They were courteously received by an elderly widow, who claimed to be the grandmother of the missing girl. No, she hadn't seen Isabella for several months and was under the impression that she and her boyfriend were presently hiking around India, or was it Thailand, she couldn't remember. Typical of young people these days, just taking off without a word to anyone! On leaving the apartment, the senior of the two officers expressed admiration for a small Impressionist painting hanging over a table in the entrance hall. Yes, isn't it charming, a copy of an original by Paul Cezanne done by my late husband, a talented artist in his own right. Sergeant Lecomte would never have described himself remotely as an expert on art; he just knew what he liked. He went away wrapped in thought. His superior officer saw no justification whatsoever in applying to the courts for a warrant to search the property on the basis of Lecomte's wild imaginings. Nevertheless, the coincidence of names *was* curious and information would perhaps be passed to Interpol as a courtesy. It was only a matter of time before the property was searched. Smaller items of the paintings stolen from the Galiano Collection were discovered propped against bookshelves in the study, with the exception of a charming one by Cezanne that was hanging in the hall because the widow was particularly fond of it. One thing led to another and the search of a warehouse property on the edge of town belonging to the widow's late spouse revealed four renaissance Old Masters including a Caravaggio; the Robber Barabbas was still railing at Jesus despite a hole in the canvas close to his head. A case could not be brought against the widow and her deceased husband was now blissfully beyond the reach of the arm of the law.

The second event took place many miles from Geneva in the deserts of Libya. A detachment of Libyan government forces launched an operation on a terrorist training camp where it was known that twenty-seven oil workers from a nearby plant were being held hostage by the Soldiers of the Caliphate, together with a number of individuals of other nationalities. The operation proved entirely successful. The captives were released without loss of life and all but six of the terrorists were killed during the action. Upon release, the hostages were taken under safe conduct to Tripoli where they were admitted to a military hospital for medical examination.

One of the foreign nationals, an Italian-American woman, was deemed fit enough for immediate discharge. She gave her name as Signora Lucia Neroni, a former aid worker with the charity, Action for Somalia. She left the hospital but her subsequent whereabouts became something of a mystery. There seemed to be no record of her leaving the country. The charity issued a statement to the effect that the safety of the members of its staff was paramount but declined to comment further. One month later, Lavinia Dyer walked into the offices of the *New York Times* and gave Ferdy Keymer the fright of his life.